RETURN
OF THE
Richmond Vampire

Musings

For all who hearken for the Intangible

In the years ahead, I suspect that more stories will emerge about the Church Hill Tunnel when spirits, ghouls, vampires and other assorted creatures of the night assert themselves.
– Professor Walter S. Griggs Jr.

The day science begins to study non-physical phenomena, it will make more progress in one decade than in all the previous centuries of its existence.
– Nikola Tesla

And the women conceiving brought forth giants, ... These devoured all which the labour of men produced; until it became impossible to feed them;
When they turned themselves against men, in order to devour them;
And began to injure birds, beasts, reptiles, and fishes, to eat their flesh one after another, and to drink their blood.
– The Book of Enoch the Prophet, Richard Laurence translation

...for there is nothing covered, that shall not be revealed; and hid, that shall not be known.

– Matthew 10:26

Contents

Preface

Fact or fiction?
As a whole or in part?
It's for you to discern;
This one thing rings smart.
Put down this tale!
Toss it away!
Call your friends
To folly and play.
For venturing into a vampire's keep
Shall only bring sorrow
As your blood will run steep.

~ Jon Rakestraw

Author's Warning

by Jon Rakestraw

Greetings to you, inquisitive reader! Whatever way you may have come by this book, I entreat you to put it away, or better yet, make use of it as tinder on a cold and dark winter's night. At the very least, read not beyond this chapter unless you are of a stable mind, not given to embarking on ill-advised journeys.

For, on October 27th, the day of Diwali, I met the most mysterious and beguiling figure of a man, if you could call him that, dressed in a dark frock coat. I was musing over some poetry whilst conversing with the staff and clientele at Church Hill's WPA Bakery in Richmond, Virginia, when this disheveled and somewhat eccentric man entered with a fox-like demeanor.

He was lightly rain-dampened and held a large, leather-bound journal. The cover had an embossed triskelion with a pewter ouroboros at its center. Three brass latches secured its heavy parchment pages, exposing only their frayed edges.

I made the mistake of uttering a passing comment about its craftsmanship. He thanked me, in a Hungarian accent, then sat down beside me with a steaming cup of Moroccan mint tea. While he sipped I noticed his long fingernails, more like claws, and on his right hand, a grandiose reddish golden ring depicting a dragon encircled by Greek inscriptions. He placed his tea upon the bistro table and unbuttoned his coat,

revealing an embossed leather belt with three straps and its corresponding brass buckles. He began fidgeting with his napkin; tiny rips made upon its edges.

My eyes moved upward fixing upon his face. He had a middle-aged pale visage: tiny sagging folds under his eyes, scar on his right cheek, a creased forehead, but his skin seemed older, almost ancient, like the cover of his book. His brown hair had sprinkles of grey in a dilapidated tonsure hairstyle, finished off with a stubby goatee. My initial perception was revised from eccentric to bizarre.

While he nicked at his napkin, he explained the book was a compilation of his personal journal and the Society of the Dragonists' Chronicles, illustrated with whimsical drawings. He showed me one of a dragon with a spiked tail. At my questioning expression, he launched into a rambling explication that he was the master scribe of this old Hungarian order. When he mentioned he was soon to be off to an "otherworldly place," I turned the conversation to the abatement of the light rain, and the flowered bicycle out front.

Soon, however, he steered the conversation to a more serious topic: a series of strange murders which he said in no uncertain terms would soon transfix Richmond. I took this man as partly mad but kept an open mind. Looking over at Tully and Alexis, the servers, and Paula, the principal baker, their expressions convinced me I was not alone in this assessment. Still, his narration was fascinating, and I was determined to listen to the rest of his tale.

He said his compilation, the thick tome he'd carried in, gave a full account of these murders and other bizarre events that would soon happen. Confused by his stern manner, I asked him how he could be so sure of future events. He replied his time frame was lodged within a different dimension. Uncomfortable and befuddled by this statement, I nodded politely, deciding it best to switch the subject once again. I told him that I, too, was a writer, but of lighter topics enjoyed by children. He smirked, drank his tea then resumed fidgeting with the napkin. I ended the silence, which in hindsight was a blunder, for I declared my interest in reading his chronicle.

Without a word, he pushed the book before me, and said it was mine. Astonished, I asked why, and he replied he was in a hurry; he had no time to edit the writing, much less publish it. Being a bibliophile and bewitched by its provenance, I said that

I might. His requests were that I add a foreword preparing the readers to understand its style of prose, instructed me where to add it, and, overall, that I employ poetic license as I saw fit–not to distort the tale, he stressed–but rather to enhance the story. He stated if a fortune came from sales of the book, that it would be mine to garner, for he had no need of lucre.

With that assertion, a ray of sunlight pierced the overcast sky sending a shaft of light into the bakery and across our round bistro table. Immediately, he rose and smiled, revealing unusually sharp teeth, which gave me pause. He put his hand on my shoulder and thanked me for taking on this burden. He stated, "There is a key to the pool." Then, in a mere moment, he had made his way to the door and had opened it slightly. He spun to face me once more and said, *"Szia! Úr. Rakestraw. Kulcs a poolhoz."*

"Szia," I only managed to mutter, and with that he was gone before I could ask what he had spoken in Hungarian. *What have I got myself into?*
I thought, staring at his mug half-full.

Looking back on it now, I wish I had burned the book, or better still, never laid eyes on it. Over the coming days, the more I read of it, the more the story unbalanced my temperament, jarred my faculties, and worse–as though it had a life of its own–induced a hypnotic urge to fashion the work for publication. I kept saying to myself, *What are you doing!?...he's a madman...talk of an Otherworld...Society of Dragons...this guy's gonna come back and suck my blood! Trash the book!*

But I didn't. It seemed I couldn't. Why, I can't explain. To this day, I still can't fathom why I pressed on amidst the mental anguish. In the waning months, I gave myself over to its influence so that the words originated from my subconscious mind. In a Jungian sense, I wrote while I slept then transcribed it when I awoke. To bolster this rumination, I researched several sources including a work by the late professor Walter S. Griggs Jr., whose principal book mentioned Bob Harrison, a resident expert of certain historical events covered in the tome. Thanks to him, I added detail of Richmond's people and places, which the scribe knew little about, but I believed were essential to understanding the story.

For those of you who do not heed my admonition, I trust you belong to a readership who possesses an inquisitive mind objective in nature and are stoic in heart. One who is given over to curiosity and wonderment of obscure and esoteric things, yet, can retain sanity amidst the inquiry. If so, read on at your own risk!

Admonishment of a Master Scribe

With a heavy heart and a guilty conscience, I now recount all I have seen and done in Richmond, a city defeated in its aspiration to be the capital of a new country, but which has since transformed itself, rising from the ashes as the gateway to the South. At your reading of these words, I, perchance, am still in exile, having fallen from my former estate as the chief scribe of the Order of the Dragon; ***Societas Draconistarum*** to be exact, known in the common tongue as the Society of the Dragonists, or, as I prefer, in the Latin: ***Ordo est Draco.***

I confess before you this tale, which I have transcribed from the Order's chronicles and my own journal, as well as from the journals of others near to me, and the diaries and reports of familiars: those imps possessing animals–some felines, canines and varied exotic avians, though mostly crows or ravens.

My heart has been heavy for some time, over a century, I would say. Though time, for me, is a travesty at best–inconsequential, since the clock differs here from whence I reside in relation to where you are reading this at present. I trust you are perusing these pages several years prior to that daunting year of 2025 *anno Domini*, for I entrusted all of my accounts to an amiable writer–dare I say naive, as well, whom I had foreseen in a vision, in your year 2019 of the Gregorian calendar. If this account is initially being pored over after the Fall of 2025, then all that I have written is in vain. That said, you would do well to pitch this book aside. If this is not the case, then leaf through these pages at the risk of your own wits.

By your dimensional time of November of the year 2025, my usually composed temperament was overtaken by remorse, or something nearing that state. Perhaps, once this work is published, I will have flushed out whatever allegorical demon lies so heavily within my heart. Nevertheless, this ill-natured state is the result of the events of that Autumn, which transpired in the City of Richmond, in the loosely united Southern American states.

We of the Order of the Dragon have, by and large, kept a low profile in the events of your world, partly for survival, but also from a lack of necessity. We have no desire to become publicly renowned; our existence lies in the background of your hectic and often meaningless materialistic lives, and that is sufficient for us. However, beginning that Fall, the head of our Council asserted us into the world in a most unusual manner; consequently we can never return to anonymity. Was it for the good of our Order, or for her own ends? I shall ask you to be the judge of that, and, by "that" I mean what was our motives and the eventual outcome. I am merely recounting the tale for my own cathartic affair.

If you are determined to embark upon reading this dark and oh-so-twisted tale, then I admonish you to first consider the following foreword, which I advised the cordial writer to set forth. . .

Rakestraw's Foreword

Yes, I have inserted the Foreword here, as the scribe instructed, because many readers do not bother to read opening remarks, preferring to dive straight into Chapter One. That said, I advise you to heed this part, else you will be lost to the tale's point of view, direction, and most importantly–its warning. Yes, your eyes do not deceive you. You read the word, "warning."

Whatever way you have come by this book, I adjure you to put it down, unless you are of a proper disposition. Let me explain:

Henceforth, I give you an admonishment not to read past this foreword unless you are of a stout constitution and are not given to overt curiosity. For if a reader should decide to "fact check" this tale using smartphones/smartwatches (i.e., dumb-phones/dumb-watches), databases and libraries, one will likely go swirling downwards into an ever increasing whirlpool of desire, craving to find the exiled and esoteric master scribe, the seat of the Dragonist Order, and the otherworldly places referenced–not to mention in our earthly world–the living people and places he expounds upon. At best, this book will grate your sanity and at worst, lead to your demise as your blood satiates the appetite of one of the Dragonists.

Regarding this book's point of view–I can't stress it enough–please forbear with me as the perspective ebbs and flows employing first, second, and third person points of view. Much of this is the master scribe's doing and I felt compelled to retain his style. He used the first, because he personally witnessed some of these events. The second, for he desired to keep the reader engaged, despite his ramblings, and to persuade, most of all, self-reflection. The third, for he conveyed the recollections of eye witnesses and familiars.

As for the overall content, much of it I had to revise, as the scribe's account is lacking in readability in regard to flow of prose, proper grammar and punctuation, though that is understandable, given his native tongue is Hungarian. Speaking of languages, he along with others employ foreign salutations and expressions which I have indicated by *italics*. As for his penmanship, however, it is second to none, and it was a joy to feel the parchment pages between my fingers and to behold his writing, no doubt created by a quill pen, though it visually was not suitable for long term reading. For those who revel in such calligraphy, I have not forgotten you. In the subtitle of chapters, I incorporated the Trattatello font as the closest approximation to his penmanship. Moreover, some excerpts from the *Draculian Chronicles* and journal entries of the scribe's overseer display this font as a delight for your eyes.

There are numerous sketches throughout. Many of the original drawings were hastily done, and, dare I border on being terse, they lack necessary artistic qualities such as balance, proportion and contrast. However, two of the drawings are unique, not only in subject but in the medium itself, so I hope you find these of interest. The first is pictured below on an old railroad ticket stub. I found it sandwiched between the pages of his musty tome. I scanned it and placed it here to satiate your curiosity. No doubt it is his doodles evidenced by a Hungarian word scribbled upon the passenger's receipt. Notice the fringe tears. These are indicative of his nervous habit to rip the edges of paper.

So, to bring his scribbles to life, I hired a talented artist, Meam Hartshorn. She transformed the scribe's sketches into something which I hope will be pleasing to your eyes. Moreover, I employed her services since many locations in our world were cited, but were not depicted by the scribe; hence I thought it would be helpful to add such scenes in moving the story forward.

Now, you may ask yourself, why did this writer put so much effort and time into

bringing this obscure piece of work to light? The answer is quite simple: I printed it on a deduction. I surmised he had hopes its publication would somehow thwart the tragic and terrible occurrences which he believed are soon to occur in our quaint city of Richmond, and, more importantly, would have repercussions in the wider world.

So, for those who do not heed this admonition, I wish you the best of providence, and hope your faculties remain intact, the deeper you delve into this tale.

Do not tread upon the Thin Places, turn back from the mist of Tír na nÓg!

Ruxandra's Dream

Transcription of Collette cel Rău's Journal, November 11, 2019 & Draculian Chronicle excerpts

I, **Bölcsem Kertész**, Master Scribe of the Dracul Order, have charge over chronicling the history and exploits of the Society of Dragonists and its Archons of Nine. For under me are scribes from each respective lair, who, with diligence and fortitude, have penned the accounts of our obscure and lengthy past in the voluminous *Draculian Chronicles*. Within this archived collection, secured in a vault far from prying eyes, are portions of the tale set forth in these pages. Its sources consist of my own journal entries, memoirs of the Archons, and the eye witnesses of mortals as well as the testimonies of familiars residing in ravens, cats, and other nefarious creatures. These familiars, I did summon, or they came to me of their own volition, enhancing or verifying much of what I have weaved into prose. Hence, I am able to distill from various perspectives much of the discourse and events you will read. That is...if you dare. For these events once known to you, will in some subtle way, entangle your life in matters most unsettling. With that said, turn the remaining pages in trepidation.

Our tale begins in an unassuming year, in an unassuming city with a most notable figure, that is, Ruxandra cel Rău, one of the Archons of Nine and the granddaughter of Count Dracula, whom I know well. For in the year 2019 in Richmond, Virginia, Ruxandra paid a visit to her grandniece, Collette cel Rău. It was a chilly,

overcast November day when they began an interesting chat at the quaint WPA Bakery in Church Hill, a cozy neighborhood upon a hill overlooking downtown.

Collette piped up, "Look here, auntie," knowing today marked the 100th anniversary of her aunt's break up with William Wortham Pool.

"What is it my dear?" she asked, peering at the cover of a magazine, while Collette read the lead article.

"It says here, and I paraphrase, that Beth and Chris Houlihan, Haunts of Richmond owners, were interested in a dowsing session surrounding the Church Hill Tunnel collapse. Ah, later Chris and Beth recounted that an outfit called DorEn Channeling did do a Yes-and-No dowsing there, and the spirit said he was Benjamin Mosby.

"Hey, that's the fireman guy who was with train engineer Tom Mason, right? Mosby has a street named after him, just a few blocks from here." Collette put the magazine down and enjoyed her coffee and macaron.

"Ahh. Fascinating," remarked Ruxandra, who began casually tapping the circular table with her pitch black-painted fingernails, the tips of which made dents in the wood. "What else does the article say?"

"Oh, yeah, let me see," she replied, putting down her coffee and riffling through the magazine. "Umm...Ben had taken a liking to Beth. He would touch her back, pull her hair, blah, blah. She didn't know who the ghost was, so she got together with DorEn Channeling to find out."

"Yes, you went over this already," replied Ruxandra, who ceased tapping and drank her tea.

Meanwhile, a customer browsing baked goods stopped and stared at Ruxandra's hair, draped over her stunning, slender figure.

Ruxandra noticed. "May I help you?"

The lady replied, "Oh, no. I'm...I'm sorry, I–I was just admiring your lavender hair–and–"

Ruxandra smiled, "And now my varied eye coloration."

"Well, ah, yes." The onlooker winced.

"It's heterochromia, thank you," she explained, and turned back to look at the no less stunning, but more youthful, Collette.

Collette continued, "The dowser went through all these names.... Beth said they got a 'yes' on Ben...talked for about twenty minutes...'Ben's happy we tell the history, and he doesn't want us to stop doing that. He wants to keep that history alive. He doesn't like it when certain tour groups come over and say he is the vampire (part of Richmond's urban vampire legend). He's a ghost in his own right, and he's proud of that part.' Whoa, that last part I was quoting, maybe there's something to this. What I mean is, the Mosby and vampire part...we definitely have a wandering spirit! Could it be he met Willie in the Tunnel?"

"William, to you," said Ruxandra sternly.

"Yes, William, perhaps there's a connection."

"Perhaps," Ruxandra mused. She finished her mug of tea, left it upon the cafe table, and promptly stood up without another word. She walked out to the corner of 27th and Marshall Street, Collette in tow.

They strolled towards Collette's house, a couple of blocks over.
Ruxandra smiled and said, "Thanks for the coffee and *canelé*."

"Is something bothering you?"

"Sunt bine," replied Ruxandra in Romanian.

"Like my new earrings?" asked Collette, brushing aside her jet black hair to show black onyx earrings.

"Whoo! Very nice...prospects on your jewelry biz?"

"Well, it's coming along. I do farmer's markets up in Lakeside and such, set up around breweries in Scott's Addition sometimes. I've got some private clients through the Soa-Gild."

"So, your RVA Oasis has some traction?"

"Yeah, just last month, around Samhain, I got three more for the next gathering."

"I'm proud of you for taking this on. Brannbjørn showed?"

"Nope, he's cooled off."

"Good to hear. Ah, the sun is poking its ugly head out," said Ruxandra as she winced, a block from the row house. "Time for a nap." They entered and she asked, "Do you have a vial on you?"

"Yep," Collette handed her a pewter vial in the shape of a twisting dragon ensnaring fine glass. "Thanks for sending me the styrofoam cases.
What's your source?"

"I'm going to pretend you didn't ask me that," Ruxandra replied then knocked it down shot glass-style saying, "Ah, *multumesc*." She went to the guest room. "Has the coffin been cleaned?"

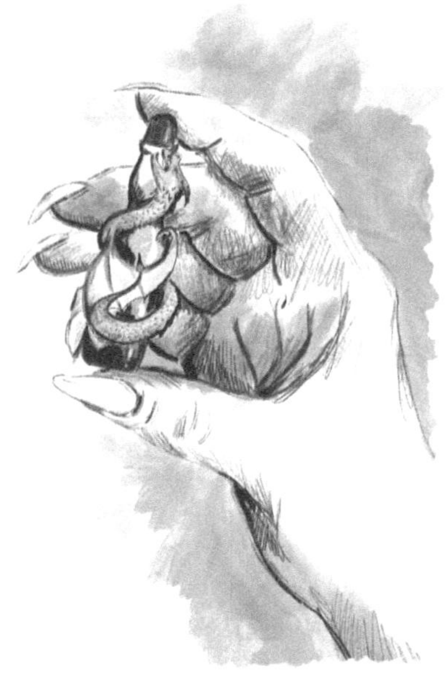

"Really! Just for a nap? You're so old-school."

"*Mă scuzati*. No one else dares speak to me with that tone."

"That's why you have a niece."

"Hmm," Ruxandra said, narrowing her eyes, "I suppose so. As I was saying, yes, it's a habit. Well, is it clean?"

"It is, since Antonio used it."

"What did you say!?"

"It's not what you're thinking–just friends. Anyway, the nice one's down in the basement."

"Latched from the inside? I don't want to wake up and find a piece of oak in my chest."

"You read my thoughts," Collette said.

"Very funny."

"The answer to your question is, yes, it can be."

"Thank you."

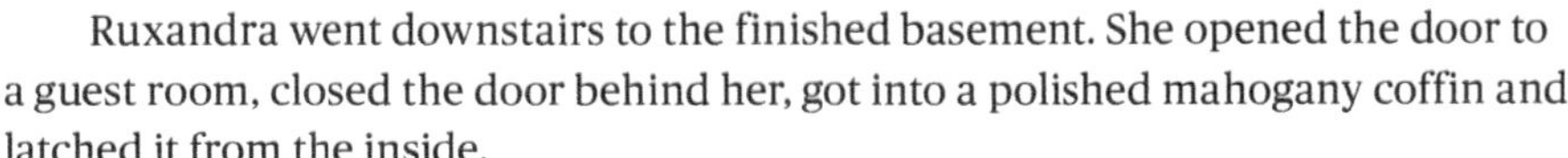

Ruxandra went downstairs to the finished basement. She opened the door to a guest room, closed the door behind her, got into a polished mahogany coffin and latched it from the inside.

She drifted off. Hours into her rest she dreamed she was at Hollywood Cemetery. She was standing on Westvale Avenue before William Wortham Pool's mausoleum. A fog cradled the foreground before its iron lattice door. She was moved to tears standing before its understated iron fence. Behind that, a small grass-covered courtyard with a short, marble chessboard walkway led to an Egyptian facade. The imposing dark entrance was topped by a relief depicting a child leading a flock. The lion and the lamb verse from Isaiah that once accompanied it was long gone. The sepulcher was barred by a wrought iron lattice door, crowned with an archway of iron vines. The gravedigger had secured the entry from tomb raiders long ago, its padlock and chain now rusty. For this was the famed burial site of the Richmond Vampire, and for decades college students, the Cult of Pool, and other pagan dabblers had forcibly entered to perform rites. Some ad hoc, others with the distinct purpose of summoning a strigoi, a vampire of unusual strength and morphing ability.

What happened next is best read as it was recorded in Ruxandra's own diary...

Jurnal de Ruxandra cel Rău, 11 Noiembrie 2019 (translated)

I had a feeling...a voice from far away.

The voice said, "D-r-a-c-n-i-a."

I felt disoriented; was the voice inside my head, or was it coming through the trees?

"D-r-a-c-n-i-a, Oh, Miss Dracnia."

Startled, I swung about as in a dream dance looking southward down a mist blanketed Westvale Avenue. The voice seemed to echo off the tombstones. I had not heard my nickname spoken in a century. The voice was deep, authoritative, even dignified. It was a man's voice, a Southern accent of African descent. I saw no one.

Louder now, he said, "Miss Dracnia, ma'am, are you a-comin' Miss?"

For a brief moment, out of the mist, I made out a tall black man wearing a sturdy, white collared shirt underneath overalls. He came and went as the fog passed before him, and stood at the fork of Westvale and Freeman Road. I felt an urge to follow, but then an overwhelming shroud of fear came over me. Fear...fear of what I would find if I followed. I hadn't felt deep-rooted fear since the start of the War to End All Wars. Then I felt grief, anger, and lastly betrayal.

"Miss?"

"No!" I replied. "No, no, go away!"

"But, Miss, it's been a hundred years to the day," he implored with his palms held upwards at his waist.

The last thing I remember, I was running away north toward Haxall Avenue. Then I awoke.

Tears were running down my

face, soaking my pillow. I hadn't cried in so long. Moreover, hearing my nickname was unnerving. I simply could not bear this.

For my own sanity I must dismiss this vision. Let it go, lest it draw me into an abyss of grief, anger and sorrow.

Hoia Baciu Forest

Ruxandra ascended the stairs to find Collette napping on the sofa. She came to. "Auntie, are you alright?" said Collette, sizing up her aunt's countenance.

"I'm fine...just a bad dream." She sat down in a wingback chair.

Collette handed her an embroidered handkerchief. "You've been crying, auntie!

Whatever for?"

"Oh, I was remembering grandfather, how he use to put me on his back and ride me in the moonlight through stretches of the Hoia Baciu Forest. Do you remember the time I took you there, when the mist was heavy, swirling about the snake-like tree trunks?"

"Yes, I do. We must go back. I love The Clearing. Up for some vamp tea?" said Collette.

"Absolutely."

They got up and walked down the hall toward the kitchen.

The Origin of Pool

Transcription of Collette cel Rău's Journal, November 12, 2019 & Draculian Chronicle excerpts

In the kitchen, Collette prepared vampiric tea: a mixture of blood, local honey, and rose petals. Once it was finished steeping in a Ceroc teapot, Collette joined Ruxandra in the living room adding rugelach to the tray. Gusts of wind occasionally rattled the paned glass. Moonbeams broke now and then, adding ambiance to the dimly lit room. Ruxandra sat in a wingback, opposite Collette on the couch.

Collette broke the silence saying, "How did it all start? I mean, exactly how did he become one of us?"

"My dear, you're not 'one of us,' you're more human. Count your blessings you're not like me, or even more so, like your great uncle Mircea. You don't have to deal with sun scorching, a voracious appetite for the red stuff, annoying fangs–"

"–Auntie, you're lecturing."

"Forgive me; I guess you are ready to hear this story. Is your mind prepared? It is a lengthy tale."

"We have all night," Collette insisted as her black familiar, Catterina, jumped into her lap and immediately started purring.

"Well, I shall tell most of it. Then I must be going," said Ruxandra.

"He came from New Orleans? I remember you saying that's where he transformed."

"Indeed, but he came originally from Mississippi."

"Tell me the whole story, auntie, please."

"Very well. William was born in 1842, the son of a Mississippi merchant. He was a good bookkeeper and worked in the city of Jackson. When he turned eighteen, in April, he went to New Orleans with a friend to celebrate. He was getting sauced at Old Absinthe House and vented to his friend about losing the love of his life, to a rival no less. He described the rival as quite tall, handsome, and too strong for him to deal with. Well, a lovely lady was also sitting at the bar, she piped in, offering her sympathies. She and Pool hit it off and began a friendly banter. She claimed she had just the remedy to solve his problem. But she warned him the solution had its side effects. He was skeptical, but that soon gave way when she told him she was Marie Philomene Glapion."

"Who's that?" Collette inquired.

"Who's that!? My dear, none other than Marie II, the daughter of the famous New Orleans Voodoo Queen, Marie Catherine Laveau. Everyone in the French Quarter knew her, and no doubt her fame and her daughter's antics had even been known by Mr. Pool. He was so enamored with her charm, beautiful copper skin, and her sincerity regarding this potion she offered, he was willing to pay dearly for a swig of it.

"Marie II was true to her word. This potion was like nothing our Order had or probably ever will see. It contained the blood of the vulture bat and blood from a vampire who was a Lilithian shapeshifter. She promised that this potion would give him the strength to overcome the invading suitor, and he would be successful in the duel to win her love."

Here, I, Bölscem must interject, for Ruxandra, in her retelling of this story to Collette, did not fully describe what she meant by the "vulture bat." The vulture bat is related to the extinct species called *Desmodus draculae*. It was literally the size of a vulture. You might have supposed it drank blood, and your assumption would be correct. It lived amongst the Mura people deep in the Amazon Jungle. Antonio Jararaca, head of the Brazilian lair, and a vampire, sly, skillful with a forked tongue and charming eyes, brought such a preserved creature to the vaulted archives, of which I am the principal curator. I classified it as a relative of *Desmodus draculae*, which I coined as: *Desmodus Draculae Caoera*.

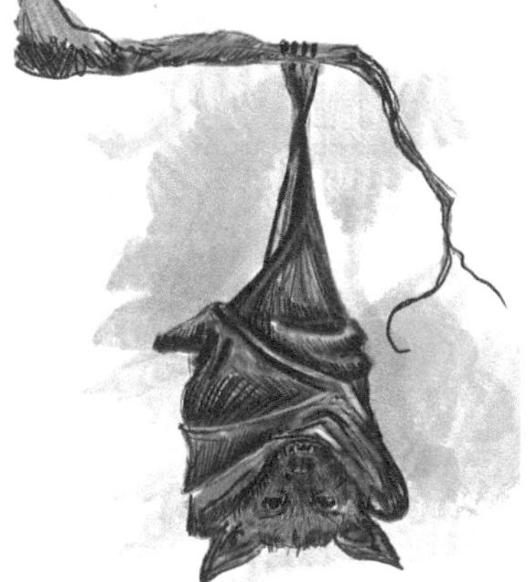

And why not? For to this day, neither man nor angel knows of all the creatures and places which that dark greenish ecosystem contains. Moreover, tales of this great bat were circulated

among the Zapotec, The Cloud People. They spoke of it rising like a great death knell from the Zotzilaha cave, in what is present day Guatemala. Now, let us return to Ruxandra's account.

"Well, he was bitter at his loss, and whether he gained her hand back or not, he wanted to teach his rival a lesson. So that Sunday, Marie II took William to Congo Square to meet her mother and pay for the potion."

"Did Queen Marie tell him what was in it?" Collette inquired.

"Yes, but Willie was undaunted, and her admonitions went unheeded."

"What is Congo Square?"

"Ah, well, Congo Square was an outdoor area where people of color, both free and slaves, could convene without restrictions. They would setup makeshift stands to sell their wares. Of note, the Voodoo Queen and her daughter were free people, and highly respected for their craft. The flea market occurred on Sundays, after church, near St. Augustine's; buyers would come from all over."

"Really, auntie, 'people of color?' You're so old fashioned.
Can you say 'African Americans' please?"

Ruxandra laughed, "Well, you're right, I am rather 'old.' Five hundred thirty-five years, to be exact.

"So, the African Americans would gather, both free and slaves, to sell things like *calas* cakes and *nkisi* objects. They danced and sang songs of their native lands. Willie loved it all. He was awed by Queen Laveau even more so than her daughter.

"He paid a hefty sum for the small vial of potion contained in a *gris-gris* bag. She warned him to dilute it with mineral water, lest if he take it straight he would surely die, or at the very least, have a sudden and unquenchable appetite for blood. Moreover, she said the powers one would gain from it varied from person to person, but that all who took it gained incredible strength and speed of foot.

"He dismissed her warnings as mumbo-jumbo and took it straight. The dark red potion had a heavy taste of iron, but smelled and tasted a bit like molasses."

Collette leaned forward and asked, "What happened next?"

"He became ill to the point of near-death. He had seizures and respiratory issues for days. At one point he had such a swoon Marie thought him dead. Much like what happened to Midnight Mary later on, in the 1870s. Her mother, the Voodoo Queen, was apathetic, knowing he had disobeyed her and had drunk it straight. He was unconscious for several days. Using her mother's manner of healing arts, Marie saved him. After about three weeks of being penned-up in the French Quarter, he recovered."

"How was he different, auntie?"

"'Different' is not the right word...more like the beginning of a *khpr*, a 'becoming.'"

"I don't understand," said Collette.

"My dear, in short, he had become a strigoi vampire. The likes of which we have not seen since your great grandfather's time. The potion had made a change in his DNA. A genetic change so comprehensive, even down to a structural level. He had the strength of twenty men. He moved like a gazelle. His nails hardened, became more like claws than fingernails. He could transform himself. A dark, foreboding creature, though he could not fly. That is but the stuff of fairytales. He could blend with things in nature like tree trunks and large boulders, a shapeshifter. Very strange...not even your great grandfather many times over could do that!"

"And where is the infamous grandfather?"

"Ah-ha, where's grandfather–he's dead, my dear."

"Yeah right. Where's his remains? Some say they're at Sveti Georgi, others at Snagov Monastery–but they only found ox bones. And still others say he's near where he fell, at Comana Monastery."

"He is at Comana Monastery. They found his bones there."

"Hmm, but where's his head?"

"It's perfectly logical. Bölscem Kertész's theory is that the Turks severed the head and took it back to Istanbul as a trophy," said Ruxandra.

"There's no definitive proof then. And what is it with this Bölcsem guy anyway? He's just some odd monk who thinks he knows it all. He hardly speaks, but oh how he rambles on in those chronicles, about you, Nastya, Chorti...blah, blah," she exclaimed.

"Really, Collette, be respectful. Besides, you like his stories about Edana."

"Yes, that's true. But what's with him muddling about with noble and base metals? I'm tired of checking the athanor's temperature."

"Have you done so today?"

"Umm, auntie, I will. Oh–but let me finish venting...he leaves his creepy formaldehyde jars and cipher wheels on my jeweler's bench. Urgh! Plus his invasive herbs and roses overtake my thyme and lavender in the garden box–and that goulash he makes, mixing in rabbit's blood. Yuck! He's downright weird."

"He's quite fond of you. You know he knew your grandfather, was his trusted advisor and chronicler. It is natural he's the Order's head scribe."

"You're probably going to recount our visit to him, aren't you?"

"Naturally. Besides, my penmanship is atrocious. His transcriptions are outstanding, with those crow quills of his. He writes such flowing characters and adds wonderful drawings. My memoir he keeps under lock and key. It's tradition. Without him, our history would be disorganized, disheveled, possibly lost! Now...do you want to hear the rest of William's story or not?"

"Sorry, do continue."

"As I was saying, Willie recovered. Marie aided him in adjusting to what he had become. He had to drink some measure of blood within a week, lest his whole body shut down. At first he was reviled at the thought of drinking blood. He stayed another week with Marie who nursed him. She provided him elixirs, part blood, tea and honey. Later, Willie joked that Marie was the inventor of the Bloody Mary, albeit with a Renfield twist, shall we say? He quite enjoyed that. He could still eat food, but it had lost its appeal in comparison."

"Now you've got me thinking about a Renfield Mary," said Collette.

"Ha! Good one! So, Willie went back to Jackson, but his rival was nowhere to be found. He had enlisted. Willie followed suit, joining in May, 1861. He entered as a private. He was adamant over State's rights, but was a passionate abolitionist. He found slavery detestable and fed on no one of African descent. He was saddened that those poor folk had no choice in coming here.

"He served admirably in the Franklin Rifles of the Mississippi Volunteers. He sustained himself on the blood of Union soldiers. However, he got sick off the blood of one of them. Of course, at Sick Call, he never revealed the cause. The camp doctor tried bloodletting, to no avail. By November of that year, he was officially removed from combat and was laid up for months back at his parents' home. He was off the role by the fall of '62."

"Sounds like he learned his lesson in choosing entrées."

"Easier said than done. Like I've said to you for years, be thankful your vampiric strain does not constitute the core of who you are."

"Point taken. What happened next?"

"Eventually he made his way to Manchester. Back then, it was independent from Richmond. During Reconstruction, unlike Petersburg to its south, Richmond blossomed. Its business leaders embraced the railroad boom with its goods and services pouring in from the North. And the North wanted its tobacco and flour. Work was to be found, and for a skilled clerk like William, it took little time to secure such a position in a tobacco factory. He supported his wife, Alice Perdue, and had four children with her."

"Is there any connection between her and the Perdue chicken family?"

"I don't know. Nevertheless, he loved her so. She kept his secret...perhaps she even made him concoctions of tea and animal blood from birds, squirrels and other such creatures. They kept quite a front, made easier by the fact that though sunlight was a nuisance to him, given the modest dress code of the time he could manage. He was actively involved in civic society and a member of the Methodist Church. His children never showed active symptoms, although one of his kids loved very rare meat. Bölcsem explained vampiric genes were recessive, hence his children did not inherit the condition. Except, I think the child who liked very bloody meat was an exception."

"Wow amazing."

"Yes, isn't it," she said, as Catterina made herself comfy in Ruxandra's lap. "Bölcsem learned about this genetic attribute thanks to a secret correspondence he kept using an alias with a fellow monk the world knows as Gregor Mendel. The one who did the landmark experiments growing recessive and dominant pea plants. His results still blow my mind, considering this was way before Watson and Crick."

"Figures, explains why Bölcsem is so into gardening, pea plants, roses..."

"Precisely. He is obsessed with genes and blood types and such, now he's working with me to produce synthetic blood, so we can exist even more off-the-grid.

"Anyway...the rest. On the pedigree of his father, Samuel Pool, Willie joined the city's Masonic Lodge which, in those days, was very powerful. It didn't take long for the head of the lodge to find out that Pool was a vampire, since a clandestine group within its ranks adhered to practices involving blood rites. So secretive was this group, that not even the Rosicrucian branch of freemasonry, which William belonged to, knew of it," said Ruxandra, holding up a golden ankh. She took the relic out of an archaic leather handbag engraved with an *Anunnaki* ruler, "Hence why the Rosicrucian rose is in the center of our ankh keys," she explained, brushing her fingers over the smoky red quartz petals.

"Fascinating," said Collette, petting Catterina, who'd been dislodged from Ruxandra's lap. "Are we the only ones with these keys?"

"No, there's a third one. The original was William's. Where it is, I have no idea, lost with Willie, I suppose. What time do you have?"

"It's 2 a.m.," replied Collette.

"Alright, we're good."

"Pool's mausoleum..." said Collette, "that's Egyptian in style, right? For his love of Freemasonry?"

"Quite so, but it was built initially to house his wife's remains. She died in 1912, or was it '13? Nevertheless, Later I formed it into a portal with Bölscem's assistance.

"Willie was devastated by her death. But I am putting the cart before the horse. So William, with the help of his Mason brothers, acquired both status and income, moving up amongst Richmond's elite. He rose from a tobacco clerk to a bookkeeper to, eventually, a position as the private secretary to the Bryan estate."

"The Bryans of Bryan Park?"

"The same. Joseph Bryan is remembered for taking the *Richmond Times-Dispatch* off of Major Lewis Ginter's hands."

"Your man was running with the big dogs. That explains how he had the jingle to put up such an impressive mausoleum."

"Oh yes, and a nice house in Woodland Heights as well," said Ruxandra.

"Was Bryan one of us?"

"Certainly not. But his friend and Masonic brother, Samuel Owens, though not vampiric by nature, was by hobby. After Alice's death in the winter of 1913, he and Samuel spent many evenings in Manchester, visiting ladies of the night to satiate their lust for blood and...other amusements."

"Where do you play in all of this?"

"I'm getting there."

"Cool. Do you want some more tea?"

"No thank you. So, to put it bluntly, Willie got careless. Just like he did when he was feeding on Union soldiers. He and Samuel had a favorite. I've forgotten her name. She consented to their desires. The problem was, by early '22, her blood was already tainted, likely from another client. Samuel and Willie became very ill and ended up dying on the same day, February 26th, 1922. Supposedly, they died of pneumonia. Well, at least that's what the papers said.

"Indeed, Samuel did die, but secretly, Willie survived. He wanted out of Richmond. The loss of his precious Alice, the blood sickness, the death of his closest friend, not to mention America's ceaseless drive for more profit, had tired Willie physically and emotionally. The Rosicrucian Masons in the Lodge arranged to put a hobo's body in his coffin, disguised to look like him. Albeit, even they were disgusted by Samuel and Pool's reckless behavior, unbecoming of the civic-minded Freemasonry. It was quite a public funeral, Pool and Owens brought much of Manchester out to pay their respects. A few days later, his Rosicrucian brothers shipped him in a trunk to Paris, care of the Masonic lodge there, and, once there, he took on a new name. In time, that's where I met Willie."

"How romantic!" exclaimed Collette.

"Oh it was. I met him through the lair there. Paris was the place to be: art and music, outlandish fashion and a most Bohemian way of life. More importantly, it was away from the endless drive for money that was America. T. S. Eliot's "The Waste Land" inspired him to go there, where art and creativity took precedence over the daily grind, and over the disillusionment left behind by World War I. Many artists and writers felt that way: Gertrude Stein, Hemingway, Beckett, Picasso.

"There he swept me off my feet with his charm, his debonair," she said smiling. A tear swelled; she brushed it away.

"Ah, auntie, it's alright," said Collette.

"Thanks...by the time I met him," she continued, "he was back on a diet of good blood; his handsome looks had returned. Though he was well over seventy, he didn't look a day past thirty. Amazing what healthy blood will do! What can I say? I'm a sucker for handsome men who can dance well."

Collette chuckled.

Ruxandra continued, "The roaring '20s in lovely Paris, the Lost Generation, Josephine Baker...what a time! Oh how I miss those days! I could stroll down the Champs-Élysées with a flapper hat and black parasol. Waste away the hours reading in Shakespeare and Company or people watching at Le Select.

"Our love affair and adventures lasted for quite a time. I introduced him to the Dracul Order and its Council of Archons. He loved Romania and its Carpathian Mountains. For the Council, he was bookkeeper; he also assisted Bölscem in curating the Records we unearthed from the House of Darkness.

"Of course, it all went wrong on November 11th, 1924, as you know. But here's the part you don't know. It was more over ideology than anything personal. Here in the US, we call our holiday 'Veterans Day,' but over there it's called 'Armistice Day,' in celebration of the end of World War I.

"Willie and I were enjoying the allure of Rome when we got swept up in the violence of an Armistice parade. I was decidedly a fan of Mussolini and his Blackshirts; William was not. He had an altercation with an anti-Fascist veteran in the Piazza del Popolo. Angry words turned to fists, and soon Liberalists and Socialists joined in against the Blackshirts. Soon enough, the violence escalated and clubs and knives came out. I was appalled by William's behavior.

"Afterwards, we realized we could not remain together without continually dredging up bad memories. It was over. The world was changing and so were we. He went back to Richmond for good later that year. I never saw him again," said Ruxandra, another tear forming in her eye. "There. Now you know."

Collette handed her the tissue box, "I'm so sorry."

"It's fine, child. It's been long overdue to tell you all this. I think part of the reason he went back was he missed his home.

"From then on, the only reports I got on Willie were from familiars...crows and cats, the usual. You get the picture. They told me he kept a low profile, used makeshift disguises. He had to. Despite the fact that his youth had returned, many people would have recognized him.

"He spent his time sleeping in his mausoleum by day and feeding on hobos and ladies of ill repute by night. Doubtless he became sick; many such people have tainted blood. At night, he took victims into the abandoned Church Hill Tunnel. At that time the tunnel was of no use to the railroad, having been replaced by a more direct, river-bank viaduct.

Although defunct, the tunnel had a life of its own known amongst locals as a mysterious place holding unknown dark forces. When the C&O decided to reopen the tunnel, many by then had dubbed it the 'Tunnel of Death' because of all who had died in its construction. Later, its byname would take on more potency with the tunnel's collapse. During its construction, a few laborers were done in by Pool himself."

"Really!?" exclaimed Collette.

"Oh yes. Among them a young night watchman," said Ruxandra.
"It all started with a bit of a falling out with his wife, Alice, in January, 1872. In his depression, he grew restless for human blood. He'd heard about the Church Hill Tunnel project and devised an audacious plan to feed on the crew and then cover it up as

industrial accidents. Deep in the Tunnel, laborers passed right by him. He disguised himself as one of them; moreover, he could completely morph himself by merging with rocky red clay and shadow. Still farther in, he had partially buried a coffin in which he sometimes slept and would occasionally stash away a victim. Workers reported the place was cursed, haunted even, but could never bring forth any hard evidence of evildoing.

"However, sometime in March, 1873, his coffin was discovered. Workers found it in an abandoned side of the tunnel. This forced him to patch things up with Alice and resume his meager diet of Earl Grey tea and animal blood."

Again, my friends, I must interrupt their chatter to properly tell all that Mr. Pool did in the Tunnel's birth and its falling into disuse. Here are those excerpts from the *Draculian Chronicles*:

Draculian Chronicles, Winter of 1872 to Fall of 1873

The saga of the construction of the Church Hill Tunnel began on February 1, 1872, in the early part of the Gilded Age. The Chesapeake & Ohio Railroad Company needed a way to get freight all the way to the Atlantic Ocean. At the time, there was not a connecting rail line, so the shortest route to connect the northern C&O line to the southern rail system down to Newport News was to cut through Church Hill via a tunnel. On top of that hill sprawled the neighborhood of Church Hill; both were named after St. John's Church, which sits, still, at the apex. St. John's is famous as the place where Patrick Henry gave his eloquent and galant speech: "Give me liberty or give me death."

However, the tunnel was an ill-conceived idea. The hill's composition was unstable; the soil was clayish and retained water. The Earth's omen hailed: seek fortune elsewhere.

Sadly, the capitalists heeded her not. Their ardor for progress rallied their laborers to sever her bosom. Moreover, the engineers decided to use the Block System (a stone block arching schema) which works well in holding up loose rock soil, but not Miocene clay! What were C&O engineers Whitcomb and Bolton, as well as tunnel advisor, Henry Drinker thinking!? Sadly, the appetite for riches overrode their common sense. So it was not surprising there were many deaths and several cave-ins during construction. Of note, the earth trembled in deviance on the morning of January 14, 1873 swallowing several homes on and around 24th Street. Even Mr. Drinker later had to admit in his final analysis that the engineers wrestled "with the unknown forces of darkness."

In the Spring of 1872, two shafts were in place to facilitate removing dirt from the tunnel. The western portal of the tunnel was at 19th Street (now called Cedar St.), and the eastern portal next to what would soon be called Chimborazo Park. The eastern construction site looked more like scorched earth, recalling to mind the predictions of Native American Indian visionaries who said the white man's iron horses would rape Mother Earth. At this time, Mr. William Wortham Pool, better known in today's folklore as the Richmond Vampire, had made a habit of going into the tunnel at night to dine. Most of his victims were ladies of the night, train hobos, or out-and-out criminals. But Pool fed not on former slaves, as he felt those people had suffered enough and deserved to live free from fear. Needless to say, many of the laborers were former slaves working in horrific conditions, while many of their supervisors were previous Confederate officers. Pool was inclined to feed on the privileged, such as the assistant engineer, James M. Bolton. However, the tunnel had an appetite of its own, beating out Mr. Pool by snuffing out Mr. Bolton's life with a chunk of earth in May of 1872.

Ah, but I digress. In late 1872, his first victim of the Tunnel construction crew was a young Charles Owens. It was an easy kill, as Charles was nearsighted and was standing near Shaft No. 3 when Mr. Pool accosted him, sucking the blood from his neck then gashing the puncture wounds with a serrated brick to cover up his deed. Next, he threw Owens down the shaft. The newspaper of the time reported that he'd got on the wrong side of the dirt bucket as it was coming up to the surface, due to his myopia. The ninety-foot fall, combined with his neck hitting the side of the shaft, was the cause of death.

Pool would later jest it was like a gift from Santa, as it happened in December, 1872.

His next tunnel crew victim was watchman George Dorsett. On January 26, 1873, George was on first nightshift, watching the tunnel for interlopers. It was a few minutes after 5 o' clock; darkness had already begun to blanket the site. Pool pounced on him, performing the same serrated brick cover up then throwing him down Shaft No. 1. It was reported Dorsett must have accidentally fallen into No. 1, because the steamy vapors around the work site had obscured the shaft.

Pool had, at the time, placed a casket in an unfinished part of the tunnel; there he would sleep or store victims until he could quietly dispose of them–usually into the deep and swift James River.

By March, 1873, the workers had found his coffin. In it was one of Pool's recent victims, a corpse slashed beyond recognition. The story never made the papers. It was covered up by the C&O so work would not be delayed by a criminal investigation.

By then, the tunnel's nickname had begun to circulate around town. It was called the "Tunnel of Death," and the name has stuck to this very day. The Tunnel of Death was ready for use on the morning of November 30, 1873. At that time, it was one of the longest train tunnels in the United States. The cost of C&O's greed and flawed planning was many lives. The first official train to go through was the David Anderson Junior. The Reverend Paul Whitehead summed up the entire venture best when he said:

> *James Bolton's life was sacrificed by the caving in of the Chesapeake and Ohio Tunnel under Church Hill–an ugly, dark hole that I never go through without a feeling of recoil, and which should have never been constructed.*

Draculian Chronicles, Winter of 1915

The Church Hill Tunnel is closed to trains. This cavernous monster is now docile! The beginnings of its demise all started back in the late 1890s with the commencement of construction of a viaduct bypassing Church Hill. This viaduct has proven to be a more efficient way of moving train traffic than using the detour route running beneath Church Hill. The viaduct is a more direct route to Fulton Yard and Newport News beyond. On June 24, 1901, the first train, engine no. 299, passed over the grand viaduct. The viaduct was, and still is, heralded as an engineering marvel in railroad history.

It crossed two other lines of track, making it the only three-tier crossing in the world: at ground level are the Southern Railway's tracks, the next up is owned by Seaboard Airline Railroad, and then at the top is the new C&O viaduct which runs along the James River bank.

These grand iron arteries will be the precursors to a booming Richmond market. As of this writing, Church Hill Tunnel is no longer in use and deemed impassable due to fragile timbers found in its bowels. Subsequently, it has been boarded up. Perhaps the Tunnel of Death will no longer devour men, whether it be by cave-in or by vampire.

Only time will tell.

"He didn't go back to the tunnel?" asked Collette.

"No, not until he returned in 1924. Like I have said, he slept in his mausoleum by day and hung out and fed on people in the tunnel by night. He kept this up until misfortune struck in the fall of 1925. As you know, they reopened it."

Collette enquired, "Why did they do that?"

"Because there was too much train traffic over the viaduct. They needed another route. The problem was they had to widen the tunnel. Trains by then were bigger. The C&O engineers were blockheads. They used the wrong method to widen it...some type of Block System and of course that's why it collapsed.

"Here I come to the part of the story where I possess little knowledge of what happened next. Between the papers and our familiars' accounts, it is all so muddled. Hence Bölscem's chronicles leaves more questions than answers. What I do remember was that on October 2, 1925, Willie was seen entering the tunnel at around 4am. This report was conveyed to me by a raven familiar named, Grip. From a tree near Chimborazo Park the avian witnessed Pool sneaking in disguised as a laborer. A bit before 3 o'clock the same day, a train with some flat cars entered from the eastern side."

Collette said, "I know that train number, it's 231. Jefferson Park has playground equipment that looks like the train and bears the number.
The flat cars, did laborers load dirt on them?"

"Yes."

"Tom Mason was the fella driving the train, and was Benjamin Mosby the man who tossed the coal?"

"Correct."

"I bet that Mosby was a stud."

"Oh, ok, so,"
Ruxandra cleared her throat and proceeded, "as the train was chugging along, its presence vibrated the tunnel. Around a hundred feet or so from the tunnel's western entrance, bricks started falling from the arched roof. Bricks continued to fall, taking out the work lights and sending the tunnel into darkness. Men started panicking, screaming, running this way and that, most made it out the eastern side."

"Yeah, later people say Mosby was yelling to Tom: 'she's a-coming in!'"

"Why am I retelling this part when you know it better than I?" asked Ruxandra.

"Oh, I don't know Willie's part; it's not like I have a copy of the Chronicle."

"Well I don't know it well either!" Ruxandra boomed.

"Whoa, no reason to get all flustered."

"Sorry."

"Not a problem...so, some say it was Mosby who ran out of the east side with severe burns, hanging flesh and broken teeth like fangs. They say he looked like

a vampire."

"I don't believe that," Ruxandra interjected.

"Uh-huh, but most people I've talked to think it was W. W. Pool who had been spooked out of the cave. He came running out and a bunch of workers chased him to his mausoleum. This is where it gets dodgy. Some say the mob killed him and others say it was a monster-like vampire that ran into William's tomb and disappeared."

"That is what I believe. I think that fox is still alive somewhere. He portaled out."

"Auntie, that doesn't make any sense."

"Sure it does!"

"No, it doesn't. He wouldn't have gone on this long and not told you."

"I don't want to talk about this anymore," stated Ruxandra.

A few minutes of awkward silence pervaded the room. Collette left then returned, handing her aunt a pewter brooch. The jewelry depicted a winged serpentine dragon with tongue protruding. Its eyeball had a labradorite crystal. "My gift to you," said Collette.

"Ah, my dear, this is precious...just like our Order's crest...marvelous," smiled Ruxandra.

Collette pinned it on her black cashmere sweater. "There."

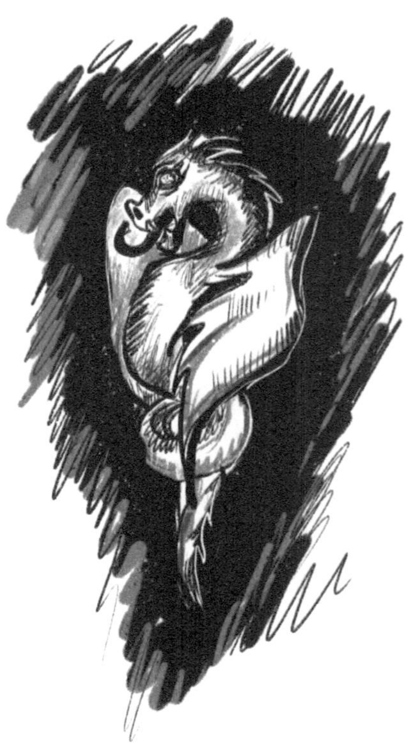

"Now, my dear I must be going back to San Jose. Will you drive me to Hollywood Cemetery?"

"Of course, auntie. When will you be back? I so love having you here," she said. Collette tidied up while Ruxandra finished her tea.

"Give me a moment to answer you," said Ruxandra, going to the vanity to collect her things.

They jumped in Collette's car and headed to Hollywood Cemetery near Oregon Hill.

"I don't know," said Ruxandra. "Hopefully not too long. Beautiful night. It's almost a full moon," she said as she gazed upward. The moon briefly peeked through the clouds. Tufts of snow were still on the ground. The pockets of clouds ushered on by a blustery sky.

Collette parked opposite the Superintendent's House at Hollywood Cemetery. The moon was reaching its apex. They opened the house's front gate and proceeded down Hollywood Avenue onto Confederate then Westvale Avenue.

As they walked, Collette noted, "Cold and windy night for a stroll."

"Yes, for you, but refreshing."

They walked in silence until they were in front of W. W. Pool's mausoleum, decorated in snow clumps and icicles. The words "W. W. Pool 1913" etched onto a stone tablet above the iron lattice door.

Collette piped up, "Do you know what they say about the 'W. W.' part?"

"No."

"They say Pool put his initials there instead of his name to portray vampire fangs," explained Collette.

"Ah, clever, but I doubt it. Willie deliberately filed down his fangs to avoid suspicion he was a vampire."

"Well, anyway, it's a good story. Auntie, were you really dreaming of grandfather?"

"Yes," replied Ruxandra as she opened the courtyard gate.

Collette followed saying, "Hmm, just seems strange that you were so upset about something that happened so long ago."

"It feels as though it was just yesterday. Going to and fro from this world to the Otherworld distorts your sense of time," explained Ruxandra as she placed her glowing left hand on the door's lock chain. The heat from her hand made the links malleable for easy opening, steam rising from melted ice.

Ruxandra pried open a link then loosed the chain from the door.

"Wish I could do that. Beats picking the lock," said Collette.

Ruxandra hugged Collette and opened the lattice entrance. "Be grateful you're not as vampiric in nature. Magick and vampiric power is not all that it's cracked up to be."

Ruxandra closed the entrance then pinched the chain link back together then adjusted the chain around the door and its frame. Collette grinned, now in the courtyard and said, "Auntie, I may not be a full

blooded vampire, but I can tell when you are holding things back. What were you really dreaming about?"

"You'll have to come and see me.

La revedere!" replied Ruxandra as she turned to face the notched wall.

"La revedere!" waved Collette.

Ruxandra pulled out her ankh key, holding it by its loop, then inserted the other end in the slot. Her body hair stood on end. She glowed an electric blue, her body resonating an earthly hum which replicated in the ankh, then in the chamber wall. From the wall appeared a small neon blue swirl that grew into a vortex encircling the entire wall.

She removed the key from its hole, placed it in her bag, then proceeded to walk into the tunnel. One moment Ruxandra was there, the next she was gone. The tunnel swirled in the opposite direction, shrinking in size until all that remained was a wall, warm to the touch. Melted ice pooled upon the chamber floor.

The Bateaumen

Draculian Chronicle, 2025

Many years had elapsed since Ruxandra's last visit to Richmond. By 2025, Collette had made a name for herself amongst the locals for her talented jewelry work. She had been dating a Chaos Magick practitioner, Steve Bilsharn, an artisan blacksmith, whom she met at Studio Two Three in the city's Scott's Addition neighborhood. He assisted Collette in bringing her jewelry ideas to life, forging settings of pewter, iron and other metals. They had been dating for about two years, but that was starting to fizzle.

Collette began feeling lonely, although attending gatherings of local pagans and written correspondence with Ruxandra helped. Every winter solstice, Collette visited her aunt either at her contemporary home in San Jose, California, or her modest retreat in the countryside near Cluj-Napoca, Romania.

But by September of that year, Ruxandra sensed that she needed to see Collette before the solstice. She decided to make an impromptu visit. She texted Collette letting her know she would be coming on the 5th with Evermore, her pet raven. Collette was delighted and they agreed to meet at Pool's mausoleum around seven o'clock.

Collette arrived in front of the sepulcher a few minutes before the appointed time. She unlocked the gate and stood just outside the chamber in the tiny courtyard. A few moments later the ground quivered. The glowing tunnel emerged from the wall illuminating the cold dark chamber. A faint smell of sulfur wafted

into the air. Ruxandra stepped out onto the crypt's vestibule in a black leather frock jacket. Evermore on her left shoulder.

"Hey, you're early," said Collette.

"*Servus*! Like to make a habit of being on time," replied Ruxandra.

"*Kraw, kraw*," hailed Evermore.

Collette petted him on the head, "Good to see you too." Evermore flew off toward one of the trees. The ladies hugged then exited the chamber. Collette padlocked the door.

"Ah, you finally put your own lock on," said Ruxandra. Collette just smiled. They walked back toward the front gate of Hollywood Cemetery.

"So, this visit is a pleasant surprise. What brings you here to RVA now?" asked Collette.

"Well, I've been worried about you. You seem lonely in your letters."

"My relationship with Steve is starting to fizzle out," said Collette.

"Oh, I'm sorry to hear that."

"Thanks. By the way, your blouse...so Romanian, folk eyes and ram horns; it goes well with the coat."

"*Mulțumesc*. Nice leather jacket. Goes well with your usual lace blouse. Is that red velvet?"

Collette smiled and swept back her long hair replying, "It is."

They were nearing the cemetery gate when Collette asked, "Hey, do you want to go get a bite to eat?"

"Sure, who?"

Collette laughed. "I'm sure we can find a dark, tall, handsome man for you."

Ruxandra smiled. "Sure, you pick. Did you get the new blood I sent you?" She eyed Collette's purse.

"Yeah, just a sec," as she pulled out a coiled dragon vial.

Ruxandra drank then gave it back. "*Vă mulțumesc dragă*."

"You're welcome, but really, thank you. After all, where would I be without your company, Sânge Nou, shipping me cases of this stuff."

"Did you notice a difference in taste?"

"No, why?"

"Oh good, it's a beta version that coagulates."

"Wow, that's wonderful. Are the others using it? Even Edana? Or is she still stealing farmer's sheep, or dare I say, others on foot?" enquired Collette, as they headed up Hollywood Avenue.

"Yes, they are, except Edana, and they like it. But only as a substitute. The real thing is still required, otherwise there are consequences, such as aging, loss of unnatural powers... Unfortunately, blood only has so much–"

"Calories, vitamins, yada-yada."

"Among other things, yes."

"So, with that in mind," gleamed Collette, "what are you in the mood for?"

"Something light," answered Ruxandra as they reached the car. "What do you recommend?"

"Oh I recommend The Hard Shell. It's a great seafood place down in Shockoe Bottom."

"I'm dying for a *bite* of seafood," laughed Ruxandra as she clipped in her seatbelt. Evermore flew ahead to Shockoe Bottom, exploring its rooftops and alleyways.

"All right," Collette touched the nav screen and spoke, "Drive us to Hard Shell."

They took a late dinner over a glass of white wine and assorted seafood delights. Afterwards, they took a stroll along the canal then over to Brown's Island. They passed in front of The Headman Statue, depicting a 19th century James River African American boatman. Evermore landed on a shoulder of the statue. He made a rattling sound.

Ruxandra turned at the sound and stopped in her tracks, looking up at Evermore then at the heroic figure. "Who is that?" she called out.

"Oh that, that's The Headman," replied Collette.

"What's a headman?"

"A headman is another name for a boatmen from the 1800s. Often they were African Americans who steered the canal system in a *bateau,* transporting materials up and down the river. Later the railroads came and they were no longer needed."

"I've seen someone like him before," Ruxandra said softly.

"What did you say?"

"Oh nothing. Let's go back to your place. The sun will be up soon," Ruxandra replied.

When they arrived back at Collette's house in Church Hill, they sat up the rest of the night catching up on old news, drinking blood tea, eating *gogoşi.* They chuckled when Collette's black cat, Catterina, and Evermore engaged in a tug-of-war over a biscuit. Evermore won when he nipped Catterina's tail, sending the cat scurrying upstairs. As dawn arrived, they both retired.

Ruxandra fell into a deep sleep. Towards the middle of her rest she drifted off again to W. W. Pool's mausoleum. Her diary recorded the dream.

Jurnal de Ruxandra cel Rău, 6 Septembrie 2025 (translated)

There I was again standing in front of my old love's mausoleum. Just as before a mist embraced its courtyard. Tears began to swell. The Egyptian pillars bidding me to gaze upon its dark lattice door. However, this time the rusty padlock was gone, replaced by a newer one; it was Collette's.

Then I heard the voice, far away once more. That same deep, authoritative voice of the black man I had heard so many years before. It echoed off the trees, the tombs. . .

"D-r-a-c-n-i-a, D-r-a-c-n-i-a..."

I could not tell its source. I looked about. No one. The sound left a resonating hum in my ear. The voice got louder; gusts of wind swelled up.

"D-r-a-c-n-i-a, Oh, Miss Dracnia..."

Vertigo set in...spinning, reeling...I had to grab the courtyard fence to steady myself. The echoing, that blasted humming persisted in my ear.

I cried out in irritation, "Where are you?"

I saw a man's leg momentarily breach a fog bank from the bottom of Westvale Avenue.

"Miss Dracnia, are you a' comin'?"

Now, the voice felt less inward more audible, beckoning. The trees swayed, but the fog lumbered along ambivalent to the wind's puppeteering.

Suddenly the mist surrendered. There he was. Steady amidst the wind, dressed as before in a sturdy white collared shirt wearing brown overalls. A towering man of African descent, dignified nose and forehead. His eyes penetrated into my soul. I looked away, in his, I saw the undiscovered; some gruesome knowledge of my loss.

I turned about heading toward Haxall Avenue, as I had before when I first dreamed of him.

"Miss Dracnia, I ain't a-comin' back."

Jarred, I looked back and stared at him, tears rolling down my face.

"It's alright Miss. Ya' gotta face this or it'll keep on a-hauntin' ya.'"

"Has Morpheus sent you?"

"Ma'am, that be my business."

Without another word he began walking toward Waterview Avenue, toward the James River.

I composed myself and embarked into the unknown. He went in and out of the mist. He seemed to hover over the ground.

Once at the ellipse of Waterview Avenue, I could see and hear the river's rapids.

I barely made out his figure vanishing into the mist down the North Bank Trail running near the river's edge.

"I ain't a waitin' forever!" his voice boomed near the Belle Isle Suspension Bridge.

With greater pace I trekked the North Bank Trail parallel with the tracks. A steam locomotive shattered the stillness with its toting horn and blistering headlamp. I caught a glimpse of the engineer waving to me. I stopped and stared at him as I read No. 231 emblazoned on its coal car. Bewildered as to what time period I was in, for there was no skybridge in the Age of Steam, I pressed on nonetheless.

At the North Bank Trail Head I heard him again at the river, "Miss Dracnia, I'm docked down here."

I turned toward the river, crossed Tredegar Street past the road lamp. Just below me, docked in the lamp's light, was a bateau. I made out the silhouette of a younger black man holding his sweep in the fore. He looked just like the Headman Statue; collared button down shirt, oversized chest pockets, rolled up sleeves, workman's pants and boots. The statelier one who had been beckoning me was in the aft. I boarded. The aft man gestured to the bowman.

They shoved off, poling westward under the Robert E. Lee Bridge toward the rapids. Looking up, I saw the walking suspension bridge held up via a web of steel wire from the car bridge. Stillness pervaded; not a bird, not a person or car was heard only a slight

breeze and the poles disturbing the waters. Soon we were past the bridge. A slithering fog rolled in at the foot of the rapids toward us.

The boatmen staked firm. We were a good quarter of the way from shore. The aft man said, "Miss Dracnia, look over the port side." I did so.

Bubbles began bursting open at the surface. First small, then they grew in size, breaking as they met the air. Swirling hair strands appeared in the current. My heart started pounding. Mixed with the hair was a pool of blood oozing outward like an oil slick. It spread, surrounding the boat. My eyes enlarged, my hands began to tremble. I turned from the sight.

"Dracnia!" a voice called out.

"No," I cried.

"Dracnia, look at me!"

I swung about.

"William, my Willie."

My eyes beheld his severed head hovering just above the water. He was covered in river mud, blood seeping from his crown and neck.

"Dracnia, forgive me! I was coming, injured by the cave in, overpowered by the mob."

Tears streaming down my face, "Yes, yes my dearest."

"Avenge me."

"But how, Willie, how!?"

By my blood,
Avenge those who were buried.

Their souls long to be ferried.
Ferried, from Death's Tunnel
To their resting place.
Seek my blood, in he who is At Rest.
Surely my love,
He shall pass the Test.

"Your blood? I don't understand," she exclaimed.

He began sinking back to his watery grave, "Seek my love, seek he who is At Rest!"

He disappeared, his only remains the pooling of blood floating past the bateau.

I awoke. Unlatched the coffin. Sat up disheveled from all that I had envisioned. My thoughts were scattered, but one thing was certain. The bateau man who had beckoned me years ago, the same man whom I followed today, had shown me a truth from the world of the dead.

Was the old legend true? Was it William who had staggered from the Church Hill Tunnel's eastern side, with his razor-like teeth broken and shards of flesh dangling from his torso? If so, he must have had one thing in mind. Escape to safety. Escape to his mausoleum, to his portal, back to my arms. The tunnel workers, the onlookers, chased him to his mausoleum. They accosted him there, before he could enter. There they overpowered him for lack of blood. Cut off his head and hid the deed in the depths of the James. Surely, surely I will find a way to avenge him! And not only him, but all those who died that fateful day.

Retribution upon the mob's ancestors who severed his head—perhaps? Assuredly, vengeance upon those generations whose forefathers sanctioned the Tunnel's reopening. Had not the Ancient One declared:

> ...he will by no means clear the guilty, visiting the iniquity of the fathers on the children, to the third and the fourth generation.[1]

Ruxandra staggered out of the coffin then penned all the account in her diary. Later she went upstairs and called up to the second floor, "Collette, Collette?"

"Yes auntie."

"Please come here."

"Auntie, you look like you've seen a ghost."

"I have."

"What happened?"

This time, Ruxandra told Collette what she really had dreamed during her visit years ago and that she had just dreamed it once again with its startling outcome.

After the retelling, Collette responded, "Astonishing! A message from the Underworld. 'At Rest,' what does it mean? Are you going to find out?"

"Yes, yes. What was the name of that dowser? The one you read to me back when I first had this dream?"

"Um, I don't remember, but I think the outfit is called DorEn," said Collette.

"Perfect. Get in contact with them, and tell the dowser we want a session at his grave."

"Um, ok, when?"

"Tomorrow's full moon at midnight, if she can manage it," Ruxandra replied. "We'll meet at Hollywood's gate. "

"How do we...at that hour, with those temps.... She's gonna ask for payment upfront."

"Here," she said, handing Collette her card. "Ask for her rate then triple it.

Hopefully she won't pass it up."

Dowsing for Truth

Draculian Chronicle, September 7th of 2025

"Ahh, this is brutal," said Lunia. She looked out from her parked car unto a frigid and blustery mess, traces of snow amongst midnight's shadows. Across the street she saw the mural sign: VICTORY RUG CLEANING Hollywood Cemetery. Both had arrows pointing toward the spooky place. The rug ad was on top. Perhaps a weird thought came to mind that the dead may need a good clean rug where they're going, hence all its letters in caps.

As she got out of the car, leather pouch in hand, she heard a cawing sound and looked up over the roof of her car. A raven was perched atop the row house displaying on its side the street mural by M. Lively. It depicts a fox rising on a cumulus cloud above tumbling sheep. Perhaps she viewed herself as one of the sheep and the ominous dark raven as the fox.

As Lunia walked west toward Hollywood Cemetery's iron clad gates, she made out two darkly dressed figures: one hooded, one slightly taller with radiant pale skin and ruby lips in a concoction of mist and lights. One light from a street pole irritated her; the other was a solitary, faint glow from the corner tower of the Superintendent's Queen Anne-style house.

"Hello," said Lunia, as she approached Collette in a black duster coat; next to her, Ruxandra stood in a dark leather frock. Both wore black leather boots. Only Collette

wore gloves to match. Her shiny black hair glistened in the street light; Ruxandra's lavender hair glowed. Their lips naturally ruby needing no lipstick.

"Hi," replied Collette, shaking Lunia's hand. "This is my auntie, Ruxandra. Auntie, this is Lunia from DorEn Channeling."

"A pleasure to meet you, Lunia," said Ruxandra with a slight bow of her head.

"It's nice to meet you as well. And who is that?" Lunia asked looking up at the raven perched upon one of the gate's pillars.

"That is Evermore," answered Collette. "He is Ruxandra's familiar."

"Oh, I see. Nice take on the Poe bird." She paused to size Ruxandra up. "You're not kidding about the familiar, are you?" Lunia said.
"Why would I?" retorted Ruxandra as the bird landed on her shoulder. "He is a faithful companion, reporting all that I require." The raven returned to his perch.

Lunia asked, "Aren't you cold?" looking at Ruxandra's bare hands and no hoodie donned.

"Not at all," Ruxandra replied.

"May I be frank with you?" said Lunia, looking squarely at her.

"By all means," she said.

"What are we doing here? I'm freezing. What I mean to say is, can't we do this tomorrow, when the cemetery's open and it's warmer?"

"Entertain me for a moment. Please take off your glove and give me your hand," said Ruxandra. Lunia complied. She held her hands for a good ten seconds then said, "Better?"

"Well, yes. How did you do that? My whole body is warm."

"Oh, I have my ways," she replied. "It's a full moon, after all, despite the gloomy sky. Dowsing works best on such a night. Besides, you know Benjamin; we do not."

"Is the payment satisfactory?" said Collette.

"Yes, more than I expected. Thank you."

"You're welcome," replied Collette.

"You all don't intend to go inside, do you?" said Lunia, staring at the main gate's lock.

Ruxandra walked over to the Superintendent's iron gate and pushed it open. "TA-daaah!" she exclaimed, walking in. "Or should I say, *Voilà!*" then bid us enter with an outstretched hand.

"Haha," said Lunia.

"*Kraw, Kraw,*" screeched the raven, flying just ahead of them as they walked down Hollywood Avenue.

Lunia led the way to Benjamin F. Mosby's grave, walking up Confederate Avenue past Westvale Avenue. While in tow, Collette noticed Ruxandra looked down toward Westvale. She squeezed Ruxandra's hand. "I'm okay," whispered her aunt.

"We can visit him on the way out," replied Collette.

At the top of the hill where Cedar Avenue intersects, Lunia stopped to catch her breath. Ruxandra and Collette came up from the rear and stood with her. Lunia pointed at a cast-iron Newfoundland dog saying, "That's our famous iron doggie. Supposedly he's guarding the grave of a little girl who died of scarlet fever back in the 1800s."

"That would explain all the toys," said Collette, standing over the girl, Bernadine Rees' gravesite, littered with plastic dolls, tokens, notes of affection and such. "Yes, a nice way to pay respects," said Lunia.

"Charming. Now, on to Mosby's grave," said Ruxandra.

Lunia led them past Cedar and Western Avenues. They turned left onto Clark Springs Circle. She stopped where the Maynard-Mosby plate faced the road. She pointed at a small arched tombstone and said, "That's Benjamin Mosby. On his left is Marie, his wife, and on the right is Dorothy, his daughter."

"*Minunat!*" exclaimed Ruxandra. "Let us begin the questioning."

"I take it that means 'great'?" inquired Lunia.

"Close. 'Wonderful,' in Romanian," explained Collette.

"*Kraw, gluck,*" sounded Evermore from a tree branch above them. The tree's trunk partially covered the road's curbstones, appearing at any moment

to shake its roots, rise up and walk.

"Ok, give me a moment while I setup," said Lunia. She untied a leather pouch, pulling out a pair of copper L-rods. "By the way, Ruxandra, your eyes are beautiful. I have never seen such a mix of hazel and blue offsetting one deep brown eye."

"Thank you. It's called sectoral heterochromia."

"Does it affect your vision?"

"Not in the slightest. Do you see the crow perched on an obelisk, there, near Cedar Avenue?"

"Auntie, really, even I can't see that far," said Collette.

"Ah, no, I don't even see the obelisk. Wow, I'll take your word for it," exclaimed Lunia.

"Why do you look so excited?" whispered Collette to her aunt.

"It says: 'AT REST' on Mosby's grave," she replied. Collette looked bewildered. "I'll explain later."

"Ladies, are we ready?" Lunia asked. They stood in the grass facing his gravestone.

"Yes," said Collette.

For a few moments all were silent. Lunia held each rod slightly downward toward the ground. "Good evening Benjamin Mosby," she called out. "This is Lunia; do you remember me?"

A few moments of stillness passed, her rods unmoved. Puffy vapors whisked away from their breath.

"Mr. Mosby are you there?" she asked again. The rods were still. Evermore ruffled his wings.

Ruxandra said, "Allow me to help you tune in." Lunia nodded in approval. Ruxandra laid a hand on her shoulder. "Relax, settle into your spirit. The rods are a part of you."

Lunia's eyes closed. Her hair began to rise. "Good," said Ruxandra speaking in a dream-like tone. "Now, ask again."

Lunia, at a pitch and amplitude mimicking a deep echo spoke, "M-o-s-b-y, Mr. M-o-s-b-y. This is Lunia...are you there?"

A breeze broke the stillness. Ruxandra let go. Lunia kept her eyes closed.

Collette stood still with bated breath.

The rods began to cross then move outward. Lunia opened her eyes. The rods slowly began to spin. The twirling quickened then stopped.

"He is here," said Ruxandra. "Ask him again."

"Are you Benjamin Mosby?" The rods pointed and Lunia walked forward halting just in front of his grave. Collette and Ruxandra followed suit.

Lunia asked, "What is 'yes' to you?" The rods crossed. "What is 'no' to you?" The rods parted open at an outward angle. "I am Lunia; do you remember me?" The rods crossed. "May we ask you a few questions?" The rods crossed again. "Thank you. With me is Ruxandra and Collette who is the shorter one. They will now ask you some questions."

"Good evening Mr. Mosby," said Ruxandra. "When the Church Hill Tunnel collapsed, was there someone under the flatcar with you?"

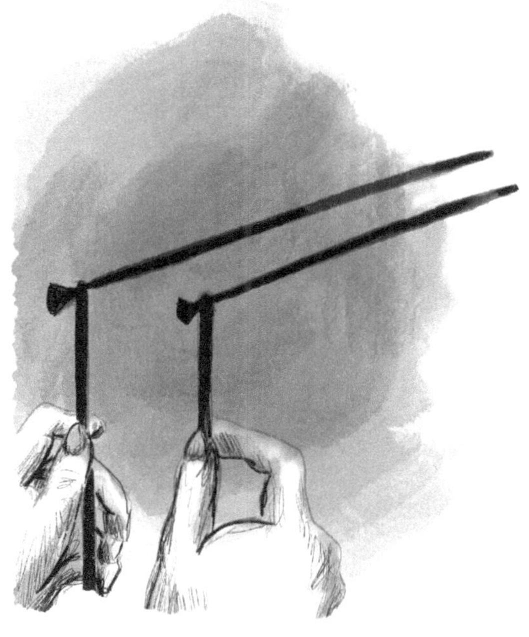

The rods crossed.

"Was this the person?" Ruxandra held out a black and white photo of William W. Pool.

The rods formed an X. Ruxandra and Collette let out a collective gasp and looked at each other.

"Did he bite you?" Collette asked. The rods went outwards. "Did, did you drink his blood?" she continued.

The rods crossed. Lunia dropped them in horror.

"Willie, *kraw...baw!*" shrieked Evermore. Ruxandra narrowed her eyes at the bird.

"Be calm," said Ruxandra, gazing into Lunia's eyes.

Lunia was breathing heavily. "*Who are you!?* That bird, it, it spoke," she cried.

"You're safe. There is no need to be afraid," Ruxandra said, maintaining her gaze. Collette picked up the rods, handing them back to Lunia. Ruxandra motioned to Collette with her right hand to stay near.

"This was all in the past," Ruxandra said, soothingly. "Breath. Yes, you're safe, that's it," she held Lunia's hand. Lunia locked onto her eyes. "Yes, that's it."

Lunia's breathing slowed.

Ruxandra affixed her gaze. "Say, 'I'm safe.'"

"I'm safe," Lunia said, maintaining eye contact.

"Say, 'It was all a dream,'" stated Ruxandra, her voice a quiet-pitched echo.

"It was all a dream," repeated Lunia, her eyelids weighty.

"Yes. It was not real. You are feeling heavy, drowsy," declared Ruxandra. Lunia's eyes became glassy, the only expressive part of an otherwise blank face.

"Follow me," Ruxandra commanded. Lunia was shepherded back to her car; Ruxandra held her hand the entire way. Evermore trailed, flying from tree to tree. He came to rest upon the building bearing the Hollywood mural across from Lunia's car.

Back at her car, Collette pulled Lunia's keys from her coat pocket and started her car, turned on the heat, and left the driver's door open. Ruxandra guided Lunia to her seat. "Sleep now, s-l-e-e-p. All was a d-r-e-a-m," whispered Ruxandra in her ear. Lunia closed her heavy eyes and nodded off. Ruxandra closed the door. Evermore swooped down and landed on her left shoulder. Ruxandra petted him. He made a warbling sound.

"Auntie, you're brilliant," said Collette.

Ruxandra smiled at her. "She'll be fine."

"What now?" asked Collette.

Ruxandra replied, "Walk with me to Pool's." They strolled toward the mausoleum. "Did you notice what Mosby's stone said?"

Collette answered, "Besides the usual: his name, date of death–ah, his epitaph, 'At Rest,' on the front side. That's right, you mentioned it in your dream, Pool said, 'Seek he who is At Rest.'"

"Precisely," Ruxandra exclaimed. "I remember hearing:

Seek my blood, in he who is At Rest.
Surely my love,
He shall pass the Test.

"So Mosby is our man. You're not suggesting a Midnight Mary, are you?" asked Collette.

"Perhaps," answered Ruxandra as they reentered Hollywood Cemetery.

"What is 'the Test' part?"

"'The Test' is Mosby passing the Remanifestation, the Becoming, and finally the Avenging."

"That's a lot."

"Indeed," agreed Ruxandra as they came to the bottom of Hollywood Avenue, the moon illuminating their way.

"But why?"

"*Grevă echilibrul,*" Ruxandra replied as Evermore landed on a tree near the mausoleum.

"Sorry, my Romanian is–"

"Roughly, it means, 'Strike the Balance.' The world is out of balance. Too much of the Right Hand Path. Masses blindly submitting to conventional direction, both economically, emotionally and metaphysically. Perhaps the Great Balance has begun," she chuckled. "Who would have thought it could start here of all places, in this humble city of Richmond."

"Start with Mosby; he's just a fireman."

"It is amongst the unknowns: the peasants, the bookkeepers, the firemen, my dear, who often ignite the beginning of the Balance. The French Revolution for example. That was a political balance, but what the world needs now, is something more comprehensive–a metaphysical balance."

"Definitely," said Collette as she opened the courtyard gate.

"Besides," explained Ruxandra, entering the mausoleum's yard, "if the dowsing proves true, Benjamin Mosby is now a strigoi, a vampiric shapeshifter, as was Pool. Let loose in the world, he has the power to avenge and to ignite the Fire of Balance."

"What would it take to Remanifest him?" she inquired.

"A Remanifestation requires a unanimous vote of the Nine Archons. And, the approval of this city's demonic ruler," answered Ruxandra, standing before the tomb's entrance. Evermore alighted on auntie's left shoulder. The familiar made a warbling sound.

"I'll miss you too," said Collette, brushing his wings with her hand.

Collette embraced her aunt, then unlocked the lattice door. She said, "Let's do winter solstice in Cluj."

"Sounds grand," agreed Ruxandra. "Take care–write." She made a finger heart gesture. "*Pa.*"

Collette did likewise. "*Pa,*" she said, waving.

Ruxandra pulled her ankh from her purse. Placed it in the notch. Enveloped in a hue of electric blue, she vanished.

An Old Flame

Transcription of Collette cel Rău's Journal, September of 2025

After Ruxandra was gone, loneliness set in once again. Her mingling with fellow pagans and her participation with an online Setian Oasis wasn't enough. Occasionally Brannbjørn, her old flame, would attend the online sessions. He offered small talk about the topic at hand but nothing more. Yet she wanted *more*, and felt an urge to restart things, but in the end didn't. For as much as she wanted to, he was of a bloodline her aunt did not approve of. Brannbjørn, though Norwegian by citizenship, actually came from the ancient Fomorian bloodline which was, and still is, known for its brutality and covetous inclinations.

However, one day in mid-September, seemingly out of the blue, he texted her.

Brannbjørn: Hey there, what's sizzlin'
Collette: Nothin, nothin @ all
Brannbjørn: U sound sad
Collette: I am
Brannbjørn: Why
Collette: Think Steve's OOO 4 good
Brannbjørn: Bummer
Collette: Yeah, wht u up 2
Brannbjørn: Kayaking fjords
Collette: Swweet
Brannbjørn: Yeah, wish u were here
Collette: Hmmm
Brannbjørn: Hmmm, wht

Collette: U still seeing Nadia
Brannbjørn: Nope
Collette: NOOO! She found out bout ur biohacking biz or ur a shapeshifter?
Brannbjørn: Both. She weirded out when she saw me morph
Collette: Sorry, similar here, gone cold over my vamp story
Brannbjørn: Eww
Collette: I had grown 2 trust steve so i confided. Told him my real age and my dracul bloodline bit. He got distant
Brannbjørn: We r a freak of nature u and I
Collette: Yep
Brannbjørn: K, ttyl. Heading up to Bergen
Collette: Come c me
Brannbjørn: When
Collette: Mabon fest
Brannbjørn: ok, Fallfeast 2 me, haptic-chat me anytime on 21st
Collette: K cool

The twenty-first arrived. Collette started a haptic video chat at around nine in the morning Atlantic Coast time with Brannbjørn.

Collette: Hey u comin'?
Brannbjørn: Sure check this out

He held an object in haptic mode. She examined a hologram of a hooped rune earring made of garnet and selenite cast in gold. She felt its edges in the rune writing, the hard coldness of the garnet stone.

Collette: Ah, nice work
Brannbjørn: Tks, keeps da bad stuff away
Collette: Gotcha. Meet @ ur Comet. Midnight UK time work?
Brannbjørn: Ja
Collette: K, c u then. Bye
Brannbjørn: Ha det

Around six in the evening, Collette spoke to her car then it drove her to a small parking lot across from Hollywood Cemetery. She walked down to Pool's mausoleum. Opened the lock, entered the chamber and closed the door. She withdrew an ankh from her purse and inserted it into the notch. The wall manifested a spiraling tunnel of blue light which she stepped into.

Far away in Orkney, Scotland, the Split Stone at the Ring of Brodgar began

Split Stone

vibrating and humming. A glowing swirl appeared on the side of the stone facing the center. Collette wobbled out, veering to her right before steadying herself. She took a few deep breaths then looked around. No Brannbjørn. "Late as usual," she said, checking her haptic smartwatch. She donned her cloak's hood to protect herself from the wind. She noticed a shag perched on the Head Stone. It made a grunting sound. She grinned, then moved toward the Comet Stone, just a short walk from the Ring.

She admired the Loch of Harray's glistening water in the starlight. A car passed by on the roadway, but didn't notice her. Once the car was out of site, the Comet Stone began glowing. She moved closer to it. She felt the ground under feet vibrating as a vortex of electric blue appeared.

Out stepped Brannbjørn, though he had to duck to exit since the vortex's height, in accordance with the stone's dimensions, was not adequate to align with his stature. A rock solid, formidable man of the North, his carefree demeanor, rustic auburn beard and azure eyes belied his antediluvian frame, impervious to the elements. Metal objects were clay in his grip. He wore an unbuttoned Tuscan style sheepskin jacket. A leather drawstring held up brown leather side-stitched pants. Finishing off his look, a pair of dark brown buckled leather boots. His rigid cheekbones, cleft chin and dignified nose enhanced his Nordic looks. He was adorned with tattoos; one on his right forearm of Fenrir, on the other, of Vegvisir. For jewelry, he wore copper and lava rock bracelets and rune earrings made of garnet cast in gold. Around his neck, a pyrite talisman inscribed with an Algiz Rune crowned by three wolves dangling from a leather thong.

Shag bird perched on Head Stone

He smiled at her. Juggled his four-knobbed crystal petrosphere, which depicted

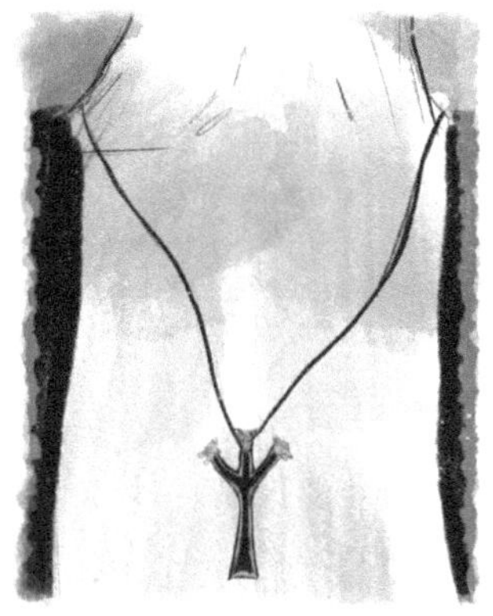

spirals of differing increments on three sides and concentric circles on its fourth side. He put the sphere in his coat pocket then walked up to her.

"Not bad," she quipped.

"I'm getting better," he held up a balanced EMF haptic watch.

"Oh, nice," she said. "Maybe an old bear–"

"Can learn new tricks," he finished for her, then they hugged. "We poking some old coals."

"I'll take that as a question," she said, "which I may or may not answer later."

"Oookay!" his brows elevated. "You look a bit disheveled."

"This portaling is not my cup of tea. The vertigo is brutal," she replied.

They started walking toward the Split Stone. "What a night that was," said Brannbjørn pointing with his thumb at the Lightning Stone and its plaque. "Does your auntie still conjure up storms?"

"Only if need be," eyed Collette.

Once at the Split Stone, Brannbjørn passed his hand through the gap. "Well, she's still holding up," he said, eyeing the split. "You know it's amazing she toppled that stone," he smirked, looking back at the Lightning Stone," and the ricochet split this one," gently touching the Split Stone.

"Yeah, well, if you hadn't trespassed and whisked Lydia away you wouldn't have this," she said feeling the burn mark on his left forearm.

"Whew, forty-five years ago and the scar is still there. Anyway, I admit I could have been more tactful in apologizing to Dracnia. Didn't know Lydia was a vamp... she wasn't exactly forthcoming," Brannbjørn countered.

"Do you know it took her two new moons to recover from these claws," she said as she felt his stone-like fingernails.

He smiled and said, "Keep doing that." Collette withdrew. He continued, "Well, at least I don't *bolt* folks. Wonder if a human witnessed our scuffle."

"Ahh no, no *Homo sapiens*

Lightning Stone

coming out here in a lightning storm...good thing she's not a crack shot," laughed Collette.

"What did you do with the fragments?"

"I took them back to Østfold."

"Still getting here by the Hunnfelt?" Collette asked.

"*Ja*, works like a charm. I'm grateful your vampires solidified these ley lines. Hey, what's with this bird?" he asked, pointing at the Head stone.

She looked up at the obstinate shag. "You know, it's a boobrie."

"Boo! A Dragonist spy," he exclaimed with pursed lips. The boobrie stared at him with its top hat tuft of feathers then squawked at him.

"Hey, it's not like that," she piped up, "it's good to have 'em around."

"All righty, shall we?" he asked, rhetorically tapping her purse.

"Let's." Collette placed the tip of the ankh key upon the heart of the Split Stone facade facing the ring. Her body glowed and vibrated. "Your hand," she ordered.

"My pleasure," he smirked.

The quivering key sank to its hilt into the radiant monolith, which shook the ground under them. A blue tunnel appeared. The pair were whisked away.

Brannbjørn's Folly

Transcription of Collette cel Rău's Journal, September 21st and 22nd of 2025, Mancho's Account, & the Draculian Chronicles Fall of 2025

They arrived inside Pool's chamber in the early evening hours of Sunday. Collette wobbled out, veering into Brannbjørn's arms. He held her steady.

"Whoa there, you Ok?" he asked.

"Yeah, thanks," she replied. She regained her bearings. She opened the gate's lock.

"It'd be easier if you just put on a Touch ID lock."

"No, that would be too easy," she chuckled. "Besides, I don't do this portal thing too much."

"Yeah I can see why," he said.

They exited and she reattached the padlock. She admitted, "The price of being too human and not enough vampy." A crow cawed in a nearby tree.

"No sweat, it's all good," he said.

They exited the cemetery by the house gate and then went to her car. Approaching, she said, "Hey Alfred, home please."

"Cute," smirked Brannbjørn. The vehicle autonomously drove them to her home in Church Hill. Once inside, her cat, Catterina, nuzzled up against Collette's legs.

"Ah, you missed me," she said picking her up.

"I missed you too," interjected Brannbjørn.

"Hmm." She dropped Catterina on the sofa then put her fingers through Brannbjørn's straight blond hair. He placed a hand on her waist. They kissed lightly for a minute. Their breathing deepened, tongues meeting.

Gently she stopped, whispering, "You'll be here for a few days?"

"*Ja*," he whispered.

"Good," she pulled away and went into the kitchen, "then we have plenty of time to catch up. There's a guest bed, second door on the left. I'm weak from that portaling." She put a hand to her left temple.

"Ah, ok, got it. Drink plenty of blood and water. Nite," he said with a resigned tone.

On Monday after lunch Collette and Brannbjørn hopped in her car to head off to the Mabon festival, a pagan celebration marking the Autumn equinox.

They headed to a field not too far from the Richmond airport. A creepy place called Elko Tract, dubbed The Lost City, built as a decoy airfield in World War II.

The weather was crisp, cool and dry; it hadn't rained for weeks, but it was overcast, ominous, dark grey churning billows. Fellow pagans, Wiccans and nature worshipers gathered in a field near an abandoned water tower to give thanks to the Universe and various gods and spirits for another year of harvest. Harvest, not only of gratitude for sustenance but for family, friends and the beauty of nature. Revelers and worshipers donned flowering garlands around an equinox altar. The altar table's centerpiece was a beeswax pillar candle, three feet high and stout. Beside it, an athame and a plate of crescent moon cookies. Each worshipper contributed an offering. This amounted to a plethora of gourds, squashes, various nuts as well as Indian corn, stalks of grain and colorful leaves, symbolizing the changing seasons, along the periphery tiny pumpkins. Collette added a basket of apples. Brannbjørn brought nothing.

Once the preparations were complete, devotees gave thanks and lit candles for each element of the earth, call outs to each quarter invoked. Some placed lighted tapers in remembrance of ancestors, others uttered pronouncements of good fortune for the coming season, but one issued a warning.

Afterwards, a bonfire was built and a harvest feast set on makeshift tables, accompanied by fold out chairs. Collette introduced Brannbjørn to her pagan friends. She knelt down and rubbed the top of a shaggy black dog's head. "Ah, Mancho, you're such a good dog, so glad you're here," she smiled.

As Collette was petting Mancho, an imposing shadow covered them. The muscular Steve Bilsharn looked down on her. The Goth biker was wearing a Sigil of Chaos ring she had collaborated with him on. He had forged the ring, she had inset the sigil of rose quartz. She wore a matching lady's version, though not on her wedding finger, as he did.

Steve said to Collette, "Hi, we gonna talk?"

"Yep, but not here," she replied.

"Ok, well, I have some owning up to do."

"Oh really," she said. "You've been drinking whiskey," she sniffed and raised an eyebrow.

Brannbjørn approached, seeing how close Steve was to her. He asked, "Hey, is there a problem here?"

"Who's asking?" as Steve stepped up slightly staring up at him. Steve was solid, an imposing figure to match Brannbjørn's height. He had shoulder length, jet black hair to go with his studded leather jacket, half hooped nose ring and array of doom tattoos.

"You don't want to go there," warned Brannbjørn.

"Look, bud, you're encroaching. Step away or you'll be hurting," threatened Steve.

"Oh, I'm terrified," said Brannbjørn sarcastically, not flinching. He glanced at Collette and asked, "Thought you ended this?"

"Ah, umm, not totally," she grimaced.

Brannbjørn rolled his eyes, and when he turned back, Steve landed an upper cut to his chin. He teetered backward a few steps, tripped over a log and landed in the bonfire. Burning logs rolled out of the pit. Some of them past the dirt barrier, igniting dried field grass and foliage. Brannbjørn regained his footing. However, the back of his sheepskin jacket's collar had caught fire.

The revelers stopped their festivities. Mancho began to growl. The men ignored the dog.

Collette yelled out, "Brannbjørn you're on fire!" Others joined in warning him. Still others were putting out the grass fire.

Brannbjørn examined himself and replied, "No I'm not."

"It's your collar! It's spreading!" said a bystander.

By the time he realized it, Brannbjørn's backside was in flames as was his shoulder length blond hair.

"Awww!" he cried, then hit the ground and rolled to smother out the flames. People were screaming, others speechless in shock, still others busy throwing beverages on the ground fires. One man took off his jacket, attempting to snuff out the fire on Brannbjørn. Steve took off down a curbed trail toward the woods.

Brannbjørn sat up, groaning in pain. He felt for his hair. The whole backside of it was gone. "Errr," he growled. He brushed the charred hair loose from his head. His scalp was blackened and bleeding.

"Ahhh, you bastard!" he roared, grinding his teeth, looking around for Steve. His eyes burning, becoming darker, fists clenched, muscles enlarging. His appearance became bearish, wolf-like: his skin slightly covered over with shaggy auburn hair...his forehead and ears rounded, amber eyes, cheekbones drawn, nose snout-like, his teeth elongated as did his nails. People screamed in shock at his transformation. One of the smaller logs that had rolled into the field unnoticed had now started a blaze.

Bystanders scattered. Mancho stood his ground, his eyes now gleaming red.

Brannbjørn stood up growling and jerked his head about, hunting for Steve.

"No, stop," cried Collette, stretching her palms out in front of her. Brannbjørn pushed her aside. He sniffed the air in all directions then locked his head toward the trail. Sniffing once more, he took off with blazing speed in the direction Steve had run. Mancho followed after Brannbjørn. Collette took a short cut to the clearing where vehicles were parked.

Brannbjørn was gaining on Steve. Steve arrived at the clearing and straddled his Harley. He looked up and saw Brannbjørn had shape-shifted, with Mancho trailing. A look of terror crossed Steve's face, he started the motorcycle, gunning it down a dirt road in the opposite direction.

Collette appeared. "Let him go," she implored.

"No! Give me your keys," demanded Brannbjørn.

She pulled out her keys. They got into her car. Bjorn floored the compact electric vehicle. Steve got on a road near Canal Swamp. At its end, he headed east on Portugee Road then south on Elko Road, Brannbjørn in hot pursuit. Mancho ran after them at unnatural speed for a dog, his tongue dangling from his sharp teeth, eyes a blazing red. A train's horn sounded in the distance.

Up ahead, the railroad crossing gates, lights were flickering, *ding-ding* bells tolling. The train horn blasted again. Steve slowed down. The gates were closing each way. Another blast. Steve came to a stop behind a car and a flatbed truck carrying sheets of glass.

Brannbjørn rounded the corner. *Ding-ding-ding*, a longer blast. Steve saw him approaching in his side mirror. The train horn blared longer. Bjorn was closing in.

The train blare grew louder. Steve went around the car and truck, heading straight for the tracks. A prolonged blast. He veered around the gate then rode diagonally over the tracks. Bilsharn stopped just before the bend in the road. He put out the bike's kickstand and stretched forth a hand toward his pursuers.

Brannbjørn went into the incoming lane. The train blare sustained. Bilsharn was in a trance, hand spread forth, pronouncing destruction in an archaic tongue. The front tires on Collette's car popped.

Brannbjørn veered around the gate, wobbling onto the tracks. "Let 'em go," Collette pleaded. The train engineer hit the brakes. The back tires popped–stuck. "We're not gonna make it!" she cried, her hand grabbing his hairy forearm. Screeching, train wheels on fire...sparks flying.

Horn and brakes deafening.

The train T-boned the passenger door. The collision sandwiched Collette's head between the door's mangled metal and glass, severing her head right off. The rest of her body was smushed into Brannbjørn's lap, while her head was propelled from the scene, landing near the truck. Her car jettisoned off the track, landing on the roof of a nearby storage building.

The truck driver looked down at Collette's bloody head and screamed. The train's horn petered out, grinding guttural brakes ceased.

Brannbjørn sat dazed, caught between the driver's door and the passenger seat with a decapitated Collette.

Steve Bilsharn retracted the kickstand, started up his bike, then continued to head south on Elko Road.

Mancho arrived, eyes blazing. The shaggy dog ran up to the head of Collette. Her long, bloody jet black hair, encrusted with glass shards. Mancho sniffed it then howled three times with his snout lowered. Everyone at the scene looked on in horror.

At the exact moment Mancho howled, over on the Pacific coast, Ruxandra was heading toward the portal on the East Bay Mystery Walls when an owl hooted three times in a moaning way. Evermore, on her shoulder, sounded out short, eerie shrills. On Monument Peak's slope, a dog near the trail leading to the

telecom towers set about howling with its head down.

Meanwhile, in Edana's chamber of *Dún Dreach-Fhola*, high in *Na Cruacha Dubha*, the oak framed painting of Collette cracked. While in Ruxandra's chamber, Collette's portrait fell off the wall impaled by a halberd. Simultaneously, at the Edgar Allen Poe Museum in Richmond, someone had spun Poe's Wheel of Misfortune. Its arrow landed on "DECAPITATED."

Back in Elko, Virginia, Brannbjørn cried, "Wait! Don't do that!" Mancho had locked his jaws upon the roots of her bloody hair, then took off down the railroad track toward Richmond.

Mancho's Dispatch

Mancho's Account, September 22nd of 2025

Eyes flaming red with Collette's bloody head in his mouth, Mancho ran over fifteen miles along train tracks. Though a stocky beast with a long shaggy tail, he scampered on the single track's rail ties with ease. The line took him through White Oak Swamp then under Interstate 295 where the track split into two sets. On Mancho ran, past the Air National Guard Blackhawk Base and Million Air Richmond terminal, by the East End Landfill, and alongside Richmond's posh Rockett's Landing. At Gillie Creek, an engineer of an oncoming train barreling down the opposite track cried, "What da Hell?" witnessing Mancho's baggage of a bloody head, its flowing black hair waving in the wind. On the black dog went, rising onto the James River Viaduct. Dock Street was below on one side and the Kanawha Canal on the other.

At the crossing of the James River Viaduct with the Mayo Island Bridge, Mancho, imbued with devilish power, leapt a good twenty feet, landing onto the deck plate girder railroad bridge running south over the James River. Without slowing his pace, he pounced upon the bridge's rail ties, going over Mayo Island, until he reached the South Side of the city, called Manchester.

He jumped from the tracks, landing on Manchester Road. From there he proceeded westerly, going parallel to the Rich-

mond Slave Trail. Across from the Southern State Silo, he arrived at an abandoned red brick building with multi-paned industrial windows spanning two stories in height. Two sides facing the road have giant, smoky-glassed rectangular windows. The panes are strewn with ivy, some panels covered in mural paint. The Witch mural dominants the building with her tall wide-brimmed black hat overshadowing her eyes, the nose and mouth denote solemness on a canvas of lunar glowing skin accentuated with long jet-black, wavy hair rooted to stone sills. At the hat's crown is a white ribbon garnished with a white rose. She has four arms: two in a namaste gesture, the other two hands outstretched, held high, absorbing the lunar bodies above her. The side facing easterly has a partially broken-down plywood door leading into a large space, now the residence of occasional hobos.

Mancho wiggled his way through the broken door. He dropped Collette's head in the center of the concrete floor. Pallets, scraps of paper, tin cans littered the area, along with splotches of water, mortar, pebbles strewn here and there. The walls below the smoky panes were marred with street graffiti. A cockroach scampered along the floor, climbing over the bloody visage. Mancho looked around and sniffed for the sulfurous presence of his master. He howled in a spine-chilling fashion several times. The echo reverberated into the high ceiling, and quivered the windows, sending sonic waves into the streets and dark alleyways of Manchester and into downtown Richmond beyond.

At first, only stillness between his intervals of calling, then a murder of crows appeared, three in all, each one landing on a defunct appliance. Mancho continued howling. A few minutes later, a clowder of nine black cats tiptoed behind him, settling in a far corner. Then entered a pack of eleven dogs, including a white dog with brown patches, next a swarm of bats filled the ceiling then hung from the rafters. Finally, rounding out the chorus of familiars, was a mischief of chattering rats with beady red eyes, who poured out of the damaged brickwork opposite the feline's corner, some faintly hissing at Mancho.

A faint sulphuric smell wafted in from the entrance. A desert red glow began forming near the back wall. It garnered shape; a swirling, dusty red orb hovered over the room's center. All clattering among the familiars ceased.

"Why do you summon me at my seat?" questioned a voice from the orb.

Mancho bowed and spoke, "Oh, most eminent Chief Choíros of Richmond, I bring you the head of Collette cel Rău."

Choíros boomed, "W-h-o did this?" The orb pulsated on each word. "H-o-w did you let this happen?"

"I, ah. Brannbjørn the Fomorian, my master, he did this," replied the trembling Mancho. "Brannbjørn was pursuing your servant, the blacksmith, Steve Bilsharn, when he drove her car into a train. The collision of metal and glass severed her head."

"Where is Brannbjørn now?"

"I know not master. I suppose he's taken the body with him."

"Perhaps." Choíros' swine-like visage emerged from the orb, eyeing the mischief of rats. "Punish him!"

"Don't devour me!" pleaded Mancho.

The rats scampered over, encircling him. Chattering, rasping, gnashing their teeth...Mancho's body shuddered, his eyes darting back and forth, wondering who would strike first.

Simultaneously, the mischief pounced. They tore at his fur and flesh. Three gashed his tail.

Mancho yelped and wailed, falling to his side. A vermin blanket covered him. His blood, innards, flesh all becoming a feast for their ravenous appetites. The imp spirit inside the canine could be seen exiting the mutilated body as a tiny, dusty reddish mist; it first swirled about the room then vanished through the western wall.

Choíros cast his eyes upon the murder of Blackburn, Morrigan and Coronis.

"Wash the head in the James. Keep it secure. Find the body! Find Bilsharn! The rest of you, tell me of any movements of the Dragonists in my city. Now, be off!"

As the horde of creatures exited the Witch building, Rudy, a scraggly homeless man, witnessed the spectacle from a passing boxcar heading over the James.

The Dark Flame

Draculian Chronicles, September 22nd of 2025

High in the *Ériu* Mountains of *Na Cruacha Dubha*, The Black Stacks, known today as McGillycuddy Reeks, a lone cry echoed the Otherworld in the halls of that forbidding fortress, *Dún Dreach-Fhola*.

Edana Siόg Fola, who, for countless centuries, was and is its keeper, cried out with a blood curdling scream, making her handmaid drop an ivory comb. The cracked portrait of Collette cel Rău could mean only one thing: she had died.

She turned to her handmaiden and commanded, "Bring me blood offering!"

Edana, a *Dearg-Due*, stormed out of her chamber, spiraling down the Serpent Stairs in the highest of three towers. Her maids accompanied and her attendees succored the train of her cloak. Edana entered the castle's keep pass guards attending the arched entrance then down into its bowels. There, in the dungeon, she came before an ominous circular stone door; twelve spans in diameter, three spans thick. Embedded in its center, a cipher wheel of yew consisting of three concentric circles. She dialed the wheels of cryptic text: Aegean numerals, Ogham, Greek, Enochian, and Runes.

The dungeon shuttered as the boulder rolled into a granite channel, revealing a murky spiral stair. An attendant preceded, igniting each sconce of lava rock. At stair's end Edana stood before the doors of *Geata Ulchabhán*. In ogham, "Wisdom" and "Lilith" were etched into the stone floor. Her Wyverian servants formed a semi-circle about her. Her mistress bore a goblet of blood. The gate only opened during Black Moons, the last being August the twenty-third of the Gregorian calendar of this year, except in time of need or distress. Edana placed the Archon Eponymous' signet ring of a screeching owl encircled by an ouroboros into its matching slot in the portal. The twain crystal doors, having no knobs, opened of their own accord. The doors, unimaginably heavy, and two palms thick, were fashioned from solid slabs of labradorite mined deep within the Earth. Its apex crowned with a *Crann Bethadh*, the Celtic Tree of Life. Etched in its upper heart, the relief of a Pharaoh Eagle Owl surrounded by nine triskelia below a quarter moon.

Edana's maidservant handed her the golden serpentine goblet filled with fresh blood. She entered alone. Edana placed the goblet upon the altar's avian head before a modest flickering murky flame. Then she flung herself, emerald silk gown, ruddy blond hair and all, before the Dark Flame. Once the Perpetual Flame glowed rose red, but it had been twisted, turned against its will, centuries ago, so in this present age it was a smoldering, dark blood red flame. Edana invoked Lilith, our Dark Mother, her frame covering the Screeching Owl's sigil embossed on the quartz floor.

In response, the Dark Flame grew to the height of three cubits emanating from an ancient iolite brazier. Its column, labradorite, fashioned as an oak trunk rising to three creatures, and its bowl, orichalcum. The rim, a screeching owl perched at the fore and at

the owl's flanks, twain Wyverns.

The flame illuminated the Archon Stones, nine smoky crystal spheres upon their respective stands encircling the great flame, each one belonging to a Dragonist lair. The visage of a scarlet haired being appeared, Lilith, the mother of all vampires. Her silky red gown was embroidered with dark quarter moons, hems gilded in gold flashing in concert with her vibrant hair. The attire was girded by a tasseled orichalcum belt studded with labradorite, maiatonium, and rubies. Her supple limbs stretched forth from the flames, cradling the goblet. She pursed her ruby red lips and consumed the precious liquid in three gentle swallows. She returned the chalice upon the owl's crown and licked her lips. Her large, penetrating eyes fashioned upon Edana. Her voluptuous lips opened and uttered words as smooth as Naphtali oil demanding an explanation for her summons.

Meanwhile, Ruxandra surreptitiously had entered the *Geata Ulchabhán's* chamber. She kept silent remaining in Edana's shadow. But during Edana's offering the now lofty firelight had revealed Ruxandra.

"How dare you enter here in such fashion! Granted you are the Archon Basileus, but you are not the principal Archon!" boomed Lilith.

Ruxandra bowed before Lilith and said, "Your leniency is implored, my mother. Does Edana's presence–"

"Silence!" stated Lilith, glaring at her with eyes as blazing as the fire around her. "Your niece has passed."

"Noo, ahhh!" moaned a crying Ruxandra as she clutched her face, dropping to her knees then falling prostrate upon the floor. "Where is her body!?"

Lilith answered, "Choíros has her bloody head. Brannbjørn her mangled body."

Edana pleaded, "We beseech thee for Collette's body. So her soul may repose in the *Tuama Crann Creathach* till the Last Days. Is she not worthy to abide in Edom, amongst the Stones of Emptiness?"

Ruxandra looked up at the flame tears pouring from her face and said, "Yes, is she not worthy?"

"I behold a rarity among you. The two of you agreeing upon a matter.

"What you request is a tall order, for Collette is more mortal than vampire. Nevertheless as your Dark Mother, vow I to entreat for her head. As for her body, does this not rest with the Council of Archons?"

"I shall persuade the Nine," stated Edana.

"Present the seal of signets in three days' time. Now be off," said Lilith. She receded within the flame, after which the Dark Flame resumed its accustomed state.

Then Edana removed the Harken Stone from her gown's pouch and placed it in a niche on the Dark Flame's column. The engraved ouroboros upon it began to resonate and glow. The reverberation echoed in the Archon Stones which also began glowing. Thus were the Archons from their various lairs beckoned in the time of Mabon.

Long live Lilith!, our beloved Mother!

Deeds of the Murder

Synopsis of Morrigan's Account transcribed in Bölcsem Kertész Naplója, 2025. Szeptember 23

Bölcsem's journal (translated)

Blackburn and I each grabbed a tuft of Collette's hair, and flew low south-easterly over Manchester Road. Then we landed nearby at the bank of the James River. There we washed the head.

Coronis flew over the highways and byways looking for Steve Bilsharn on his motorcycle. No sign. Then to his flat in Scott's Addition. She pecked on his window. Still no sign. Off to Studio Two Three. Again, no sign. Coronis staked out upon his apartment's roof, waiting for his return.

Later, under the cover of darkness, Blackburn and I took Collette's head to a homeless man, Rudy, for safekeeping. We trusted him for we have grown accustom to feeding from his hand. Countless times he has brought us table scraps from the area restaurants and food trucks that dot Richmond's Canal Walk and business district. Rudy lives behind a Canal Walk barricade situated at an underpass, a fence, ironically designed to keep his type out. Rudy's abode is a makeshift tent in the bowels of the underpass just northwest of the Turning Basin. In this shelter, Rudy has managed to jerry-rig an electric line so he has power to a small refrigerator. In it he has placed Collette's head in a freezer bag. Blackburn remained in the vicinity keeping watch.

Meanwhile, I took flight to find Brannbjørn and the body. I waited in a tree across from Collette's flat in Church Hill. Soon Brannbjørn arrived in a rental car. Once inside, I flew up to the living room window and lightly tapped.

"Who is that tapping?" said Brannbjørn. He went to the door. No one there.

Tap-tap-tap.

"Blasted, who's that tapping?" He looked out the kitchen window.

"Have I gone mad?"

Tap-tap-tap, louder now.

Bjørn went to the living room. There, on the sill, he caught me in the act of rapping. He opened the window slightly.

"What is your name, familiar? And what do you want?"

"Morrigan am I, *caw.* Wants body, *caw...argh...* Collette's key."

"You shall have no such thing. Tell your master he shall have body and key when my terms are met."

"*...hiss, ha-rra-w-w...*what terms, *caw!?*"

"A foundation amulet, Dragonist forged, bearing my Rune fashioned in the Helm of Awe against their magick. Oh, and tell your master, no intrusion, whatsoever, in my slaying of Bilsharn."

"Hmm...*caw...*Master want Egregore of Andromalius, Bilsharn has."

"Consider it done," said Brannbjørn. "Now listen bird, Collette's body shall be at the Comet Stone, the sixth day at midnight. No amulet, no Collette. Now, out of my sight, buzzard!"

"*Hiss...caw, caw,*" cried I and flew off.

Archons of the Dragonist

Bölcsem Kertész Naplója, 2025. Szeptember 25

The Archons, the Nine, assembled over the matter of Collette cel Rău's death. She was beloved by all of the Nine, one of only a few things they all agreed upon. I had an affinity for her as well, though I fellowshipped with her sparingly. She was a curious phenom, born within the garnet curtain walls of *Dún Dreach-Fhola,* known in the common tongue as the Castle of Blood Visage. I remember the day of her birth. Ruxandra beckoned me climb *Túr Ulcachán,* the Owl Tower, one of three castle towers formed from iolite crystal, to see the infant. The babe had lively eyes and a vibrant cry. In the castle's countless centuries of existence, Collette was the only hybrid ever to be born there. Nevertheless all loved her, for she was kind and sympathetic to our vampiric life and only thought of others, whether in our world or the world of mortals. In time, she blossomed into a striking beauty adept in all manner of decorative arts. She assisted all the Nine in adorning their liars and most of all in fashioning jewelry for them such as: amulets, talismans, necklaces and rings. She will sorely be missed.

At the convening of the council, the Archons, decked in their tau robes, presided at the Nine's bench, a crescent moon of obsidian. When I entered the chamber, they were looking down upon a small-boned canine familiar. Mancho it was, once Choíros' imposing familiar, he had now been relegated to the body of a small black terrier. He was giving his account of how he had witnessed Collette's death and his subsequent retrieval of her head. Mancho concluded with how his master had humiliated him. Clearly his downcast demeanor suggested he had taken sides with our lot. At this point in the proceedings, I extracted excerpts from the council minutes:

Edana: Mancho, thanks be to you for adhering to our summons and imparting your story of our beloved Collette's demise. On behalf of this council, we express our gratitude for securing her. Moreover, we know your testimony is true, for we have upheld your witness with that of your crow friend, Morrigan, who has returned to his master. You, however, will remain here for a time, lest Choíros apprehend you and thus confine you to a dark pit.

Mancho: Grateful am I, my lady.

Edana: Guards, have a Traveller fetch us a sheep for Mancho. Pay the gypsy tribute in gemstone.

Guard: Very good, my lady.

Edana: Sophar!

Sophar: Yes, Chief Archon.

Edana: Release the poet from the dungeon.

Nastya: My Lady Edana, forgive my crassness, may I partake of him?

Edana: Nay, Nastya. Sophar and his Wyvern soldiers will bring us, shall we say, several sweet dishes for the feast, for I do have pity upon bards.

Sophar: Very good, my lady.

Edana: Bölscem! Tally the rods.

Bölscem: Yes, my lady.

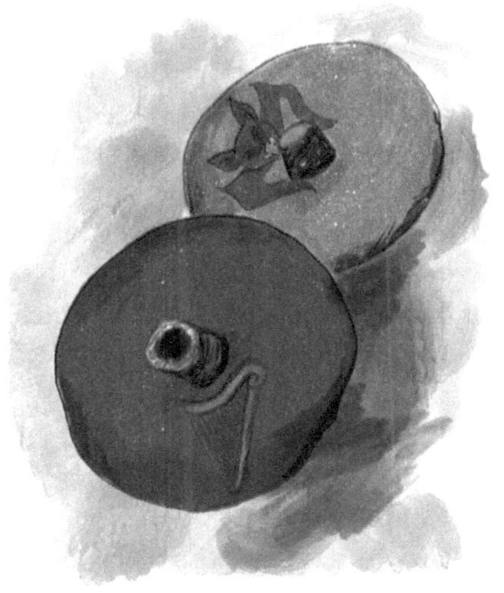

I withdrew and counted the ballot rods with Edana and Ruxandra's handmaidens as my witnesses. This was conducted in the manner that the Athenian Archons had done so long ago. Every Archon possesses a disc bearing a rod through its core. The sides of the disc bear an inscription of their respective lair's coat of arms. The ends of the rod differ: one tip rounded, denoting a submission of "aye," and the other hollow, denoting a submission of "nay."

The Archons had judged on two matters. Of note, Ruxandra, on behalf of her Romanian lair, had cast a hollow end upon the first and a rounded end upon the

second. Those matters were...

...Firstly, forge a foundation amulet for Brannbjørn in exchange for Collette's body
...Secondly, put to death those Choíros has decreed for judgement in exchange for Collette's head

Bölscem: My Lady Edana and Principal Archon, the Council has spoken. As for the first matter, we have two dissents. Need I remind you, Principal Archon, it requires a unanimous ruling to forge an amulet from the Foundation Stone of *Dún Dreach-Fhola*. For the second matter, the casting is six-to-three to adhere to Choíros' bidding.

Edana: Whoever has dissented upon the first ruling, take liberty to voice your reasoning.

Ruxandra: I dissented.

Kojo Aboagye: You? Of all Archons, why? Your own flesh and blood?

Ruxandra: With all due respect to the Archon from Africa, giving the amulet to Brannbjørn is tantamount to insanity. He will no doubt lead his Fomorian horde upon us and storm these castle walls.

Kojo: Is not our strength of arms and magick ample enough to resist him?

Ruxandra: *Nu* with the amulet. Even here, our magick of all crafts would be limited. Moreover our walls and the strength among us is no match for a Fomorian siege. Yes, they are few; thirty remain pure in blood, yet they tower over us and are skilled at arms, able to behead with swiftness, and Brannbjørn, a shapeshifter, has the strength of twenty men. Moreover, with the amulet he would incur no injury from our perimeter defenses, chief of which, the Ouroboros Ring of Fire.

Nastya: Kojo, truth she speaks. Ruxandra, can you not *block* the portal to here? Cast a new path to our stronghold?

Ruxandra: I can, but it would only be a matter of time until Brannbjørn found the new way.

Kojo: Then what do you propose?

Ruxandra: I propose the blood of Pool destroy him. With Brannbjørn dead, his clan leaderless, they will scatter, knowing we will hunt them down, one-by-one.

Edana: Pool!? Your William Pool? You speak madness; he is dead.

Ruxandra: *Da și nu.*

Edana: The common tongue, please.

Ruxandra: Yes, and no.

Lothar: *Was meinst du?*

Edana: Please, Lothar.

Ruxandra: His blood lives on in Benjamin F. Mosby.

Lothar: *Was!?*

Ruxandra: Pool's blood lives on in a humble fireman named Mosby of Church Hill. Bölscem, please explain.

I stepped forward from my lectern before the Council, arrayed in their silken black tau robes embroidered with gold displaying lair and ouroboros symbols, save Edana's robe of a deep emerald. Edana, directly above me, chaired the high seat, the Eponymous Archon, as signified by the golden ouroboros brooch and matching signet ring. Ruxandra, the Archon Basileus, sat at her left petting a black cat. Kojo, an *Asasabonsam*, and the Archon Polemarch, sat at her right with his black mamba coiled around his left arm. Then the other six were Nastya, a beautiful blond Upir, Antonio, her lover and a Brazilian vampire of the Mura people. Next, was Lothar, a tall Neuntöter bearing a hideous visage of disease and bloodshot red eyes. His only equal in grotesqueness was the large and furry Chorti, whose name bears his kind, having backwards feet with claws. Also of note, Chiyo, a fair-skinned, long-necked *rokurokubi*, whose Japanese name means "a thousand generations." And lastly, was the Pole haling from Wilno, Ontario, Grzegorz. He was a Vjesci, having bloody spots upon his face and fingernails, ever vigilant red eyes, and long fangs. These Nine were illuminated by nine flames sprung forth from iron dragon sconces. It was, and is, an intimidating sight when they convene, even for a vampire such as I to behold.

I then explained all that transpired in the Church Hill Tunnel collapse and how Mosby was mistakenly thought to be dead, but is now only sleeping. Furthermore, I explained that if a Rite of Remanifestation was performed, Mosby, having Pool's strigoi blood, would possess abilities making him a formidable adversary for Brannbjørn.

Edana: Extraordinary!
Kojo: I motion for a Remanifestation.
Chiyo: I second that motion.
Edana: Any objections? For a Remanifestation we must all agree.
Lothar: *Ja, ich habe eine Frage.*
Edana: Can you please speak the King's English?
Nastya: *Urod*...there's a black sheep in every family.

Edana: Haha. Continue, Lothar.

Lothar: *Wie werden wir Mosby kontrollieren?*

Ruxandra: Lothar asks, "How will we control him?" With this:

Ruxandra displayed an implant in the form of a scarab.

Edana: What is that?

Ruxandra: Antonio?

Antonio: It's an AI implant. I can monitor location, emotion, send data. Best of all, I can paralyze the wearer. I wrote the code; made my own asynchronous event-driven engine, a spinoff on the latest Node.js code.

Kojo: My Brazilian brother, that is way too much info. Where did the hardware come from?

Ruxandra: A subsidiary of my company, Sânge Nou, Inc.

Kojo: So, *another* shell company. I wouldn't be surprised if you had a demo planned?

Ruxandra: But of course. Guards! Bring the subject.

Kojo: Figures. Another staged dissent.

Three guards brought forth an emaciated twenty-year-old man who had not been sedated, hands and feet shackled. One guard turned him around, pointing at his bare neck. He was barefoot, standing in the dead center of the ouroboros craved into the stone floor, directly below the Nine, perched high upon their crescent bench. He wore only a burlap gown.

Ruxandra: Give him bread.

A guard handed the prisoner a small slice of bread.

Antonio: Eat.

The man took a bite and swallowed.

Man: Why am I here? What is this place? You bastards drugged me, didn't you?

Ruxandra: Silence! We have decided to show you mercy. Unless you would rather be a meal?

The man ceased his bantering at the sight of Ruxandra's fangs.

Ruxandra: Free him. Take him back to his farm.

One guard spun him around then unshackled his hands and feet, tossing the chains to the side, while the other placed the scarab at the base of his neck. Instantly, the scarab merged into the man's skin where it looked more like a tattoo than an implant. He winced and scratched at his neck. From the open doors, the third guard beckoned the man exit. The man began to leave. Antonio pointed a fob fashioned as a gargoyle at the man.

Antonio: Now watch!

Antonio touched a pad on the fob. The man halted, placing his hands upon his head. Antonio moved his thumb clockwise over the pad; the man buckled over, falling to his knees, crying out in agony.

Kojo: Interesting. What else can it do?
Antonio: Observe.

Antonio ceased touching the pad. The man regained his composure and charged toward Antonio. Antonio pushed twice upon the pad button. The man ceased his charge and began gasping for breath, standing before them paralyzed.

Kojo: Impressive. So you can track him anywhere?
Antonio: Yes, and there is an app version as well with full capabilities.
Ruxandra: Guards, return him to the dungeon.

The man was shackled and taken away.

Edana: Satisfied Lothar?
Lothar: *Ja, sehr gut, Antonio.*
Antonio: *Obrigado!*
Lothar: *Bitte.*
Edana: Enough, let's shepherd this. So, if there are no further objections, I motion for the Remanifestation of Benjamin Mosby during the Ivy Moon, with an amendment.
Ruxandra: And what is your inclusion?

Edana: The amulet set with maiatonium be forged, but a corrosive additive be stealthily inserted, thus rendering it, in due time, powerless. In this way, we meet Brannbjørn's terms, attain Collette's remains, but foil his pillaging inclinations. Bölscem, you are adept at alchemy; is not such an erosive means possible?

Bölscem: It is, my lady, though a full lunar month must transpire to decay maiatonium sufficiently.

Kojo: Ruxandra, no amulet, no niece. It's a risk we have to take. Besides, if Mosby is all you claim that he is, he will at the very least delay Brannbjørn's schemes, if not all together thwart them. At the very worst, the Fomorians will be timid if they lay siege to this castle. After all, the amulet only protects the bearer not his minions. Moreover, it is high time, we lure these barbarians to our fortress walls. The amulet shall be our bait. Once here, Chortu and I have devised a trap to catch the roguish bear.

Chortu: Kojo speaks wisely.

Silence pervaded the chamber. All eyes upon Ruxandra.

Ruxandra: Very well, I am swayed.

Edana: Ah, *excelent*, as you would say in Romanian. Thus I put forth the aforementioned motion with its amendment.

Chortu: I second that motion.

Edana: Thank you for that, Chortu, and thank you for saying it in *English*.

Chortu: *Sí señorita*.

Edana: Are there any objections?

The Archon chamber was silent. She slammed the war hammer upon the bench.

Edana: The motion is passed. Guards! Bring forth Mancho and Morrigan to my chamber. Sophar, have the amulet forged. Now, let us feast!

The Archons adjourned to the Banquet Hall of Blood. The hall was bathed in candle and torch light and fumigated by sage and dragon's blood smoldering in bronze incense bowls. Upon its walls, various escutcheons hung, mostly of each Dragonist lair. Also adorning the hall were finely detailed tapestries depicting Lilith, ancient *Ériu* epics, and various vampiric heroes of age's past. Edana, as fair as Etain, fair locks of strawberry blond hair, her silk cape held by a golden ouroboros brooch signifying her honorable position. She sat at the head of a long obsidian table, tapping the principal chair's arms, fingers adorned with gold rings, some with visages: the Green Man, the Dara Knot; others crowned with Kerry diamonds...emerald, amethyst. While Ruxandra sat opposite, her rings darker, foreboding, visages of gargoyles, dragons, bats...darker gems–black star sapphire, onyx, spinel.

The Wyverians, the lower degree in the order, as denoted by their tabards, offered melody upon recorder, bodhrán and lute; still others served the Nine blood wine. Most gorged on rare, roast lamb steeped in rosemary from a shallow cauldron, amongst other victuals. Only Ruxandra, myself, and Nastya, ate from a black cauldron of bloody goulash.

I drank my fill of blood wine; the jovial atmosphere enhanced my intoxicated state. Edana played a strain of wonder upon her harp. She caught my ear when she sang the *The Isle of the Blest:*

On the ocean that hollows the rocks where ye dwell
A shadowy land has appeared as they tell;
Men thought it a region of sunshine and rest,
And they called it Hy-Brasail, the Isle of the Blest.

From year unto year on the ocean's blue rim
This beautiful specter showed lovely and dim;
The golden clouds curtained the deep where it lay,
And it looked like an Eden away, far away.[2]

This isle of the Otherworld, I discovered many moons ago. During my sojourns to find ancient mariner maps, I came upon an Arabic star map protected by only a simple wooden door in one of the Libraries of Chinguetti. The custodian there was a humble man who dared not part with it. Suffice it to say, I drew a copy, paying him in gold coin. It was far more accurate in showing the Isle's locale than was Angelino Dulcert's vague map, and indeed, its Islamic cartographer was renowned. Legends spoke of a time during Beltane, in the seventh year, when it revealed itself among the misty ocean. True to the map's direction, at the appointed time, I sailed solo upon a single-masted dhow and found the Land of Maidens–in the ancient tongue, *Tír na nÓg*. There I was met by beautiful maidens and fell in love with the noblest and fairest of them all, *Clíodhna*, whom you know as Cleena. Her wave of beauty and song soothed my weary soul. Now I long to go back and be separate from this devilish crew who, even now, are gorging themselves on the flesh of humans the Wyvernians brought them. I have grown weary of human blood and have found the blood of other

creatures upon this isle will suffice me. It will not be long till I hearken back to the Land of Maidens, whom none in the Order know of, save Edana.

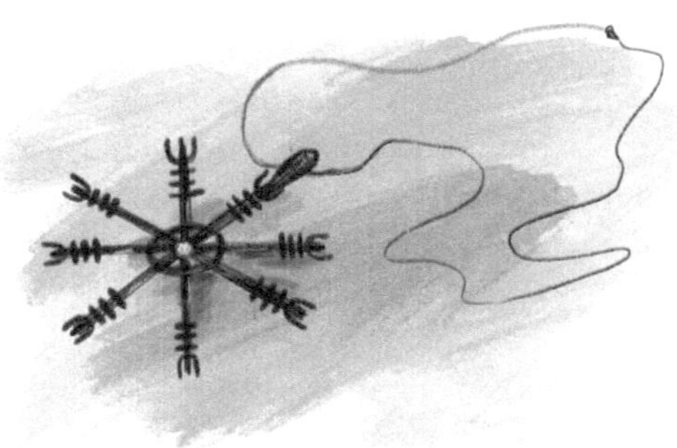

Ah, but I digress.

As for the amulet agreed upon for Brannbjørn, it was formed from part of the foundation stone, made of maiatonium, on which this hidden castle was built countless moons ago. A living, swirling stone, not of this world. In recent time, from a Hall of Records, we discovered nuggets of it, from the famed House of Darkness, deep in the Labyrinth of Yaxchilán. With it was a scroll in the Enochian tongue, which told of the stone's properties, its operations, and its origin. The origin story included a star map pointing to a planet in the constellation of Pleiades. This maiatonium stone strengthens our bond with the elements: earth, fire, water and air, linking our subconscious with it. A breathing, adaptable stone, pulsating in ebbs and flows and resonating at a frequency which I shall never disclose, not even in this journal. For this knowledge in the hands of humans would bring untold terrors upon this earth.

The feast ended with Antonio and Nastya going into a chamber, while Lothar and the others drank and made merry for a time. As for Edana, she retired to her chamber high in the Owl Tower where she had her fill of yet another poet from Waterford. Meanwhile, Ruxandra oversaw the forging of the amulet, a Helm of Awe, fashioned by Izurg, the blacksmith and lapidary, who skillfully set the tiny caustic additive in its hub. Then he placed the cut maiatonium crystal upon it. Once complete, this Helm of Awe now glimmered and swirled at its heart. To bind it to its wearer, upon a branch of the Helm, Brannbjørn's runic was engraved. Once in his possession, if wielded before it diminished, could this Fomorian descended from the *Jötnar*, become the new Orion of vampires?

Ruxandra summoned me to the forging chamber. I made haste, knowing all had been set in motion for Ruxandra's vengeance.

I hasted into the chamber, bowing on one knee. "You beckoned, Countess."

"Ah, Bölscem. When is the election for a new Eponymous Archon?"

"In eight moons, my countess."

"Edana is reckless. This gorging on humans and lambs about the countryside has got to stop, lest this fortress be found out," Ruxandra exclaimed.

I replied, quoting lines from an old Irish poem:

But the time will come.
When mortal eye – our work shall spy,
And mortal ear – our dirge shall hear.

"Who said that?"

"One of the keeners witnessed by Connor Crowe. They ferried the coffin of Flory the Cantillon," I answered.

"How fitting. Our Collette could be our Flory, our Connor Crowe, one of Edana's amusements. Needless to say, these pesky humans increase in knowledge daily: quantum computing, NASA's MMS, CERN's latest discoveries, and no doubt the elite among them have found another Hall of Records. Soon such knowledge will be more than enough to spy our gate."

"What would you have me do?"

"Deliver the amulet to Brannbjørn. Sophar and the Balaurian Guard will escort you. Have them bring Collette's body here. Ensure you get her ankh key. Then go and petition Choíros for the Remanifestation and comply with his bidding. That should satisfy him for her head. Now make haste!"

The Body, the Key, the Amulet

Bölcsem Kertész Naplója, 2025. Szeptember 26

The monstrous mouths of the Dacian wolf banners swallowed the wind. Their frightful fangs caught the moonlight while their serpentine bodies wiggled. I and Sophar stood amidst the Ring of Brodgar, flanked by six of the Balaurian Guard poised to brandish their falx swords, three on each side. Four Wyverians attended us: two in front bearing torches, and twain pole-bearers in the rear.

Brannbjørn and Ivor, his captain, skilled in arms, approached, flanked by two torch bearers forming a party of nine Fomorians. The others of the party, an archer in the rear with four warriors who bore Collette's body in a simple spruce coffin with a sliding lid.

"Hail Brannbjørn, Lord of the Fomorians," addressed I.

"Hail, Bölscem and brave Sophar. My heart grieves for your loss of Collette," said Brannbjørn.

"Yea, I sense you speak truly. How fair you, Ivor, and your beauty, Asta?" said I.

"I am well, but my Asta gave stillbirth. Your concoction served well for a time, but alas, death had its day," replied Ivor.

"My condolences, noble Ivor," said I.

"*Tusen takk*," replied Ivor in subdued Norwegian thanks.

"Let us not succumb to acquiesce. I will refine my potion."

"Enough, Bölscem! Where is the amulet?" exclaimed Brannbjørn.

"Does it contain a piece of the foundation stone?"

From underneath my tau robe, I pulled out a velvet pouch and dangled it before him.

"Open the pouch, Bölscem."

I complied, dangling the Helm of Awe upon its orichalcum chain.

"Good. Now hand it over."

"Where is the key?" I retorted.

Brannbjørn displayed the ankh.

"Very well; now let us see the body," I requested.

Brannbjørn beckoned the pallbearers. I motioned to Sophar and his guards to examine. Two guards pulled on the t-notch lid, sliding it open, while two others stood by as Sophar examined Collette's body. He saw her clutch purse at her feet, in it her wallet and broken phone.

"It is her body and belongings," said Sophar.

"Release the body," ordered Brannbjørn.

Sophar's men bore the casket.

"Excellent. The key, please," I requested.

"Hand me the amulet first, Bölscem. No tricks," said he.

"Toss the key whilst I toss the pouch," countered I.

The deed was done.

I inspected the key. It was hers; the inscription on the ankh's loop gave proof it was genuine: a butterfly between two stars depicted in the style of Romanian folk symbols.

"Hmm...how do I know it works?" inquired Brannbjørn as he held the amulet in his hand.

"I suspected you would ask–Kojo!"

Kojo appeared from behind the Head Stone and pointed toward a Fomorian torchbearer. In Twi, he commanded an attack, "*Toa!*"

A black mamba apparition unfurled from out of his left arm then wriggled in the air toward the torchbearer. The snake bit upon his free arm. The man cried out, fell to his knees clutching his other arm and dropped his torch. Its flame lit a tuft of grass illuminating a nearby monolith. The Fomorians closed rank and drew their Ulfberht swords. Sophar's men drew their falxs.

“What is this!?” Brannbjørn exclaimed.

“You wanted proof. Toss him the amulet,” chuckled Sophar.

“This is madness,” said Brannbjørn.

“Do it or he will die,” I said.

Brannbjørn tossed the amulet. The Fomorian, still on his knees, caught it. At the amulet’s hub, the maiatonium gem glowed and swirled. Instantly the punctures in his arm mended, and life came back to his countenance.

Brannbjørn looked in amazement then said, “And the fire?” For the blaze had spread, illuminating much of the henge and sending strands of glittering gold over the lochs.

Without taking my gaze off Brannbjørn, rain did I invoke, stretching forth my hand and uttering an Enochian spell. Where I pointed, over the Loch of Harray, a fog of vapor began to form. As I twisted my hand it amassed into a dark cloud. With both palms I gestured toward the center of Brodgar’s henge. The ominous mass submitted to my will, poised over all concerned. With one fell swoop of my hands, the cumulus unleashed its burden.

All stood transfixed, forbearing the downpour. Their swords clenched, each troop fixed their gaze upon the other, ready for some deed of trickery. But alas, none came to fruition. All the warriors’ armor clinked under the tentacles of rain, shimmering in what stubborn flames briefly held sway, their eyes barely blinking, affixed on their foe.

Ah, what a sight upon the Isle of Orkney; the smoke rose in the Ring of Brodgar with drenched Fomorians and Dragonists. A source of mirth for us vampires, a source of indignation for our rivals. Our magick at its peak, during the Witching Hour, in the Land of Caledonia.

“N-o-t amusing, Bölscem,” exclaimed Brannbjørn, wiping droplets from his brow. “Merriment will be mine the next time we clash, for I’ll enjoy watching your head roll!”

He turned with his company and proceeded to the Comet Stone. I grinned, knowing Collette would have been pleased.

Choíros' Demands

Draculian Chronicles, September 27th of 2025

The Witch Building had not changed since Bölscem had visited it more than five years before. The master scribe stood in the presence of that dusty red orb, Choíros, the chief demon over Richmond. His cadre of murderous crows, Blackburn, Morrigan and Coronis, looking on from a stone sill, as was a scruffy black dog, more beast than canine. It had the head of a pit bull with the mane of a lion, its fur, midnight black. Obviously the creature was an important familiar, for he flanked Choíros on his right. The demon spoke of Richmond as a city ripe for harvesting malevolent souls. No doubt he had been given approval from an arch demon to initiate a reaping. All he needed was an instrument to fulfill this principals' wishes.

Choíros declared, "Certain families, up until the fourth generation in this city, have ripened and are now fit for a scythe. How do you propose to fulfill my cravings?"

"In an expeditious manner oh great Chief," I said in a flattering tone, bowing my head slightly for added effect. "Where is the head of Collette?"

"Her head is kept guarded in a safe place, not far from here.
Now, answer my question."

"The Society of Dragonists will raise our new servant, Benjamin Mosby, to do so. For he lies at rest with the blood of Pool coursing through his veins. He will do your bidding, great Chief."

"Enough with the pleasantries, scribe! Mosby's been buried almost a century. Just how do you know his blood is strigoi?"

"By a dowser. She summoned Mosby in the company of Ruxandra."

"That is not enough proof. Is there more?"

"The spirit of Pool visited Ruxandra and pronounced this riddle:

By my blood,
Avenge those who were buried.
Their souls long to be ferried.
Ferried, from Death's Tunnel
To their resting place.
Seek my blood, in he who is At Rest.
Surely my love,
He shall pass the Test.

"Ah, you speak truly, Bölscem. For my master, Count Andromalius, has, for many a moon in the halls of Hades, heard this plea of William Pool. Apparently the time to heed Pool's petition is near. Hmm...the death of Pool will be a century past, this second of October. Very well, Ruxandra and Pool can have their revenge, and we can have our new souls.

"Now, what is *your* motive–you, and the other vampires, in asserting yourself into the mortal world? Are you not like the bats of the Mafra Palace Library who only do their work under the cloak of darkness, yet leave your excrement upon marble floors?"

"Indeed, Chief Choíros, you speak wisely. Yet, from time to time, we emerge from the shadows. We need this strigoi, albeit in a new form, to rid ourselves of Brannbjørn.

Can you secure Bilsharn for bait?"

"Bilsharn–your blood dealer, with pleasure!"

"*Caw, caw,*" cried Coronis in glee.

"Now, why are you so keen on ridding yourself of this Fomorian?"

"That lumbering bear has been a thorn in our side for as long as I can remember. He seduced, and later took the life of, our Lydia. Now he has gone too far with his careless actions ending the life of our beloved Collette. Rumors abound that some in our lower Wyvern ranks, and possibly even some within our Balaurian ranks, might, shall we say, *defect*. In short, the Draculian Order is threatened. If we rid ourselves of Brannbjørn, they will be leaderless and scatter."

"I see," he replied. "And why can't your lairs do it alone?"

"We are not in the habit of making ourselves known in the world, as you have said. We tread lightly. This Mosby has Pool's blood in him, and he shall do our bidding. And if he succumbs to true death, it is his loss, not ours, for he is not of our clan."

"Very well. What do you require of me?"

"The head of Collette returned to us. And with your permission, your aid in the Remanifestation ritual."

"Hmm, when do you want to do this?"

"Naturally, a century since Mosby's death: October the second. We gather at midnight."

"Ah, you are such the romantics...you vampires."

Choíros motioned to Morrigan, who promptly landed on my left shoulder. The demon stated, "You shall have Collette's head once you possess the names of the souls I desire. Morrigan here, will keep a watchful eye upon you to fulfill the reaping."

At that phrase, Morrigan nipped at my ear, drawing blood.

Damn, crow! "And who has these names?" I replied as my wound began healing within seconds.

"This very night I will speak the names into the dreams of a homeless man. He is called Rudy, aptly labeled such for his shaggy red hair. Remember, all within the immediate family must be cut down. For, is it not written, that those who transgress up to the fourth generation must die?"

"Indeed it is. And where shall I find this 'Rudy?'"

"You shall find him on the Canal Walk. He lives in the recess of an underpass just northwest of the Turning Basin. There, he lives in a makeshift shelter behind a fenced wall. Once these lives are harvested, I shall give the command to release Collette's soul back to her body."

"And if we fail in getting all those upon your list?"

"Then her soul is lost to our layers, never to join you in the wilderness of Edom at the End of Days."

"I agree to your terms. Please make aware to Brannbjørn the whereabouts of Steve Bilsharn upon my cue. We shall use Bilsharn as bait. Now, the way to her head, please."

"Very well." His ghastly arm motioned to a black canine. This shaggy and ominous black beast, part Tibetan Mastiff, came before me and growled, revealing his grimacing teeth.

"This is Mávros, the son of Richmond's Black Dog. He is my right hand familiar. He shall be keeping an eye on you as well.

"Meet him and Blackburn just before midnight at the head of the Pipeline Walkway. They will lead you to Rudy and the precious head you seek."

Rudy's Nightmares

Bölcsem Kertész Naplója, 2025. Szeptember 28

True to Choíros' words, on that brisk drizzly night, Mávros and Blackburn emerged from the shadows before the steel ladder leading to the Pipeline Walkway. More a trek than a stroll, the narrow walkway jutted out over the raging James River rapids. The quarter-mile, meshed metallic catwalk was bounded by railings that sat atop a massive storm water pipe. Below it flowed the Pipeline Rapids, which can swell up to a deafening tone.

When I arrived, the noise was bearable and I could make out Blackburn's cawing, which led me to their location. No doubt Blackburn and his murderous crew found haven on Bailey's Island and Devil's Kitchen Island, which are viewable from the walkway.

Mávros said nothing but merely stared at me with consternation. He turned and started trotting toward the train tracks. We saddled the tracks past a flood wall gate at which I hooded myself, then briefly we went onto 14th Street. Traffic was sparse, as it was the wee hours of the night. Blackburn appeared now and then as I followed the black lion-like beast down flights of stairs to the Canal Walk. The canal, running

parallel with the river, was once a vital artery to Richmond's warehouses of flour, tobacco and such. Its shorelines were pathways traversed by mules towing goods up and down the river. These paths now paved walkways which we trotted underfoot, heading northwest. On our right was the Turning Basin, a body of water wide enough for a canal boat to do an about-face. Such boats, called *bateaux*, from a bygone era, were elongated, flat-bottomed cargo boats with a shallow-draft. This means of transport became obsolete with the advent of trains and later, trucks, both of which drove the noble boats into the pages of history.

Past the Basin we went, Mávros not lessening the pace as we approached the Virginia Street overpass. In the distance, right before us, a dark and forbidding underpass; in front of it, a foot bridge spanning the Canal Walk. Beyond that, a makeshift shelter of sheet metal and cardboard and a sallow tent propped behind a breached chainlink barrier. Along the back wall, a nylon clothesline held a few plaid shirts and ripped jeans. On the north side of the sidewalk, silhouetted by the underpass' canal lights, I made out several emaciated figures, zombie movements, hallmarked by tattered clothes and scruffy hair. A faint odor of weed entertained the air. Obviously, during dark hours, this was a part of Richmond where the homeless, vagabonds, and derelicts ruled. I was on their turf. Momentarily my heart was snared in a net of fear. To recover, I reminded myself of my qualities of swiftness, vision in night, and the strength of five men, not to mention menacing teeth and knife-like nails, all of which, in short order, would make mincemeat of them.

Mávros came to a halt before the fenced rift, poised over a large manhole with the letter "R" for *Richmond* engraved upon its center. Mávros howled three times. In response, a shabby-looking man appeared, shrouded in long, lavender hair. He eyed Mávros, then responded with three claps. A dozen or so figures retreated into the darkness of the overpass. "Yo, boss man. The dog's here with a goth," he said as he retreated back toward the shelter.

Coming toward us I could make out a muscular man of medium height with oil-tanned leather skin and scruffy, dirty red hair. He moved with a limp, as half his calf

was gone, taken out by what looked like gunshot spray.

He opened the barrier's padlock and pulled back a patch of fencing. He wore camouflage cargo pants and a black t-shirt stating "F' da' Rich!" above an all-seeing pyramidical eye. He said with a penetrating blue gaze, "Hey there. I'm Rudy. What brings you here, vampire?"

The word "vampire" jarred me. *How did he know?* I pondered. Plenty of people in this town donned gothic wear. I held my tongue and instead inspected my host. Besides his damaged calf, the scars on his forehead and left cheeks let me know he had seen combat. The tattoo branded on his right forearm symbolized the Electric Strawberry unit. This last observation caused me to raise a brow in admiration.

"Impressed, are you?" he said. He took a drag from his joint, flicked it away, then motioned us to enter. Mávros and I stepped inside the opening.

"Yes," I said. "Airborne infantry?"

"Yep, Electric Strawberry 25th Infantry. You know some stuff," he replied. We entered his courtyard, strewn with an assortment of porn and soldier of fortune magazines as well as empty, crushed beer cans and a blanket of butts of cigarettes and ganja.

"Yes, I read up on military history. That unit's mission speed is admired. By the way, how did you–"

"Know you were a vampire?" he interjected. "I may not know your title, but I know what you're up to just the same. I had a dream of you last night, transforming from a bat to a man with quite the dental work."

"Well, I am not a Strigoi. What I mean to say is, I do not transform," I explained.

"Do you have something to write with?"

"I do, but memory serves me well. What do you have for me?"

"Some hoity-toity names," he answered.

"Excuse me?" I was bewildered by such a phrase, I could not begin to imagine how to pronounce that in Hungarian.

He ignored my confused look and told me how the names had come to him in a nightmare. He described a swine-faced demon that appeared within a vortex of darkness. It boomed:

These names I speak are doomed to die.
The blood they spilled continues to cry.
Messenger you are,
Waiver not in your call
Lest I come again
And that be your final fall.

Then the spirit pronounced the names thrice. He woke up, wrote them in his diary, then settled back into sleep. He dreamed again of a bat coming out of the Church Hill Tunnel's eastern portal. It fluttered before him, screeching, then transformed itself into a sinister cloaked figure. Part shadow, part spirit, the nefarious being clutched a scroll in his clawed hand, a quill in the other.

At first, Rudy admitted to me, he was shaken by the vision. The dark apparition entreated him for the names of the doomed. He was utterly speechless then petrified when the spirit unhooded itself, revealing amber glowing eyes and sharp fangs. Then the ghost hissed at him with a sulfurous breath jolting him out of his sleep. He looked about for the dreaded specter, but no one was there. The specter he claimed bore a striking resemblance to me.

"Extraordinary," I said. "But I have come for more than names."

"That will cost you," Rudy replied.

"Will this suffice?" I held up a wad of bills, fifties and hundreds.

"Chimera," he ordered. A few moments went by then a freezer door opened, spilling its container light from the underpass' darkest corner. A red, zipped freezer pouch was removed, then the unit was closed. From the shadows an orange-dread-locked Caribbean woman appeared, holding the ruby-colored, metallic sack.

"Here she is, well, part of her, anyway. But first, handover the money."

*"Caw, caw...*the names. Master scribe wants the names," cried out Blackburn, who swooped in through the barrier's opening and landed on my shoulder.

Rudy's mouth dropped open, as did his companion's. A few homeless men, sitting against the wall, voiced some: "What the...?" expletives.

"Whoa! What devils are you dealin' with?" exclaimed Rudy. "Here...here are the names," he said, showing me a page from his journal.

I briefly studied the page and said, "Thank you. Now the head, please."

He reacted with astonishment, since I did not transcribe the list. Humans never cease to amuse me with their limited brain power; only a few of them have a photographic memory. Although, the recent chip implants among the well-to-do have shown some promising enhancements in their brain processing. This vet obviously could not enjoy that privilege, as he, like so many Americans, had been left behind in this post-pandemic economy. He showed all the signs of PTSD: assertive and irritable behavior plus a hyper-vigilance to his surroundings. Flashbacks and nightmares were likely his unwanted guests.

Chimera held out the bag and Mávros snatched it from her, delivering it to me. I checked the contents. Sure enough it was her, blood-covered but preserved. I handed him the wad.

As he examined the bills, I quelled my sorrow by remembering that soon the blood of Pool would exact the revenge my Order and I seek.

Before I turned to go, Rudy handed me a program and lamented these words:

Tormented spirits to this very day
In the haunted tunnel, a train and crew,
No peace, no rest, they're in there still
As the fires of hell burn in the hill.[3]

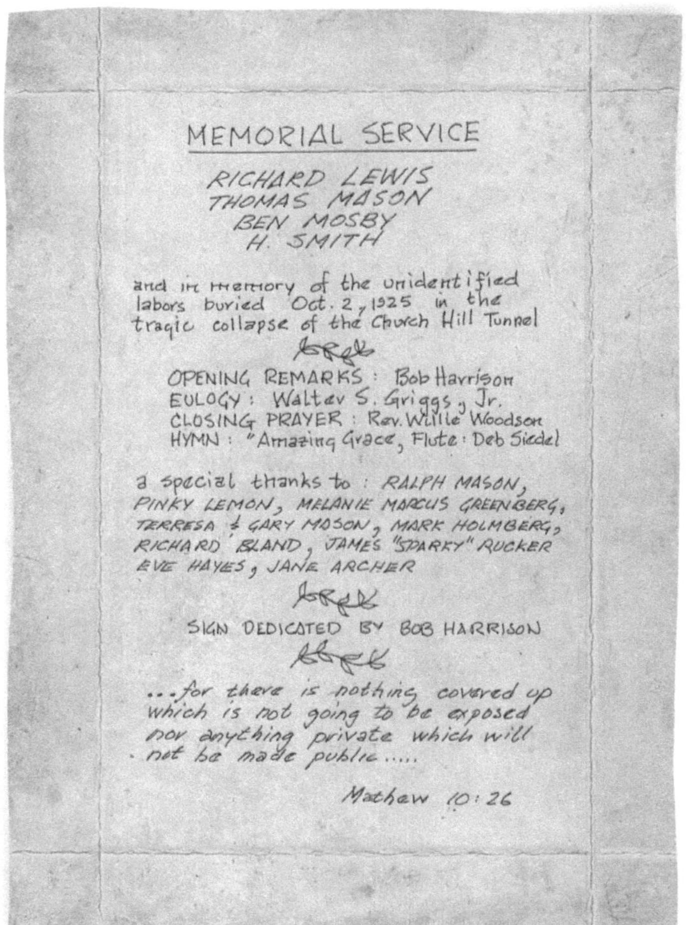

MEMORIAL SERVICE

RICHARD LEWIS
THOMAS MASON
BEN MOSBY
H. SMITH

and in memory of the unidentified labors buried Oct. 2, 1925 in the tragic collapse of the Church Hill Tunnel

OPENING REMARKS: Bob Harrison
EULOGY: Walter S. Griggs, Jr.
CLOSING PRAYER: Rev. Willie Woodson
HYMN: "Amazing Grace, Flute: Deb Siedel

a special thanks to: RALPH MASON, PINKY LEMON, MELANIE MARCUS GREENBERG, TERRESA & GARY MASON, MARK HOLMBERG, RICHARD BLAND, JAMES "SPARKY" RUCKER EVE HAYES, JANE ARCHER

SIGN DEDICATED BY BOB HARRISON

...for there is nothing covered up which is not going to be exposed nor anything private which will not be made public.....

Mathew 10:26

The Keening of Collette

Draculian Chronicles, September 29th of 2025

Deep below the keep of *Dún Dreach-Fhola*, Bölscem handed over Collette's head to a Wyvern seamstress. She carefully sowed the head back onto her torso. Her fleshly temple was then mummified to house her soul. Only Hades' demands remained to be met.

As Edana played "La Serenissima" on her harp, accompanied by Nastya on the violin–a favorite song of Collette's–guttural groans and wailings echoed within the burial chamber, *Tuama Crann Creathach*, known as the Tomb of Eadha. Three great wrought iron candelabrums lit the catacomb. An aperture at the vaulted ceiling's apex invited the candle's fumes. The slit was in the shape of the chamber's name in Ogham: four flush strokes, cleaved by one core vertical line. Its recesses held coffins carved from ancient aspen trees. Many a vampire kind lay in repose, but mostly those of the *baobhan sith, leannán sídhe*, and *moroi* nature. The walls were adorned with tapestries of *Donn*, the Lord of the Dead, chieftain Abhartach, various banshees, and *Morrígu*, The Phantom Queen, in all her aspects as well as our Dark Mother, Lilith.

Ruxandra's tears fell on the veil of Collette. Her mutilated head covered by a *borangíc* scarf, a *zgardana* about the neck, and her body in an embroidered, pearl strewn dress of fine linen silk. Collette lay in a peaceful repose nestled within a baroque coffin made of aspen. Romanian folk cravings adorned it; her personal symbols of butterflies and stars framed by zig-zaging lines representing the snake of renewal. All the Archon women, Nastya, Chiyo, Edana, and Ruxandra let their hair down. They keened for Collette, wailing and singing for three days, occasionally stopping to reminisce of her and eat *coliva* in remembrance of their young follower who lay forever stilled before them.

The Remanifestation of Benjamin F. Mosby

Draculian Chronicles, October 2nd of 2025

As it moved toward W. W. Pool's mausoleum, the levitating scarlet orb cast a crimson glow upon Hollywood Cemetery's headstones. The swirling mass emanated noxious sulphuric fumes that augmented the already malevolent atmosphere–a waxing, bloody gibbous moon peered down upon the sepulcher's chamber. Saturated in glowing hues of otherworldly cerulean and coal black, it seemed to be breath itself; the crypt's iron mouth inhaled the stale air through its lattice then exhaled a foul, odorous zephyr upon its courtyard.

In an instant, its frame shuddered. The vigor of a vampiric hand lay hold of its lock. The rusty door creaked ploddingly open. Ruxandra cel Rău emerged from the doorway with Evermore on her shoulder. She took in her surroundings then descended the stone stairs unto the diamond-tiled marble walkway while Evermore took flight and perched upon Isaiah's lamb statuette which crowned the Egyptian Revival mausoleum. Next, the rest of the vampiric clan filed out from Pool's gate into the enclosure bounded by sloped retaining walls and an iron clad fence. The dark tau-robed wraiths blackened the courtyard then thronged Westvale Avenue. Lastly, Edana Sióg Fola appeared, flanked by Sophar captaining three Balaurian Guards. She glided down the steps, settling amidst the black mass of Archons and Bölscem Kertész, *Maestro Scriba*. All looked up and bowed slightly, greeting the ominous demonic orb.

"Greetings Earl Andromalius," said Edana. "Does this Remanifestation rite arouse your presence?"

"Greetings Edana Sióg Fola," hailed Andromalius, his stern visage peering forth from the orb, accentuated by an encircling serpent held in his grip. "Indeed I am roused, for I come to preside over this rite. Choíros, Chief over Richmond, has been delegated to matters elsewhere. I, the Earl Andromalius, thirty-six legions at my command, have come to punish the thieves–the wicked and their generations in this principality; an unassuming city of vice enamored with tobacco and banking."

All of us Dragonists subdued our surprise at so principal a demon delving into our affairs. Moreover, his words had weight, for his underlinings arrived en masse. Familiars of all kinds came forth from seemingly every obelisk, gravestone, tree and shrubbery in Hollywood Cemetery; packs of black dogs, a murder of crows and a mischief of rats. Others too, demonic apparitions, more hideous, mingled with the movements of bare branches in the wind.

Andromalius declared, "It is high time to reap a harvest and fulfill our respective vengeances. Has not Benjamin F. Mosby been at rest for a hundred years to this day? And do not his veins course with strigoi blood? Let us raise him to do our bidding."

"Yea, we affirm your declaration, Earl Andromalius," stated Edana.

Then, without another word, as midnight approached, Andromalius' orb drifted northward along Westvale Avenue. Following the high demon, the hooded Nine would have only been monastical in appearance had it not been for their cloaks' fringes, embroidered with silver and gold serpentine dragons. Over the left chest, a golden stitched ouroboros, the cross on its dragon's wing long since abandoned. On the back, the sigil of Lilith, sewn in silver thread, our Scarlet Mother Goddess of the Black Moon.

Besides the footsteps of our charcoal boots, a clatter of squeaking and pattering broke the din. Then in the moon's bewitching light, one could make out an amorphous mass of black and brown, clustering from our rear. The chattering grew louder. The orb's glow revealed a mischief of rats scurrying past our party, ascending up Haxall Avenue. Their squeaking soon faded into the night.

Forward we and the demons proceeded on Westvale then up Confederate Avenue. From Evermore's perspective it looked like a dark swarm, save for the scarlet orb and the reddish brown and gray overtones of the cloaks of the Balaurian Guards led by Sophar. They bore tunics tightened by a three-looped hunter's girdle, black strapped boots and were armed with falx swords, though Sophar bore

a khopesh instead.

Where Cedar and Confederate Avenues met, a pack of eleven canines sat at attention at the Iron Dog, the cast-iron guardian monument. The molten sphere continued onto Clark Springs Circle and stopped before the marker stone reading Maynard-Mosby. Then we Dragonists formed a semi-circle about Earl Andromalius, facing the gravestones.

The pack, led by the black lion dog, Mávros, formed a perimeter guard about us. A murder of crows made up of Morrigan, Blackburn and Coronis kept watch in nearby trees. A clowder of nine black cats sat on tombstones. Evermore held the highest ground, perching upon the apex of the Confederate Soldiers' Monument.

Andromalius' sinuous arm emerged from the orb. His slithery finger pointing at the grave of Benjamin F. Mosby. "There lies the Richmond Vampire in the body of Mosby," he declared.

It was a humble stone with a convex top, its corners garnished with petals. On its front it read:

AT REST

On its crown:
BENJAMIN F. MOSBY
DIED
OCTOBER 2, 1925.

Next to Benjamin, his wife. The marker read:
MARIE T. MOSBY
DIED
MAY 21, 1968

On the other side of the shrub, his daughter:
DOROTHY MOSBY WICKHAM
DIED
MARCH 26, 1985

Edana raised a gold scepter of a winged scarab declaring, "By the authority vested in me as the Eponymous Archon of the *Societas Draconistarum*, I now commence the Remanifestation of Benjamin F. Mosby. Ruxandra cel Rău, the Archon Basileus, proceed."

The vampiric coterie encircled the Mosby graves. Ruxandra eyed Grzegorz and Nastya, "Encircle him." From a leather pouch, Grzegorz set lava rocks from the foot of Mosby's grave to the Maynard-Mosby ledger stone in the form of a pentacle. Halfway between marker and ledger he left the pentagram's center bare, and anchored larger molten rocks at its elemental points. Grzegorz withheld three stones from completing the circle. Next, Nastya laid hands upon each principal stone, causing them to vibrate at first, in unison with the earth, then foment to a volcanic radiance. Each lava stone's core throbbed and glowed in a rhythmic, smoldering pulse. Once done, Nastya and Grzegorz filed back to the newly formed ring of Dragonists about the graves. From that point on, all who traversed the pentacle went through the gap.

Ruxandra took three steps forward from the circle, looked up at the moon, then, with her left hand, formed a pentacle before her and beckoned Andromalius' spirit enter. The orb engulfed her, her hands and arms rising to receive him.

Ruxandra lowered her hands and said in a deeper tone, "Chorti, unearth him!"

Chorti, the earthen, hairy vampyre with backward facing feet stepped into the pentacle's center. On his knees, he thrust his claws into the terra firma, causing a brief tremor and the lava stones to flare. The dogs howled, cats hissed, crows cawed and the rats chattered.

In Enochian, he beckoned the earth do his bidding. Then, he plunged his right arm up to his armpit into the dirt. Next, his left arm slightly swiveled while simultaneously raising it so his wrist emerged. During this, the terrain frayed, Mosby's turning coffin rippled the surface. Our feet quivered with the ground. His left arm rose ever higher, palm downward, fingers in a grasping position. Then, suddenly, the ground ruptured, and the tip of the coffin burst forth. The more he raised his hand the more the coffin arose. He stood to his feet, his hand

rising to his chest then above his head. He ceased when the casket's lid was clear of the ground, though it fell not over, for it was rooted to the earth; the Underworld would not let go just yet. The rumbling dissipated. He returned to the circle.

Ruxandra then motioned to the bloodshot-eyed, boiled-skin infused Lothar. The imposing Neuntöter stepped before the casket. With his puss-covered hands and talon-like fingers, he wrenched open its lid. The splintering and cracking of wood and nails jarred the still air.

Mosby lay face down in a dusty black suit, both his feet pressed against a corner, his hair and his hands indicating no sign of decay. Lothar smiled at this wonder then flashed a jagged-tooth grin at Ruxandra and Antonio. Antonio stepped forward. He placed the scarab implant on the surface of Mosby's neck. Then, with his smartwatch, he opened an app and triggered the activation. The scarab dug its legs then body into Mosby's neck, becoming flush and thus appearing more like a tattoo than an implant. Antonio backed away and nodded an affirmative to Ruxandra.

Next, Lothar grasped Mosby's frame and turned him face up. As with his hair and hands, his oval face showed no signs of aging, his cheeks not overly drawn, dark eyebrows still full, a prominent forehead, well-proportioned nose and mouth. Lothar then returned to the circle.

Chiyo, the Japanese *rokurokubi*, kept lookout using her elongated neck to peer from on high. She spoke out, "Strangers are present. I hear them."

Edana glanced at her, "Who? Where?"

Chiyo's neck lengthened more, rising eighteen cubits in the air. Her periscopic head scoured the cemetery. "I spy them looking over the wall of the Cabell monument."

"Guards, bring them here," ordered Kojo. Soon after, Sophar and his two guards seized two young men retreating southward on Western Avenue. They brought them before Kojo.

"What have you seen?" barked Kojo.

"Hey man, nothin'! Just some furry guy," said the slim, jet black-haired man who wore a Virginia Commonwealth University hoodie. The other, a shorter, heavier young man wore a beanie and an xtra large Gelati Celesti t-shirt stating on its backside: WITHOUT ice cream THERE WOULD BE DARKNESS AND CHAOS.

Kojo flashed his fangs at the spies then, with radiant amber eyes, stared down the smaller, pudgy man and said, "Where's the ice cream? Did you bring enough for all of us?" He motioned to Lothar and Chorti with his long nails.

"Well, ah, no," the man said, trembling.

"That's not good," declared Kojo. "We are all hungry. Without it we have darkness, and chaos–yes?"

"Yes, yes...of course, sir."

Lothar, more ghoul than vampire, began to lick his lip and reveal his jagged enamel. The slimmer man's eyes popped wide; he broke free of the guard's hold and bolted. Lothar gave chase. He caught up to the man at the intersection of Western and Confederate Avenues and with one swipe of his clawed hand, knocked the slim man down. Then Lothar dug his claws into his shoulder and dragged him back, blood oozing onto the road. The rats scurried from the rear, lapping up the precious fluid. The pudgy one was held fast by the grip of a guard upon his shoulder.

Kojo never glanced upon on the chase, instead looked at the plump peeper and said, "Well, we can't have folk hungry, can we?"

"No sir, no, please don't eat me," he pleaded.

"Ah, well, without ice cream, we need to have a substitute. What do you suggest?"

Lothar brought the VCUer before him. He said, *"Er ist schnell und er ist dunkelbraun."*

Pudgy asked, "What's he saying?"

"Oh, he said your friend is fast, quite a compliment. But, he also said he's dark brown," replied a somber Kojo.

"Uh, he's white," said the pudgy man.

Kojo chuckled and replied, "He means his aura...that's the only color that really matters. His aura's no good; he's full of darkness and chaos." Kojo grinned at Lothar and said, "Enjoy!"

"And m-m-my aura?" asked the ice cream lover.

"Oh...it's greenish; that's someone who has a love for life and room for growth," explained Kojo.

Lothar sunk his teeth into the slim man's neck, gorging upon his blood. He flailed for a bit then went limp, turned pale, and fell flaccid to the ground.

Meanwhile, Kojo took a bite of the pudgy man's neck. He too flailed then went limp and pale. Once satiated, he pulled out a hanky and wiped his face. "Ah," he licked his lips and dropped the man to the ground.

"Guards, watch over my friend here. Lothar and Chorti, enjoy the speedy one," ordered Kojo. They dragged the body behind the imposing upright oval-topped headstone of the Slaughter family and devoured him to the bone.

"Are you done?" said Edana, rolling her eyes.

"Yes, and, I left plenty of pudgy for you and the others," answered Kojo.

Edana turned to Ruxandra and said, "Continue."

"With pleasure," she replied. "Nastya, place the crystal."

Nastya, the Russian Upir with long, flowing blond hair, slender visage, lascivious eyes and lips stepped before Mosby. She delicately opened his suit jacket, flipped his tie over a shoulder then unbuttoned his shirt. From a purple velvet pouch, she brought forth a petite, chrysoprase crystal cut in an obelisk shape. As she rested the sharp end upon his chest right above the heart, the obelisk began to quiver and glow, as did her staying hand. She then punctured his skin; burying the tip into his flesh. Mosby's body flinched, his mouth slightly opened, then he went rigid. She released the spike. A tiny glob of blood pooled then began sliding down his torso. Using a silk handkerchief, Nastya dabbed the droplets. With her other hand she touched the tips of her fingers near the wound; the blood coagulated and the skin firmed up around the incision. The bleeding ceased and Nastya stepped away.

"Excelent," said Ruxandra in Romanian. She stepped up to the rigid Mosby and placed her glowing left hand on the base of the obelisk. She spoke an Enochian commandment of Re-manifestation, exhaling into his gaping mouth. The crystal quivered, her spirit and Andromalius' spirit intensified in an electric blue hue, the hair on her head and arms stood up, as did the hair of all in the circle, the crackling sound of magnetic energy permeated the air. All the familiars were puffed and silent.

Ruxandra cried out, "M-o-s-b-y-y-y, *khat* and *sahu* come forth! The Earth beckons you." Mosby's body loosened and the wind blew upon him.

"M-o-s-b-y-y-y, *ka, sekhem,* and *jb* come forth! The Fire beckons you." His heart began to beat and blood began coursing through his veins. He gasped for breath. Ruxandra removed the chrysoprase crystal. The wound from the crystal instantly healed. Bölscem entered the circle and extracted a vial of Ben's blood using a vintage glass syringe. Ruxandra let him breathe for another minute or two then continued.

"M-o-s-b-y-y-y, *ren* and *ba* come forth! The Water beckons you." His face twitched and his eyelids flittered. He exhaled. She buttoned his shirt and flipped his tie back down.

"M-o-s-b-y-y-y, *akh* and *šwt* come forth! The Air beckons you." His eyes opened and closed with more purpose. Ruxandra backed out through the pentacle's gap. Grzegorz placed the last three stones in the gap, sealing the shape. Then, with a deep voice in Enochian, Ruxandra invoked a spell of containment upon Mosby's soul. Once finished, the pentacle hummed and crackled with the vigor of enchantment.

After a brief span of time, Mosby's breathing established a rhythm. His eyes progressed from gazing straight on, to surveying side-to-side. Then, within moments, he took a deep breath and said, "Wha', What is going on? Where am I?"

"Welcome, Mr. Mosby. You are in Hollywood Cemetery," said Ruxandra.

Benjamin looked around, perplexed at the strangely-clad figures in their black robes.

"Who are you people? Am I alive!?" he asked.

"Yes, you are alive. We are vampires; as are you," said Edana.

Mosby sized up Edana from head to toe and noticed her sharp fangs, accented by a mole slightly above her upper ruby lip. She had silky, pale skin, with a few freckles here and there, and brilliant reddish blond hair. Then he said, "Are you an Irish vampire?"

Edana chuckled and replied, "Oh yes, all Irish. And you?"

"Well, I imagine I have some in me." His breathing returned to a steady tempo.

"Do you remember what happened to you when the tunnel collapsed?" asked Ruxandra.

"I remember some; I saw a brick fall from the ceiling and I hollered out to my engineer: 'Watch out Tom! She's a-coming in!' And after that a brick or two falling around us... Then the top of the tunnel started caving in. I jumped outta the engine and dove under a flatcar–never saw Tom again.

"I was torn up real good. The engine's boiler ruptured spewing steam and hot water on me. I heard a lot of men running, screamin', even some praying, as I dragged myself underneath several flatcars. Horrific, ma'am, I tell ya. I still hear their cries.

"After that I, umm..."

"Go on," said Ruxandra.

"Well I crawled along, and under one of 'em, there was a faint light. I made out a ghastly figure. Said he was William Pool. Fella was in bad shape; gouges in his face and hands. He was bleeding real fast. He looked me straight in the eye and pleaded with me to drink his blood. He said it would give me strength, strength enough to survive the ordeal, and through me he would...what was it? He would 'execute vengeance upon those who were the cause of this tragedy; revenge for all those who would die here in this death trap,' that's what he said.

"I was stunned of course. He grabbed me and said, 'Do it or you're a dead man!' True enough, I was barely alive. My mind, body, was going quick. I was bleedin' heavily. Bits a' dirt, glass and steel embedded in my skin...lots in my chest. Reckoned I had only a few seconds to live. Outta desperation, I drank his blood, from his forearm. Instantly the dizziness went away, an iron aftertaste of his blood sickened me. My body started shaking and I went into a seizure. Meanwhile, Pool crawled away towards the eastern portal."

"Did you catch up to him?" inquired Ruxandra.

"Nope. Never saw the man again."

"Please continue," said Edana.

"At first I thought I was a goner. Not to mention the feelings of guilt and shame for

drinking a man's blood. But after a few minutes I felt new strength, new life surging within me. I began on all fours moving eastward through the rubble for what seemed like forever. Later, I managed to right myself and staggered toward the gray daylight; I emerged from the eastern portal into a crowd of people.

"Once out–it was raining–I asked for water and told some folks to call my wife and tell her I got out and I'm not badly hurt. Men tried to help me up, but their touch pained me–burn marks all over, you understand. I half crawled up the slope to the road. There a taxi had just dropped off a reporter. So I got in and told the driver lickety-split to the hospital. As I was riding, my body was changing from the blood I drank. By the time I got to Grace Hospital, I'd started to go rigid. My heart beat real low and faint, but at the same time I could feel my body healing itself; I knew it had to be this new blood; it had real power. I went in and out of mindfulness, telling my Marie and our daughter Dorothy how much I loved 'em. 'Course I never told 'em what I'd done. The guilt lingered. After awhile I didn't remember anything, my mind went foggy. Now...well. Here I am with you strange looking folk. Y'all witches or something?"

"My, my, a verbose man of the fire aren't you," chuckled Edana.

Bölscem whispered to Ruxandra, "His manner of speech vacillates between a simple fireman's lexicon to that of your Pool's."

"Poor, poor Mr. Mosby. You have been through much. The doctors thought you dead and mistakenly buried you, where you stand now," explained Ruxandra, gesturing to the headstone.

"How long have I been here?" He began to stretch his arms and legs.

Ruxandra paused, cleared her throat and said, "You, Mr. Mosby, have been dead, to this very day, exactly one hundred years."

"Excuse me? But I...I remember going about Richmond like it was the other day, speaking to this and that person... None of this makes sense. It doesn't feel like I've been gone–that long," he exclaimed.

"Yes, that was your ghost, Benjamin. Your spirit has been wandering Richmond for decades while your body has been in a preserved, dormant state. We simply woke you up," shrugged Ruxandra.

"And why exactly did you wake me?" Mosby asked, taking a step out of his casket. But before anyone could answer him, Benjamin cried out in agony as he felt the pressure of blood pushing against his nerves and stiffening his joints and muscles. Using the coffin as a crutch, Mosby looked about and saw the gravestones of his wife and daughter. Tears began welling up in his eyes.

A few minutes went by, as all let him grieve, and let his blood circulate fully to his appendages.

Finally, Ruxandra said, "As you see, your wife and daughter are buried next to you. Their life was difficult once you were gone. We are here to help you exact the revenge you so seek. Not only for you, but for Tom Mason, Richard Lewis, and all who had their lives stolen from them, from their families. All of you knew widening the Tunnel was folly. Even before the construction started, the place had been dubbed 'The Tunnel of Death.'"

He let out a long groan. He knelt over and began to cry. Yet again, all gave him space to mourn. Over time, Mosby gathered himself and walked to the edge of the circle. He bumped into an invisible barrier. "What is this!?" Mosby exclaimed, placing his palms high and low on the magical shell.

"Let us call it a *cocoon,*" replied Ruxandra.

"Huh?"

Then the supreme scribe stepped forward and spoke, "Mr. Mosby, allow me to introduce myself, I am Bölcsem Kertész, historian and master scribe of the Order of Dragonists. You have been grafted into our kind by the blood of Pool. You are one of us now.

"However, we could not be sure how you might react, given the shock of waking up in your own grave and beholding your wife and daughter buried next to you. Moreover, the realization that you are now–well, no longer human–this might shock a man out of his wits. You see, Mr. Mosby, we are a prudent species disposed to precaution, please understand."

"What d'you mean, 'no longer human?'" inquired Mosby.

"I mean, good sir, you are now a vampire," replied Bölscem. "You said it yourself: You made the choice, albeit out of desperation, seizing Mr. Pool's forearm and drinking his life source. Then, and now, you experience its wondrous power."

"Ah, figures. I expected some just punishment on that. Explains why y'all are dressed in black robes, sharp teeth, nails and all."

"Precisely," said Ruxandra, grinning.

"Well then, how are you all letting me outta here? What's the terms?" he inquired.

"Well," began Ruxandra, "once you have given us your word you will aid us in our endeavor, then we will release you."

"What endeavor might that be?"

"To exact justice. Justice on those who have been wronged, those such as yourself–and your family–Mr. Pool, for Richard and Tom, and all the rest who were destroyed by this catastrophic misjudgment. Moreover, your efforts will help to 'Strike the Balance.'"

"Strike the Balance?"

"Indeed. The inequality, bigotry–racism, abuse of the working classes, the ever widening gap between rich and poor–all is out of balance. You experienced it yourself, in your time of the Roaring '20s. We too have endured persecution. For centuries, we were hunted, sought for dissection and the discovery and destruction of our lairs. Now, the imbalance is more acute than ever. This country, for instance, is a fractured land. Your assistance would be most welcomed in this noble pursuit as

well," said Ruxandra.

"Why me? Clearly you've got dark arts and are immortal. Do it yourself."

"Ah, Mr. Mosby, we have our strengths and our limits, but you, Benjamin, have very unique qualities, deemed valuable at this hour. In time, I will elaborate," stated Bölscem.

"If what you say is true, and I agree to your terms, then you will release me from this bubble?"

"But of course," replied Ruxandra.

"Hmm," he replied. There was a long pause. "I agree to help you. However, if I think your ways ain't right, I'll stop helping. Well?"

Ruxandra surreptitiously looked at Edana. She winked and gave a faint smile; she turned to Mosby and said, "Yes, that is fair. Nastya, release him. Bölscem, assist Mr. Mosby."

Nastya stepped forward uttering a lyrical string of words in Enochian to break the spell. Then Grzegorz removed six stones, side-by-side.

Bölscem stepped through the gap and extended his hand to meet Mosby's. "Come, Mr. Mosby." The two clasped hands and Ben tottered out of the circle. Bölscem steadied him, then Grzegorz came to his other side to assist.

"You're exhausted and frail. Antonio, your wine sack," requested Ruxandra.

Antonio opened his leather wine sack and gently poured sustenance into Ben's mouth. He drank. "Ah, that was delicious wine," said Ben. Then the scab on his chest fell off and was overcome by new skin.

"Ah! *Americano*," chuckled Antonio, "my own concoction. More blood than wine; I'm pleased that you liked it."

"What!?"

"*Fica tranquilo*," smiled Antonio.

"Antonio, English please," sighed Edana.

"What's he saying?" Ben asked.

"He's saying something like, 'Don't worry, it's all ok.' In other words you are fine," explained Bölscem.

Color came to Benjamin's countenance. He no longer looked pale, but more pinkish beige in skin tone. "Well, I'm feeling better," Mosby exclaimed.

"That goes without saying, Benjamin. You're one of us. Blood is water to us," said Edana.

"I'm good," he said, looking at Bölscem and Grzegorz. They let go.

Benjamin put a finger in his mouth to examine his teeth. "Oww!" he cried. Blood oozed from his pointing finger. "I've got fangs, like you," he exclaimed, looking at Edana.

"Indeed," said Edana, "and quite the figure," she mumbled, eyeing him up and down.

"It's healed!" Ben looked with amazement at his pointing finger, then wiped away the drying blood.

"Welcome to the world of immortality," exclaimed Ruxandra.

"But, but... this is all too much to take in," he replied, walking over to his wife's grave.

Meanwhile, Andromalius' orb departed Ruxandra's body and darted southeastwardly toward The Witch Building. Nastya snuffed out the elemental stones while Grzegorz collected the others. Then, Edana led them all back to the portal at Pool's mausoleum, the pudgy survivor in tow, escorted by the guards. Mávros and his pack gnawed on the bones left by Chorti and Lothar.

Bölscem stayed with Benjamin, who was still kneeling at his wife's grave. He brushed his fingers over her name and the dates engraved upon the flat slate. Tears struck her first name, Marie. Droplets filled the crevices of the engraved "8" making up the last number of her year of death–1968.

Bilsharn's Cage

Morrigan's Account & Bölcsem Kertész Naplója, 2025. Október 2

The stench of verminous feces pervaded the air of an abandoned warehouse on Richmond's South Side. On its second floor, sunlight sifted through pale lavender panes revealing Steve Bilsharn suspended in midair by an otherworldly force. He revolved slowly in an unconscious state, enveloped in a red dusty glow. Below him, a pentacle painted on the marred concrete expanse barred the occasional scurrying rat. Instead, the rodents maneuvered around its rims, which were inscribed with the Egregore of Andromalius and his minions, a shoal of sigils. Mávros and his pack stood guard. Three packs of three dogs each rotated watch; one band on the second floor, another on the building's perimeter, and the third, either resting or wandering the streets for food and water.

The bait for Brannbjørn was set.

Bölscem's Scuffle

Bölcsem Kertész Naplója, 2025. Október 3

"What's this tower of glass?" said Benjamin, looking up at a skyscraper through the car's passenger window.

"Oh, that's the supplier of electricity for the state of Virginia," said I. "It's the Dominion Energy building."

"I reckon Edison's lightbulb has come a long way. First National still here? Huh, Bank of America. What's the tall building there, looks like a big steel radiator?"

I chuckled, "That's the Federal Reserve Bank of Richmond."

"Whoa, the govie's gotten huge!"

"Indeed." I raised a brow as we headed north on 9th Street. "What was it in your day? Two, three percent income tax?"

"'bout that," replied Mosby.

"Well, it's over twenty percent now, collected by the Feds' henchmen, the Internal Revenue Service. Plus, paper money is no longer backed by gold."

"So the Fed's a big paper mill...so I'm guessing the dollar ain't worth much," smirked Benjamin.

"You could say that, but things are stranger than that...most people don't pay with bills, they carry around mechanical devices they tap upon a register to purchase things, like this." Stopped at a traffic light, I propped my left forearm so my coat sleeve slid down, revealing a trapezoidal shaped smartwatch.

"How much's an ice cream cone?"

"That will set you back five dollars."

"Hooh boy! Heavy sugar!" exclaimed Mosby.

Ahh...I'm in for a long escapade of Twenties lingo, I thought to myself.

The vehicle turned onto East Cary Street. Mosby commented, "Hey, I've counted about a dozen drifters. What gives?"

"The world had a pandemic a few years back. Out of it, the poor got poorer,

especially in America, where money means more than people. Politicians blamed each other instead of working together to find a solution. Welcome to a divided America, Mr. Mosby."

"Same crap as the Twenties, just worse now..."

"Yes, worse. Humans tend to repeat the mistakes of the past. They just put a new spin on it."

"Speaking of spin, how are you not turnin' the steering wheel and we stay on the road?"

"This car, like many now, has gadgetry called 'artificial intelligence.' A machine under the hood drives the car, and it runs on electricity. No gas."

"This heap has a brain! No gas! Bee's knees!"

I did not bother asking what the bee expression had to do with it.

After a few blocks, we were on 14th Street heading south to bypass an accident and he asked, "Where are we going?"

"Well Mr. Mosby–"

"Call me Ben."

"Ben, we are going to a friend of mine's. A flat in Church Hill. Unfortunately, she is recently deceased."

"How'd that happen?"

"She was killed in a car accident caused by a man named Brannbjørn."
We were now on Dock Street.

"This Brannbjørn...someone I should know?"

"Yes. He is a threat to the Dragonists."

"The Dragonists, you mean, your vampire club."

"Ah," I sighed, "you could call it that."

"I reckon you want me to dispose of him, among other things."

"Yes, if at all possible. You catch on fast."

"What makes me the man for the job? Why not you? Appears you've got experience in fighting...what with that scar on your cheek. Looks like you been in a scuffle or two."

"Indeed I have. It was a unique blade. As to your former question, what makes you our man, well, that may be hard to stomach. Are you ready?"

"Throw me the pitch."

"Excuse me?"

"'Throw me the pitch,' it's a baseball saying. Get the picture? I'm supposed to take what you throw at me, and, hopefully, I can hit it outta the park."

I could tell this guy was gusty. Although how much of him was now Pool and how much of him was Mosby, was hard to tell. He was quite social, showed flashes of eloquence, and cavalier, as was Pool, yet his argot reverted back to a Southern blue collar man, especially when he became emotional.

"All right, well, here goes." The vehicle was on 21st Street heading toward Broad. "You, sir, are a Strigoi."

"I'm a street goer–did I say that right?"

"You are a Stri-goi," I pronounced it slowly with my best Romanian accent.

"And what, exactly, is a Strigoi?"

"It is a very special kind of vampire, originating from Romania. He or she is extremely strong. The strength of twenty men. Able to transform to camouflage, to conform to one's natural surroundings. See in the dark, perceive the auras of people, and run over seventy kilometers an hour. Among other things."

"Can you run that by me again? Seventy kilometers...what's kilometers?"

"Kilometers, my dear young man, is part of the metric system of measurement, which is now used across most of the world, except here."

"So tell me in miles per hour?"

"It's around forty-three or forty-four miles per hour."

"Berries, I could've used that back in the day, when I was runnin' the bases."

"Bases?"

"Yeah, bases. Running the bases, you know, baseball. I could've hit an infield ball–scored a homer!"

This was the Mosby side talking now. I must admit, it was entertaining conversation.

"And what's this 'aura' business, vampy? Nice Friar Tuck haircut, by the way."

"I once was a Benedictine monk; I prefer having few hairs on the top of my head. I used to possess a tonsure."

"And the goatee? What are you, a friend of the devil?"

"Ah," I sighed again, "–no."

"Hey, a few blocks back we passed the Triple Crossing–there's a sight for sore eyes."

"Indeed, a railroad engineering marvel," I agreed. "Back to your question. All life, especially intelligent life, such as humans and angels, possesses a spiritual body, an etheric anatomy.

"It's composed of seven parts, and each part possesses a corresponding aura, or atmospheric reverberation, which, all considered, emanates up to three feet from one's physical body. Vampires can see these emanations, based on an awakened pineal gland."

"Pine needle gland? Whoa, that was a lot of information there, Friar. I'll take your word for it. Anyhow, so that's the haze I'm seein' floating around folk on the sidewalk?"

"Exactly. With time, you will see the colors, then the layers, more clearly. At that point, you can discern people's character without them saying a word to you. Also, you will be able to communicate with me, and, with practice, with animals."

"That's pretty cool."

"Yes, as you Americans would say, 'cool,' as in amazing. But there are some drawbacks, restrictions, to the vampiric life."

"Spill the beans."

"You might not like sunlight or garlic, and you need blood to survive," said I as we entered the neighborhood of Church Hill.

"Great, so I'm like Dracula."

"Well, we shall see when the sun comes up. Your blood donor didn't have much problem with it. But his blood combining with your blood can produce some strange effects."

"Hey stop the car! That's my old church."

"Hey, Besom, park." The car slowed down and parked a block away near Proper Pie Company.

"Who's Besom?"

"That's the name I have given the vehicle. It's an old English term for a witch's broom."

"Ohhh, boy," Mosby rolled his eyes. He pulled the lever and the gull wing door opened upward. I got out on the other side.

My patience started to wear thin with all of his questions, though I can't say they came as a surprise. Luckily, Antonio had installed the Scarab app on my smartwatch, which hooked up to his implant. Hopefully, I would not have to use its paralytic feature. If he should really annoy me, or worse yet, became noncompliant, I could put him in his place immediately. Its range was global via 6G cellular, or so said Antonio. As backup, I had Evermore, entrusted to follow Mosby's every move.

He jaunted down Broad Street toward St. John's Church. I tagged behind him, giving him space to reminisce, and he was probably going to recognize some of the names on the tombstones. But the iron gate was locked. He asked more questions about the church becoming an historical park. I assured him the Episcopalians still gathered here every Sunday for service.

Then he did something unexpected. Reflecting back, as I log this in my journal, regarding what happened next, I realize now this was the side of Pool working in his mind and spirit. Ben looked around the outlying sidewalks and streets, loosened his tie. Then, since it was two in the morning, and he figured no one else was around, he scaled the iron gate with ease. However, he landed haphazardly on the top of the stairs then rolled down, hitting the bottom of the inside of the gate. I was impressed with his agility, but more amused by his slow acclimation to his new abilities. I laughed then covered my mouth to muzzle the sound. He lay there, nursing his bruises.

I looked at him and said, "Here's how to jump a gate."

I surveyed first to ensure no one was watching, then launched myself in one leap over the gate and iron wrought archway above it. I landed perfectly on the other side. Evermore *krawed* with admiration. He was perched on a tree just above the grave of Elizabeth Arnold Poe, the mother of Edgar Allen Poe. It was his favor-

ite perch in St. John's cemetery.

He grimaced a bit then looked up at me and said, "Show off. That's not funny. I reckon you've had a century or two to work on your fence jumping." He brushed some leaves off his jacket then stood up. "This vampire thing will take some getting used to," he said under his breath.

I gave him a hand up, and he ascended the stairs to the winding brick path. He passed the graves and went straight for the church entrance. He stopped in front of the main doors and read the sign next to them. I sat down on the bench nearby. The lamp overhead cast his shadow on the walkway.

"How come I've got a shadow?"

"Because you're standing in front of a lamp," I replied matter of factly.

"But I'm a vampire. Remember Count Dracula? He didn't cast a shadow," said a surprised and mildly perturbed Mosby.

"That's the stuff of books and fantasy. It's simple physics. You have a material body, hence it casts a shadow when you're blocking the light. You're not dead; we vampires never died. We're the *undead*. We've *undone* death; outwitted it, you might say."

Ben shot me a disappointed face, then set about meandering the grounds. I remained at the bench.

"He was a good man, a kind man, and he had a grand mustache," said Ben, looking at the inscriptions of the late Reverend Robert Archer Goodwin at the base of

a cross monument. "He gave me good advice about a crush I had on a redhead. I was an early bloomer."

I stayed quiet, letting him recollect. He walked about for a few more minutes then paused at the grave of the church's former sexton, Antonio Graffignia.

"Antonio was lovable. Fun to be around as a boy. He recited Patrick Henry's 'Give me liberty or death' speech. Folks wanted to know the history of the place."

Then, after a few moments of silence, he asked, "The tunnel runs right over there, doesn't it?" He pointed across the street where a sign memorialized Henry's speech.

I nodded. Then it hit him; everyone he knew was dead.

"Damn, Friar. I wish I'd been sick that day. I wasn't even supposed to go. I miss Marie...my little Dorothy, the way she skipped around the neighborhood. All because of the blasted C&O! We all knew that tunnel was a death trap. It was just a matter of time before something happened. I'm gonna make those bastards pay," he exclaimed. His tirade finished, he sat down against the base stone of Antonio's grave and began to weep.

I said nothing. I left him to mourn. I could not understand the depths of his sorrow, since I had never married nor had a child.

After several minutes I went over to console him. He said, "Hey Bölscem, did you hear me crying?"

"Yes, Ben, we vampires have keen hearing. I can even hear the footsteps of two policemen approaching," I motioned with my eyes in the direction of Broad Street.

At that moment, the beam of a flashlight filtered through the ironclad fence and momentarily blinded Ben. He put up his forearm to cover his eyes.

"Hey you two! You're not supposed to be in there," said a tall, Caucasian officer.

Meanwhile, a shorter, Asian officer moved toward the gate.

"How'd you get in there?" he said.

"We jumped the gate," replied Ben. "We'll jump back out, too, right there on Broad Street."

Not amused by Ben's honesty, I motioned to Evermore for action.

Ben continued, "Yes Officer, we're sorry. It's just I haven't seen people that I know in many years and I couldn't wait 'til morning."

At this point, I knew I would have to dispose of the officers because they would ask us next for ID, and neither of us had any; well, I did, but it was not legal. Moreover, I did not want the policemen to run a background check on someone who had been dead for over a century. On the bright side, I knew the cops would not shoot us, thanks to the new guidelines that had come out of the 2020 riots, and neither had activated the livestream on their body cams–yet. I motioned to Evermore with my left hand to attack: fingers spread then brought together with my palm moving in a downward motion.

As I was walking towards them, I could make out the white officer was about six foot two inches, and his Asian partner looked like he could fare well in a hand-to-hand. At the very worst they would tase us, which would probably bring me down for a minute or two, but not Mosby. Nevertheless, I could not risk the exposure. At this point, I was only pondering what I would do with their bodies.

The Caucasian officer came over to be with his partner in front of the gate. As Ben and I started walking down the main brick path towards them, I saw the taller officer hit the body cam button. At that instant, Evermore swooped down and set about pecking on the officer's head. His hat went flying. He keeled over, bits of hair and blood staining the brick landing, but the raven would not relent. The other officer struck Evermore, sending him in retreat. I knew I had to act fast. Now in range, I switched on a cellular jamming app on my smartwatch.

Then, in what seemed like only seconds (and I guess it literally was), I took off at blazing speed, climbed the fence in two moves dropping right in front of them. The two officers backpedaled, each one going in opposite directions against the brick wall cove, which held the double doored iron gate in place. Coming out of my landing, I swiftly punched the taller one between his nose and upper lip and simultaneously elbowed the other in the same area. Their heads bashed up against the brick walls, knocking them out. Then I turned off the Caucasian officer's flashlight and smashed his cam lens.

I then heard chatter over the officer's walkie-talkie. I looked down at his name tag and, mimicking his voice, I said, "This is Officer Bratzke. I accidentally fell and broke my body cam. Everything's OK. Be in later for repair, over."

The dispatcher replied, "Roger that, take it easy."

I replied, "Will do, over and out."

I looked around and, to my good fortune, no one had witnessed the scuffle. Although I did see a hipster walking his mutt on East Broad Street, coming toward the corner at 25th; luckily he headed north on 25th and didn't notice as the gate was set-in from the street, providing cover.

I brought my keys out of my pocket and held the mic button down and said, "Besom, come to me." The car's lights came on. It did a U turn and then another before 24th and parked in front of the gate. I opened the trunk. By now Mosby had cleared the gate.

"What are you doing?" he asked.

"I'm taking care of the situation. Put the tall cop in the trunk." I then walked up to get the Asian one.

"Did you kill them?"

"No, they're alive, just knocked out. But I intend on disposing of them." I picked up the Asian officer and put him on top of the other cop and slammed the trunk. Afterwards, a van drove by–another close call.

"No, we're not doin' that. I ain't no cop killer," Ben exclaimed.

"These men had dark gray auras with a tinge of deep red–basically not pleasant folk," I clicked the door button. Both gull wings opened up and I asked, "Well, Mr. Mosby, what do you suggest?" We both climbed into the car, and I continued, "Bear in mind, you don't have any ID, and in case your memory has had a momentary lapse, you're supposed to be dead!"

He looked befuddled.

I said, "Besom, home please." The car started down Broad Street toward Collette's house. "I don't think it would look good, going down to the precinct and dropping off two unconscious cops. Which reminds me...I need to get you a fake ID." He stared at me, saying not a word.

"Saint Florian help here," I said softly.

"Hey, I heard that. Who's Saint Florian?"

"The patron saint of firefighters."

"Very funny friar vamp."

"Hey, I was a Benedictine. We didn't use that term."

"Whoa, sorry."

"Forgiven," I smiled.

"Hey, why don't we just stage it so it looks like these two coppers were drunk on the beat. Leave 'em in front of their precinct, propped up against the wall, with whiskey bottles in their laps."

I mused over his idea, fiddling with my goatee, and then said, "OK, not a bad idea."

When we got to Collette's flat, I told Mosby to wait in the car. I got out and entered the house then rummaged through the kitchen for liquor. I found a bottle of gin and a bottle of tequila.

Then I returned to the car with the two bottles wrapped in brown bags and drove back towards the scene of the incident. I went around a block or two and found their vehicle on 24th.

I started the car with Bratzke's key and left it in park mode. Then Ben and I propped them up in the front seats. I poured a few drops of liquor in their mouths and on their hands. Then I got on the walkie-talkie and said in a drunken voice mimicking officer Bratzke, "Dispatch, I have a request."

"Go ahead," said the dispatcher.

"We need a tow truck at 24th and Marshall. Some jerk slashed all four of our tires. Over."

"Roger that," replied the dispatcher. I dropped the walkie-talkie in Bratzke's lap and closed the door.

"Wow, that was a great imitation," said Mosby.

"You haven't seen anything yet," I replied.

"I don't know how much more of this I can take," said Ben.
He sat down on Collette's sofa.

"Vampire. I'm a vampire? This whole thing is crazy, Ben," he was talking to himself staring at his fingernails. He touched them. "Wow...they're sharp, stone hard. How do y'all cut these things?"

"We use an iron file," I replied standing in the hallway, studying my own.

"Nice crib."

"Yes it is. May I get you some tea or coffee?" I said, rummaging through Collette's kitchen cabinets.

"Yeah, coffee, that'd be great. I'm starving. Whatta you have to eat?"

"Well, let's see here...I have some lentil crackers, granola, some flaxseeds." *Collette really ate healthy,* I thought to myself. "As far as cold stuff, let's see here." I opened the refrigerator. "There's nothing in here," I lied. There were several bags of blood. Most synthetic labels reading Sânge Nou Inc., and a bag of the real thing named: Tru Sânge. Thankfully, it did not have the symbol for *Scarletvin* on the bottom, which I detest. "No one's been here in a while."

"That's just great," he replied. "I'll just settle for some crackers, thanks," Ben propped up his legs on the coffee table.

A few minutes later I brought out a French press, two cups, and some crackers on a dinner tray. I sat down in the wing-backed chair opposite him. "The sun should be up in about thirty minutes. Would you like some sugar in your coffee?"

"Oh, no thanks. I prefer it black and thick as tar."

I poured him a cup. We made small talk about the weather and the neighborhood. Ben took a few sips of the coffee not bothering to look at its reddish tint. His skin tone took on a new richness; the more he drank, the deeper the sound of his voice got, his movements became smoother, and his speech more refined.

Ben took another sip, looked up and said, "What is in this? It's really good. It's like a meal onto itself. I'm getting a buzz...I feel like I'm at a speakeasy."

"A speakeasy, you say?" I inquired.

"Yeah, a speakeasy. Back in my day, drinking was illegal, so we would go to these secret bars–you'd have to know the password to get in, and of course you'd speak it real easy-like, so no one would overhear you."

"Yes of course. Anyway, take a guess as to what's in your coffee."

"You added blood to this, didn't you?"

"Correct," I replied. "You were hungry, and that's all there was, besides these crackers. And you need sustenance; you've been through a lot."

"It's the berries!" He took another swig. "I think I'm getting zozzled," he grinned.

Laughing, I replied, "Precisely. Your body is now evolved for consuming blood. The result, extraordinary virility and heightened senses. Plus, especially in the beginning, the after effects are intoxicating. I gave you the real thing; there are also bags of artificial blood in there, but it doesn't do quite the trick. The synthetic keeps your system going for a while, but every now and then you need the genuine article to keep from aging and to keep your intangible senses, shall we say, sharp and honed."

Then he got somber on me. The Pool side of him loved the drink, but the Mosby side kicked back in. He put down the coffee, removed his feet from the coffee table, but still seated said, "I never wanted all this. Just wanted a normal life with my Marie and Dorothy. I never got to see my little Dotty get married." Tears fell from his eyes. I handed him my handkerchief. This guy was all over the place–personality and mood wise. He wiped away his tears.

Then he continued, "Uhh, least she married into a good family, the Wickham's. I was enjoying my time on the rails with Tom and the boys. Life was much simpler then, not all fly-boy like, none-a these gadgets and slick machines y'all have now."

With gravity and sincerity I said, "I'm sorry this happened to you, Ben. I get it. You loved your wife and daughter very much. But you didn't have a future; you were in a desperate situation. One would do anything, and you did that anything, to get back to your family. I don't blame you, and I don't think many people would blame you for doing such a thing," I paused and looked him straight in the eyes.

"But, alas, now you are with us. I welcome you into the family. We will take care of you and help you adjust. Pool's blood runs through your veins. He was one of us, thus you are one of us. We share the same blood, you and I, and the Dragonist Order which brought you back."

"How did ya'll know to wake me?"

"Pool called to us in visions and dreams, insisting we wake you. It is he that seeks revenge, not only for you and your family, but for his own, too. The time is ripe; a time when the privileged few (more so now than in your day), have become fat cats at the expense of the commoner–folks like yourself and the men in that tunnel. It is now a season of cleansing, a time of balancing. You're valued by us, and we need your help."

Sunbeams started intruding into the living room. I watched with curiosity how it would affect him. At first he didn't notice, but as we continued our conversation I saw him wincing.

Then it happened.

"What's this I feel? Like I've got hard vinegar on my skin," said Mosby.

"You're reacting to the sunlight," I explained.

Suddenly, the morning sun delivered a full blast of light into the living room.

"Whoa," said Mosby. He looked down at his arm; it shriveled like paper too close to the fire; steam began rising from his forearm.

"Stay there much longer and we won't finish this conversation," I exclaimed.

He stood up. "What's with you? Why isn't this affecting you?"

"Unlike storybooks, not everyone reacts the same to vampire blood. When I became a vampire I had little issue with sunlight, certainly not as severely as you have, but if I sit here for another thirty minutes or so, believe me, I will start to grimace in pain as well. On the flip side, I am nowhere near as strong or as fast as you. So each of us has our gifts and weaknesses."

"Ok, I guess." His eyes started to glaze over. He stumbled out of the living room and into the kitchen.

"Take it easy there big fella. You need to get some rest. Your body's still adjusting to being awakened and to drinking the red stuff. There's a daybed just down the hall there."

"Yeah that sounds like the ticket," Ben said, exhaling strongly. He walked down the hall and entered the guest room, promptly plopping himself onto the divan.

I arose, cleaned up, and was putting the dishes away when he came back into the kitchen.

"I can't sleep. I feel so *exposed*; it's so strange. What's going on?" Ben asked.

I chuckled, "Look, you've been in a casket so long, that's what your comfort level is. It will be hard for you to sleep unless you are in one of those contraptions."

"What! Now that's looney," Ben exclaimed.

"Suit yourself."

He went back to the daybed and tried to sleep, tossing and turning for the next twenty minutes.

By this time, I was doodling in my diary when he came into the library.

"Hey–this is torturous," he exclaimed.

"Listen to me. Go downstairs. There's a casket down there. Try it out. I'll take the divan; I'm fading myself."

"You're pulling my leg."

"That sounds bizarre, and painful, I imagine."

"Whoa there, Mr. Scribbler. It's just a figure of speech." He wiped his forehead.

"Hmm, I detect a tad of attitude in your tone."

"Sorry. I am really wiped," Ben said with a sigh.

"Apology accepted. Now, use the casket downstairs. After all, you are in a vampire safe house."

He took the stairs to the basement. "Hey, what's with this furnace?" Ben hollered.

"It's chemistry–please leave it alone."

"Alright, alright, no need to be touchy."

After that, I heard the casket lid close with a slam. Enough for one day, I went to the daybed and sat there. I gathered myself then began to write in my journal of the recent events. No more stirring emanated from downstairs and I supposed that he was fast asleep. When I looked at my smartwatch, the scarab app verified he was still in the house and had not fled out the back door, as I had half expected.

Bölscem's Excursion

Bölcsem Kertész Naplója, 2025. október 4

Ben and I rested and laid low the rest of October third and part of the next day as well. When I awoke, the sun was midway in the sky. I found myself still in a drowsy state on the fourth. In my spirit, I felt Ruxandra and Kojo beckoning me, no doubt to hear how Benjamin was adjusting to his new life.

I reached into my leather pouch and placed in my right hand a pyrite crystal for protection and in my left hand a bismuth crystal to ease the transition from the physical to astral, and iolite, for clarity. I remained on my back, closed my eyes, and soon my corporeal body began to vibrate in tune with my spiritual body. A few moments later, I was looking down upon my figure; I double-checked that Mosby was still asleep. Sure enough, he was lying in the casket, breathing normally.

I then swiftly traversed the Atlantic looking down upon the shores of *Éiru*. At first, I spied the craggy cliffs of the Skellig Islands then shortly thereafter the mainland at St. Finian's Bay. From there, into Kerry, over Ballaghisheen Pass, I ethereally flew by *Éiru's* tallest, *Corrán Tuathail*. Beyond this, a heavy mist clung to the peaks of *Na Cruacha Dubha*, whereupon I settled my feet near *Cnoc na Péiste*, Hill of the Serpent. I walked up to the eastern most monolith of the Ouroboros Ring of Fire, and entered the Otherworld via *Dorus Nathair*, the Serpent

Portal. The nine obsidian pillars are trapezoidal in shape, tapering to nine cubits in height. Etched upon its edges, warnings and declarations in *Ogham*. These stone sentinels encircle Edana's fortress, known as *Dún Dreach-Fhola*. Each pillar oozes volcanic lava, and sulfurous gases. They absorb man's harmful electrical and magnetic forces. Mother Earth's core energies are drawn through the stones and drive the spinning of smoky quartz spheres, three cubits in diameter, floating atop each concave horn-tipped pillar. One palm's breadth separates sphere from pillar. These ethereal orbs emit bolts of lightning and serpentine fire. Some bolts break forth high into the mist, others to another sphere; still others curl back into the Earth. The vibrating, crackling, roaring and snapping of the atmosphere is incessant. This, in collaboration with the sinuous volcanic flames, composes a cacophony of death and destruction to any being who would dare attempt to breach it, being they physical or otherwise. And, truly, this first defense has held sure for countless centuries.

For even astral sojourners have attempted to pass between the stones, our betwixt and between, only to meet their demise, forever cut off from their physical bodies. Occasionally, in the natural realm, wayward hikers stumble onto our castle, having climbed the roof of The Black Stacks on a misty day of Beltane or Samhain. The Balaurian Guards have found their charred carcasses upon the slopes of *Cnoc na Péiste*. Others, not attempting to pass, were even less fortunate; accosted by our guards falling prey to our voracious appetite for human blood.

The bard and folklorist, Seán Ó Súilleabháin was fortunate and wise. He knew better than to try and pass. He read the ogham warnings inscribed on each pillar, as did his predecessor, William Butler Yeats. We spared them both. However, Seán Ó Súilleabháin caused such a stir amongst our ranks, being the first mortal to publicly disclose our locale, though not in great detail. Save it not for Edana casting a hollow rod in the Council's tally, he surely would have been put to death, his bones cast in Lough Googh. But, I digress, my dear journal. There is no need to recount these tales, for such encounters with Séan and Yeats have been recorded in the *Draculian Chronicles.*

So, with my signet, I passed betwixt and between the Ring of Fire unscathed, my vibration in synch with the Ring's vibration. I arrived at our castle's drawbridge bearing entrance beyond the ramparts, chemise, and flanking towers crowned by battlements. Since the Great Pyramid of Giza has lost its golden apex, is there a more spectacular sight than the bolts and flames from the Ouroboros Ring of Fire illuminating the dark garnet ramparts of *Dún Dreach-Fhola*, its three, dazzling iolite watchtowers, and its foreboding keep hewn from blocks of precious pyrite and garnet? The Balaurian Watchmen lowered the drawbridge and raised the portcullis. I strolled under the barbican and stepped into the cobblestone courtyard set with nine impaling poles for the disobedient. In its center, set in a depression, a cast iron grill to catch what blood we did not drain. This excess for the dark dogs, more beast than canine.

Today, only one unfortunate soul, a *Lucht Siúil*, known in the common tongue as a Pavee, or Irish Traveller, was there, succumbing to a slow and gruesome death. Likely, he had failed to appease Edana's wishes; perhaps he had botched the restoration of her dragon clawfoot tub, for she bathed after the manner of Elizabeth Báthory. Opposite the impalement gallery, stood the memorial commemorating The Watchers, the two hundred angels who forsook heaven's pleasures for the companionship of women. The monument consisted of an iolite marker engraved with all their names. Behind that, eighteen marble statues of their prefects, the grandest in the center, Samyaza, their leader.

Past all this I traversed, in etheric form, into a wide octagonal foyer. From there, flanked by guards, past the great keep doors of yew *Crann Bethadh*, the Celtic Tree of Life, craved in its center encircled by a Draculian ouroboros and about that, nine triskelia. From there, I ascended a spiral staircase until I came to the floor of Kojo's chamber. A guard bid me enter.

"Good, good, Bölscem. We've been expecting you," said Kojo.

"Greetings Archon Polemarchos," I said, nodding before Kojo, who was in his physical body. Likewise to Ruxandra I nodded and said, "Greetings, Archon Basileus."

"I've been waiting," replied Kojo, without looking at me.

"How is our awakened vampire?" questioned Ruxandra fixing her gaze upon me.

"He is settling into his new life. He sleeps in Collette's guest casket. He is enamored with television, especially old movies that have to do with the railroad," I replied.

"Like what?" asked an amused Ruxandra.

"*Murder on the Orient Express, Stranger on a Train, Silver Streak*–"

"Oh, I love that film! The best parts are every time George Caldwell gets thrown from the train."

"Is he drinking from the blood bags?" inquired Kojo.

"He is, my lord."

"That is well, but I sense there's something you are not telling us," said Kojo.

"Well, my lord, we got into a bit of an altercation..."

"Altercation? Go on," said Kojo.

"Well...with the Richmond City Police. It occurred the other night, on the way back from the cemetery."

"You had contact with mortals?" Ruxandra glared at me.

"My lady, he insisted on seeing his old church and meandering about its graveyard, reminiscing of those who'd passed on. I...I felt it was an appropriate thing to allow since he had been through so much. Besides, he wanted to endear himself to me."

"I see," she demurely replied.

"Did the police attempt to arrest you for trespassing?" Kojo asked.

"No my lord. Before they could get to that point, they ordered us out of the graveyard, and, as one of the officers switched on his webcam, I dispatched them both. To make a long story short, I framed them for being drunk on the job."

"Did any of this altercation make it onto the cam?"

"Doubtful, my Lord Kojo, nor did I see anything in the papers the next day."

"Things have not started off on the right foot. I do not think that we can wait till Samhain," said Kojo, eyeing Ruxandra.

"Yes, Kojo. I agree we must accelerate his recovery. The moon is full on the 7th of this month."

Kojo looked at me. "Continue to give him blood; let him go about the city and explore his newfound powers. Help him become accustomed to seeing in the spirit world." He paused and fed his black mamba a mouse from a cage.

"Very good, my lord."

"Also, take him by the Tunnel. Surely that will stoke his passions to do our bidding. Perhaps, by the seventh, he will be ready to reap the souls that Andromalius and you, Ruxandra, so desire. If all else fails, you have the scarab at your disposal," he said then hurled a mambele into a target stand.

In reply I said, "On a fortuitous note, I have noticed much of William in him."

"What are you saying?" asked Ruxandra.

"What I mean to say is, he vacillates between the personality of Pool and Benjamin Mosby. The very fact that he has not fled is a step forward."

"True," said Kojo, throwing another mambele.

Ruxandra consoled me and said with a hand on my shoulder, "I will come and see you soon. May the blood of Pool run strong in him. We should surely engage him soon in the vengeance we seek. Now, be off."

"Very good, my lady."

Flying westward over the James River, I entered Richmond's city limits. The moon was glistening upon the water and making the skyline glimmer. Some buildings accentuated the effect, such as the Wells Fargo building, its three concentric neon lights at its rooftop vivid and glowing. The city showed its cards; as in so many other American cities, the tallest buildings were primarily banking companies. In my medieval days, churches were the tallest and most prominent structures. Before that, in antediluvian times, great monoliths, temples and towers reigned, and magick ruled the world.

Not yet ready to fuse with my flesh nor mentor Benjamin Mosby, I hovered over the city, taking in its nightlife, clubs down at Shockoe Bottom. College girls scantily dressed, looking for a tall, dark handsome prince to party the night away with. Homeless people shuffled along the Canal Walk, passing by the occasional couple taking a midnight stroll. Then I heard some groaning and the clinking of chains down in Tobacco Row, where Libby Prison used to be. There they were, a chain gang. All the apparitions still reside there, hung in perpetual misery between this world and the next, looking to be free. They were working out their agony and frustration with Elizabeth Van Lew looking on, the Civil War spy who often visited the Union prisoners, shuffling amongst them, occasionally skipping as she walked, and I heard her humming–likely why they called her "Crazy Bet."

I hovered up the hill, one of the supposed seven hills in Richmond, Church Hill, on my return to see if Benjamin was meddling in some mischief. As I went up Broad Street toward Patrick Henry's Pub & Grille, I saw a child pointing out the top most window shouting, "Look! The fire! See the fire?"

I could not help myself. I responded, "It's over, child. The City of Richmond is no longer burning. The Civil War is over! Find rest in your grave, child. Find peace."

The boy looked up and said, "No, good sir, it's not over; I see the fire."

It was no use. The spirit was held in a cycle of distress at his beloved city smoldering in the intense heat.

If more humans had the ability to perceive the spirit world and, more specifically,

the traumatized dead who cannot make peace with their former existence, then, I think, humans would be a better lot; definitely more respectful of the past and their ancestors. Perhaps there would be less chaos, violence, and inequality in the world if their empathy were engaged by such perception.

Are we not all in a never ending cycle of purging from the drama of our past? Never reconciling, always regretting, looking or feeling our way to a harbor of escape, whether that respite be drink or be prayer, or meandering by the golden ripples of a midnight James River.

Workin' the Tunnel of Death

Bölcsem Kertész Naplója, 2025. Október 4

Once back in my body, I searched everywhere for Ben. He was not in the living room or kitchen, nor was he in the casket downstairs. I even checked upstairs, seeing if he was in one of the coffins up there. *Where could he have gone?* I peered outside the window. The day was fading. Evermore was nowhere to be seen. He was most likely following Mosby at a good distance. Then I remembered the Scarab app on the custom smartwatch Antonio had made. Mostly, I loathe these gadgets, but on this occasion it would prove useful.

I opened the Scarab app and clicked the GPS arrow; up popped a holographic map of Richmond with a blinking dot. That dot was Ben, walking down Mosby Street, of all streets in the city. I reckoned he had put two-and-two together and figured the street was named after him, it was not far from the Church Hill Tunnel. From the vector of the blinking dot, it was apparent Ben's walking pace had improved; he was strolling faster than a human being. He was heading toward the tunnel's western portal–the scene of the most tragic tunnel collapse of the twentieth century.

Quite amazing in its time. It was the longest train tunnel in America. It ran through most of Church Hill, starting at 18th Street and running under Franklin and Broad Streets then opening out to the world again just below Chimborazo Park. From there, it hooked up with Fulton Yard and unto the east and to the ocean ports, where flour, cotton and tobacco, among other cargo, could be loaded onto ships destined for world markets. Even to this day this is the case, albeit now by the James River Viaduct, running parallel to the river.

It is still astounding to me that many of the trainloads bear coal. Humans can be so primitive, burning fossil fuels which poison the air, when all about them is safer, cleaner technology which should have been implemented a hundred years ago.

With a sigh, I gathered myself and went after Mosby. Rounding the corner at Marshall and 18th, I caught sight of him under a streetlight which had just flickered on. He was reading a Virginia Historic Marker, that told a brief history of the Church Hill Tunnel collapse. Ben stood there looking at it in awe, like a tourist standing in the Louvre gasping at the sheer compositional genius of the Mona Lisa. He even changed his posture, as if viewing it from different angles might reveal nooks of his memory.

SA 90
CHURCH HILL
TUNNEL

About 200 feet east is the western portal of the Church Hill Tunnel. On 11 Dec. 1873. Chesapeake and Ohio locomotive number 2 passed through the tunnel, marking the completion of one of the longest tunnels in the United States. The tunnel was being repaired on 2 Oct. 1925. when Chesapeake and Ohio locomotive number 231 entered the tunnel heading west, pulling ten flat cars. The train was near the western portal when suddenly 190 feet of the tunnel collapsed, trapping and killing railroad workers, some of whom remain entombed in the tunnel along with the train.

As I got closer to him, I spied Evermore out of the corner of my eye, perched on the roof of the T. W. Wood & Sons' warehouse, now an apartment complex for mostly twenty-somethings. The ground in front of the Tunnel's western entrance was fashioned into a fenced-in gathering area for tenants. Farther back, the portal itself was zoned off by a short, stone barrier wall.

"Good evening, Ben," I said. He snapped out of his cerebral sanctum and looked at me standing behind him. He had ditched his black tie. His suit jacket had been replaced with a brown leather shearling coat. Mosby must have found it in one of Collette's closets; it was probably Steve's or another of her ex-boyfriend's.

"Hello, Bölscem. Figured you'd find me here."

"Well, this would be the logical place for you to end up," I said.

"You got me there. What's the deal with cementing the tunnel entrance? It's like the city's trying to hide what happened here," Ben exclaimed, gesturing toward the fence barring us from entering.

"Hiding what?"

"Hidin' what!? Are you trying to stoke my flame?" shot back Ben.

"No, I just want to understand you. Are you referring to the fence around it, or the fact that the Chesapeake & Ohio Railroad cemented the entrance?"

"All of it! Why, this is an important place! The folk of today don't understand that. If they did, they'd take down this fence. Everyone should be able to get up close to it. It's history. The C&O and city should've put a museum here. This was one of the longest train tunnels at the time. Why doesn't it have "1925" on it?" asked Ben.

"Because the C&O did not seal it until '26," I answered.

"Well, that doesn't make sense."

"Agreed. Tell me about that fateful day, October 2nd, 1925," said I, then pursed my lips.

"Well, I remember everything. A bit brisk and a steady rain. I was slated to do other work. The fireman who was supposed to help Tom was ill, so I got the call to replace him. Fate, I guess. Wish I'd never gotten that call..."

"Perhaps fate, Mr. Mosby," I interjected.

"As I was saying, it was routine. I was just needed to stoke No. 231 a bit. Tom was chatting about his daughter getting her tonsils removed," he chuckled. "Said she was scared. If she weathered it, he'd promised to get her a doll and five bucks."

"Five dollars was a lot in those days," I grinned.

"Yep, sure was," he replied, then his face turned stern. "As we were heading out of Fulton Yard, about to enter the eastern side of the tunnel, Tom said he had a bad feeling about this day. I said, 'Nah, it's just 'cause it's cold and rainy is all.' 'No,' he said, 'I kissed my wife then I turned to go to work. Something in me said, *Tom, kiss her one more time.* So, I turned and did.' Tom was a fine man, and I liked him a lot.

"I'll never forget what he spoke next. He got all serious, and mind you he was a solid, jolly kind-a fella, and spoke to me straight, 'Ben,' he said, 'that second kiss felt like the first kiss I ever gave her, and oddly, like it was the last time.' Well, I got a lump in my throat on those words. I went back to shoveling coal into the box."

"Hmm," said I with a somber look, "wonder if the fireman who called-in sick really was sick? Perhaps he had a premonition and heeded it."

"Oh, that's a thought. So, after that, I felt uneasy, but I didn't tell Tom. Didn't wanna jinx things. It was supposed to be an easy gig: haul ten flat cars. Drop 'em off. The laborers load 'em up with dirt, and it starts all over.

"Then it happened again. When we entered the tunnel's eastern side, just after three, I got that same lump," he declared, pointing to his Adam's apple. "Goosebumps, too. Felt like we entered the gates of hell. Mind you, the work lights lit up the tunnel, as did the engine's light, but, despite that, I felt a coldness in my spirit."

"You should have heeded your heart."

"Sure should've. We had a full crew. Conductor McFadden, he was always polishing things, including his Hamilton–"

"Hamilton?"

"His pocket watch, like my Elgin here," he pulled out his Elgin pocket watch, dangling from a gold chain. "Come on Bölscem, you're sounding like a sap."

I gave him a hard stare.

He continued, "This watch ain't ordinary. These don't deviate more than thirty

seconds, unlike your wrist watch there. If one's off-synch with the timetables, it can mean death–trains running into one another. Get the picture?"

"I got the picture. And for the record, this is not a wrist watch," I said, holding it up. "It's a *smartwatch*, and it never deviates from the correct time."

"Smartwatch? ...More a dumb-watch to me. Why, you have to touch it to make it do anything."

I acquiesced and said, "You were saying?"

"Oh, yes," he continued. "There was Kelso too, that day, and Adams, the brakeman; he had the same Elgin as me. Anyhow, I shoveled coal into the firebox. It glowed real nice in the blackness of the tunnel. All went well as we went underneath Broad Street, and we ran a ways down the tunnel without a hitch. At the other end, overcast light showed dimly at the Tunnel's west end. We were 'bout a hundred feet from it. On both sides of the track were workmen. They made quite a racket with their shovels and pickaxes. Others, more skilled, were putting concrete arches in place for widening.

"Tom applied the brakes; the hissing reverberated around us, echoing down the passage. Tom told Adams to uncouple the flatcars. He did so, gave the OK, then Tom released the brake. Steamin' and hissing started up again. The train moved slowly forward.

"Then it happened. A brick or two fell from the ceiling. One bounced off the boiler, another made a splash in a pool of water. Then more bricks with dirt. Tom was leanin' out the window, peering down at the exit. The last thing I said to Tom, I yelled, 'Watch out Tom she's a-coming in!' He ducked back inside the cab; dirt and debris still fallin'. The work lights flickered twice then went out. We were all in darkness. Poindexter, the foreman, took off shouting, 'Run for it!' Then I heard a rumble and felt a whoosh of wind, like a tornado. The whole tunnel was caving in." He paused, looking back at the historic marker, tears swelled in his eyes.

I stood still for a moment. He gathered himself, then I said, "What happened next?"

"Next, I jumped out of the cab as the boiler burst under the weight of the collapse, sending searing steam upon Tom and I. Shrapnel, too. We screamed out in pain. I felt blood coursing down my chest and over my right eye. Thought I was a goner then; it was pitch dark. Fear gripped me. I heard-a sharp cry from Tom. I stumbled and crawled managing to get to the first flat car where I saw a faint light. It was hellish. Men screaming, runnin', some praying, others crying out in agony. Lord, a scene outta Hades, the sounds of tormented souls." He stopped his anecdote. A thought popped into his head. "What...what happened to Tom?"

I said slowly, "After several days of digging down a shaft, they found him slumped over. The reverse lever had struck him, trapping him there. I'm sorry, Ben."

He wiped the tears from his face, "Why God? Why him, why me? I wasn't even supposed to be there that day!"

He walked over to the faux iron gate securing the apartment complex and the tunnel entrance. He peered through the rails, eyeing the concrete-blocked pathway leading to a cadre of table and chairs for residents to sit on. Behind that, a short retaining wall held in a small field of medium sized drainage rocks, which stretched to the arched portal. Etched in the middle of the massive concrete wall, "1926." Above it, the original stone block arched work. The barrier acted as a gravestone, sealing the locomotive and the half dozen or so souls buried deep within.

Without a word, Ben tried the gate. It didn't open. He climbed the fence with ease, landing on the stone block pathway. I followed suit. We must have looked like gang members, two guys in leather jackets, his just below the waist, mine more a vintage goth frock coat with black leather laced boots.

As we walked toward the western portal I asked, "What was the faint light under the flat car?"

"It was William Pool. He had swiped Adam's lantern. Adam likely'd got walloped by a falling brick."

We sidestepped past the chairs and umbrella stand tables stopping at the petite stone block wall. "What was that? Do you hear that?" said Ben. I nodded in affirmation. He stepped over the short wall.

I followed and said, "It's the sound of pickaxes."

We maneuvered over the courtyard of stones, more, I think, a barrier rather than a drainage system. The clinking became more pronounced as we got closer to the portal. The cement entrance was over 10 cubits high by 15 cubits wide. A few cubits directly below the engraved date, 1926, Ben put his ear to the wall.

"Sure enough, I hear men singing and digging! Wait, wait...I...hear Richard!" Ben put his mouth toward the wall and hollered, "Richard, Richard! Is that you?"

The clanging and shoveling ceased. The footsteps of someone at a distance echoed in our ears and grew louder.

Richard Lewis' ghostly figure slipped out through the concrete barricade. He wore a raggedy porter hat, grey, collared shirt, and a tattered belt holding up well worn workmen's pants. His dark brown workmen's boots had several scuff marks, and clay soil clung to his soles. His pickaxe rested upon his shoulder.

"Whatcha owls doin' out here!?" Richard exclaimed. Then paused, taking a hard look at Mosby and shouted out, "Ben! Benjamin Mosby! Why, is that you?"

"Richard! You ain't changed a bit. Still a Baby Grand," both men chuckled. Richard put down his axe then propped up his arms and flexed his guns. He showed a broad smile accentuated with a perfect set of pearly white teeth.

"Still got great teeth," exclaimed Mosby, laughing. "Man, I remember you pullin' Kelso's bad tooth. He screamed like a baby. You always had quite the hands for pullin'."

Richard chuckled, "Yeah that be right, Mr. Mosby. You got quite a pair of pearls yourself." The two men shook hands.

Mosby eluded the statement about his canines and said, "Well, I guess in your present state, there's not much more teeth to pull, but you sure are busy with that pickaxe there." Ben pointed at the pickaxe. "Don't you think it's a bit late to be doing that now?"

"Noo. We bolstering it, it's a' cursed, could cave in on folks any time, plus we'd like to get old 231 outta there."

"Applesauce! What...what are you talking about?"

At that, the tunnel groaned, its reverberations upon the soles of our feet. I placed a palm upon the tunnel to affirm what we all had felt.

"Golly! Was that the tunnel?"

"Like I said, it's cursed, it's seekin' new souls to devour–but above ground. A couple a years ago there were some sink holes. Luckily no one got hurt, or worse yet killed. But next time, Ben, I fear folks won't be so fortunate. Ya see it's been over a hundred years since it's, well, a' eatin'–if ya get my meaning. Smith and I, here, with the others, well we won't rest, 'til the curse is lifted."

"I don't know about a curse. Richard, I've done some readin' and no one's died since. Maybe ya'll are making it quiver 'cause you're messin' around in here. Needless to say, I'll check out the other end of the tunnel to see what's goin' on. But as for locomotive 231, leave it in there," implored Mosby.

"Now Ben, why don't you believe such a thing?" Richard spoke rhetorically, his strong hand upon Mosby's shoulder. "We the one holdin' the beast at bay.

Besides, we've been paid to do this job. I know it's not much, but it's our purpose.

It's our fate, till the good Lord calls us home."

Benjamin rolled his eyes and looked at me, then back at Lewis and said, "Richard, this is my companion in adventure, Mr. Bölscem–and don't ask me to pronounce his last name."

We shook hands. "Well, it's a pleasure to meet you, Mr. Bölscem."

"The pleasure is all mine, sir. I'm impressed with all your spadework. I have heard it for several years, off and on, as I pass through Richmond every now and then. If it is any consolation, I believe in your labors."

Richard smiled and replied, "Well, I appreciate your kind words, sir. You know, I know a little nail polishin' lady down in Shockoe Bottom who could file those down for ya," he grinned as he looked down at my hands.

Ben interjected, "Yeah, I agree with you there. Those things look rather hideous to me. Even more hideous are his teeth. Here, Rich, check out his teeth." Ben looked at me. I acquiesced and smiled.

"Whoa! You some kinda vampire or somethin'?"

"Yes, is there an issue with that?" I replied.

"Oh...no sir! No, no, I'm not here to pass judgment; that's the Lord's business."

"So, Ben, you too? Your teeth ain't exactly normal," quipped Richard.

"Yes, Richard. Sadly, but at least not as sharp as his."

"What happened to you?" Richard said with an intense look at Ben.

"Well, it's a long story, so, seein' as you're busy, I'll keep it short. When the tunnel came crashing down, I went under one flat car, and lo and behold, this fella named Mr. Pool was there already hiding."

"Yeah I heard 'bout him, the Richmond Vampire, right?" Richard sized up our expressions then continued. "Folks over the years mentioned his name when they came to this wall. So, he was the one behind this...all that feelin' of death down here? He was the one feedin' on us amongst the work lights. One time, I swear, if I could–on my mama's grave–I saw a ghastly figure meld right into the rock face!"

Ben looked to me to answer. I said, "Yes, that would be him. He fed on workers when the tunnel was first constructed."

"I knew somethin' weren't right," Richard shook his head. "The first day on this job I felt it in my spirit. No wonder folks call this the 'Tunnel of Death.'"

Ben continued, "Anyways, William Pool was there, under the first flat car.

I was all torn up from the steam and metal spewing out of the engine. By lantern light, he gazed at me and said, 'If you want to get out of here and see your family again, you had better drink this.'" Ben shivered. "He thrust his gouged forearm under my nose. 'It'll give you the strength to heal and carry on,' he said to me. So, desperate and not really thinking clearly, I did it. Well, you put the two together and there you have it."

"Oh...so, in a way, there's really two Richmond Vampires," said Richard with a

gaping mouth.

"Now wait a minute here! I ain't takin' on the burden of that legend. I haven't been feeding on nobody. Get that straight in your head," exclaimed Ben.

"Now, now, Ben, ain't no reason gettin' all huffy and such," responded Richard, showing him the palm of his right hand. "So that explains why you both can see me. You got supernatural eyes."

"Well, I reckon so, Richard. Look, you can drop the axe bit. Rest in peace. It's over Richard, the train ain't never goin' nowhere. It's stuck in here."

"No sir-e-e, ain't no rest for me. Feel it in my spirit. As for you, Mr. Mosby," Richard poked Ben's chest with a finger. "Something's not right. Some souls tied up with this mess...souls still alive, they need to be dealt with, ya hear. And you, you sir, are the man to be dealin' with it."

Ben's eyes got real big.

Richard went on, "Don't ask me why. Don't ask me how. It ain't by accident you're back, that you're a, ah–well, I won't say it.

"Back in the 60s," he continued, slapping a block, "Smith and I one time tried to get this here train goin'. Get it on outta' here. Well I couldn't get it to go; reckon I needed a stoker. Got the whole tunnel a shakin'.

Guess it rattled some a' Church Hill, cave-ins, and such. And, like I said, this tunnel is leakin' somethin' fierce. Reckon there'll be more cave-ins a-comin'.

"Ya' see our spirits can't rest til' there be a fixin' of it, and some justice, and when that be done, then, and only then, will me and the boys rest. We are a-countin' on you, Ben, to bring the train–sort a' speak–into the station. We wanna go home. Besides, these apartment folk will finally stop complainin' bout' our pickaxin'. Can't say I blame 'em. You understand me?"

"Yep, I understand you, Richard," replied a grave looking Ben.

"Mr. Lewis," said I with gravity, "it's a crime what they did to you and the others here. I came in the aftermath and saw firsthand that your families were not given the justice or proper compensation for your sacrifice.

"However, back in 2005, they had a memorial service in remembrance of you and Mr. Mason and the others. In fact, descendants of yours showed up at the memorial service and they had a framed picture of you. They paid their respects. Isn't that enough for you to lay down your pickaxe? Let Ben take it from here."

"Nooo, not layin' it down. We ain't resting til' Mosby done do, what he needs to do. Meanwhile, gonna stay busy, idle hands be the devil's playground," he stated. He picked up his axe and moved to enter the tunnel.

But just before he departed, he turned to Ben and said, "Some of this mess, you got a skin in the game. But some of it ya don't. Be careful, Ben."

Before we could say goodbye, he vanished. He slipped through the imposing tunnel's western bulwark as though it were a curtain. As we maneuvered over the rocks back toward the wall, we heard the pickaxes commence.

The workmen started singing:

Remember the Church Hill Tunnel
Near a mile under Richmond town–
There's a story I want to tell you
Of a train that'll never be found.
Many shovels and picks were diggin'
For their pals in the buried train–
But the cold slimy clay held its victims,
Soon their hopes were found in vain.
Many hours did they search for their comrades
Who might live in the cold, cold cave,
But they never found one who was living
Way down in their untimely grave.
Brothers keep shovelin'
Pickin' in the ground.
Brothers, keep listenin'
For the train that's never been found.[4]

Maggie's Prime

Magnolia Jones' Diary, October 5th of 2025

Dear Diary,

Today some strangeness came my way. Though at first everything was enjoyable and quite pleasant. This afternoon, it was unseasonably warm, so my medical aide, Delores, was kind enough to help me get in the pool. It was nice, gliding on the water in a float. I even burned some calories paddling with my hands. After my swim though, that's when things got weird. I saw a black cat. But it was not just any black cat, it was sneaking about the place and just before it bounded over the fence, I swear, when it glanced at me, its eyes were glowing. Then, a little while later, while talking to Mom, I noticed a crow. It hung out in a tree above the cabana. At one point our eyes locked, the cold black pupils nefarious and intrusive. The feathers on the top of its head spiked. Weird! Very weird. Hope this is not an omen or something.

But other than that, it was just a-n-o-t-h-e-r day in the wheelchair. I feel trapped, like a pretty bird in a pretty cage. I used to fly, but that was long ago. Back then I was so adventurous and carefree. I miss those days when Vickie and I went riding. We were always bugging mom to take us to the stables. Plus the hikes. All those hikes along the river. Mom took us everywhere: Belle Isle, Reedy Creek, North Bank Trail..., me and sis would pretend we were wood fairies, labeling landmarks with Tolkienesque names. It was all so goofy and so much fun.

Now, here I am, twenty-one, in the prime of life, no boyfriend, and still a virgin—well, *technically* still a virgin. I haven't been with a guy I want to be with. Diary, I guess I should explain that technicality someday in these pages.
Maybe that would be therapeutic?

My father, as usual, is off on some business trip. Early this morning a limo whisked him away to Million Air RVA terminal to catch a Lear, probably to some big city. I'm guessing New York or Boston. I don't know. It's usually NYC.

I feel so isolated, stuck in this chair. Living in hoity-toity Windsor Farms doesn't help either. The most secluded, snobby and homogenous area of Richmond. Old Moneyville on steroids. Sometimes I feel like a prisoner—not just because of the wheelchair, but because my default crowd is a bunch of elitists who shut themselves off from the real world. It's so bad here, even if a white guy in a late model car meanders down a side street he gets "the stare" along with non-verbal looks like: "What are you doing here? You're not from here! You're not driving a pristine Audi, or Beamer!" However, if it was a Bentley, well, I s'pose he'd get a favorable look. Anyway, enough of that...

Earlier today the phone chat with my mom didn't go well. She's fearful. She thinks I'm gonna hook up with some artsy guy; no income, living in Carytown or Oregon Hill, tons of student debt racked up from earning some worthless FA or BA degree. LOL—I'm such a hypocrite, with my soon-to-be BA in English Lit. But I digress. Like I was saying, dear Diary, it's amazing how many guys are saddled with student loans, plus a huge car note and credit card debt. There's even guys in their 20s who've got *healthcare* bills—sheesh!

So I'm supposed to marry somebody in my "class," but that's pretty impossible when I can't even get around like normal people, let alone play tennis at the country club with some hot guy, or dance at a gala. Yeah, I can see it now—a picture of me in a Valentino gown stuck in a wheelchair with my bladder bag hanging out. Makes a great photo op for the *Richmond magazine's* socialite column. NOT!!!

Well it's 9pm, and I've arrived at the same mood I had yesterday. I'm feeling day by day more and more depressed—thoughts of ending it. I'm taking depression and mood swing meds; can't even pronounce them. Maybe I should stop reading Camus' *The Stranger*—LOL.

Thank God for my online classes to distract me. Of course, UofR is where I attend. The go-to school for my elitist clan of *Homo sapiens*. This morning was online, a sociology class, the topic: The Validity of the Asch Experiment. Pretty interesting...place a naive "guinea pig" with a bunch of stooges who all say the graphic line on the page is long so it puts the "piggie" under peer pressure to agree, even though it's short. Today, thanks to social media, there's even more "piggies" in our world.

When I physically show up for class, it's because it's a senior seminar. Most people are friendly with me, but I hate that sympathetic look. Too much pity breeds misery. During our second week of class, I wheeled up to this guy named Cornelius. He wore a "Geek Inside" *Intel* shirt. He didn't mind, didn't give me the sappy *So Sorry For You* look. So we got to talking. Turns out he's pretty weird—kind of a nerd, he made a robot lawn mower using something called Raspberry

Pi. He's kind of funny, in a quirky way. He's big into Modernist lit: Yeats, Pound, Eliot. I find that sort of stuff melancholy and romantic all at the same time. He came over to play chess the other night and we kissed.... But I doubt it will go any further. Let's just say he is not the type of dude that has raging hormones. Anyway, it's just more of a friendship than anything else, so I'm grateful for that I guess.

Au revoir!

Magnolia Jones' Diary, October 6th of 2025

Dear Diary,

This day was so uneventful. In my boredom I found myself ruminating about my father. I'm really concerned about how he's behaving. His moods are getting darker and darker. I wonder just what he's doing at his business? It seems these days he's gone all the time. Every time he comes back from a business trip he tends to act all somber like; he's got his mind full of something serious, and he's over-the-top narcissistic—and cynical too, which I've never really seen before. His recent actions at the company he helps run has been to reduce costs by any means and keep enough liquidity in the accounts. What I mean to say is, I've overheard him talking about slashing middle management and lower ends with such an indifferent tone. Apparently, he and the rest of the board don't hesitate in writing them off the ledger.

I overhear a lot...when he is at home in his office, I eavesdrop on his conference calls; it gives me a little drama in my boring life. Dad can be a cold and calculating ass, and sometimes that spills over at the dinner table. I think he knows what Uncle Roger did to me on and off when I was, like—nine and ten, before the riding accident. I was vulnerable, gullible, and didn't fully know what was going on. The guilt and shame I feel is not justified, I know that now from listening to psychobabble podcasts. I was just a kid, couldn't do anything to stop it, but I was too embarrassed to tell anybody about it. Then one day, when I turned eleven, it all stopped, and Uncle Roger barely came around after that. I'll always be wondering, did my dad confront his brother? I'll never know, because I'm definitely not gonna bring that stuff up to him, not now.

But the other night I found myself telling Cornelius about it. I guess I needed to vent. He looked at me with such consoling eyes and understanding. In an indirect way, he probably can relate since he got dumped by his mom in Oregon to live with his remarried dad here in Richmond's Elysium, aka, Windsor Farms. What I like about him is, he didn't try to tie the issue with my depression. He just listened. The bottom line is, it's a real relationship, a friendship, and I haven't had many of those. It's genuine—unlike with the rest of my fake fam, except for my eccentric, no-filter-on-her-mouth grandmother, Nellie.

Speaking of real relationships, there's none with the Father at church. Sometimes I go to confession, but I've never exposed my deep, dark secrets, like the uncle thing or my sexual cravings. I just have this dread that if I ever told the priest, it would sooner or later get out somehow in the gossip, and I would be mortified. I can see it now. I'm at the country club for brunch and overhear some somebody whispering my name, after they had had a mimosa or two, and it included the name of my uncle. I know, dear Diary, this might seem irrational, but you should see the way he looks at younger women during mass. He seems like the kind of priest who really wants to have a sex life. The way he stares at me during mass, especially during communion, it's totally creepy. I mean, I know I'm a hottie from the waist up, but seriously, I'm young enough to be his daughter and I'm in a wheelchair.

Anyways, he even looks at younger girls in ways he shouldn't. But for some strange reason it's like he's got some kind of fixation with me. I've heard about guys that have fantasies about women in wheelchairs. Maybe it's something to do with control, that their every fantasy can be realized without the woman putting up some kind of fight, whether it be emotionally or physically. Where do they get these priests? I miss the Father we had when I was a teenager. He was so kind, benevolent, and really listened to his flock.

Well, dear Diary, I've gotta go. My orthopedic therapist is here. Another session of pain to try to stimulate the muscles in my waist and legs. Hope that black cat doesn't show up again. That cat gave me the creeps. I think its eyes were glowing, though maybe I was hallucinating, these mood drugs can do that sort of thing.

Au revoir!

Spying the First to Fall

Morrigan's Report (synopsis), October 5th of 2025
& Bölcsem Kertész Naplója, 2025. október 5

After the tunnel encounter with Richard Lewis, we made the rounds of Church Hill in the wee hours of the morning. Ben took me around, visiting old stomping grounds such as where he and his wife, Marie, and his daughter, Dorothy, used to live. We went by where Tom Mason had resided and where Ben got his groceries, haircut, and other bygone places.

As night receded with the rising of the sun, Ben retired back to the basement casket while I stayed up, drawing the curtains to keep out the morning sun.

It wasn't long after, I heard a tapping on the living room window. Morrigan, the crow whose familiar canine friend, Mancho, had been brutality mauled by a mischief of Choíros' rats, was the source of the rapping. The hospitality of Edana at *Dún Dreach-Fhola* had evidently stuck with Morrigan. He had followed her counsel and sought me out on my return to Richmond. I opened the window and Morrigan popped in, cackling away in a mixture of crow speak and English.

Morrigan had been busy. As instructed by Ruxandra, he brought a report about the souls he had been spying upon in Windsor Farms, the wealthy, west end side of town. These were the first souls desired by the arch devil of Richmond, Andromalius, for hell hath enlarged itself to make room. Andromalius insisted their time was up. They were an "old money" family with roots one could trace back to a C&O Railroad baron.

Morgan verified their surname, seeing it on his flyover. The family's initial, 'J,' for Jones, was on a grand iron gate, barring entrance to their estate, and the surname was upon their mailbox.

Mávros, that lion-like dog and servant of Choíros and Andromalius, was wandering about the perimeter. Beyond the gate, a long driveway was flanked on both sides by two reflecting pools, each with its own sculptured fountains at the center.

The drive led up to an antebellum style mansion. Its front was dressed with inlaid doric columns, black shudders with multi-paned windows, and its side porch was adorned with oversized hanging ferns. Morrigan peeked through the windows of the estate, carriage house, and the poolside cabana, which had an attached pergola. In the backyard lay a putting green area and a clay tennis court. The neoclassical-shaped pool had a handicap lift with arm rests.

By the pool, on an Indian summer's day, he was drawn to the sound of a young lady having a phone conversation on-speaker. She was seated in a rattan chair, wearing a one-piece swimsuit, partially covered in a pool robe. Despite the cat eye sunglasses taking up much of her face, she was a stunning beauty. Next to her was a wheelchair, and a tube ran from a bag attached to the mobile chair. At the cabana's bar sat what he presumed was a female medical assistant or perhaps a maid. He did not know which.

Morrigan said he staked out on a tree branch between the carriage house and pool. From the chat, he discerned the caller was a daughter talking to her mother, Linda, about when her father, Harold Jones, would return home. Also, her mother had a cautionary tone when she spoke of a man named Cornelius, at which the daughter was visibly displeased and refused to talk about further. The girl's name was Maggie, or at least that was her nickname.

I reiterated to him these people were the souls Andromalius sought, and that Maggie's given name was Magnolia. Morrigan understood and added he had overheard that she had a sister named Victoria. I instructed the avian to keep an eye on them and to report their whereabouts the night of the seventh of October.

He nodded, and at that moment, Catterina, Collette's black cat, jumped into my lap and started purring. He asked why he should continue to report to me, since he saw Catterina snooping about the estate. I replied that I wanted to gather as many viewpoints as I could. Morrigan comprehended and complied, especially when I gave him some carrion beetles from a tin box. He eagerly gobbled them up. As Morrigan took flight, he cawed and said, "Harold, your time's up, *caw*. Your time's up!"

Peculiar Footage

Internal Affairs Division Memorandum by Investigator Clayman, City of Richmond Police, First Precinct, October 6, 2025

Source: RICH Police Intranet - hacked by Antonio Jararaca

MEMORANDUM

FROM: INTERNAL AFFAIRS DIVISION, CITY OF RICHMOND POLICE

TO: OFFICER JIM BRATZKE

DATE: OCTOBER 6, 2025

SUBJECT: INTERNAL INVESTIGATION

This is to inform you, Officer Bratzke, of an inquiry initiated by the Internal Affairs Division regarding October 3, 2025.

An IT analyst of the City of Richmond Police came forth and advised us that the recording on your body cam on October 3, 2025, at 3:33 AM, showed the presence of two subjects inside the historic St. John's Church graveyard, which, at the time was locked to visitors.

This video record contradicts what you said on the radio to dispatch at that time. The following is the conversation with dispatch:

Officer Bratzke: *This is Officer Bratzke. I accidentally fell and broke my body cam. Everything's OK, be in later to repair it, over.*

Dispatcher P. Evans: *Roger that, take it easy.*

Officer Bratzke: *Will do, over and out.*

Later, at 4:30AM, we found you and officer Desang on 24th Street near Marshall Street, seated in a police vehicle passed out with bottles of tequila and gin. This was reported to us by the tow truck driver, who was dispatched to assist you based on your call for a tow due to four flat tires on your cruiser.

The first precinct office will be notified of the final ruling of this internal investigation.

Based on the contradiction between your body cam and your statement and the inebriation event, you and Officer Robert Desang are hereby put on administrative leave until further notice, pending a resolution to this inquiry.

Bewitching Mosby

Jurnal de Ruxandra cel Rău, 6 Octombrie 2025 (translated)

"How fare you?" I asked Bölscem as I closed the fire door behind me on the roof of the former First & Merchants National Bank Building. It was an historic bank building turned into a luxury apartment tower.

"Good evening, my Lady Ruxandra, quite well, despite the routine police drone," replied Bölscem.

"How so?"

"Well, midway in Mosby's ascent the UAV zoomed toward the building so I had to conjure up a gust." Bölscem pointed down the street. "See the wreckage at the corner of 9th and Cary?"

Lights from squad cars smeared the fog, then an interlude amidst the haze and drizzle revealed two officers roping off the debris site.

I smiled. "Very good. Did it see you?"

"I doubt it. I sensed its buzzing sound just as it turned onto 9th. Ah, here he is," said Bölscem, watching Mosby pull himself up onto the roof's cornice. Ben appeared, wiping rain from his forehead serenaded by a symphony of skyline luminescence flickering behind him. Bölscem and I walked over to greet Benjamin, who remained on the roof's broad eave.

"Brilliant climb!" Bölscem said then, gesturing to me, stated, "Ben, the Lady Ruxandra cel Rău. She has come to witness your progress, remember her?"

"Yep, I sure do. Hello there; what's with 'the lady' biz?" said Benjamin.

Bölscem explained in a rambling reply, "My lady's formal name is Doamnă Ruxandra cel Rău. She married into the Moldova royal family—her husband was Bogdan III of Moldavia. Her title is Doamnă Ruxandra of Wallachia, Doamnă means 'lady'; her father was the eldest son of Vlad Drăculea."

"Oh, o-o-oKay. Any relation to Count Dracula?" asked Benjamin, focusing on me.

"Yes," I replied. I leapt up onto the eave. Then I unpinned my brooch, my lavender hair landed upon my shoulders, complementing my countenance of sharp teeth and heterochromia eyes. "I am the granddaughter of Count Dracula." There was silence, except for my dark leather frock coat and lavender locks waving in the wind.

His expression displayed skepticism.

So I called out several times, a haunting, high-pitched cry. Moments later, a low rumble of screeching and fluttering wings emanated from the river's forest. The expanding sound took on the form of a black mass emerging from the skyscape of mist and neon lights. Mosby's eyes widened. The cauldron of bats swirled about a cowering Mosby.

Then I said with raised hands, "These are my children!" The bats encircled me in one moment, and in the next, they jettisoned off back toward the river. Mosby's jaw dropped, and he said nothing.

Next I moved within an arm's distance of him. "You are an impressive climber," I commented, smiling.

"Yes, isn't he? He clung to the side of the building like a bug," Bölscem exclaimed.

"Indeed, and his physique has solidified. I can see he's been drinking," I concurred.

I could discern Benjamin's trepidation. His face was constrained, his head emanated a dark grey aura, denoting mistrust, perhaps a measure of fear, while his heart shown a murky brown, indicating an apprehension to embrace the future. We stood for a moment, the wind filling the void of silence between us.

Then Benjamin asked, "Why's this building seem familiar, even the newer ones?"

"Your spirit has been roaming these streets for a hundred years. Does the name Beth Houlihan ring a bell?" I replied.

"Why, yes. Yes it does."

"What about her do you remember?"

"I remember her like she was from a dream. A voice echoing through a long passage, asking me if I remember what happened in the tunnel."

"Yes, Benjamin. That woman, Beth, is a spiritualist," I explained.
"While you were in your ghostly state, wandering the city, you were brushing up against her. At some point she employed a dowser to communicate with you.

Later, I employed that same dowser to verify that it was you. My niece, Collette, and I communicated to you through her dowsing rods."

"Yes...yes, I remember vaguely your niece. She was a knockout," he said,
and I grinned. "And your strange eyes—I remember those too. Though I don't recall the exact things you asked."

"My heterochromia is what you speak of; a discoloration of my eye."

"Ma'am, I didn't mean it to sound like that. You're rather bewitching to look at," he said in an apologetic tone.

"Why, thank you."

"Can I be frank?"

"Sure, what's on your mind?"

"Why'd you wake me? I was doin' fine as a ghost."

"Do you remember why you contacted Beth?"

"Vaguely."

"She is a ghost hunter, but more importantly, a storyteller. You asked her to keep telling people about what happened to the tunnel workers, that tragic day in October of '25. She has been faithful to your request, reciting the story of the Church Hill Tunnel and its vampire, like many before her time."

"What are you getting at?"

"Ben, do you want this history to take on more than just a story? Think of Tom Mason's horrific death. Richard Lewis and H. Smith, among others, buried alive. These men are forever toiling away in the bowels of that tunnel as we speak. Do not their souls deserve resolution?" pressed I upon Mosby as the wind pelted our faces.

He stood speechless and dumbfounded.

I urged him even further, declaring, "More to the point, you saw what the C&O did to the tunnel's western portal. Sealing it, without proper recognition. It is, in fact, a mass grave. How the city has fenced it off, keeping it out of the memory of the citizens of Richmond, and of the world."

He nodded.

I continued, "Surely you have noticed that today's people are so enamored with gadgets and technology that your history is nothing more than a local color write-up in the Richmond Times-Dispatch." I motioned to Bölscem to hand him the October 2nd Dispatch.

Ben read the headline:

City & RailOne Consider Sealing Church Hill Tunnel's East Portal:
100th Anniversary of the Church Hill Tunnel Collapse

Benjamin said, "That's it? No memorial service? No speeches?"

"That was it," affirmed Bölscem.

"Who's RailOne?"

"The company who acquired CSX, which had acquired C&O."

Mosby turned my way and I said, "Benjamin, now is your opportunity to turn this all around, to bring to light what happened, to fix the injustice this collapse has incurred. It's essential you act. Those men still pick away at the unsteady earth, poised to collapse again, for you heard the tunnel rumbling. The lives above ground are at risk. You can

change that and bring to rest their labors. Avenge them and their progeny."

"Revenge? The people who did this are dead," he quipped.

"True," I responded, "but not their descendants. Those most responsible must pay; it is only just and right. For does not the good book say: 'The iniquity of the father will visit their children unto the third and fourth generation.'"

"Well, it sure does."

"You, Benjamin, will visit upon the children their due. For these children have inherited the same malicious behaviors as their forefathers. They have and will continue to subjugate others. Their scourge upon the land must be stopped.

Besides, for what other purpose are you yet alive? And not just alive, but you now possess great prowess that can right the wrongs too long delayed. It is time, Benjamin, you stand upon the earth exactly one hundred years to the month of the Church Hill Tunnel collapse."

As I held my gaze upon him, he asked, "What would you have me do?"

I replied, "Testify who you are, your legacy to these descendants. Admonish them to demand RailOne reinforce the tunnel preventing any further tragedy, as well as reparations to those families of the deceased. Plus would not a memorial to the dead be fitting?"

"How can these descendants force RailOne to do all you say?"

"These people have a controlling interest in RailOne. It is high time you pay them a visit."

"Look, proper amends weren't doled out in my day. What makes you think these folk will do it now?"

"Benjamin, you're a vampire; display your power. Tell them if they refuse there shall be consequences. I doubt they would want you to visit them again in a less cordial manner. Understood?"

"Yeah. If I do what you ask, then what?" Mosby queried.

"Then you can walk away, start a new life. Forsake the Dragonist Order; if it is your wish, we will bother you no more," I promised, smiling.

"And just how am I supposed to start a new life? I'm legally dead."

"Not an issue. We have means to give you a new identity: birth certificate, license to drive, bank account~"

"Dough?"

"He means money, my lady," interjected Bölscem.

"Ah, of course.... Bread was bartered when I was a child. Will three million suit you?" asked I.

"Whoa! That's the berries!" he piped up.

I looked at him quizzically about "the berries" remark, but decided to ignore it. I then proceeded, "In Ameros or dollars?"

Bölscem cringed saying, "My lady, I have not explained that yet."

"Ameros? What kinda scratch is that?" exclaimed Mosby.

"Bölscem will explain later. Suffice it to say, your country has splintered into pieces. Either currency can be exchanged for the other. Which will it be?" I asked sternly.

"In that case, I want half in dollars and half in the other."

"Consider it done. Anything else?"

"I want to be human again," he demanded.

I chuckled and gazed at Bölscem to take over.

Bölscem said, "Ben, I am afraid that's impossible. You cannot be changed back; this is something I researched extensively in my lab. Once our endeavors are finished, I will assist you in assimilating into the world of humans. After all, William Wortham Pool was able to hold down a job and have a family. The only real bitch is that you will need to ingest blood every three days, else, without it, you will die. Think of it as a kind of blood asphyxiation."

"Ah, great."

"Remember, Ben, this was not our doing. You made the choice. You drank Pool's blood. I'm sorry, I can do no more in that regard," stated Bölscem.

"Gentlemen, we are digressing. Mr. Mosby, now let me be terse. Is your fear of the future and what you've become, greater than your desire for justice?"

"No, no...of course not! I seek justice."

"Excelent! Then we are agreed."

I sounded optimistic, though I knew Mosby's words said one thing, but his spirit another—he wavered. He vacillated between the old side of him, showing resistance to our plans, and his new side, the William Pool side, which showed an eagerness to aid us. His demeanor and his aura waxed and waned between a brownish glow of apprehension and hot red glow for action.

My desire to use Mosby to dispose of Brannbjørn and the Fomorian threat, and to satisfy Andromalius' demands, was on a knife's edge. I dared not mention the most pressing matter: the exchange of souls—Andromalius' souls for my niece's. My ex-love's demand for revenge was of a lesser concern. I knew I would have to employ other means to persuade, coerce, and possibly even force Benjamin to do my bidding.

During our lengthy conversation, my bewitching gaze and beauty had an entrancing effect on Benjamin. Initially I made minimal eye contact, but as the conversation drew on, I gazed into his eyes, putting a spell upon him. Once hooked, I telepathically told Bölscem to exit the roof. He did so without a word.

"What else do you want, Mr. Mosby?" My eyes fixed upon him as I undid the top buttons of my coat. He looked shyly at my cleavage.

After an awkward moment of silence, save for the wind, he managed to say, "You're some dame."

"Why, thank you," I replied. "Now, Benjamin," I continued, inching ever closer, "may I call you 'Ben?'"

"Sure, why not."

"Ben, what do you desire from me?" I asked as I brushed the hair from his forehead. "Are you not lonely? Do you not long for some company?"

"Well, uh, I do feel a tad lonely."

"Ben...Ben, give over to your passions, your needs." My hand glided down his cheek. "Embrace what you want." My lips moved near to his ear. I spoke softly, "Satisfy your desires; it will make you stronger. Do you not want me?"

"Yes, yes I do," he whispered back.

I softly kissed his cheek then his upper lip. I paused. He leaned forward. My lip touched his other cheek. Then he kissed me like Willie used to do. I sensed the blood of William Pool rising in him.

"Bite me," I whispered. "You know you want to. You haven't tasted fresh blood."

Ben kissed the lobe of my left ear then worked his way down my neck. His teeth and tongue brushed my neck, making my skin form goose pimples. "Yes...ah, yes, do it," I entreated.

He lightly pierced my skin. Drops of blood formed on his tongue. He kissed and licked my neck intermittently. The aroma, taste, and physical high from my blood excited him. He bit again into the indentation he'd made in my skin and drank some more of me. After a few moments, I gently pushed myself away from him, and his eyes met mine. My wounds healed within seconds. I declared, "How do you feel?"

"I feel high as a kite...and there's something else. I, I feel somehow connected to you."

"Ah and so you are. Do you not feel a surge of power? You are an immortal, as am I. No longer one of 'them,'" I said as I pointed down at the pedestrians below. "You are now one of us, and we are in need. Soon, you will meet the one who aims to destroy us and to take what is ours. But first, we must right the wrongs and the greed that began it all. We must avenge what happened to you, to your family, then, and only then can you move on with a new life. Do you not feel vengeance rising in you?"

"Yes, yes—I see that now. I feel that now."

"Good, good! That is passion for balance, for order. Nature abhors the uneven. Imbalance is fleeting."

"Yes—yes, that makes sense. I am different now—a vampire. I must embrace a new life. You're right," Ben admitted.

"Excelent! Bölscem will be with you. He will instruct you in the first task," said I then turned and walked away. Simultaneously, Bölscem opened the maintenance door and passed by me. As he did so I muttered, "He's ready."

The Omen of Victoria

Magnolia's Diary, October 7th of 2025

Dear Diary,

I had another day of strangeness. My older sister, Victoria, saw a dog which looked like the infamous Black Dog. Years ago, this sizable King of Strays roamed the West End. Dubbed "That Dog Again" by animal control, he eluded capture countless times. Perhaps he had a sixth sense. No one knew his origin story; some said the Orient. Anyway, here's what I recall of my peculiar day:

I was hanging out in the sunroom, when Vickie walked in with a big bandage over her left knee.

"What happened to you?" I asked.

She replied, "Maggie, do you remember when we were little, that Black Dog of Richmond? He used to wander our neighborhood."

"Vaguely. Remember, sis, you're older than me," I grinned.

"Not that much older," she countered. "Anyway, I saw a dog today that looked a lot like him. Had some Chow in him, scruffy fur like lion's mane, but bigger."

"So?"

"So, the Black Dog was sort of friendly, kids—not adults—kind ones, could walk up to him and pet his raggedy mane, but *not* this dog." A look of trepidation crossed her face.

"What are you saying?"

"I'm saying, I was jogging on Dover Road when suddenly this dog jumped out from the bushes just a block away."

"So?"

"Let me finish," exclaimed my sister.

"Okay, go ahead."

"I got closer to the dog and realized it kinda looked like the Black Dog, so

I tried to pet him. When I got within an arm's length, the thing started growling at me and showed its teeth. I backed up and said, 'I'm sorry,' and then started jogging the other way."

"Okay, what's the big deal? Maybe you scared him."

"Well it wasn't so much that, but the dog started following me. Then it picked up speed, so I started running."

"Oh, my god! Then what happened?"

"Before long I was sprinting, I looked back to see where the beast was. He was gaining on me. That's when I hit a bump in the sidewalk. I fell face first—well, I landed pretty hard," Vickie said, pulling the bandage away, uncovering a nasty red scrape on her knee.

"Eww, that's gross."

"When I got up, the dog was like, within twenty feet of me."

"Wha'!?"

"Nearby was Tuckahoe Women's Club, so I ran inside. Blood oozed down my leg—so gross!"

"Ugh! Is that where you got that bandage?"

"Yeah. Staff there were really nice. They cleaned it up and dressed it."

"Sorry that happened to you. Was the dog still there when you left?"

"Nope. I peeked out the club's front door, looked all around. No sign of 'em. So then I left. But then on the way home, something spooky happened."

"Spooky?" I said skeptically. "Really? What?"

"When I got back here, just as I closed the gate I saw a crow up in a tree, cawing at me. I swear, Mags, *at me*. And then, when I looked down through the bars of the gate, there was that dog again, across the way. The whole thing gave me the creeps."

"Whoa! I saw a crow too! It was two days ago. I was sunning myself near the pool. That is creepy!"

"What did it do?" Vickie asked.

"Nothin', it just felt like it was watching me."

"Was its plumage sort of spiked on its head?"

"Yeah it was! And, okay—don't laugh at me, but it seemed like its eyes were glowing."

"Next time I see that bird...I'm gonna borrow dad's pistol."

"That's a bit extreme," I stated.

"Going to Jack Brown's later. Text me what burger you want," my sis said as she left the sunroom.

Hmm, now as I'm retelling this dear Diary, it just hit me that's the most conversation I've had with my sister in a while. When she's not jet-setting in Capri or Aspen, she's usually off with some guy on a local rooftop bar. She's like Rita

Hayworth in *Gilda,* going from place to place, guy to guy, except she's got a trust fund, so she's not someone's laundry.

It's late as I write this. I'm fading, but it's worth noting that just an hour ago I swear I saw that crow again, but this time outside my window; I'm probably just freaked out from Vickie's story and so I'm just seeing things. Still it's Spooky!

Au revoir!

Covach's Intrigued

Breland/Covach Phonecon, October 8, 2025 14:21-14:25

Source: Breland's cell - hacked by Antonio Jararaca

Parties: Detective R. Breland, Homicide Division, City of Richmond Police; FBI Special Agent Lenora Covach, Criminal Investigations Division, Human Trafficking Task Force

Covach: Special Agent Covach. May I help you?

Breland: Hey Lenora.

Covach: Richard! It's been a long time; how's my old precinct doin'?

Breland: You're missed, except for that Rothlisberger bobblehead you left on your desk.

Covach: Were you the one who put a wad of gum on its head?

Breland: Not snitchin'.

Covach: Figures. You Richmonders are all alike. What's up?

Breland: Covach, I think I've got a *paranormal* down here.

Covach: Richmond? Nothin' happens there, except craft beer and statue drama, and even that's old news.

Breland: Seriously, Lenora, I know you're a big-shot agent now, but you're the only one who will take me seriously on these things.

Covach: Why? 'Cause I steered the Lockgreen case?

Breland: Precisely. You were the only one who made a connection between *Scarletvin* and that "vampiric" suspect. Well, that's what you and I called her.

Covach: Yeah, that never made the FBI report...so much for joint task force cooperation.

Breland: That's beside the point. All I'm askin' is you take a look at some clips–bodycam, drone footage; it's only a couple seconds' worth.

Covach: Ok, ok, snail mail it to me, encrypt it.

Breland: Nope, can't. Have to do it via private channel.

Covach: Oh, that's why you called me on my personal cell. Let me guess, Clayman, the IA guy, he leaked you the clips?

Breland: Hey, who knows. I opened my desk drawer and there it was, a thumb drive.

Covach: Yeah, and this morning after my dental work, I found a fifty dollar bill under my pillow, from the tooth fairy no less. I'll look at it. Send it to my personal cloud account, the one we used to share bootlegged music on. And Richie, if there's something to this, you owe me a drink.

Breland: You got it!

Shadow on the Door

Magnolia's Diary, October 8th of 2025

Dear Diary,

Not much happened today. The usual physical therapy in the morning, Instagram scrolling...but later in the day, my online Lit class was interesting. We analyzed W. B. Yeats' fantastical poem, *Byzantium.* When we got to stanza two, Cornelius, who's also in this class, loved the first two lines in stanza two:

Before me floats an image, man or shade,
Shade more than man, more image than a shade;

He remarked, "Yeah, I can totally relate to these lines. Some nights when I haven't eaten much for days, my senses are more keen. I've looked out my window and seen the shades of spirits, really more images, traveling to and from AgeCroft Gardens to Virginia House."

At that comment some students chuckled, their teleconference mics not on mute. I was speechless.

Given Cornelius' tendencies toward the techie stuff, I was surprised to hear he believes in the supernatural, but I believe he's seen what he describes, because tonight I didn't feel like eating dinner, and, just an hour ago, I swear, dear Diary, I glimpsed glowing scarlet eyes in a cat's silhouette before the cabana. I was gazing through my window pane when suddenly I blurted out, "There's a shadow on the door!" I pondered: *Was it the black cat I spotted the other day?* One instant it was there, the next, it had vanished. Then, not a minute later, the spikey-headed crow landed on the back fence. It cawed a few times then took flight. A preposterous impression seared my heart: the feline and the avian were scoping out the place.

But why? *Hmm*, I thought, *I bet the cat and crow are out to get me!* LOL! Which brought me to the dog Vickie saw yesterday. *Is he their boss?* I can't believe I entertained such speculations. My harebrained fears are getting the better of me.

Well, dear Diary, I'm done for the night. Just one more thing, will tonight's nightcap be an exception? Cognac XO or just the usual hot cocoa? After what I just saw, not a tough decision.

Au revoir!

Unexpected Visit

Bölcsem Kertész Naplója, 2025. október 9

Under a waning gibbous moon, we smelled the odor of a cigar mingle with the towering cedars. "Leave the help alone. You need only confront Harold Jones," I whispered to Ben. We stood placid just outside the perimeter wall of the estate.

Our avian scouts, Morrigan and Evermore, were in position. Evermore, the larger, kept watch upon the roof while Morrigan was perched upon a branch above the pool and cabana. I detected heavy footsteps, a faint splash, then a whiff of cognac. A rear door slammed shut.

"Kraw, kraw," Evermore sounded the "all clear" signal, while Morrigan echoed his sentiments.

We vaulted over the stone wall then worked our way across the grounds to the pool's cabana. "Why's this fella so important?" asked Ben.

"He, Ben, is an ancestor of a C&O exec from your day. Moreover, for RailOne, he is a principal shareholder and sits on the board."

A desk light flickered on through a kaleidoscope of stained glass. We could make out the outline of Harold Jones puffing his Havana, his legs propped up on a desk.

We were wending our way past the pool when Mosby hit a wrought iron pot pedestal and toppled a tropical plant upon the pool's deck.

Harold spun about on his wingback swivel chair. He stood abruptly and cupped a hand, peering out through a translucent diamond pane. His frame became clearer; he was a tall man, amply built with a prominent forehead, most of his white hair crowning the sides of his head...that *typical executive look*, I thought. To avoid detection, we shuffled over to the shadow of a wisteria-laden trellis.

Nearby, a possum scampered along the top of the wall. Harold must have observed it since he resumed sitting in the wingback, puffing away.

I motioned to Ben. We moved to the back door. I grasped the doorknob, where-

upon my hand began to radiate upon the knob and its locking mechanism. Next I turned the knob and opened the door. Ben's eyes widened as he examined the molten latch bolt.

"How'd you do that?" he whispered.

"I'm a hot guy." I entered the doorway.

"Funny." We stood inside a dimly lit mahogany-paneled hallway.

"Now, it's time to give Harold Jones your piece of mind," I said, looking at him sternly. I started to walk toward an adjacent hallway leading to the study.
Mosby hesitated. "Why are you not budging?" I asked in an insolent, yet soft voice.

With a hushed tone, he replied, "Why can't we do this somewhere else? Like, I come to his office or meet him on the street?"

"No Ben, nooo," I replied, ushering him into a billiards room right off the hallway. "We cannot risk public attention. We have gone over all this. Remember, our force-able entry sets the tone; puts us in charge. Besides, he deserves a good scare. Like we planned, I address him first, explaining we know his lineage, then we explain who you are. Lastly, we state our terms. Got it?"

"Yeah, only, I've never broken into a place before."

"Well, there's a first time for everything," I answered. I turned and resumed my march toward the man's study, Ben close behind.

"What the devil!?" a startled Harold exclaimed, looking up from his cognac and still clinging to his cigar. My vintage goth apparel must've shocked him, let alone we were trespassing. Ben shuttled in behind me.

"Good evening, Harold," I replied.

"Who are you!? How do you know my name?" he demanded.

"As to who we are, it's of little concern to you. As to who you are, I've known of your crimson addiction for quite some time." I began tapping my long fingernails upon his desk and flaunted my fangs.

His face went white. He retreated from his desk to the rear bay window bench. There, on the bench's cul-de-sac was an unlatched Huey gun case.

"Smart. You keep it unlatched," I smiled. Harold pulled out the pistol, aiming it at my chest. "Relax, Mr. Jones, I'm not here for your *Scarletvin*." His eyes narrowed. "We vampires don't need oxidized infant blood to stay alive. Even animal blood will do for a season. Besides, the gun will not stop us. Observe."

Keeping my hands near my waist, I utilized my left pointing finger's nail to cut the veins on my right forearm. Blood pooled for a moment then dripped onto his oak wood floor. Like a Pavlovian dog, at the site of blood, his mouth opened just enough to reveal his tongue push up against his lower gums.

"Aw, you are quite an addict," I teased. His breathing became heavy, fixating on my forearm. His countenance changed to mild shock as he witnessed the slit close, the bleeding stop. I brushed the remaining droplets onto my middle and index fingers then offered it to him. "Would you like some, or should I say, do you *need* some? This is far more potent than any you've ever had."

The gun started wobbling in his right hand and he said, "I, I thought it was all a fantasy. Some at the Bohemian Grove said your kind existed. I, I laughed it off."

I fixed my gaze upon him and said, "I'm surprised at you, Mr. Jones...not believing your friends higher up on the food chain." His boldness began to wane under my stare. "Now, Harold, put the gun down, and listen to my offer. Unless you would rather find my teeth buried in the side of your neck," I said sternly. He placed the Colt 38S on the desk.

"Good, now give me your hanky," I commanded. He complied. I wiped my blood remains onto it, then handed it back to him. "Go ahead."

Harold placed the handkerchief under his nose, all the while keeping his eyes on us. He sniffed it. The rosy sulphuric aroma brought a slight smile to his face. He licked the hanky. "Ahh," he uttered. Gaping mouth, goosebumps appeared. Eyes half shut, his body went into a mild orgasmic tremor. When he recovered he noticed his gun twirling in my left hand.

"Glad you enjoyed that," I voiced.

Then I tossed the gun to Mosby, who looked befuddled.

A look of bewilderment also set in on Harold's face. "How'd you–"

"Grab that?"

"That's not–"

"Possible? I'm afraid a great many things are possible, Harold. You are dealing with a vampire." Without looking at Ben I ordered, "Just put it in your pocket."

Ben placed the weapon in his outside pocket.

"Who the hell is he?"

I continued, "Ah, Mr. Jones, good question. You've heard of my friend here, Benjamin Mosby. He's back from the grave–just to see you. He has a request (or two) to make of you."

"Huh? *The* Mosby!? The fireman from the tunnel collapse?" Harold asked in disbelief. "Your shittin' me!"

"Nope. I'm back," replied Mosby, moving to stand next to me. He unfolded a raggedy newspaper clipping from the *Richmond Times-Dispatch* dated October 4, 1925. It showed his mugshot below Tom Mason's.

A look of shock fell over Harold's face. He admitted, "That, that looks exactly like you! You–uhh...this makes sense...the story in the paper about your grave being tampered with. I, I thought it was a hoax."

"No hoax, Mr. J," said Mosby.

"Look, I'm sorry that happened to you, you and your family. My grandfather should've never approved that widening." He paused for an instance, inspecting me then Mosby. "Is it reparations you want?"

"Yeah, in a way," answered Mosby. "I wanna museum there, a plaque listing the dead. And the tunnel fixed."

"A plaque *maybe*, a *museum?*" Harold said sardonically. "Look, that's a tough one. As for the tunnel itself, it's fine."

"No, it's not. It's starting to cave in," Ben said with conviction.

"So," countered Harold, "let the lawyers deal with it." He paused and took a sip of his drink then continued, "Besides, my RailOne engineers would need the city's help to do any repairs. And frankly fellas, the city drags their feet on nearly everything, even schools. But money... money is not an issue. I can wire you some funds right now. You fellas drain me some of your juice and we can settle this tonight. Whatd'ya say?"

BENJAMIN MOSBY.

"We are not here for money," stated Ben as he began to round the desk. "We're here to stop a cave in, for some pay back, for remembrance for those who died. Your family needs to make amends. I told you what I want West Ender. It's not negotiable."

"Hey," said Harold, eyeing Ben's pocket, "I can't promise all that, but I can look into it. There's already a plaque at the western site, and the city put in a jungle gym that looks like your train 231. Isn't that enough?" He eyed my medieval, lace-up boots and Ben's rustic brown leather jacket. Then he chuckled, took another sip of his cognac and put it back on the desk. He uttered offhandedly, "You guys look like you need some new threads. Come on, I can swing three mil in exchange for some vials. That's my offer–take it or leave it."

"Look here, you dapper scumbag," Mosby shouted and swiftly grabbed his neck. Harold held close, easily got the Colt out of Mosby's pocket. He released a round, grazing Ben's head. In response, Ben's nails punctured Harold's neck in three places, one caused by the thumb, the other two from his fingers. Blood gurgled onto the starched white collar then onto the Persian rug. Harold dropped the .38, attempting to stay Mosby's hand, gasping for breath. I heard a whizzing sound from the doorway behind me.

I spun and beheld a platinum blond in an electric wheelchair, wearing a silk nightgown. It was Magnolia. A look of terror crossed her face; she gaped, but no sound escaped.

Ben, unaware of the lady, was fixated upon his hand, saturated in blood. Horrified he released his grip. “Ahh, crap, what’ve I done?” he exclaimed, glancing at me, then realized the woman nearby. Harold had dropped to the floor, clutching his neck with one hand and going for the gun with the other.

The situation was spiraling out of control. I needed to neutralize Mosby and finish off Harold. I opened the scarab app on my smartwatch, intending to trigger the paralytic component in his implant. I was too late.

Just as I was about to turn it on, I saw Harold out of the corner of my eye, still on the floor, roll to one side. He pointed the .38 at me. Sparks flew from the muzzle, then a snake of smoke. I slammed back against the wall from the force of the round. Unexpectedly, my legs became immobilized. I knew then I would suffer a few minutes of incapacitation, flat against the wall, while the nerves in my spine self-healed. What unfolded next, I could not have dreamt up.

“Oh my god,” said Ben, blood gelling in his hair, “are you gonna make it?”

“Look out!” I shouted. Harold had aimed the gun at Ben, but then directed it at his own daughter, Magnolia. “Before I, ah...go,” he voiced with a husky breath, “I... I’m gonna make sure you’re getting nothing. I let your uncle have his way with you because you’re a manipulative bitch–just like your mother!” He released a round into her stomach. She keeled over and cried out.

He then swiveled awkwardly to shoot Ben. Ben sidestepped. Harold missed his vitals but grazed him again. This time it was the skin on his right hand between his thumb and forefinger. Mosby’s blood mixed with Harold’s on the Persian rug. Ben stomped on Harold’s gun hand. He let go of the pistol. The bullet was lodged in a Frederic Remington statue called, *The Outlaw.* Magnolia sat back up, clutching her stomach area as blood spread out, soaking through her pearly white nightgown. She was groaning in agony and crying out in shock. Her voice caught abruptly in her throat when she beheld Mosby’s hand heal in seconds.

A chorus of footsteps sounded, coming down the hall. Then I heard the back door burst open. Tingling sensations trickled down my legs.

Magnolia stared at Ben and pleaded, “Help me!”

Just then, Harold’s wife, Linda, entered from the rear door. She screamed, and right after her, from the hallway, came Victoria and Magnolia’s medical aid, who joined in the chorus. Victoria placed her palms on her cheeks and the aid waved her arms like a baby chick learning to fly. My thighs twitched.

Magnolia’s mother gathered herself and grabbed the gun from the floor. Harold had turned pale, he fought to focus his eyes.

Mosby put up his hands and stated, “Lady, I didn’t mean to hurt ‘em.” Linda didn’t say a word as she shot him in the chest. He stumbled backwards, landing in a guest chair. Then she aimed the .38 at me, still married to the wall, and demanded, ”Who the hell are you? What’s going on here!?”

"Mother! What are you doing!?" Victoria exclaimed.

"Mom! Help!" uttered Magnolia.

Her mother ignored her and said to Victoria, "Clearing a way for you."

I wiggled my toes.

"What! Maggie's dying! Delores, call an ambulance," ordered Victoria.

"Shut up!" Linda yelled at her.

Delores went over to pick up Harold's desk phone. She got as far as placing the receiver to her ear when she took a bullet. Her body glanced off the desk, falling opposite Harold. Her right hand dropped the handset. Her left hand dragged the phone housing onto the rug.

"No witnesses," the wife said stoically.

Victoria screamed again.

"Would you shut up! Now, what's all this about?" she coolly asked, aiming at me.

Shocked she didn't attend to her daughter, I said, "I'm Farkas, a bill collector for a *Scarletvin* dealer. Your husband's behind."

"Bah, figures." She pointed the weapon at her husband. "Harold dear, your time's up. Any last words?"

Indeed Harold was fading fast. A red pool had formed on the rug near his neck. He rolled onto his back and said, "Yeah. Linda, Olivia was a better screw."

"Couldn't have been as good as our gardener," she countered and shot him in the heart.

Victoria cried out, "Daddy!" She knelt over, shaking him to respond. "Daddy, Daddy!" tears poured down her face. Edges of her hair absorbed and became stained by his red pool.

"*Kraw, err, kraw,*" sounded Evermore as he swooped into the room via the back door. He pecked and pried several times at the widow's face. Linda screamed and flailed, and lost her grip on the gun. Blood spattered onto the carpet. (I wanted that carpet, such a fine Persian made of silk.) She fell over, hollering in agony.

Victoria and Magnolia both let out a cacophony of screams. Evermore kept pecking. Then Victoria picked up the gun.

"Evermore!" I alerted. The bird jettisoned, bounced off the window, careened and flew out the door.

To my surprise, Victoria turned the .38 on her mother. Sobbing, she exclaimed, "You murdered Daddy! You killed him!" she pulled the trigger, ending her mother.

She then rushed over to examine her sister. Magnolia was fading. She checked on Mosby; he just sat there, moaning in the chair. She spun about, fixing the gun on me, and declared, "You're taking the fall for this."

Flutter, flutter...back came Evermore, this time landing on Victoria. He unleashed an onslaught of pecking and pricking. She swiveled and fought, finally pulling the trigger to bring him down. As I had guessed, the gun went, *click, click*. The Colt had

a standard magazine, eight rounds; seven had been loaded in the magazine, plus the one that had started the whole mess in the firing chamber. "That's a nice piece in your hand," I said to Vickie. "It performed grandly tonight. I'll give Harold Jones one thing, he had good taste in firearms."

Unabated, Evermore resumed his assault, her face and right ear all turning crimson.

Suddenly, Mosby pushed up out of his chair to swipe the raven away. Evermore dodged him then exited the room. But the deed was done. Victoria fell over onto the desk, the force of which popped her mutilated right eyeball out of its socket. The gooey sphere rolled onto the carpet, right in front of Magnolia. Her sister was dead.

"Ahh, nooo!...Vickie!" Magnolia sobbed. The sight of the eyeball shook her out of her fading state. She was slipping fast, much of her blood collecting in her seat, some dripping onto the wheels then unto the rug. She managed to lift her head; she knew she was almost gone. Magnolia locked eyes with Mosby.

Mosby explained, "My blood it does the trick."

She reached for his right forearm, imploring, "That's disgusting, but I don't wanna die. Please, please give me your blood! Let me drink." With his left hand, he slit his forearm, then gently grabbed her hair, holding her head up. He placed his bloody arm upon her full lips. Her eyelids half open, greenish hazel irises and pupils teetering between looking straight on and rolling to the back of her head.

She managed to lap up his blood. Some of it dripped down her pale, creamy cheeks.

"Stop, Ben," I adjured. I could bend my knees.

"No," he replied. She kept consuming. I got to my feet.

"Ben," I advised, "if she keeps drinking, she'll die an excruciating death." I walked over to the window and surveyed the yard.

"You act like I don't know that. I sat for hours in Grace Hospital convulsing on Pool's blood. It's worth a shot."

I made out a man lying on his back next to the pool; it didn't look like he'd be getting up again. "Ben, we've got to go."

"Yeah, I can hear the sirens too." Though still out of range to the human ear, Ben exhibited yet another vampiric ability; he could hear distant sounds. I opened the study's window and deduced the cause of the sirens. Next to the dead gardener was a cellphone, still on a call. A stream of blood meandered from his disfigured face down his shoulder, to his arm, and into the pool via a hand submerged. His eyeballs had been plucked out and were bobbing about on the water. At least his fluid had not mingled with the rug.

Evidently, he'd been copulating with the wife in the cabana. The gunshots had aroused them and he'd called 911. Later, Evermore recounted that Morrigan had done him in.

"Let's go! She's had enough," I pressed him. The sirens were closing fast.

He pulled his arm away from her lips and looked her in the eye, promising, "I'll come back for you." His arm stopped bleeding.

"Ben! Move! I'll frame it on the wife then I'll meet you where we jumped the wall. Now, go!"

Ben exited. Using my hanky, I planted the gun in the widow's firing hand. Just before I left the study, Magnolia's dermis had revived from a deathly pale white to a rich, pearly cream. Never had I seen skin like hers before, nor such beauty, only surpassed by the maidens of *Hy Breasal*. Her skin was similar in color to a magnolia petal, hence why she was called such.

The sirens had ceased. Cruiser lights strobed upon the trees. The front gate was shut, thanks to Antonio. Before we had shown, he had hacked into the estate's security system, locked the gate, turned off the cameras, and deactivated the alarms.

I reflected for a moment. The situation had indeed gotten out of control. Maybe I should have turned the paralysis on Ben sooner? If I had done so, then I could have finished off Harold with little effort as well as the rest of the family. Why did I allow Mosby the opportunity to get on his soapbox? Nevertheless, it was now all water under the bridge.

I recalled the pact with Andromalius. He required certain souls, including Magnolia's. Once they were all dead, then, and only then, could the Dragonist Order get Collette's spirit. All considered, the agreement suited us. Andromalius and his imps were aiding us in our destruction of Brannbjørn, using Bilsharn as bait. Once dead and the amulet retrieved, the Fomorian clan would be leaderless and pose no more of a threat.

At the sound of the police scaling the walls, I jolted out of self-reflection. Their guns and flashlights clattered against the barrier's blocks. Instantly, all the mansion's lights went out, both inside and out. Its generator kicked in, lights flickered, then the backup unit cycled down. *Good man, Antonio,* I said to myself.

Why had I not left Harold's study yet? I kept hesitating to finish the job. Ruxandra and I knew Mosby wasn't up to killing; we figured the reparations bit would be as far as he would go. I would never have guessed that Mosby would have accidentally done it for me. His desire for amends, Pool's blood inside him, and his short fuse turned out to be a potent mix, but not to the extent that he could kill. After all, he was just a fireman, and from a good, God-fearing, Episcopalian family. It was not in his pedigree. In the end, his clumsiness, his lack of familiarity with the strength of his hands, and his fingernails being more claws than nails, had got the better of him.

I saw flashlight beams strike the trellis.

It was now or never. I must kill her. I reached for her hair; she came to. Those dazzling hazel eyes peered up at me with gratitude. Magnolia said nothing, just smiled. I smiled back and left.

Brannbjørn's Return & Dark Blood

Morrigan's Report, October 10th of 2025
& Bölcsem Kertész Naplója, 2025. október 10

"Caw, caw, Master Scribe Kertész," sounded Morrigan, "I spotted Brannbjørn alone. He go in Goth store...*braw*...Rest in Pieces, *caw*... near Hollywood Cemetery."

"Interesting," said I, fiddling my fingers upon the armrest of Collette's wingback chair. "Perhaps his blacksmiths have fashioned a replica of Collette's ankh." I pulled out the portal ankh key from my leather pouch. "If he does have such a device, I doubt his has the petals, but where would be he get the necessary metals to pull it off? Hmm."

"*Craw, caw*...am I not pleasing Master Scribe?"

I knew he was desiring his favorite food, unsalted Virginia peanuts, which are larger and more flavorful than the runner kind. I kept him hungry. In this way, he was more congenial in imparting all he knew. However, I sensed I was reaching the end of his patience.

"Yes, yes, Morrigan, I am pleased. What else have you for me?"

"Indeed, Master Scribe *rattle-rattle–click, click*."

"Yes, understood. You are hungry–have patience, my friend. What else have you to report?"

"Brannbjørn looted Steve Bilsharn's place, *rattle...click*. He drive rental, *caw... craw...rattle*, looking for Steve: Studio Two Three, Fallout, blah...*craw*, Taboo, no find there Bilsharn, *craw*."

"Rental? Make, model, color?"

"R8 e-tron, dark gray, nice–*craw*."

"Figures. Keep an eye on him. What of Harold's estate?"

"Ah, *caw*, man I pecked landscaper. Wallet had biz card, said so, *craw*.

Police there, *rattle…click, click,* overheard saying old lady did it. No press, *hiss…click… caw,* police closing case fast. But, *braw…click,* Detective Breland show, *hiss.* Some police mock him. He take many photo, *hiss…coo,* use tweezer."

"What did he pick up?"

"Hair, *craw–hiss,* dried blood."

"There was lots of blood, Morrigan. Any particular shade of red?"

"*Craw, caw,* burgundy."

"Hmm, very good, Morrigan. You may go."

"*Rattle…rattle…click…click.*"

"Forgive me. Just a minute." I went into the kitchen to fetch the peanuts. I looked at my watch; Antonio was calling. "Greetings, Antonio, give me a moment."

"No problem," he said. I put a bowl of peanuts on the sill and closed the window behind Morrigan.

"Yes, I'm back. *Como está?*"

"*Muito bem.* Hacking the estate's system was fun. Jones had a system out of the UK; man radar, biometric gate access, even UGSs. The A/V console hadn't been patched so I walked right in."

"UGS?"

"Oh…unattended ground sensors."

A buzz interrupted us. "Antonio, it's Ruxandra…I'm merging her with our call."

"*Szia.* Good evening, Bölscem."

"*Szia,* my lady. Antonio is on too."

"*Olá, Antonio!* Can you get me some Manga Rosa?"

"*Sim!* You in a need of a heady high?"

"*Sim!* It's been a tough day here in San Jose. The FDA is giving Sânge Nou Inc. crap over the specs on our new version of synthetic blood."

"The coagulation part?" I asked.

"Yes, our pig trials went well, but we've had some hiccups in our human pilot. Bölscem, I still have you on the payroll, do you not want to return to us?"

"I'll consider it after this Mosby business. Edana has slated me for chronicle tasks; one has to go through her, I'm afraid."

"Yes, yes. Now, where's Mosby? How's he taking Harold's death?"

"Let me see," I said, looking at my Scarab app's GPS tracker. "Ah, he's at the tunnel's eastern portal. No doubt he's reminiscing."

"Is Evermore following him?" she asked.

"Oh yes."

"Do you think he believes us?"

"Yes, I think so. His aura gives off that impression. I explained to him it was not his fault. He's still learning his own strength. He is certainly stronger and quicker than any of us."

"Hmm, yes, and that is why I'm concerned, Bölscem. Use the app's cybernetic features if you have to."

"Will do."

Antonio piped in, "I updated the app the other night."

"Really! Oh do tell," said an excited Ruxandra.

"Bölscem, open the Scarab and touch the cyborg icon," instructed Antonio. The icon looked like a retro robot head with a third eye. "Now, next to the paralysis icon, there's a new one: a dot capped zig-zag line entering a brain."

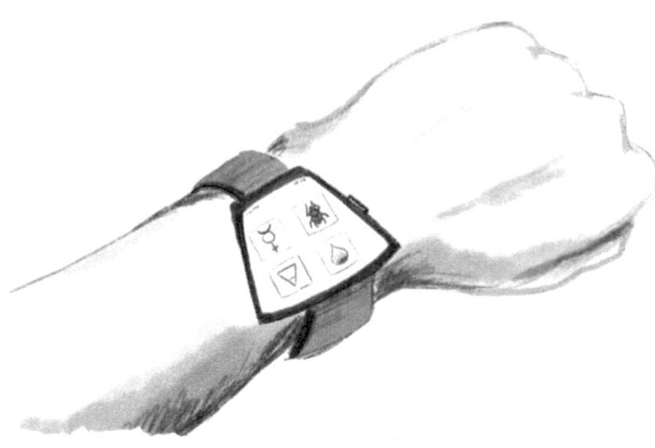

"Yes, I am there; it's prompting me for an 'endoword.' What's an 'endoword?'"

"An 'endoword' is a thought–a word, a suggestion the user wants to insert into a subject's frontal lobe."

"Fascinating," exclaimed Ruxandra. "Do put in an–"

"It can be a phrase," interjected Antonio. "There's a one-hundred-fifty character limit."

"I typed *'park might cave in,'* since he is currently taking an evening stroll at Chimborazo Park. It is near the tunnel's eastern portal."

"*Excelent.* Do tell us if he brings it up," asked Ruxandra.

"I will."

"I got your message. All told, who died at the estate?" asked Ruxandra.

"Everyone. The two daughters, Harold, the mother, and a landscaper," I stated.

"*Grozav!* Andromalius will be pleased."

"My lady, are you not wary of Ben's performance?"

"No, not at all. True, I did not expect he would lay a hand on Harold, let alone accidentally breach his jugular vein, but this does not worry me. Brilliant thinking to frame it all on the wife."

"Thank you."

"And the grandmother?"

"Yes, Nellie. Mávros took care of her for us."

"Oh, that must have been messy."

"According to Evermore's report, it was. The eccentric old bird died a half hour before the others. She and her aide were taking a moonlit walk when they got mauled by Mávros."

"Ah, he's so vicious! I am not surprised."

"Ruxandra, we have a more pressing matter."

"Go on."

"That detective was there; he got a sample of Ben's blood."

"Detective...umm, what was her name?"

"Not Covach, her sidekick."

"Covach's partner...Breland, is it not?"

"That's right, Breland."

"Ah, Breland. I remember now...from the Lockgreen case; they found *Scarletvin*."

"Keep tabs on Breland's phones and computer. What could he discover?"

"Nothing. There's no DNA on record to match with Mosby, nor his fingerprints," answered Antonio.

"No, I disagree. He will flip when he's told his telomeres look brand new," I stated.

"Telomeres?" inquired Antonio.

"Antonio, Bölscem, let's table that discussion. Breland will no doubt reach a dead end and drop it. Bölscem, did you fetch Harold's *Scarletvin*?"

"No, my lady. I did not have time."

"No matter. *Scarletvin* is so passé, especially compared to Sânge Nou's new synthetic adreno-oxidation method. By the way, we are making quite a profit out of our Southeast Asian lab from it. Ah, the dark web is such a blessing."

"The magic of offset cluster routing!" said Antonio.

"Yes indeed. Down with the Tor browser and Tails OS, up with your Shallot platform!" replied I.

"Now, before you two digress further into geek speak, what others are on Andromalius' list?" asked Ruxandra.

"Harold's brother and the descendant of the Chief C&O Engineer–the one who signed off on widening the tunnel," I answered.

"What was the engineer's name?"

"C. W. Johns. I have sent both of you a photo. I found it in the C&O's archives."

"Have we located this descendant?"

"I have," said Antonio. "He lives in a posh penthouse at The Prestwould. Bölscem, I'll text you

the address."

"My lady, I hate to sound like a broken record, but we have another pressing concern," said I.

"And that is?"

"Brannbjørn is here. Morrigan has spied him around town. As expected, he ransacked Bilsharn's place. He likely found our planted clue to where Bilsharn is caged."

"Ah. Then in that case, we must take care of him first. I'll let Kojo know. He's dying to dismember Brannbjørn. Perhaps I will toss in Nastya, for good measure. Bjorn's got a soft spot for her."

Eastern Portal

Bölcsem Kertész Naplója, 2025. Október 11

Since the ordeal at the Jones' estate, Mosby and I laid low at Collette's flat. The shock of killing Harold, albeit accidentally, had taken its toll on him, as did the family shooting each other. We had a chat that night that took a scientific turn, when he asked what happened to the bullets we had both taken. I explained to him our bodies broke down the slugs and their pieces would pass naturally through our digestive tracts. The conversation petered off when I tried to explain his biological makeup had, in some respects, more in common with a starfish than a human in that a starfish can regenerate damaged parts.

Later that evening, he said he needed a walk to clear his head. He was heading again to Chimborazo Park. He enjoyed the panoramic view of the river and trains going by. I asked him how it had gone, the other day when he had walked there. Amazingly, he confessed he had an overwhelming feeling that the park was going to cave in. His theory was, he thought because the park is near the abandoned tunnel, it might do so. This account confirmed that the scarab implant could indeed insert thoughts into a recipient's mind.

Before he went out, I handed him a new wallet containing a fake National ID, debit and credit cards, as well as some cash. His ID read "Edgar Willis."

My new ID came too. I was "Peter Novris." All this came courtesy of a package from Nastya' front company in Sochi, Russia.

Surprisingly, he did not ask me much about the packet. His mind was elsewhere. He took the wallet, looked at the new identity, said his thanks, and left.

Via the Scarab app, I tracked him. First, he went to Chimborazo Park; later he moseyed on down to East Franklin Street just below Libby Hill Park. From there, near a row of contemporary townhomes, he entered the woods below Chimborazo Park. Down a steep hill he hiked, heading toward the abandoned entrance of the tunnel's eastern portal. No historic state marker–or any signage, for that matter–informed a

stranger its entry was an infamous tunnel. Thorns and poison ivy, bogs and rotting wood dominated the terrain surrounding it. The arched stone opening, strewn with hanging ivy, more resembled a humongous troll's mouth than a railroad tunnel. It cast an ominous mood over a rivulet issuing from its bowels. The remnants of a rusty chainlink barrier were the only clues warning trespassers the portal was too dangerous to explore.

But knowing Mosby, he would be undeterred in snooping about. He was there for quite a while, which lined up with the story he narrated later that night.

At around three in the morning, while I was playing my recorder, the front door creaked open. Drips of water struck the foyer's tile floor as Ben said, "Hello, Bölscem. I went to the tunnel's eastern side."

"Hello Ben," I replied, putting down my instrument.

"But of course you know that because of him," he pointed at Evermore, perched on top of the wingback chair where I was sitting.

"I don't need Evermore to tell me that. You reek of it. Strip down and shower please."

He resolutely stomped off to do so like a child caught playing in a place he should not. In the meantime, I pondered the online news about the survivor from the estate shooting, Magnolia. The story reported that Magnolia had been found semi-conscious in her wheelchair, sitting in a pool of her own blood. She had been shot in the stomach but was in stable condition at St. Mary's Hospital. The rest of the family was dead. Police said the family had caught Linda, her mother, in an affair with a groundskeeper, from which things turned violent. Linda had shot everyone then taken her own life. Her grandmother, Nellie, it was believed was killed in an unrelated attack; an animal with rabies, a Rottweiler, perhaps.

I was astounded Magnolia was still alive. Unlike the movies and Stoker's description of Lucy Westenra's metamorphosis, humans usually die within *a day* of ingesting vampiric blood. Perhaps popular culture confuses vampires with sanguinarians. The vampiric gene expression process unleashes a radical shake up of a human's genetic composition. Thus, most people do not survive the transformation. Usually death occurs by heart attack or brain hemorrhage. Rarer still, have humans survived strigoi consumption, like Ben's blood, which is far more potent than the typical vampiric strain. In short, Magnolia should have incurred massive internal bleeding and died by now. Like Mosby's drinking of William Pool's blood, she'd had a one-in-a-thousand shot of enduring the transformation. She had beaten the odds.

What was I to do now? I didn't have the heart to track her down and kill her. Something in me snapped that night. I could not finish her off. Why, I don't know.

A plethora of questions and anxious thoughts entered my mind, most notably: Mávros would eventually rip her to shreds. Upon discharge, she might look for us. If she eluded Mávros and the rest of the familiars, then found us, how would I explain this to the Dragonists? At least Andromalius would be less of a problem than

Ruxandra. He might be appeased. He could be persuaded that since Magnolia was no longer human, she was outside of his jurisdiction. But Ruxandra is inquisitive and dogmatic in her executions. She would find out somehow, if she hadn't read the news already, and insist she be tracked down and eliminated. Her termination would be a foregone conclusion, considering the Dragonist Order has plans to kill Mosby.

Mosby has been deemed a threat, for once he becomes adept at the full scope of his powers, it will take at least six vampires to overpower him. Moreover, Ben shows no signs of wanting to join our ranks. As for Magnolia, even if she wanted to join our Order, Ruxandra would vote against it at Council. She would not tolerate another strigoi as powerful as she, especially one that is a woman of such beauty. Though Ruxandra was from the House of Drăculești, the strigoi strain she inherited was not as potent, given its recessive nature. Even her father, Mihnea cel Rău, was diminished in prowess from his father, Vlad the Impaler, known to the world as Count Dracula. Though her brother, Mircea III Dracul, now in exile, fared better than she in vigor.

Mosby returned from his shower in a bathrobe. Evermore rested on a perch stand Collette had made for him in the corner of the living room.

"I'm fit to be tied," said Mosby, plopping down on the couch.

"What happened?" I asked.

"I explored the eastern portal. What a mess that is. It's all covered with weeds and tree brush. Whew! And the stench of stale water! Have you been down there?"

"No, I haven't been there in ages."

"Well, you should see it. It's a disgrace."

"How so?"

"How so!? The damned city and the RailOne have left the place in ruins. They should clear the trees and weeds and put a memorial there! Here's a sketch of it." He handed me a pencil drawing of an arched entrance enveloped by undergrowth and hanging vines on a crumbled dinner napkin.

I examined it and said, "I told you they do not care. Corporations would rather cover up their mistakes than leave a remembrance

for future generations."

"Well, this next part's gonna sound crazy," Ben hesitated, "but...but I just had to go in there."

"Okay, what's so crazy about that?"

"*Kraw!* The place is flooded," chimed in Evermore.

"Yep, there's water dripping from the ceiling and the sides of the arched walls. Perhaps Richard's right, maybe it could cave in. I mean the brick's fallin' apart. It's all slimy–a breeding ground for mold and fungus."

"How much standing water?" I asked.

"Enough to swim in."

"Ben got wet," said Evermore, and gave a throaty chuckle, only recognizable as such to me.

"Yeah, I got in."

"No wonder you stank," I responded.

"Yeah, yeah...if you were in my shoes and had survived a cave in, lost your mates, you'd go in and check it out too."

"Well, you're probably right," I conceded. "Go on."

"So I went as far as I could go, wading through the mucky water. The farther I went, the deeper it got. So I started swimming."

"How far back did you go?"

"I don't know...about three hundred, maybe four hundred feet. I heard a lotta' clamoring back at the entrance. When I looked back, it was a buncha' guys who had blown up some rafts. In the blackness I was amazed at how well I could see them."

"Excuse me, did you say 'guys with rafts?'"

"Yep. Little blowup rafts. I wish I'd had something like that in my day. They were sucking down 'giggle water'...whooping and hollering."

"Did they see you?"

"Oh, they saw me all right."

"Ben, what did I tell you? We must keep a low profile."

"Don't worry, everything's Jake, Friar. They barely saw me."

"Who's Jake...never mind. So...they had flashlights, didn't they? Ben, I don't buy your explanation."

"Ok, ok, they had torch sticks, but I swear, they didn't get a good look at me."

"Did you do anything?"

"*Kraw, hiss*...Ben scared boys," said Evermore.

"Ah, yeah, I spooked 'em good," he grinned. "I dropped down into the water. Realized I could swim for a good minute or two without ever coming up for air. I took a deep breath and swam underwater to within twenty feet of them. When I poked the surface, this caused a faint echo. I heard one of 'em say, 'Whoa, that's freaky.'

"Then I burst out of the water with raised arms, extended my claws and showed them my fangs. Dirt and muck hanging all over me...I was some swamp monster," he chuckled, losing his composure to narrate for an instance. "Bölcsem, you shoulda' seen it. It was swell. I scared the pants off those boys!"

"Ah perfect! So they did get a good look at you?"

"Nah, go chase yourself, Bölscem! It was too dark to get a good eye on me. Besides they dropped their torch sticks."

"Flashlights."

"They were so scared they capsized their rafts...took off screaming and hollerin' for their mamas," he laughed. "Those eggs were half swimming, half crawling out of the tunnel! Except for one; he stayed behind. He was sloshed more than the others. He was an angry drunk–big guy, too. He brandished a jagged whiskey bottle he'd bashed against the brick arch.

"Then he said, 'I wanna piece 'a you.' I warned him he didn't want to go there. He replied, 'Oh I do.' Next, he rushed me, sloshing through the knee-deep water. He missed me on the first swipe, but caught me on the chin on the second. The piece stuck there. I pulled the glass out, my blood spurted, mixing with the brown water."

"What happened next?" I asked.

"I snapped. I got a hold of his hair and pulled him in and took a deep bite out of his neck. He flailed for a minute or two while I got a swig. After that he went limp. I gorged on whiskey boy for a bit."

"Did you kill him?"

"Nah. I dragged him out of the tunnel and left him by the side of the creek."

"Wonderful. So that guy definitely got a good look at you."

"Relax. I didn't kill anybody, and no one's gonna believe a bunch-a drunks. They left a flask of panther piss behind. Want some?"

"Panther piss?"

"Whiskey!"

"No thanks, I'm a gin guy."

"Oh, okay, be a bluenose." He pulled the flask out of the robe's pocket and took a hit. "As I was leaving, I heard the distant horn blows of a train down by the river. The squeaking of coal cars...it took me back."

Tears welled up in his eyes; he took another swig of whiskey. The sun breached the horizon.

Blood Sample

Breland/Covach Phonecon, October 11, 2025 14:21-14:25

Source: Breland's desk phone-hacked by Antonio Jararaca

Breland: Hello, Detective Breland here.

Covach: Richie, you're gonna owe me a drink.

Breland: So, you checked out the clips?

Covach: Yeah, I checked 'em. The body cam one reminds me of that grainy footage from the Lockgreen case. This guy moves just as fast plus he jumped St. John's gate with no problem. That's not human.

Breland: Agreed. The drone one?

Covach: Maybe it's the same guy on the roof, but it's hard to tell with the fog and drizzle.

Breland: It's the same guy.

Covach: If you say so.

Breland: In the meantime, things have gotten stranger.

Covach: How so?

Breland: Oh...let's just say I've stumbled upon some rather bizarre blood samples, one of 'em is a *match* to the sample from the Lockgreen case.

Covach: You mean the sample that was thrown out as evidence?

Breland: Exactly.

Covach: Hmm, go on.

Breland: Did you hear about the familial shooting spree in our ritzy part of town?

Covach: Yeah, I read the headline but didn't get too much into the weeds... still here in Virginia Beach. Been wrapping up a Russian mafia case–the usual human trafficking. Give me the gist of it.

Breland: Well, the way the chief is tellin' the press, it goes like this: the husband caught his wife with the gardener, who also had two friends at the same time robbin' the place.

Covach: Bah! What a theory! Guess Harrison's thinking a two-for-one? What a world!

Breland: Here's the scenario: Linda shot her husband, Harold Jones; the daughter, Victoria, tried to stop her and a scuffle ensued between Linda and Victoria which ended in them both dead. Linda gouged her daughter's eye out with a sharp implement, maybe her nails, but somehow Victoria managed to get the gun and kill her. The other daughter, Magnolia, survived a gut shot–she's in critical condition at Saint Mary's. Harrison, the lead detective, questioned her, but got little out of her, except that her old man shot her. She's been in and out of consciousness, having migraines and seizures. Oh, and the medical aide to Magnolia, er Delores. She's dead as well. Apparently shot by Linda during the tussle, or so says Harrison.

Covach: Wow, that's a jacked up mess!

Breland: Oh, it's gets better! A partially *melted* latch, and, you're gonna love this, the gardener's eyes were ripped out too. But the real gem is I found a vial in a hidden compartment within Harold's desk. The lab ID'ed its content–*Scarletvin*.

Covach: Let me guess...just like the batch we found at Lockgreen.

Breland: Bingo! But there's more...

Covach: Oh, do tell.

Breland: Well, back to those blood samples I mentioned earlier. Two of 'em were unusually dark in color. So the lab did an extraction, and whataya know... one of the samples had a match with our DNA data bank!

Covach: So this family feud is tied to the Lockgreen case?

Breland: Yep!

Covach: Amazing...the DA removed that evidence from the Lockgreen file, but it's retained in the DNA bank. You can't make this stuff up! Go on...

Breland: The darker sample has DNA that's similar but even more off the charts.

Covach: Off the charts? Richie, get to the point, I gotta run.

Breland: Lenora, it's not human. It's more like *superhuman*. They did a PCR on both samples...in other words, the DNA barcodes did not match with the reference library of codes for any known species.

Covach: Interesting...

Breland: I took it to a geneticist at VCU. The telomeres on both looked like a newborn's and they had genetic characteristics of a bat, a starfish, and a human. However, the burgundy colored sample–the darker of the two–had coding like you'd see in a chameleon.

Covach: Telomeres? What is that?

Breland: That's the caps on the ends of our DNA strands.

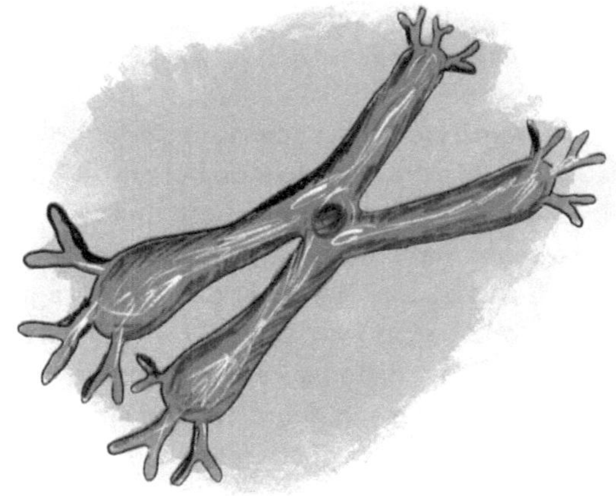

Covach: Ok, I've got about a minute left–let's wrap this up.

Breland: When humans are young, telomeres are pretty thick and protect our DNA. As we get older they deteriorate, we age. In these blood samples, the ends are like brand new, plus they've got *tentacles*, we think they protect the telomeres–or are part of its regeneration. Bottom line, the DNA is like a starfish's, the organism can regenerate itself, heal itself.

Covach: Fascinating. Do you think there's a connection between this guy in the video and your blood sample?

Breland: Oh definitely, I think this is the guy!

Covach: Look Richie, I'll patch things up on my end then I'll be in Richmond in a couple of days.

Breland: How's that...how can the Bureau have jurisdiction?

Covach: Richie, *Scarletvin*...likely dealt across state lines...it's tied to human trafficking. My superior will initiate the paperwork to open an investigation. Harrison will be sidelined.

Breland: Ah, that'll work...it'll be just like old times, Lenora.

Covach: Bye Richie.

Everything's Changed

Magnolia's Diary, October 11th of 2025

Dear Diary,

What a rough day! At least this tragedy proves Cornelius is a true friend. He fetched you and left me with a "Get Well" card and flowers. He's so sweet!

Other flowers adorn the room and cards too. I guess I should open those. Aunt June's bouquet has three magnolia stems. She's nice.

This entry is gonna be short...my mind's in pieces. My head hurts like hell—my chest too, is in pain, but it's strange, it feels muscular...like I've been bent out of shape leaning forward in my wheelchair, pruning roses in the garden.

Yesterday the Father from our parish came by to give his condolences. Despite the way he has looked at me in the past, this time he didn't do that, and he was really sincere. Father said he was taking care of the funeral arrangements with my uncle. Uncle happened to be in the room too; he started spouting off about his brother's will. All I remember is something about an executor meeting after my discharge.

Everything's changed. Everyone close to me is dead, even grandma Nellie. A detective Harrison came by and told me she died the same night from a dog attack. He said it was a cruel coincidence. I don't buy it! Something sinister is going on, Diary, I just know it.

I should've died too. I can't believe my own father shot me! What an asshole! I can't believe he hated me that much!!! I know we didn't see eye-to-eye, but I never thought he had the heart (or lack of it) to wanna kill me!

So here I am sitting in St. Mary's with an IV hooked up to me and a big bandage on my tummy. Earlier today the doctor came to see me and said it's amazing I'm alive. He said I lost a lot of blood, but he did extract the bullet. He explained he was prepared to do a major stitch up of my intestines, but that it

turned out to be only a minor operation since they were in amazingly good shape. Hmm, that's odd. Speaking of 'odd,' how is it that the wheelchair chick survives, but the rest of my able-bodied family is dead? I guess I'm a pretty lucky gal. Anyway, the doc has kept the IV in as a precaution, I guess.

Since this craziness, I've been in and out of consciousness so I don't remember much. But I do know this: I've been having seizures, vomiting, severe headaches, and, sometimes, I even scream out in pain.

I wanna write more...but my body is shaking...like I'm having my very own earthquake. *Ahh!* Just felt some searing pain up my legs. Maybe I'm gonna die after all?

Au revoir :(

Magnolia's Diary, October 12th of 2025

Dear Diary,

I'm still here...it's noon time. My mind's starting to clear. More of that terrible night is coming back to me. What the F!!! I can't believe I drank that guy's blood! Disgusting! At least he was handsome.

Now I realize, it's the blood that saved me—not the doctors. I lost too much blood to have lived, plus, intestines don't just heal like that. Well, let's just say you have a conscience Diary—don't judge me. You would have drunk his blood too. I mean, the guy recovered from a gunshot wound right before me! He was different—sharp teeth, long fingernails—like, dare I write this...? Just like a movie version of Dracula.

Whoa! The thought hit me like a freight train—he's a vampire! Which means *I'm a vampire too!?* Maybe it's true? Shortly after I awoke, the nurse drew the curtains and I winced at the sunlight. I snapped at her to close the blinds.

I've had bizarre dreams of this guy. I saw him walking in Church Hill past a glass sign saying, "But as for me, give me LIBERTY or give me DEATH." I felt like he was in my head, asking me where I was. I said,"St. Mary's," then he vanished.

Well, I can't write any more, dear Diary, I feel like I'm gonna have another seizure. The cool thing is, I can move my feet! And my toes! I haven't moved them in years! *What's happening to me!?*

Au revoir!

Brannbjørn Bleeds

Bölcsem Kertész Naplója, 2025. Október 12

At sunset, I heard firm knocks upon Collette's door so I opened it to find a steaming Brannbjørn. "Where is he!?" Brannbjørn demanded.

"Well, hello to you too," I replied.

"Where'd he go?"

"Where'd who go?" I played dumb.

"You know, that ass Bilsharn."

"Ahh, Mr. Bilsharn."

"Why aren't you being more cooperative?...I cared for Collette too. She and I were patching things up, until Steve showed."

"I understand," I said.

"Bölscem, you don't understand. You've never had a real relationship with a woman. You're nothing but a scribbler and a doodler."

"*Hiss, kraw*...be respectful," said Evermore, resting on my left shoulder.

"Shut it, bird brain! Tell me where he is and I won't bury you into that wall," threatened Brannbjørn, grabbing my garment.

"Bölscem, is there a problem here?" said Mosby over my shoulder.

"And who are you?" asked Brannbjørn, still holding me.

"I'm your worst nightmare, if you don't let that man go," said Ben. Brannbjørn refused, gesturing a taunting smile at Ben. "Stay out of this, cretin."

Mosby swiftly stepped around me and punched Brannbjørn in his right eye. The force knocked him backwards onto the walkway. He recovered and lunged at Ben, who stood in the doorway. They both fell back onto the hallway's runner rug with Brannbjørn on top, jabbing Ben in the kidneys and face. Ben countered by kneeing him in his groin and digging his claws into Brannbjørn's forehead, causing blood to flow upon the floor. (Yet another rug stained! This time a Turkish one.) Brannbjørn fell back as Ben righted himself via the wall, dazed from the Fomorian's

blows. Still clutching his groin, Brannbjørn laid eyes on the alluring Russian Upir, Nastya. She was nonchalantly descending the staircase, twirling her blond hair and smiling at him through slim, ruby lips.

Nastya said, “Now, now boys! No need to wreck the place. Bjørn, your family jewels still in place?”

“Oh, Nastya...very funny. Nice to see you,” groaned Brannbjørn, standing up. He looked back at Ben, the cuts on his brow were almost healed. He said, “I was just getting acquainted with–”

“Mosby. Benjamin...Mosby,” Ben said in anguish. His eyes expanded at the sight of the Fomorian’s accelerated healing.

“Nice claws you got there,” said the Fomorian. He grabbed a tissue and wiped the blood from his face. “Where are you from?”

“The past.”

“Well, go back there. Also, consider finding a new friend. This guy’s just using you,” he growled, thumbing at me.

Brannbjørn turned to Nastya. “See you tonight, Nastya. Only you, nobody but us–no familiars, and not him,” said Brannbjørn, eyeing me.

“Promise. Only me. I text you address; see you at seven,” Nastya smiled.

“Drinks afterwards?”

“Of course,” she replied.

Brannbjørn exited, brushing roughly past my shoulder.

Nastya half waved then shut the door.

Johns Met Morrigan

RVA Joie de Vivre! Blogsite

A Bizarre Day in RVA

Posted by Charles Johns on October 13, 2025 | 3 Comments

Today, fellow readers, I want to tell you about what an interesting day I had in RVA! It started out pleasant enough, it's been an Indian summer so far. From my condo, the trees in Monroe Park still have their leaves. Usually I jog before sunset, but since it was so warm this morning I broke my routine. However, looking back, I won't do that again on account of a bit of bizarreness. Let me tell you about it…

I awoke to the bustle of the city. Took a brief run (though, like I said, I do this just before nightfall) down to the Canal Walk then over to Shockoe Bottom. Today I went by the Edgar Allen Poe Museum where, fittingly, I saw a raven, or maybe it was a crow, perched on the museum's sign. It cawed at me three times, so I cawed back…then the creature swooped over me and pecked me on my head! "What the hell!?" I shouted. The bastard had plucked a few hairs off me! I took a swipe at it, and missed. It flew off. I swear I thought it said in broken speak, "I'll be watching you, *caw…hiss*," it cried as it flew away. Maybe the Poe Museum's cursed?

After that ordeal, I needed a good pick-me-up. I took a pit stop at Ironclad Coffee Roasters, where they make an excellent Pumpkin Spiced

Chai Latte. Delish! Afterwards, I jogged home to shower.

Since the weather was so warm, I decided to sketch in Monroe Park. The beautiful trees, three-tiered fountain, and the Checkers House were all subjects on my canvas. (The Checkers House is a two story hexagonal brick building.) Painting went well. I was only interrupted once by a homeless person begging for money. About halfway through, my stomach started rumbling. I hurried on over to Mojo's Philadeli and grabbed myself a Philly cheesesteak.

Later, my wife and I went out to Edo's Squid, an Italian restaurant near Virginia Commonwealth University. From the outside, it looks like a dive, but trust me… just go up the narrow staircase to the second floor. You won't regret it…fresh pasta dishes…and they'll help you pair it with the perfect red or white.

Joie de Vivre!

P.S. On our way home from Edo's I saw that raven/crow again. Creepy!
But hey, it's October and this is Poe town—*c'est la vie!*

Thanks for reading my post! Leave me a comment below…

A Bizarre Day in RVA

Comments

PoeBoy October 14, 2025 at 9:06 am
Homeless 'bugged' u? Did it occur 2 u they might be HUNGRY! Maybe that raven's trying 2 tell u something

GucciGal October 14, 2025 at 10:12 am
Thanks for your blog tips…now I've gotta try Ironclad…Pumpkin Latte sounds yum :)

Respect2daDJ October 14, 2025 at 1:12 pm
Next time offer the homeless guy a latte, then it'll be a perfect day…

Talons in the Chest

Nastya Upir, 12 октября 2025 г.

Nastya's Journal (translated)

On the warehouse's second floor my wait for Brannbjørn was short lived. His text read: I'm here. Kojo and Bölscem were in place.

I looked up; Steve Bilsharn hovered in a stupor. Below and encircling him rendered upon the floorboards was a pentacle with the Egregore of Andromalius. Mice here and there scurried from wooden pallets to cracks in the brick wall; half moon's light invaded the littered stockroom. Fighting equipment strewn everywhere: brass knuckles, boxing gloves, wrist tape...fight club at one time? This place...about to see more fighting.

Texted Brannbjørn: On second floor.

Stairwell echoed. Metal door creaked, Brannbjørn emerged gazing at spinning Steve. "Oh perfect," the Fomorian grinned, "...I'll make cabbage of him."

"Wake him?" I asked.

"Oh please do! I want to watch this idiot flap like a caught fish, as I choke the life out of him. What do I owe you for this bit of magick?"

"Promise you leave lairs alone. Oh, and your copy of the ankh key. As for me, vodka shots tonite at Fallout, in your company of course."

"Vodka–no problem, copy of Collette's key–perhaps. You see, it's not so easy. What if one of yours meddles with one of mine?"

"No," I shook my head, "we not bother Fomorians. We caught Bilsharn for Andromalius; he gave us her head. Now, here's Bilsharn–we both happy, no?"

"Hmm, why don't I believe you...there's something fishy–"

"AARGH!" cried Brannbjørn. Kojo's talon-like fingers punctured his chest curling around his collar bones. Kojo was dangling from a rafter beam by his morphed, hooked feet. He hoisted Brannbjørn off the ground. Bölscem appeared from hiding

and leapt from a pallet stack to yank the amulet from the Fomorian's neck, but did not succeed. Brannbjørn reached around, grasping Bölscem by the scruff of his neck, then hurled him at a wall. Bölscem was out cold, fallen like a rag doll.

Brannbjørn seized Kojo's arms then ripped his claws out. The Fomorian fell to floor, free but gushing blood. The wounds began to seal as Brannbjørn scrambled to his feet. Kojo landed on bare feet having changed back.

Brannbjørn looked at me and remarked, "This is how you invite a guy out!?"

I hissed, showed my sharp teeth. Kojo and I encircled the Fomorian. Amulet still his, our magick no good against him. Had to kill with brute force.

Without reply, Kojo and I rushed him. Kojo aimed for the back of his neck with an akrafena, an Ashanti machete, and I swiped at his face. Brannbjørn stepped toward me, dodged sword but not my claws. Blood fanned out from his cheek, coloring floorboards.

"Nice nails," quipped Brannbjørn. He felt the cut marks.

"That's for Collette!" said I.

"Steve killed her–not me," he explained. Brannbjørn backed up to brick wall.

"Look truth in the eyes," I exclaimed, "you crossed that track, knowing a train was coming. Fools must pay!"

Kojo lunged and swung, I went for his eyes. Brannbjørn too fast; avoided blade, punched Kojo in the face. He fell to his back. Machete clanged upon flooring. I missed too, then he back slapped me. I fell, bruised badly, struggling to recover.

"Mosby, now's the time to help!" shouted Kojo. He staggered to his feet, gaining the machete.

From doorway, Ben said, "Yep. Anybody messes with Bölscem, messes with me!"

"Bring it on, fireman," said Brannbjørn, gesturing with a hand.

"How'd you know?" said Ben.

"That's easy. Read about your tampered grave in the paper. Figured these blood suckers must have conjured you up."

Ben charged Brannbjørn. He managed to pin the Fomorian to the wall–Ben faster, stronger!

Bjørn cried out, "Now!"

Thunk! My heart ruptured. "*Govno!*" I gasped, collapsing to the floor. I looked down to see a dart in my chest. I ripped it out screaming as I did so. Then I turned my head around–Ivor, the Fomorian's captain. "*Zasranec!*" I was stiffening up.

He reloaded a yew crossbow. Aimed it at Mosby who still grappled with Bjørn.

Kojo bolted through air. *Whoosh, clang!*...Ivor's head fell *kerplunk* upon the floor. Kojo too quick for Ivor. All stunned, all still.

I stumbled to my feet. "Hold him!" I commanded Mosby. Kojo handed me machete. Mosby wrestled to do so, but by and large kept the Fomorian up against the brick barrier.

Thud! Brannbjørn's head rolled to my feet. I collapsed then, clutching my chest. Fireman Ben set the warehouse ablaze.

Later at Collette's house, I was slipping fast.

I feel this is my last journal entry. I'm numb, dizzy, heart missing beats...not much time. Bölscem examined crossbow bolt. "Tears of Isis" was on its tip. Too much in bloodstream–spread fast, death coming. Bölscem will immortalize me in *Dragonist Chronicles*. I hold honor slaying Brannbjørn!!! Fomorians scattered!

To my fellow Dragonists, mourn me not! Have I not lived a glorious life as one of the "little ladies" in the time of Grigori Rasputin?

Now, I go in peace. We unite at Age's End, in Edom.

Long live Lilith! Our beloved Mother!

Dasvidaniya,
Nastya

Relieved Myself

Magnolia's Diary, October 12th of 2025

Dear Diary,

I woke again to the sound of beeps and clicks from the medical machinery hooked up to me. I glanced at the hospital clock; it was two in the afternoon. How long have I been asleep? More and more I've been sleeping during the day than at night.

For a few minutes I just sat in bed, gazing at the TV. There was an ad about a robot hand delivering Halloween costumes. *Hand* delivery? As if same-day drone delivery wasn't enough. What's next? People zipping around in flying cars?

The nurse came by to redress my bandage. She was amazed to find no sign of a wound—no scaring even! The physician's assistant was called in. She too was puzzled. She made note of it in my record and said she left it to the surgeon to analyze. Of course I knew the cause. That blood did it. My head though, yikes! It is still killing me! They added something to my drip which eases the pain. I'm fading back into sleep.

3:30pm

I felt a tingle down my left leg! Wow!...blood expanding into the vessels there. I grimaced under the pain. Then...I moved my leg! I bent my knee for the first time in ten years! Stunned, I laid there slowly bending and straightening my left leg. A few minutes later my right started to tingle too. Awesome!

It's got to be that blood that's bringing my legs to life. Whew! All this movement has made me tired. Time for a catnap.

4:30ish

Detectives Harrison and Breland paid me a visit. They gave their condolences. Breland asked if he could switch the overhead light on, and I said it was too bright. Next came the questions about the night of the shootings. I gave descriptions of the two caucasian male intruders in my father's study. Breland drew rough sketches and flipped his small pad frequently so I could affirm his drawings were accurate. The one guy, with an oval shaped head was handsome: manly features, prominent forehead, cheekbones, and clean-shaven. The other: shorter, middle-aged, scar on his cheek, etched forehead, goatee and a hairdo like a monk.

I told them my own father shot me. I started to cry, then I just stopped talking. I couldn't deal with retelling the whole thing. They said they'd be back tomorrow morning.

Around 6

I can bend my right leg! I was moving it back and forth when my door began to open. I quickly straightened it before anyone could notice. I thought it was an attendant delivering dinner. It was my Aunt June. She came by with some clean clothes. I wanted to tell her I could move my legs, but then thought better of it until I could test whether or not I could bear weight on 'em. She offered her condolences and said I had been in her thoughts and prayers ever since this tragic event. She's the devoted one in the fam. I thanked her. She asked how I was doing and I told her I was recovering well, but wasn't ready to get back in my wheelchair just yet. Once she left, I just stared at it in the corner of my room.

11 pm

I can't sleep...been binge watching this show about explorers who find Atlantis in Antarctica. Of course while binging I got stiff. So since I've been moving my legs, I figured I'd give walking a shot. I pushed myself over to the bedside and dangled my feet on the floor. I gently lowered my feet, I had those funky patient socks on—the ones with the grips on the bottom.

I could feel the cold linoleum floor through the grip socks. For the first time in years I could sense the soles of my feet! I put weight on them. I wiggled my toes! Gently I leaned forward, putting more of my body upon them. Then I pushed off with my hands up onto my feet. The whole sensation of balancing had become so foreign to me, I fell to the floor. I broke my landing by rolling to one side. I ended up yanking all the tubes out of me. Oh well, no matter, I didn't need them

anyway. I grabbed onto the bed frame, pulled myself up, and again tried to stand on my own. This time my balance was better. I took a step, then another.
Cool beans! I'm walking!!!

But suddenly, in the midst of my celebration, I got an urge to pee. I stumbled over to the bathroom, grabbed the handicap bar and landed with purpose on the toilet seat. Wowzer! For the first time, in years I enjoyed relieving myself without a bladder bag! Whoopee!!! (Pun intended—LOL.)

In my excitement I bit my lip. I brushed my tongue up against my teeth and felt how sharp they were, and my canines felt longer than usual. Alarmed, I double checked them with my fingers, and, sure enough—my teeth had become sharper, my "fangs" longer. *What's happening to me!?*

Au revoir!

Traitor Revealed

Draculian Chronicles, October 13, 2025

In the annals of this long and glorious chronicle, it is with sadness we hereby record the treachery of Izurg Séidire, Head of our Three Dána, and master blacksmith.

Bithlár Biáilde, his apprentice, and three Balaurian Guards apprehended Izurg attempting to flee *Dún Dreach-Fhola* with a scroll expounding the forging secrets of the Ouroboros Ring of Fire. This, our first line of defense–in Fomorian hands–would have brought about a devastating siege. By thwarting Izurg, surely the Fomorians should be set back in their advances for many a lunar cycle. Especially bearing in mind the demise of Brannbjørn at the hands of Nastya Upir, and of Ivor, at the hands of Kojo Aboagye, has rendered the Fomorians leaderless.

The Archons of the Dragonists, by a unanimous vote, ordered the impaling of Izurg. Whereby, after a long and excruciating death, he will be burned and his ashes cast into the Portal of Hades. Moreover, the Archons have promoted Bithlár to succeed him.

We mourn the loss of Nastya Upir, a fellow Archon, and Countess of the Russian Lair. She died glorious in her deed of slaying the great Brannbjørn, our rival over many centuries. Edana Siόg Fola, the Eponymous Archon, hereby declares the Ivy Moon be a time of remembrance of Nastya Upir. Like ivy which grows everywhere, she too, will always be with us, *everywhere* we go. We will unite with Nastya again at Age's End, in Edom.

Long live Lilith! Our beloved Dark Mother!

Revealing Questions

Interview room, City of Richmond Police Headquarters, October 14, 2025, 0930~1005

Source: RICH Police Intranet - hacked by Antonio Jararaca

Parties: Detective R. Breland, Homicide Division, City of Richmond Police; FBI Special Agent Lenora Covach, Criminal Investigations Division, Human Trafficking Task Force; Roger Jones, Harold Jone's brother

(Excerpt from recorded interview file)

Roger: Just call me Roger.

Covach: All right, Roger. Have you seen these vials before?

Roger: Nope, what's in them?

Covach: Are you sure? They were found in your brother's climate controlled safe–it's *Scarletvin*.

Roger: How come the FBI is involved? Linda shot my brother–case closed.

Covach: I think you know very well why I'm here. Your name made our file in the Lockgreen case, although your lawyer got in the way for us to question you–pulled the defamation card–he's clever.

Roger: Oh yeah that Lockgreen biz, what a sham that was.

Covach: Excuse me?

Roger: Are you kidding? The rumor is, you G-men think some kinda of vampire was involved. Some big-money-for-blood scheme. You had the audacity to suggest a non-profit organ donor was involved. That was a bit far-fetched.

Covach: Were you not on their board in 2023?

Roger: I was. What of it?

Covach: Need I remind you, you also sat on the board of Sânge Nou at that time, and hmm...it says here, you still do.

Roger: So?

Covach: So, this company was also inculcated in *Scarletvin*, child trafficking–kid's organs.

Roger: Theories, no charges were made...I didn't think the FBI was really into *X-Files* stuff.

Breland: May I?

Covach: Go ahead.

Breland: The same fingerprints we found at Lockgreen showed up in your brother's study, the scene of his murder. That scenario applies to a hair sample as well. Also, we found that the DNA extracts from the hair sample match the DNA blood sample off the rug. The DNA is...let us say, unusual. So yes, it's paranormal stuff.

Roger: What?! Your man Harrison told the papers Linda shot him.

Breland: Yes, that was our initial assumption, *before* these DNA results came back. By the way, we recommend you not share these developments with anyone.

Covach: Now, R-o-g-e-r, who was that intruder? Or maybe you know the other fella who crushed Harold's larynx?

Roger: I don't know either.

Covach: You stand to inherit the mansion and a lot of your brother's dough. Seems like a motive, wouldn't you agree?

Roger: Don't be ridiculous. I got enough of my own dough; that's not a viable motive. You've got my alibi: poker playing at the club. My buddies half-joked you'd call. So you've got nothing on me.

Breland: Yes, you're right. But, place yourself in our shoes. If you were us, wouldn't you want to ask a few questions?

Roger: May I be frank?

Covach: By all means.

Roger: You're barking up the wrong tree. My brother had a terrible habit. Those guys were probably dealers, blackmailing Harold to get more than the agreed amount. There was a scuffle. Meanwhile, his wife was getting to know the gardener. The two worlds, shall we say, collided.

Breland: That's very possible.

Roger: Good, I hope you arrive at a similar conclusion. And, I expect not to see my family's good name smeared all over the papers.

Breland: We will use discretion in our final report.

Roger: Great. Well, gentlemen, it's been a pleasure. In an hour I've got a golf date at Westhampton. Thank you for your efforts in finding out who's responsible

for my brother's death.

Breland: You're welcome. And thank you for taking time out of your schedule to see us on such short notice.

Roger: Oh, not a problem. From here on out, please contact my attorney if you have any further questions. I fly back to Oakland on Thursday.

Breland: Will do, thanks again.

Relentless Questioning

Magnolia's Diary, October 14th of 2025

Dear Diary,

I was up all night, couldn't sleep. The nurse has opened the blinds again...the light's hurting my skin. It's 10am. I got up and closed them, making sure no one in the hallway saw me do it. Oh yeah! Still walking!

I miss my Vickie so much! I can process it now: Mom shot dad, Vickie shot mom. A black bird—a raven—killed Victoria, not our mom. A raven? What the hell is going on!? Who were those guys who could take bullets then vanished? I can't write anymore, it's too painful to put on paper.

1:30pm

The FBI showed up. An agent named Covach. I guess Detective Harrison is off the case. But why the Bureau? Obviously there's something bigger going on here than my family's deaths. It probably has to do with the strange men. My father was probably involved in some interstate contraband, hence a special agent is now on the case.

Anyway, I'm glad Harrison has been kicked to the sidelines. He seemed a bit cold and too much by-the-book. But Detective Breland was back, so I gave him the whole spiel: who killed who, I even told him what the raven did. They didn't look at me like I was nuts, and, I gotta say, that was a surprise.

Diary, I certainly didn't tell them I drank the stranger's blood. They would have put me in the psych ward for that! Then the conversation got bizarre...

Breland flashed some photos at me of twenty-year-old guys. He started with a scrawny looking one saying, "Do you recognize this person?"

"Ah, no."

"How about this guy?"

He was medium build; I replied, "Same...never seen him before."

"And this one?" The last fella was huge; he had two puncture marks on the side of his neck.

"No...what happened to him?"

"You tell us," piped up Special Agent Covach.

"Excuse me?"

"Look, Magnolia, we know there's something you're not telling us. Two days after the death of your father and mother, these college guys were down in the eastern portal of the abandoned Church Hill Tunnel. They ran into a man who fit the sketch you gave us the other day. As you can see, the big guy was bitten on his neck. Blood on his clothes matched a blood sample found at your residence."

"Oh..."

"Did he bite you too?" asked Covach.

I started cracking, Diary. "Umm, well, he did have fangs..." then I came to my wits, "but *noo*, he didn't bite me. I don't know that guy. Is he alive?"

"Yes. Now, how did you recover so quickly? From what we've been told, you oughta be dead. Given the amount of blood you lost, the doctors are amazed at your recovery, and no internal injuries? Awful lucky, I'd say."

"May I ask what you're getting at? Maybe my injuries were exaggerated. As you can see, I'm fine."

"Miss Jones, the college guy allegedly bitten by this man," explained Breland, again displaying the sketch, "swore he hit the fanged man square in the chin with a jagged bottle. He witnessed the fanged man pull the glass shard out of his chin and within *seconds* the cut healed over. No scar even formed. So what we're getting at is, we think you drank the assailant's blood. How else could you explain such a recovery?"

"With all due respect, that's just plain crazy. Have you gentlemen lost it? I've heard about the FBI looking into paranormal cases, but I never believed you took it seriously. *No*, to answer your question, I didn't drink the guy's blood."

Covach said, "Great, then you won't object to us taking a blood sample. If you check out, there should be no genetic change."

"Oh no you're not! Nurse! Nurse! Stay away from me! That's breaking HIPAA!"

"Miss Jones, please calm down. It's standard procedure." The nurse poked her head around the door and Breland motioned things were under control. "We have to look at everyone's involvement, including yourself. In particular, we have to rule out any dealings you might have had with these men. I hate to say this, but you're a suspect in a murder investigation. So I'm afraid you don't have a choice in the matter," stated Covach.

Next, Breland displayed a grainy photo of the goateed, monk-haired man I'd described yesterday. It had a video timestamp on it of October 3rd. "Is this the other intruder you saw?"

"Yes, that's him."

"And he was shot as well?" asked Covach.

"That's right."

"Who shot him?"

"My...my father."

"Was this about your late father's *Scarletvin* addiction?"

"His.... *What*!?"

"You see, Magnolia, we think this goatee fella is a blood dealer. Mr. Jones may have been late on his payments. The stuff's expensive."

"I...I don't know anything about it; the term you used, my dad's habit—any of it. By the time I got there, they were done talking and had started shooting," I said. Then, I started crying and shaking. Needless to say, they rattled me, especially Covach. I guess that's why she's on the Bureau's payroll. Thank God they stopped questioning me.

They ended by stating they'd be back tomorrow and left. A few seconds later my nurse informed me Uncle Roger was in the waiting room. Of course, I refused to see the bastard. Later, I got an email from the executor: a meeting was scheduled for three o' clock this Friday to go over the wills. I doubt my folks left me very much.

7:30pm

Wowzer! I fell back asleep and had a dream about that handsome guy again. It was so real; he told me to meet him tonight at Patrick Henry Park. He smiled, showing sharp teeth and I smiled too, then I woke up. Super weird!

My order for a rare skirt steak was now cold, but I ate it anyway. It was good—for hospital food. I've never liked meat rare before. I easily bent my metal fork while stabbing the steak.

I can walk and pee! My teeth have elongated and sharpened...I was hoping it was a temporary thing...and I sleep all day. Diary, I wanna see this guy I keep dreaming about. He can tell me what's happening to me...what I've become.

Au revoir!

Sample of Poison

Breland/Covach Phonecon, October 14, 2025 16:21~16:30

Source: Breland's cell phone - hacked by Antonio Jararaca

Covach: Hey Richie what's up?

Breland: More strangeness today…I'm down here at the lab. On October 12th, there was a warehouse fire down on the South Side. Just outside the building they found—of all things—a crossbow bolt.

Covach: Well? So maybe somebody was playing Dungeons & Dragons.

Breland: Yeah you'd think, but forensics concluded that it's not recently made. More like the medieval period. The real deal…shaft's made of yew wood and on the dart's head was a *substance*. Man, you can't dream this stuff up!

Covach: Let me guess, it's a silver arrowhead laced with mercury.

Breland: Hah, nice guess…you a D&D head? You're not gonna believe this, but it was laced with *Verbena officinalis*.

Covach: Okay, Ritchie, English please.

Breland: It had vervain on it.

Covach: What the hell is that?

Breland: It's a herb plant native to Europe, used by Druids and witches as a heart tonic. Legend has it, after Christ was taken from the cross, his followers staunched his wounds with it. Some legends purport it'll kill a vampire.

Covach: Wow, this is getting weirder and weirder. I thought New York was bad, Richmond takes bizarre to a whole new level.

Breland: Welcome to P-o-e town...where ravens talk and people are buried behind brick walls.

Covach: I've learned one thing workin' for the Bureau...the weirder it gets, the more sense it makes. Check every camera nearby that fire...ATM cams, CCTVs, traffic cams–the works. I bet you lunch our goatee guy will show up on one of those.

Breland: Will do.

Covach: Let's meet at 1430 tomorrow at St. Mary's. I've got a few more questions for darling miss Magnolia. Plus, we will get that blood sample. Keep tracking her locale...any calls, texts, posts she makes, I want to know about it.

Breland: Gotcha. See you then.

Time to Move

Magnolia's Diary, October 15th of 2025

Dear Diary,

It's the witching hour...when peculiar things happen. I'm agitated, uneasy...a gut feeling I've gotta get out of here. Call me crazy, Diary, but I just got a mental impression this guy's talking to me. He's telling me to come to him right now. My nurse has nodded off.

That's it...I'm gonna bolt. I texted Cornelius to come and get me. This is unbelievable, I'm discharging myself without a wheelchair. What will the hospital staff think? I've got to do this. Those detectives will come back and start questioning me again. I'll break down and confess what I did. Worse, they'll obtain a blood sample.

Cornelius just texted, he's at the parking garage. I'm glad he's unconventional; no one else would've agreed to pick me up. Without a wheelchair, no one will suspect it's me. I'll put on a baseball cap and shades just to make sure. No fam to go back to...what have I got to lose? It's time to start a *new* chapter, this is the new me! Here I go!!!

Thirty minutes later I was walking through Patrick Henry Park with Cornelius, looking for the mysterious man of my dreams. We treaded lightly on the uneven brick sidewalks checking out the park's trees and benches. It was eerily quiet. A late-night passerby spooked us walking his pit bull. It wasn't him. A few minutes later, out of the corner of my eye, I thought I saw the tree in the middle of the park move. At the time I thought to myself, *was that a man's leg moving, or was it a tree root? Noo, it must be the moonlight playing tricks on my eyes.* I kept looking, then, lo and behold, out of the side of the tree trunk a man appeared. His chest and face transformed from looking like tree bark to human skin. His legs now visible as wool pants. He put on his shirt and over it a shearling coat. As he walked down the brick path I recognized it was him. He was well proportioned, striking, late 20s, perhaps, but in an odd way, he seemed much older.

"Hello. I'm Benjamin. To-mat-o! You must be Magnolia."

"Ah, 'tomato'? What's—?"

"A head turner," he replied, "And who are you?"

"Hello, I'm Cornelius, a friend of Maggie's."

"Hello."

"How'd you change like that?" I asked.

"It's a tonic I drink," he replied.

"Thanks for the straight answer...how do you know my name?"

"I know a few things. So you survived."

"Yeah...thanks to you," I replied.

"Maggie, what do you mean?" asked Cornelius, eyeballing me.

"I..." I shrugged, "I drank his blood."

"*What!?*" stated Cornelius, looking at me in bewilderment.

"Hey, it's not a habit or anything! I saw Benjamin here, right before my eyes, heal from a bullet wound. Cornelius, I was on death's door. Don't judge me. I bet if you were in my shoes, you might've done the same thing. At the time, I felt like it was the only choice I had," I exclaimed, crying now like a baby.

"When you're at death's door, some get desperate," replied Benjamin. He gave me his hanky.

"I suppose so," said Cornelius.

"Most don't survive what ya did," said Benjamin.

"Explain..." I replied dabbing my eyes.

"Maggie, you drank vampire's blood. Most don't weather that kind of thing. You must be quite a bearcat."

"Bearcat?"

"Yeah, a fiery dame."

"Well, thanks, I think... So this explains why I'm walking. Why I see in the dark... why my teeth are stronger, and, um, sharper."

"You're not gonna bite me, are you?" asked Cornelius.

"Noo...don't be ridiculous," I retorted.

"Can you handle sunlight?" asked Benjamin.

"Not much. I sleep during the day."

Cornelius' eyes got really big then he said, "Whoa, I was freaked out enough by the blood drinking thing, but now you guys are mega freakin' me out."

"I'm a little surprised at you..." I said glaring at Cornelius. "Wasn't it you who told our Lit class you see ghosts?"

"Yeah, it's just—"

"Cornelius, let's finish this chatter inside. Aren't the coppers lookin' for you two?" asked Mosby.

Cornelius drove us a couple of blocks east to a townhome. He told me to only call him from someone else's device then dropped us off. The place looked nice, a bit Victorian. Later, I would discover it was a kind of vampire safe house. There were coffins in bedrooms, goth decor, petrified critters in formaldehyde jars and a vintage *Nosferatu* poster depicting a plaque from Wismar, Germany.

The former owner, Collette, was Romanian, which explained why some of the house's decor was from that region: wood carved wall plates, tapestries, a map of Transylvania by Ortelius, and a cross section of petrified wood from Hoia Baciu Forest on an iron stand. She was the niece to Ruxy, that's her social media name anyway. I'd heard and seen of her before in posts; she's a stunning lavender haired chic who dons cool dark threads. Some call her the "Blood Lady." She's an exec at Sânge Nou, a biotech company touting breakthroughs in synthetic blood products. Maybe there's a connection between her company and the blood running in Mosby's veins?—now running in mine. Who knows? At the very least, it's definitely got my marbles churning.

More did happen that night...too much to write here. But the gist of it was this: Benjamin was truly *the* Benjamin Mosby, the firemen whom everyone thought died on account of the Church Hill Tunnel collapse. After all, he looked exactly like a vintage photo I'd seen online about his exhumed grave. Who else could it be? He hadn't aged a bit! Wow, what vampiric blood can do! I get this guy, like me, he was in a desperate situation, which calls for desperate measures. So he drank vampire's blood to live, in this case, the blood of W. W. Pool. Wow! William Wortham Pool was the Richmond Vampire, and now Mosby succeeded him. Sometimes legends are more real than reality, if that makes any sense.

Obviously, my decision to elude the law and run off with a murder suspect meant I could never go back to my former life. That night, from the kitchen (on its wall a cool woodcut of words read "*Pofta Buna*"), I drank my first blood tea. I gotta admit, it tasted oh so good and gave me an awesome buzz. Afterwards, I'm pretty sure I spoke to a raven, but then again, maybe I was tripping. The raven said its name was Evermore. I'm gonna go with the hallucination option for now.

Benjamin and I were up all night. He told me of his adventures...his escape from the exploding locomotive, how he'd discovered Mr. Pool under a flatcar, what compelled him to drink Pool's blood, and his subsequent awakening by some archaic group of vampires; one of whom he befriended, named Bölscem Kertész. This Bölscem is a kind of chronicler, a scribe, who Mosby said would soon return from a funeral for a Russian vampire. Was this the guy I'd seen that fateful night? The one involved with my father, in some sort of blood/drug deal. I couldn't bring up the topic just yet, nor could Ben, we were dancing around that trauma. Anyway, at the Church Hill Tunnel's western portal, he claimed he'd encountered the ghost of Richard Lewis. One of several workmen buried alive along with unnamed others. He said he could see his ghost on account of being a vampire, having the ability to see the unseen. Lewis swore the tunnel was cursed, on the precipice of caving in, hence why he and his companions were there to bolster its archway. Moreover, he admonished Ben to do something about it. Well, Ben, confessed he took it to heart and that's why he and Bölscem went to my father, RailOne's CEO, to persuade him to address the needed repairs to the tunnel. But my father, unsurprisingly, was not too agreeable to their demands. At this point in his story, Ben noticed I was beginning to breathe heavier, fidgeting and overall becoming agitated—for obvious reasons. He clammed up and so did I for a spell or two.

This was all too much to take in. Benjamin Mosby, asleep for a hundred years—now a vampire, and he was in league with others of his kind—plus a ghost. If someone had asked me a month ago if such things are true, I would've said they were smoking crack.

Later that evening, I finally brought up that horrific night at my father's estate. At the time, I was surprised Benjamin had not brought it up when we first had met. Looking back at it now, he must have surmised: let her bring it up when she's good and ready. Well, however he was thinking, I was then emotionally pre-

pared to hear his account. He explained his actions—how it was all a terrible accident. He and Bölscem only sought repairs to the tunnel and reparations. They had no intention of killing anyone. To his credit, Mosby expressed great remorse and apologized profusely.

What else could I do, but accept his apology. After all, he saved my life, and of course it helped that my father had never been much of a dad to me. If he had been a dad, I can't imagine how I could have found it in myself to forgive Ben. Upon reflection, there was a big positive in all the gloom and tragedy; for since my equestrian accident, I wasn't *really* living...I mean, I was bound to a wheelchair relieving myself into a bladder bag.... Mosby, albeit via Pool's blood, gave me new life—a major glow up. I could physically do all the things I had done before the accident. In fact, I could do them even better. Now I could run as fast as a gazelle, see in the dark, lift several times my weight, even see rings of color around people. I guess that's their aura...oh, and my nails! My nails are like iron. No more emergency dashes to the manicurist's for a quick fix!

Just before sunrise, Benjamin asked me to cut his hair, which I did. In the process of shaving the hair off the back of his neck, I found a tattoo of a beetle. He knew nothing of it. I postulated this vampiric order had tagged him...how else could they keep track of him? I explained my theory, and he agreed I must be right. Ben asked if I could remove it. I said I couldn't, but that Cornelius might be able to. I almost hit the call button on my watch when I remembered what he said. Too bad Ben didn't have a phone. Hopefully Cornelius hasn't disowned me as a friend; I can't imagine him snitching on me to the police.

Au revoir!

No Need of Him

Bölcsem Kertész Naplója, 2025. október 15

After the funeral of Nastya Upir, a conclave convened in my lady's chamber. Ruxandra sat at the head of a lengthy obsidian table, the gold feet of its legs depicting dragon claws. Basilisk visages capped the arms of medieval chairs. We were deciding the fate of Benjamin Mosby and those souls still living which Andromalius required as payment for the soul of Collette.

The mood was somber, especially for Antonio, who had lost Nastya, his love. His countenance hinted at disdain for Ruxandra, whom he no doubt blamed for Nastya's death. Yet he dared not be brazen, for Ruxandra could be ruthless to those who questioned her ways.

Antonio asked, "Why is not Edana here?"

"She is occupied elsewhere...Kojo and I are to preside over affairs in Richmond," explained Ruxandra.

Kojo said, "Now with Brannbjørn dead, Izurg's treachery exposed, and the Fomorian threat squashed, we must decide if Mosby is still relevant to our plans. What are your thoughts, Antonio?"

"Remove him. He should have engaged Brannbjørn earlier, else Nastya would still be alive."

Kojo looked to Ruxandra, but she held her tongue. Kojo replied, "I must agree with Antonio. He only engaged Brannbjørn because the Fomorian assaulted you, Bölscem. Mosby has an affinity for you. Wouldn't you agree?"

"Yes, Lord Kojo, I agree."

"Why is that?" Kojo pressed. "And why have you not used the full capabilities of the Scarab app? Antonio has gone to great effort to create it."

"There has been no need, my lord. So far, he has removed all the parties we have

asked of him."

"Yes, but it was accidental," interjected Antonio. "Nastya would still be here if you had used my app! Days before, you should have been manipulating his mind. Using the endoword feature *I* showed you. Then he would have destroyed Brannbjørn without Nastya being there. You knew Kojo and Nastya were no match against his strength and speed. Her blood is on *your* hands!"

"I beg to differ! You have too much confidence in your cyber toy. Have you forgotten the inner war within him? Yes, Pool's blood runs through him. But he is a simpleminded fireman, not a cutthroat killer. Why weren't you there? Or perhaps you are too cowardly to put your own neck on the line?"

Antonio rose from his chair, as did I. He swung at me and I redirected his fist downward. His momentum carried him to the floor. He snapped back to his feet, his viperous tongue protruding between razor sharp fangs.

Kojo rose from his seat booming, "Enough!"

Antonio and I resumed our seats at the table, glaring at each other.

Ruxandra broke her silence stating, "Bölscem speaks wisely, Antonio. You know as well as I, and I say this as delicately as I can, Nastya had a *past* with Brannbjørn. She had to be the bait; it was the only way to lure the Fomorian scum into that warehouse. She did not die in vain."

"I will not speak of this further," said Antonio refusing to look her in the eye.

Kojo changed the topic. "Very well, so...is there any further need for Mosby? Brannbjørn is gone; what can Mosby do that we cannot do ourselves?"

"What of the others Andromalius desires?" said I.

"Bölscem, his usefulness is waning," replied Ruxandra. He aided us in killing Brannbjørn. What more purpose can he serve? We can appease Andromalius' appetite without him."

"So, my lady, with all due deference, this mission of vengeance, ah, the iniquity of, of–"

"Yes, of the fathers upon their descendants," said Ruxandra, finishing my thought.

"...I speak of the Tunnel's collapse."

"Naturally. Go on," she said.

"The mission was, was more of...shall I say, of a *personal*, rather than of a Platonic undertaking?"

"Oh, you are speaking of my statement, '*Grevă echilibru*,' are you not?"

"Meaning?" wondered Kojo.

"Meaning, 'Strike the Balance.' My reference to the world waltzing its way down the Right Hand Path," Ruxandra said.

"Ah," said Kojo, "and is your vengeance more *personal* in nature?"

"It is, I confess," answered Ruxandra glaring at me. "As you all know, William Pool meant a great deal to me. He would have demanded the same revenge Andromalius seeks. All this dovetails nicely into removing the rest of the souls the archdemon seeks, lest we not secure Collette's spirit back to us."

"Collette was beloved by us all. She is missed..." said Kojo.

"Now, gentlemen, unless there is a further objection, how shall we dispose of Mr. Mosby?" asked Ruxandra.

"I will do it," said I. "When I return to Richmond, I will use Antonio's gadgetry to paralyze him. Then, I will drive a yew stake through his heart."

"Why yew?" inquired Antonio.

"Oak may do, but yew, mingled with the blood in a strigoi's heart, assures the result," I explained.

"Very well, Bölscem," said Kojo, "and, upon your return, spike his head in the Court of Impaling."

"Yes Lord Kojo," said I.

"As for the other souls Andromalius requires?" asked Ruxandra.

"Countess," I replied, "the Johns' descendant...I shall dispatch him. After all, I can smell him; Morrigan brought me some of his hair."

"Ah, *excelent*! And the other, I myself shall snuff out," said Ruxandra. "Then we can close this whole chapter on Richmond...I mean to burn down the safe house... save for a few keepsakes. Finally, I will close the portal at Pool's tomb. Our exploits in Richmond will cease."

Agents, Hobos & a Scribe

Magnolia's Diary, October 16th of 2025

Dear Diary,

Thud, thud was the sound I awoke to, a pounding on Collette's front door. I sat up on the daybed, still in my velvet dress, and waited to hear Ben answer the door. He did not.

I asked, "Who is it?"

"It's Special Agent Covach and Detective Breland. Open the door, Maggie."

I was shocked. How did they find me? I looked down at my smart watch; it was ten in the morning. *Crap*, I thought, *they must've tracked me through this watch*. I took it off and placed it on the nightstand.

Thud, thud, thud! "Open up!"

"Just a minute, I'm getting decent!" *Oops, I lied. So glad Aunt June brought this dress to the hospital*. I put on my flats and a frock coat with ruffled hems from Collette's wardrobe. Next, I placed my diary in one pouch pocket, and in the other, my clutch purse. I then jumped off the daybed and ran down to the basement. Ben was asleep in a coffin. *Yikes! No time to process that*. I shook him, "Wake up!...FBI are here."

"Maggie!" I heard from the stoop. "Open up or we'll break down the door."

"Just a sec!" I yelled from the basement, I shook him one more time; his eyes opened.

"Wha' the, huh? What is it, Maggie?"

"The cops, they're here! We gotta go!"

He got out of the coffin, put on his boots, and grabbed his coat. *Thump!* The door struck the hallway's wood floor. The sounds of several footsteps rushed in. They were going throughout the house. They proceeded to come down the stairs. Ben and I bolted out of the walk-in basement and into the fenced yard.

Two Richmond City police officers and a G-man in a suit blocked our way to the back gate. The agent yelled, "Halt! FBI—put your hands up!" Ben launched into the G-man before he could get a shot off, knocking him into the stockade wooden fence. But, one of the police officers managed to let off a round. It penetrated right below Ben's collar bone, blood splattering the house's clapboard exterior. It hardly slowed him down. Ben threw one officer into the other. They both ended up in a heap at the base of the yard's privacy fence.

We exited the back gate. The G-man recovered and shouted, "Stop or I'll shoot!" We kept running. *Bang!* I felt a stinging pain graze my forearm, but I stayed on my feet and kept running. We ran so fast the agent couldn't keep up. We entered a small plot of grass then ran past a restaurant and onto Marshall Street, down 32nd. I think we were doing about thirty miles an hour. Wow! Being a vampire has some really cool perks!

As we headed south on 32nd we arrived in Chimborazo Park, overlooking the train tracks below. To our right, shrouded in a wooded vale, lay the dilapidated tunnel's eastern portal. Police car sirens echoed off the park's trees. Around us, dog walkers stopped to witness our pace. A train's horn announced its approach.

Ben halted then turned to me and said, "You ok?"

I stopped and was amazed to see my forearm had ceased bleeding. "I'm good." I showed him that my injury had healed. "We gotta move." The sirens grew louder. "What now?"

"We're about to be hobos." He pointed to the oncoming locomotive, heading west along the James River. "Follow me."

We descended a flight of concrete stairs near the corner of Grace and 32nd. From the stair's landing we hurried down a dirt trail then into the woods and from there to Williamsburg Avenue. We followed it to East Main Street then up a hilly dirt road that met with the viaduct and our impromptu ride. We jumped into a vacant boxcar.

Once I caught my breath, I asked, "Where are we heading?"

"We're getting out of Richmond. You'll see."

The iron viaduct ran parallel to the James River. The water table was high, given the heavy rain from the night before. The roar of the rapids, blaring sirens and train whistle, plus my adrena-

line beating like a drum in my ears was at the same time both terrifying and exhilarating. *Oh, to walk again is great, but to sprint like this—from the police—is surreal,* I thought.

The diesel engine took us past Shockoe Bottom: an abode of vagrant bars, the Poe Museum, and groups of homeless peddlers. Suddenly the train came to a halt. The jarring unbalanced someone whose ruddy complexion from the dark corner of the car careened into the light then back into shadow.

"Damn," said a husky voice, "I hate when we stop."

"Who are you?" asked Mosby sidestepping out of the daylight.

From the shadow emerged a rough man in fatigues. Ganja wafted before him. He wore an Allen Ginsberg t-shirt with a line from his poem, *Howl*. A forearm tattoo, a strawberry pierced by a lightning bolt...looked military. His face laden with wrinkles and scars, no doubt from conflicts fought ages ago. The beatnik vet came to mind.

"I'm Rudy. I know you," he said, checking out Ben from head to toe, then asked, "but who are you?" staring at me.

"I'm Maggie." Like Ben, I, too, avoided the light spilling into the boxcar.

"How do you know me?" wondered Ben.

"The night of October 2nd, I saw you in a dream. Two bats comin' out of the Church Hill Tunnel. The first became Bölscem, the second became you. What's your name, vampire?"

"I'm Benjamin. Hey, just so you know, I'd like to undo what I've become."

"Fair enough," said Rudy. The train jerked back to life. "Stay away from Bölscem and his sort."

"Why's that?" asked Ben.

"They tend towards the use 'em then lose 'em," Rudy said.

"You speak in riddles, hobo," replied Ben. We neared downtown and Brown's Island.

"Who's calling who a hobo?" chuckled Rudy. The locomotive's horn blew three times; he turned solemn. He went into some sort of a trance and cried out...

I dreamt a dream
Two souls to die
Collette's soul no more
In Hades will cry

At that, Ben and I were spooked. Not helping the mood, we were coming up on a cemetery, Hollywood Cemetery, to be exact. Ben glanced at me and ordered, "Let's blouse!"

"Huh?" I said.

"We gotta go."

The viaduct ended near the Belle Isle Suspension Bridge meeting up with a hill, our drop off point. We jumped out and walked down the hill toward a dirt path. Above us was the Oregon Hill Overlook. Below the overlook, to one side, the North Bank Trail Head I recognized from childhood. Vicky and I used to hike it with Mom.

The train slowed then stopped. We looked back up the hill. Rudy clung to the boxcar's ladder and sang a folksong I'd heard before...

Twenty years he rode the lines of steel
As loader-brakeman, then as engineer
When he'd get home we'd stay up through the night
To hear his tales by candle light
A moon of bone shines down on the tracks
Where Church Hill Tunnel has fallen in
The C&O man said daddy's gone
And won't be coming home again[5]

On one of the hopper cars I spied the unusually large raven, Evermore. He cawed (though it sounded harsher) and hissed at us then flew off toward the cemetery.

"Oh no, not that blasted bird," said Ben. "And he's going the way we are."

We started upon the trail.

I detoured, bearing toward a series of large, elongated rocks under the bridge.

"Not that way," said Ben, pointing west on the North Bank Trail.

"Give me a minute," I replied. Before my horse accident, I sat on those rocks with my mom and Vicky. For fun, my sister and I labeled places like this with fantastical names. We called this site: Sitting Stones, because we'd love to take a break there. I had to relive the moment. Besides, I needed to process what I just experienced, so I took a seat. I opened you, my dear Diary, to record the day so far.

"What are you doing?" exclaimed Ben, backtracking, hands on his hips. Now I could see swelling tears.

"I'm writing down what Rudy just sang."

"Dames and their diaries," Ben said, rolling his eyes but also wiping tears. "Need I remind you, the coppers are still after us."

"Did that song make you cry?"

"Yeah," he said dabbing with his hanky. "It was speaking of my old friend, Tom Mason, the engineer with me that fateful day."

"I'm so sorry, Ben."

"Thanks," he said, putting his hanky away, then began filing his nails.

"Why are you doing that?"

"I don't like pointed fingernails. Seems like every hour they're sharp again."

"Well, they might come in handy that way." I resumed writing.

"Really, we oughta be going."

I ignored him for a few minutes then asked, "What do you think he meant by the 'Two souls to die?' And what's with Evermore hissing at us?"

"Guess it's the two folks Ruxandra wants to send to an early grave. She was Pool's dame and Collette's aunt. She woke me with a mission to make amends, but I never figured she meant revenge of the killing kind." He kicked the dirt and declared, "I've been a sucker this whole time."

"So...you weren't trying to kill my family?"

He came over and sat on a stone next to mine. "No, just here to set things right...rich folk paying common folk for lost loved ones, a museum to tell the history...that sorta' jazz." He slumped over then looked me in the eye. "I wasn't trying to kill your old man...just trying to defend myself. Didn't know my own strength. Sorta' new to being a...aah, I'm not gonna say it. Again, awfully sorry."

"Apology accepted."

Ben looked over at the viaduct, exclaiming, "Aww applesauce! It's been a hundred years...who am I kidding? No one cares about the tunnel, nor the folks buried in it. I ain't gonna help the lavender gal or her friar no more. I'm not in the business of bumping folk off."

"Ruxy?"

"Yeah, Ruxandra, who paints their hair lavender and she's got weird eyes, to boot. But don't let that fool ya'. That woman's all business."

"Hmm, hope we don't run into her."

He stood up and said, "Alright, those gumshoes might show up. Follow me, I got a plan to get us outta Dodge."

I closed my journal. Westward we hiked on the North Bank Trail. Soon, Hollywood Cemetery came into view behind a chainlink fence overgrown with brush. Opposite were the train tracks and the James River, which wound in and out of view.

A few clips down the trail we came to the rickety red bridge Vicky and I called Troll's Toll. It overlooked the remains of the Richmond Waterworks and Kanawha Canal. Beyond it, the tracks and the James. We were out in the sun. Our skin began to tingle then sear in the sun. Being a vampire has its drawbacks. We passed a few hikers smoking pot. Then up a rocky staircase.

(I used to call it Giant's Spine, since it looks like the remains of a spinal cord from a giant.)

Just past the stairs, tree cover returned and the trail met the cemetery's fence line. With his bare hands, Ben ripped a hole in the fence like a kid would pull apart a toasted waffle. We passed through the opening and up a hill to Waterview Avenue. Tourists visiting the graves were dumbfounded when they saw Ben and I moving at the speed of a scooter. To avoid attracting any more attention, we slowed to a brisk walk.

From Waterview, he led me down Westvale Avenue. Within a block of Pool's mausoleum, Evermore was sentineled upon its lamb statuette. He cawed—really a *kraw*, and hissed. We slowed down. Something didn't feel right.

Then a bizarre looking man of medium build with a goatee and buzz cut wearing a frock coat and medieval laced-up boots marched down the tomb's marble walkway like he owned the place. When he turned onto the road in front of us, I knew it was him; the blood pimp responsible for my family's demise. Oh, how I wanted to gouge his eyes out!

Ben put his arm out, signaling me to halt. We stood about half a block away. He said, "That's Bölscem, you remember him?"

"Oh yeah—how can I forget that strange hairdo and goatee. Is, is that a wand in his hand?"

"Looks more like a stake to me. This ain't looking good."

Bölscem began to utter unfamiliar words and perform odd gestures with his body.

The wind picked up. The clouds darkened.

"What's he doing?" muttered Ben.

Rain pattered upon the avenue then became more intense. A dark fog coiled through the trees, grave markers, and obelisks. Visitors and tourists fled to their cars. Looking again, I realized Ben was right. Bölscem was indeed carrying a wooden stake in his hand.

"Drop Pool's key upon the ground!" ordered Bölscem.

"What are you talking about?" replied Ben. The rain was picking up. "What's with the stake, friar?"

"Don't play dumb with me, Ben. Why else would you be here? I should have known Pool left the original portal key with you. You cannot leave; your job here is not done."

The rain intensified to a steady downpour.

While I stayed put, Ben started to saunter toward him. "You're not here to stop me...you're here to bump me off!" Ben shouted. "This is Ruxandra's doing, isn't it?"

When Ben was just a couple of feet from Bölscem, the scribe jerked his left hand up, making his sleeve fall back, revealing a peculiar-looking smartwatch. He began touching it. Ben charged. Just as he got within an arm's length, he collapsed.

Panicking, I ran up and shook him, shouting, "Ben, Ben, are you okay!?" He was still breathing, trembling...he was frozen on the pavement.

What happened next was too gruesome to write down. Let's just say I couldn't believe I got that violent. Is it because of the blood of Pool running through my veins?

Au revoir :(

Change of Plan

Bölcsem Kertész Naplója, 2025. Október 16

As I exited the gate of Pool's mausoleum, the air was brisk but the leaves of fall had not yet reached their peak. The trees' tentacles clung to what little vestiges of summer persisted. However, as much as Richmond waned, the impending cold brought on by the change of seasons was inevitable.

So too in my mind, I was clinging onto what vestiges of warmth and fondness I held for the company of Mosby. But in my hand, I was clenching a yew stake, displaying what little regard I had for Ben's life. An inner war was battling away; part duty to my Society, part adherence to what affinity I felt for my new friend, and, indeed, for the part I'd played in bringing him to his current precarious state.

Hence, this turmoil played out upon this day, but in a way I never would have imagined could have happened. For before the tomb of W. W. Pool, the actions I carried out altered the course of my life and those concerned in the highest echelons of the Dragonists. Yet, much of the catalyst for this unexpected change in course came from an equally unexpected source: the very woman I should have killed but spared, Magnolia Jones, for she showed courage beyond her years. . .

As I had planned, I utilized the scarab app to incapacitate a belligerent Mosby, but I had not expected I would have to contend with his fiery new companion.

"What have you done to him!?" cried an irate Magnolia.

"I paralyzed him."

She pulled back Ben's collar. "By this? It's a chip, isn't it?"

"Yes, now get out of my way," I demanded, brandishing the stake.

"No, I will not!" she shouted. She stood up, defiant to me. She hissed and showed her fangs, unnerved by the droplets cascading down her face.

"You've got spirit, Magnolia...I'll give you that."

Evermore *krawed* and *cackled*...then took flight and landed on my shoulder.

A growling Mávros appeared from behind a nearby tree and closed the gap within striking distance of her position. I would need them. Though Maggie was a fledging vampire, her strigoi strain made her stronger and quicker than me.

Maggie changed her stance to eye us all at once. Her breathing became heavy. She remained in the road next to Ben, resolved to protect him. The rain and wind I had conjured up failed to deter her zeal.

"You're outnumbered. Step aside and I shall spare your life," I said, lying about the latter.

She didn't move. "Don't do this... you're his friend...he always said good things about you."

Mávros moved in gnashing his teeth. She turned and hissed at him. He leapt upon her, jaws of death and claws arrayed. She swatted him away his claws ripping her sleeve. Evermore launched off my shoulder and began pecking at her head. She spun and swiped at him...missing. Her long platinum hair drenched in burgundy blood. She swung again, this time knocking Evermore away. Just then Mávros chomped down on her leg. Velvet hem and blood concocted in his jaw. She was disoriented, wiping the oozing blood from her brow, losing her position next to Ben.

Seizing the opportunity, I moved quickly, raising the yew stake over Ben, poised to drive it through his heart. Just as I was about to strike, I heard a whimpering cry. I spun around to see Maggie's nails dig deep into the back of Mávros' neck. His jaw retracted. She flung him aside. Her creamy palm bathed in blood. Despite her battered state, torn velvet dress and bloody hair and hands, she was undeterred.

"No!" she pleaded. "They're using you! It's about Pool's blood, about Sânge Nou, isn't it?"

Sânge Nou? Mosby must have told her. The stake shook in my hand. *Told her about the company, the awakening...where was the blood I had extracted? The syringe? Suddenly the fog waned...all this mayhem...Ruxandra's doing.*

Sânge Nou must have needed the unique properties of Pool's blood to achieve coagulation, and God knows what else. And Collette's death, that was her catalyst to gain her beloved's blood, and to muddle in carnage again, not only to rid of us Brannbjørn, but to exploit the Dragonists, Andromalius and his imps who would all exact the revenge she so desperately yearned for. Revenge she had put off for so long to appease her grief of losing her lost love. This had nothing to do with "Striking the Balance," nor Richard Lewis and Engineer Mason or his fireman friend, Mosby. This affair germinated out of selfishness–out of profit, out of madness...it wasn't even exacted upon those who had killed William Pool, but upon their descendants. I finally faced the fact that this exploit did not hold water, I was merely a pawn in Ruxandra's chess game.

The stake made a dull clatter when it landed on the road.

Mávros, at first befuddled by my hesitation then my resolve, became undeterred, for his true master was and is Andromalius, gathered himself and attacked Magnolia again. Yet what the beast had not discerned was that through the tattered ends of her dress, one could see her leg had almost healed. Renewed vigor surged into her countenance.

"Bring it on you mutt!" she exclaimed as he pounced upon her. Gnashing teeth, he sprang at her throat. In midair she grabbed him by the neck then hurled him into a stone column of Pool's tomb. Mávros lay dazed and disoriented.

Seizing the opportune moment, I picked up the stake and ran over to Mávros, then with both hands, I drove it through his heart. The beast let out a whelping cry, his legs and body went stiff...then the monstrous creature sagged back against the column. Evermore sized up the situation and took off.

The storm I had evoked, I left churning, sending it the way the raven flew. *"Kaw...arrgh,"* Evermore cried, swirling high in the brooding sky. Resigned, he soared northward, encircled in a stormy cauldron of cumulous rain and lightning. The storm's emanations would impede Ruxandra from sensing any irritability in her familiar. The nearest Otherworld gate that Evermore could enter was at least a day's flight; the "King's Chamber," in Putnam County, New York. I had a day, maybe two, before the Dragonist Order would know of my betrayal and come for us.

Magnolia gathered herself and could only manage to say, "You stopped."

"Well...this whole thing has gone to rot."

"Why'd you change your mind?"

"You were right, I was blinded by loyalty..." I opened the Scarab app and deactivated the paralysis. Ben vibrated on the ground then blinked his eyes several times.

"Ahh...what just happened?" said Ben turning to me.

Before I could answer him, two Richmond City police cars led by an unmarked vehicle came speeding down Hollywood Avenue. "Come on, get up!" I pulled Ben to his feet. There was no time to enter the portal. *What to do, where to go...?*

"Follow me!" ordered Magnolia. She ran up a hill abutting Pool's mausoleum, Ben and I right behind.

"What about the portal?" asked Ben as we paused near the grave of Ellen Glasgow on Ellis Avenue. A fog bank camouflaged our location from the police and FBI.

"We don't have time to use it. Besides, you won't get far with that mark on you. Your every move is tracked by the Dragonists," I explained.

"I've got a solution for that," piped up Magnolia. "Now come on!" she pressed.

Why had I grown fond of Mosby? Was it, because, like me, he too, was from another time, a man who had lived a humble life, like I once had in a Benedictine monastery, so very long ago? What I did know, was the inner conflict within me had been boiling away in the recesses of my mind for quite some time. Questions about the Dragonist Order nagged at me ever since the Lockgreen affair came to light. Ruxandra's obsession to perfect synthetic blood had come with too high a price. Then her meddling with Mosby wrapped in idealistic jargon was the straw, for me, that broke the camel's back.

The thud of the yew stake upon Westvale Avenue still echoed in my mind. For with the dropping of the wooden spike came the arduous beginning of my flight to exile.

Snuffed Out

Jurnal de Ruxandra cel Rău, 17 Octombrie 2025

Since portaling back to California, my mobile watch has not worked well, although this has happened before. Traversing between worlds has its wear-and-tear on electronics. On my Bay Area land-line, there were voicemail messages, but I was not in the mood to listen. I wondered how Bölscem was getting on, but today, much of my thoughts were upon Roger Jones. Roger was an astute businessman, he had aided Sânge Nou Inc. in rising quickly as a bleeding edge biotech company. But his days were done, his soul was required. The arch demon Andromalius desired it in exchange for my niece's spirit. She did not deserve to be without her kind at Age's End. Hence, I snuffed him out as such. . .

"Wow, Roxy this is some view,"
said Roger as we both looked out from Monument Peak in California's Diablo Range.

"Yes it is," said I.

"Have you seen the earnings forecast based on our latest synthetic blood trials?"

"I have, they're fantastic."

"You were right; the coagulation piece excited our shareholders."

"Don't mention it."

"Thanks for the invite up here. But say...why here? What do you need to discuss?"

"Privacy is essential, plus, it's good to talk in nature. Clears the mind." I pointed to a formation of boulders upon a ridge. "Do you know what that rock line is?"

"No...looks like some kind of stone wall. It looks old," he said.

"It is. There are many of them. They are called the East Bay Mystery Walls. No one knows who built them. Their lineage an enigma, but yours is not."

"What do you mean?" Roger asked.

We were alone, other bikers had left the peak. Sunset was coming, and with it the closing of the park. I spoke directly. "You come from a train baron's bloodline, do you not?"

"I do," he said, befuddled, "what of it?"

"Your descendant was bent upon widening the Church Hill Tunnel. His obsession with progress over people killed William Wortham Pool, the love of my life."

"William Pool? The Richmond Vampire? That's just a legend—are you off your rocker!? So some laborers died, so what? Men are expendable in the name of progress."

"Just 'some laborers,' you say. They were men with families, sons and daughters, wives and mothers, lives, dreams...like everyone else. My Willie was my family."

"Hah, you're not serious..." he chuckled, "that would make you quite old."

"I am. Five hundred and forty-one years, to be exact," said I. Then I cut my wrist, spilling my blood upon the rocky ground.

"Hey! What are you doing!?" he burst out.

"Proving to you my age."

He watched in amazement as my forearm healed, not even leaving a scar.

A mixture of disbelief and terror came upon him. "You're a...a vampire?"

"I am. And I have been musing for quite some time how to vent my wrath," I stated.

"But surely," he said, slowly backing up towards the sun, just kissing the horizon, "you're, you're not holding me responsible?"

"Not personally, perhaps, but you and your brother will have to do." I smiled, showing my fangs.

His face turned pale, trembling. "You? You had a hand in my brother's death!" He stumbled upon a rock and fell back upon a broader stone. Dazed I pounced upon him.

"You and your brother are scum. The world will not miss a pedophile!" I exclaimed as I overpowered him and bit into his neck. His pulsing blood permeated my senses; I often find the blood of the deviant to be by far the most tasty.

After sucking much of the life out of him, I dragged his body upon the peak's portal stone. Along various ley lines, I portaled him to my lair, high atop Montură Izvorul, Dracul Castle. Whereupon my Dacian Guards enjoyed what was left of him, allowing him to nearly heal three times only to be drained again. When they tired of him, he met his final fate in my courtyard upon an impalement pole.

Now, only one soul remained to snuff out, after which, Earl Andromalius would release my dear Collette from the shores of Sheol.

Extraction

Magnolia's Diary, October 17th of 2025

Dear Diary,

We had to get this scarab-style implant off Ben. So in the early hours of the seventeenth, we went to the only person I knew who could help.

Cornelius stood in the doorway of a walk-out basement. A grand manor in the heart of Richmond's old-money district, Windsor Farms. He looked over my shoulder with skepticism at the unusual sight of Bölscem and Ben. Tunes from the band, *Strike Anywhere* fanned out from his crib.

"You need me to do *what now!?*" asked Cornelius.

"An extraction," I replied.

"Who's the friar?" he asked.

The conversation started off on the wrong foot. But then again, if I were in his shoes, I would have been peeved to see three vampires at my door, one of whom looked like a retired monk having a bad hair day.

Needless to say, my charm swayed him and he let us in. The mansion was constructed in the grand Federalist style near even grander places—now museums—namely, Agecroft Hall and Virginia House. All this grandeur nestled in a woodland above the James would be the last place the police would look for us. Avoiding the main roads, we had snaked our way along the river's various footpaths to get here. From now on, surreptitious travel would be commonplace...fleeing from the Bureau, the cops, and soon, the Dragonist Order.

In the basement was a makeshift lab / man cave, which turned out to be his parents' place; they were away from home for a spell. Under florescent tube lighting, he had computer parts strewn here and there on work tables. Books on Python, Java, even Fortran stacked here, there...everywhere. Monitors hooked up to a computer array of multi-colored blinking silicon blades in harmony with the light show of a bootleg router. This circus of luminosity revealed geek stickers upon laptops, PC boxes, workbenches, bins...a yellow elephant for *Hadoop* (my fav), *GitHub, Grunt, Java* (a coffee cup, classic), a Banksy Monkey overlaid on a *Macbook's* logo—kinda of cool. All this confirmed to me Cornelius was not some ordinary nerd, but an uber-nerd. The icing on the cake was his black t-shirt stating, "Kubernetes solves everything!" above a stuck-out tongue and tightly-closed eyes emoji next to a helm logo.

However, the standout in the lab was a cleared workspace with cleanly organized, highly specialized tools: soldering station, vacuum chamber...even bio extraction tools. I asked him why he had such items; he didn't say a word, but pointed to a white mouse in a plexiglass box, a wireless implant on the top of its head. Needless to say, that freaked me out, and I did not want to know why he'd done that. I guess this is what happens when youthful nerddom meets old money.

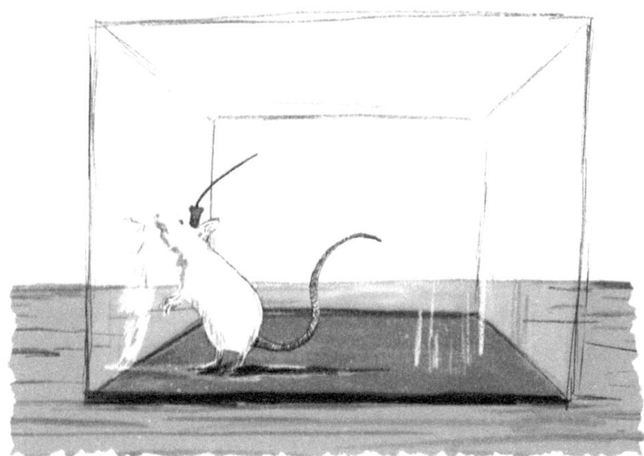

Ben, on the other hand, was a tad less subtle than me. He said to Cornelius, "So you're a west egg Frankenstein."

"Huh?" replied Cornelius, looking to me for a translation.

"He means, you're a rich guy who doesn't have to work, living like a mad scientist," I explained.

"Oh. Cool," said Cornelius. "Now, lie down here and I'll give you a local," as he snapped on medic gloves.

What happened next, my dear Diary, would be woefully pitiful to explain in writing, given my knowledge of biotech terminology. Suffice it to say, Cornelius, in coordination with Bölscem's tinkering on his peculiar smartwatch, removed the implant.

Au revoir :-)

Aunt Jane & the Castle on the James

Magnolia's Diary, October 18th of 2025

Dear Diary,

My dress was a mess! Bloody, torn and God knows what other bodily fluids—human or otherwise, were caked upon it. One thing was certain, I needed some new attire. So, since I couldn't go back to my own closet, the only other place I could go for some threads was my Aunt June. She had always been the forward-thinking planner in our family, and no doubt she likely surmised I might not go back to the estate just yet, but rather may want to spend a day or two with her. So to Aunt June I went despite the flak of my newfound companions who insisted I keep a low profile. Instead, I persuaded Cornelius, albeit I laid low in his back seat, to drop me off near my aunt's. Later, I would meet Ben and Bölscem at a cove by the river. Of course, those two opted to go by foot, keeping on-the-low from the authorities.

Now, Aunt June, a widow for many years, lives near William Byrd Park in a lovely three-story brick colonial. Every shrub hedged just right, mulch about the trees. Like her grounds, June is manicured, controlled and quaint. But this day, I put her in states of elation, shock, anxiety...it ran the gamut.

"Sugar, cream?" she asked.

"Just a cube," I replied as she handed me a cup of tea in her drawing room.

"I still can't get over it...you can walk! How?"

"You wouldn't believe me if I told you."

"You're probably right," she agreed, then took a bite of a butter cookie. "Dear, you look a wreck! You really should change. You know your lovely velvet dress, and some of your other things, are in the guest closet."

"Thank you, Auntie."

There was silence for a moment or two as we both sipped our tea. Then she said, "Well, where have you been, child?"

"I really can't say."

"I'm not surprised," she looked me straight in the eye, "...the police came by asking questions." She drank some more, then put down her cup. "Roger went missing."

"Huh?"

"His cell phone was found early this morning, Pacific time. A hiker chanced upon it, amongst some rocks, at Monument Peak in California. It had blood on it. There's no doubt it's his."

"Maggie, what's going on? You're walking...your father's dead, and now your uncle's missing...and the police are after you! I don't know who or what you've gotten yourself mixed up with. I have no idea what to say to you, child, or how to help you. I'm so confused." Auntie was working up into a fit of hysteria.

"Auntie, it's okay."

"How is it 'okay'? You made tabloid news, you know. 'Missing person escapes St. Mary's Hospital...leaves wheelchair behind.' It's right up there with that bizarre story of Benjamin Mosby. Did you read what happened?"

"A little."

"His grave has been tampered with. My, my," putting her hand to her head, "who would do such a horrible thing?"

"I... I think—"

"And did you know he's the fireman? The one who died in the Church Hill Tunnel? His body went missing the very day of the 100th anniversary of its collapse. It's all over social media. And now all kinds of nut jobs have been hanging out at Mr. Pool's mausoleum. They say the Richmond Vampire's back!"

"Auntie, do take a breath."

"I'm fine! Someone even posted footage from some kind of...hovercraft. What do you call it?"

"A drone, Auntie."

"Yes, that's it. It looked like a creature scaling the old National Bank building. And it occurred in the dead of night."

"You don't say."

"Are you mixed up in any of this hogwash?"

"Auntie, it's not hogwash...I, I can't explain...you wouldn't believe me. You didn't press me on why I can walk, so please don't press me about all these other things."

"My God! Magnolia Caroline! Are you in some kind of Satanic cult!?"

"No-o-o," I chuckled, "please calm down."

"Your uncle's gone missing, our family is all but dead...all but me. Oh Lord! Am I next? I'm next!"

"No, Auntie," I stifled another laugh. "No one's after you."

"I don't believe that! What goes around comes around. We're on the chopping block. Too much ill-gotten gain in our family; it's that old railroad money—too much blood on it...sins in our bloodline! My, oh my...my...my!!!"

"You're being ridiculous. Please relax," I said, handing her a tissue.

She blotted her tear ducts and blew her nose in that dainty Southern lady way. A few seconds of awkward silence transpired. She finished her tea.

"Maggie, this is yours." She handed me a manila envelope. "In it is your inheritance. Please take it, and don't come back until things settle down.
I love you, but I don't want to know where you're going or who you're with. I'm too old to take much more. I'll be praying for you, dear. Now please go...and go out the backdoor."

I got up and said, "I love you, Aunt June...thank you for everything."

"Oh, and before you go, draw the kitchen curtains and take some food from the crockpot. And do change out of that tattered dress. And wash your face, child."

Despite Auntie's drama, I was so glad she had brought some of my clothes from the estate: boots, scarf, and my burgundy velvet vintage dress that went well with the sable black coat I'd grabbed from Collette's closet. The garb came in handy, since my rendezvous with Ben and Bölscem had demanded I trek through undergrowth and muddy trails. This cove on the north shore of the East Branch Tuckahoe Creek was a secluded place, just north of the James, a feeder for city water.

When I caught up with them, neither of them had a plan as to what to do next. So I told them, in no uncertain terms, I had no intention of camping outside. So when darkness embraced the land and waterways, we made our way upriver to

the municipal waterworks. At night, it was a deserted water station, a great hideout.

After all, we were fugitives, not only from the police and FBI, but from the Dragonist Society as well. And it was a perfect place for vampires—an old Gothic Revival style building called the Pump House, known by locals as the "Castle on the James." Its lower levels used to be a waterworks site, pumping canal water to city residents in the 1800s. Its upper floor was an open-air pavilion for dancing and other socialite affairs. Now, it was mostly run down. Occasionally volunteers would work on its foundation and Tudor windows; they accessed it via padlocked doors. But thanks to Ben's strength, he opened a side door at the bottom of a granite stairway, away from the casual view of passersby.

Situated along the Kanawha Canal's Three Mile Locks, far from the bustling city, the castle served as an impromptu pitstop during the day for hikers and bikers. The locks themselves were now more waterfalls, since over time their wooden gates had become porous, dumping vast amounts of water into granite channels. These locks were three miles upriver, hence the name, from the Turning Basin, situated downtown. To us, the cascading water was soothing, as were the trains, which ran now and then, sandwiched between the river and canal.

Later that night, Bölscem sauntered off toward the RailOne A-Line Bridge. A grand, arched bridge built in 1919, dubbed at the time, the "Million Dollar Bridge." He said the view of the colossal structure was a necessary focal point for his musings over what he had done, and, what we must do next.

Meanwhile, around Pump House Park, Ben and I strolled the gentle trails and meandered over footbridges. Naturally, the temperature was brisk for a human's constitution, but our bodies adjusted with no discomfort. (Again, being a vampire

has some really cool perks.) We reclined near serene waters between the locked gates. Later, we sat together on top of a granite block making up part of a lock's channel, our legs dangled, soles gently swinging above the churning waters below. It felt so romantic.

"What's on your mind?" asked Ben.

"Ben, did you tell anything to Bölscem about our run-in with the police?"

"Nope, but I think he figured it out when the coppers showed up at the cemetery. At this point I'm keeping my cards close. Besides, it was just a few hours ago he tried to take my life. Let's see how this all pans out."

"That makes sense. Hey, before the police showed up, how were you gonna get us out of Richmond? Is there, um, some secret tunnel in Pool's mausoleum?"

"Could be. I reckon once the Dragonists woke me from the grave, that's the place they headed. Maybe there's a tunnel running up into the hillside...or maybe it goes south under the river, then it connects with a network of other tunnels. Who knows? All I know is, a whole host of vamps can't all fit into a small mausoleum chamber. So, with or without the friar, I plan on finding out what's going on. You with me?"

"Well, let me check my social calendar," I laughed, and got a smirk from my companion.

Later that night, Bölscem returned to the Pump House bearing *pawpaw*, an indigenous fruit, called by locals, the "hipster banana." It grows in the wild. Oblong shaped, it fit in the palm of my hand. Its flesh pale yellow meat with glossy dark brown seeds was a welcome treat. The pawpaw tasted a bit like a banana, but also a mango, with a custardy texture. I wondered if a local bartender has ever concocted a pawpaw cocktail? I could sure go for one reclining by my pool. Especially since Ben was spitting the seeds at me. I put a stop to that with a stern glare.

For a beverage, Bölscem handed out a small wineskin filled with blood. I must admit, Ben and I desired a drink. We didn't ask how he came about it, nor did we want to know. It warmed our insides, gave us a buzz, and nourished our minds and bodies.

The remainder of the night we conversed, much of it getting to know one another. Albeit, at first, conversations were strained as we were shaking off the vestiges of ill-feelings from yesterday's altercation. Some of the talk was worth noting, such as Ben recalling what Richmond was like in the 20s. Speakeasies in sleazy sections of downtown, jazz at the Hippodrome Theater, and the rising popularity of baseball—thanks to the introduction of AM radio. Richmond's economy too was booming, due in no small part to its prominence as a Southern railroad hub. At the hub's center, its jewel in the crown—the Triple Crossing—the only place in the country where three rail lines passed over one another. With the increased train traffic came increased freight delays prompting the C&O to reopen Church Hill Tunnel to offset congestion. Ben said if it weren't for the city's enthusiasm for railroads, particularly its chamber of commerce, he'd probably have lived a long and happy life with his family. This realization brought a quietness to our conversation.

As the night drew on, Bölscem played his recorder, esoteric tunes, I had never heard, of an age long since past. Such performing put him in the mood to recount dark and lurid things. Of particular interest to me was his description of Castle Dracula, which he called "Dracul Castle." Bölscem explained it was hidden from the eyes of man, deep in the Carpathian Mountains. Its battlements, even in Dracula's time, were a spectacle of dilapidation, as were its furnishings, much of which were frayed and moth-eaten. Its receiving room, octagonal in shape, was lit by a solitary flame, but its grand hall, with hearth and feasting table, was a sight to behold. The vast fortress had many doors, leading to many rooms—too many, in fact—but Bölscem's favorite, the library, held a vast collection of books on seemingly every topic from history to politics, botany to law, with, interestingly, volumes of poetry filling several shelves. In the midst of it, a table from which he could study all these grand archaic tomes. His favorites were on the subject of alchemy. Authors such as Zosimos and Geber inspired his own tinkering to such an extent, he purported he'd become adept at transmutation. During his extensive travels, he alleged he befriended a metallurgist who called himself Elias, whom, to this day, was known as the catalyst for Helvetius' infamous work, *The Golden Calf.*

I asked Bölscem if he was the librarian of the castle. He said he was not, but that he oversaw the book steward who came later, when the keep passed into the hands of the Count's granddaughter, Ruxandra cel Rău. His duties were to chronicle the exploits of the Drăculeşti lair from its inception to the present day. Like her father, and his father before him, the Lady Ruxandra likened books to "companions," and "good friends," especially on starless winter nights by the fire, with none but them for company.

I pressed Bölscem if I could go there. But in hindsight, I wished I hadn't, since the more he spoke of the place, the more his tone darkened. His reply was brusque, saying I could not. But then, after a pause, he expounded, claiming it was nestled deep in the mountains; its tree limbs were like monstrous tentacles

against a crimson sky reaching out to grab the unwary. "Besides," he said, "the calèche and dark beast which drove it, who knew the way, were long since gone. However," he said, "one night, blue flames illuminated the sky, revealing its locale and treasures concealed long ago."

Bölscem further claimed many a man had gone mad trying to find the stronghold, and, even if they succeeded, they would not survive to tell the tale. For if they discovered it by day, Ruxandra's henchmen would make sport of them. And, if by night, the wolves would tear them to pieces.

At this point, his eyes were ablaze, his hands compulsively ripping at the edges of paper, so I withdrew my presence. As day broke, we sought sanctuary in what was once the Pump House's control room. In it were two elongated crates filled with restorers' tools, the place being a pet project of preservationists. We emptied out the tools and slept inside, covering ourselves with their wooden lids. Bölscem was in one, Ben and I in the other. Oh, how I miss my own bed and linens, and silk pajamas. At least Ben's chest made for a nice pillow. Hopefully, no friends of the Pump House would show up for work.

Au revoir!

Fugitives Tell Tales

Magnolia's Diary, October 19th of 2025

Dear Diary,

On the second day of our seclusion, around the witching hour, we ventured to the North Bank Trail and from there we took a footbridge over the railroad tracks. Once over the truss bridge, at its anchor, we descended a steel and concrete staircase. Each landing to the next flight is decorated with a mural. Of course, Bölscem's favorite was a depiction of bats.

Once at ground level, we traversed the woods to a raised boardwalk then upon a narrow dirt trail until we found ourselves at a series of sandy beaches along the James River. This was Texas Beach, which is really a series of beach heads. Out upon a peninsula, we found a suitable area for making a small fire. Being far up river from the city and the fact that most of the branches still held their leaves, we felt secure from prying eyes, especially the police. We gathered branch and tinder; Ben arranged the fuel into a tepee frame and encircled all with stones. I felt like a Girl Scout. It was kinda of fun to be roughing it. Bölscem did something really cool. He fashioned cedar strips into a ball then closed his eyes and cupped the tinder sphere. Suddenly his hands radiated, a bluish glow ignited the orb, impressing Ben and I. He inserted the starter into the base of the

tepee. Ben blew upon it until flames caught the brittle branches. Scouts, eat your heart out!

We plopped down on makeshift seats made of severed tree trunks likely hauled in by earlier revelers. Bölscem entertained on his recorder while Ben poked at the fire. The beach, the fire, a few sips of vino blood, put us all in a mood to tell tales.

The monk bantered about the Society of Dragonists, but piqued my interest when he spoke of how he became a vampire. Bölscem's recorder reminded me of another recorder, my digital one, which I carry in my clutch purse. I bought it to discreetly capture lectures, but this night, I secretly recorded the scribe. Bölscem gazed into the fire and began to tell his tale. . .

"I was a seasoned Benedictine monk, yet inclined to a Hesychasm lifestyle, when I first met the Voivode of Wallachia, whom you know as Count Dracula, at his palace at Târgovişte. I was on a mission of alms from my Hungarian monastery with a fellow brother. Unbeknownst to me at the time, Count Dracula had shown my companion several of his enemies, impaled upon stakes. He asked the monk what he thought of his justice. My brother in the faith told him such a practice was barbaric and not fitting for a voivode."

"Oh! How did Dracula respond?" I asked.

"Well, the Count did not take well to this and promptly had his men impale the monk, leaving his blood to pool at the base of the pole."

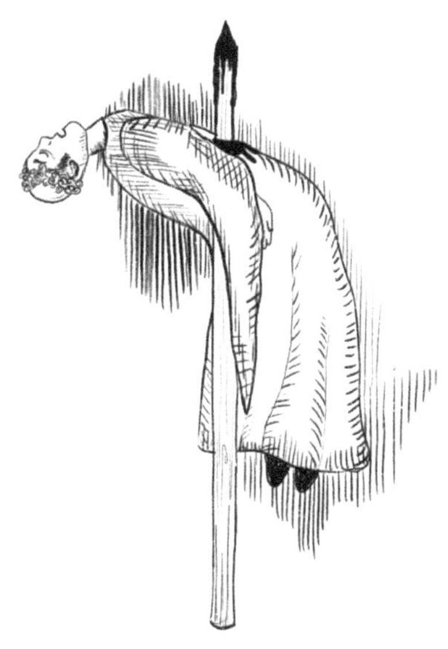

"Oh, gross! Why not just chide him? Then it avoids an awful lot of mess."

Bölscem did not respond, but merely continued his tale. "Then I was summoned before him. He posed the same question to me, desiring to know my mind upon this means of retribution. I replied, 'You are voivode. Is it not the will of God? Since the Lord has ordained you as such, so is your justice ordained as well.'

"The Count replied, 'You are a wise monk, unlike your fellow brother. Peace follow you, and may your mission be prosperous.'

"From that time forward, I was in the Count's favor. He invited me into his library, both of us being bibliophiles. We discussed many things: alchemy, folklore, poetry. He recited to me from his favorite verse, sorrowful odes to lost love and hopelessness. On the morrow, he put charge to his servants to have horse and carriage return me to my monastery."

"That's an amazing story," I said.

"There's more...for several years I did not hear from the Count. Then one day I received a sealed summons. Naturally, I obliged—under the auspices of a mission of alms. It was then, over a stay of three days, that he convinced me to forsake the precepts of Saint Benedict and become his personal scribe. Over time, I was initiated into the *Societas Draconistarum*, known in your tongue, from the Latin, as the Society of the Dragonists. I longed to be immortal, to experience the mysteries I had studied in scriptures and esoteric texts. I went through the rites of passage, barely surviving the ordeal (which many do not), to become a vampire."

"So...how old are you?" asked Ben.

"I am six centuries old and a decade and a half."

"Wow! You don't look a day over fifty," I blurted.

"Thanks, I think," he replied, smiling softly, then began tearing notches in a piece of note paper, a habit I deduced when he conversed, especially upon memory or emotionally charged subjects.

"Sorry...I just figured all vampires looked like they were in their twenties," I explained.

"You have been watching too many movies," he replied.

“Bölscem, what do you think we should do next?” asked Ben.

“Ben, I am pondering that. By now Ruxandra knows of my betrayal, and she will surely come for us. I dare not turn on this gadget,” he sighed, glancing at his smartwatch, “lest Antonio track us. In fact, I’ve no need of it now.”

He took it off and heaved into the midst of the James where its rapids would carry it to the Atlantic.

“What about our fake IDs and cards?” asked Ben pulling out his wallet.

“Hmm...we will keep them for now; perhaps they will serve a purpose,” he replied.

“Well, I’m keeping mine...it’s real,” said I. “Besides, I have an offshore account we can tap.”

“Yeah, it’s in Ruxandra’s Romania,” said a flippant Ben.

“Funny that you mentioned Ruxandra. She came up in the news,” I said, pulling out a phone.

“Where did you get that!?” exclaimed Bölscem.

“Relax, old timer. It’s a prepaid. Cornelius gave it to me; it’s loaded with minutes and data. They can’t trace it to us.”

“Hmm...you have not logged on to any of your accounts, have you?”

“Noo.”

“Good, keep it that way. So what news are you speaking of?”

“There’s a story about an ongoing search for me. How I left my wheelchair at the hospital. And, ah, in Church Hill, how I and this guy eluded police and FBI, then—“

“What!” exclaimed Bölscem.

“Oops,” said I, cowering from Ben’s glare.

“Great, Maggie. Cat’s outta the bag now,” said Ben, shaking his head.

“Is there a mug shot of Ben?” inquired the scribe.

“Ah, I haven’t gotten that far...let me finish what I was reading,” said I with clenched teeth. “Ah, let’s see here...’then they disappeared in Chimborazo Park.’ Cops couldn’t keep up,” I began to laugh, “—oh!”

“‘Oh’ what?” Bölscem asked, now perturbed.

“Well, looks like they have a photo of me and a sketch of Ben.”

I held the phone up for Ben and Bölscem to look at the images.

“Not a bad looking sketch. What else?” said Bölscem.

“Umm, there’s a hotline to call for anyone who spots us.” *Just great*, I whispered to myself.

“Wonderful! And when were you going to tell me about your little escapade with the police?” pressed Bölscem.

“Well, ah—“

“Never mind! What are the other stories?” asked the scribe.

"Hmm...let's see, ah...here's one, it's about Ben's grave. Ben, they've got a picture of your empty coffin."

Ben put out his hand, saying, "Let me see." I handed it to him.

"Whoa. Now that's a scary photo. I remember when I woke; there were all these creepy looking vampires...kinda like you," Ben said, looking at Bölscem.

The scribe just smirked. He didn't take the bait. Then Ben acted like Bölscem wasn't there and said to me, "Anyways, they were in dark robes...the lavender dame, Ruxandra, wouldn't release me. She had me in some kinda' invisible cage. Said she'd let me go if I agreed to help them." He handed the prepaid to Bölscem, who examined the photo.

"It was amazing how Chorti did that," he mused, giving me back the phone.

"Did what?" I asked.

"Commanded the earth. The photo proves it. There're no shovel marks, see? And did you notice the five scorched marks surrounding the coffin?"

"Yeah.... What is that?" I inquired.

"Heat signatures left by the pentacle stones interacting with the earth. The ceremony demands such to awaken."

"What's the gist of the rest of it?" asked Mosby.

"Hmm...let's see. Oh, it says a VCU student's bones were found. Oh, that's dark!"

"Where?" asked Ben.

"At the Slaughter family gravesite, not too far from yours. Apparently, his best friend was with him; that person has gone missing."

"Ah," said Bölscem tugging on his goatee, "they should have not have left his bones."

"*They!?*" I said, horrified, looking at Bölscem then at Ben.

"Don't look at me! I'm no man eater," exclaimed Ben.

"Ah, that. That was Chorti and Lothar," answered Bölscem. "They not only enjoy blood, but flesh as well."

"That's disgusting!" I blurted out then covered my mouth feeling like I was going to vomit.

"Agreed," said Bölscem. "Let's hope Lothar is not sent to hunt us. He is merciless." He tossed a few twigs into the fire. "What else is a headline?"

"Let's see," I said, scrolling. "Oh, here's one, it's an interview, conducted by Mark Holmberg—guess he's out of retirement. It's 'cause-a you, fireman."

"I didn't talk to him," snapped Ben.

"No—not you, he spoke to someone else."

"Who's he?" Ben asked.

"He was a well-known reporter around Richmond. He wrote about spelunking the tunnel, the Black Dog, stories about the Richmond Vampire...that sort

of thing."

"Oh," said Ben, placing more wood on the fire. "What's it say?"

"Not too much wood," cautioned Bölscem. "Keeping a low—"

"Holmberg had a chat with a dowser," I interrupted, "named Lunia. Claimed she knew you. Name ring a bell?"

"Yeah, it does...guess it was when I was a spirit roaming Richmond."

"Must be," I replied. "Lunia recounted how, just last month, before your grave, two Goth-like women hired her to do a dowsing session. One, in her 30s, had lavender hair and multi-colored eyes. The other, slim, jet black hair, in her 20s."

"The lavender lady's Ruxandra and Collette was the younger," interjected Bölscem.

"Go on..." said Ben.

"It says Ruxandra asked if you'd encountered William Pool in the tunnel collapse. You said, 'Yes,' signified by the rods crossing. You also said, 'Yes' to drinking Pool's blood, at which Lunia dropped the rods in horror. This true?"

"Yeah, I wasn't in my right mind, and I was desperate. I couldn't bear to be without my Marie and Dorothy. They'd be devastated if I died. Aww, well, in a way, I did anyway."

"I understand, it's disgusting," I said, placing a hand on his forearm, "but I would've done the same thing."

"Thanks." Ben looked at me then down at the embers. "I do miss them so." He wiped away a few tears.

For a few moments we listened to the crackling fire, then I asked Bölscem how the Dragonists began.

He cleared his throat then stated, "As I've said before, the Dragonist Order's formal name is *Societas Draconistarum*, from the Latin, the Society of the Dragonists, or Order of the Dragon. It was founded in 1408 by King Sigismund, who, at the time, was sovereign over my country. He formed such an order to galvanize galant knights and noblemen to defeat the invading Turks. Ruxandra's grandfather, Vlad the Impaler, whom you know as Count Dracula, was a member, as was her father, Mihnea cel Rău. With the death of King Sigismund, it began to morph from its initial mission to better serve the whims of her grandfather. Over time, the crusades dissipated, and the Order of the Dragon began to recede into the dust of history. Eventually, Ruxandra took the reins, transforming its chivalric bent, to, let us say, a vampiric leaning."

"How so?" asked Ben.

"Well, for one, she changed its symbol from a dragon along the lines of the St. George motif to something more primal."

"Do you have the St. George pic?" I asked.

From his coat pocket, he produced a journal and thumbed to a sketch of a circular dragon with its tail wrapped around its neck. Upon its back was a great wing with a cross.

"This is the original," he said, "and this is the current." He then displayed a gruesome ouroboros tattoo on his left forearm.

"What does it mean?"

"The dragon serpentine power of life, death, and rebirth."

"Oh, makes sense...and the ring on your right hand?"

"Made of orichalcum. It is the Master Scribe's signet ring. Before any map, scroll, or book is archived, it must pass before my eyes, then be sealed in wax with this ring."

"Master Scribe? Are there others under you?"

"There are. The others I oversee, each lair having its own. I alone am, well, was, the Master over all, hence the one ring. My main charge was to compile and write all the Dragonist's history into the *Draculian Chronicles*."

"Cool beans! Can I read it? I'm a major bookworm!"

"I'm afraid not, Maggie. It is secured behind a great door in *Dún Dreach-Fhola*, sentineled by the Balaurian Guards. The iron clad deadbolts can only be opened by a cipher wheel lock in concert with this signet."

"So 'lairs, Balaurian,' what's the hierarchy?"

"My dear Maggie, you ask a lot of questions."

"I'll say," piped Ben.

"Hey, it's fascinating stuff," I said.

"Well, we have time, but I need to take my stroll before sunrise."

Ben had had enough and went over to the shoreline, foraging for wood.

"Ok, sounds good, so can you answer my question?"

"Very well...the Dragonist Order is comprised of nine lairs each headed by an archon."

"An archon?"

"Yes, an archon. We adopted portions of the Athenian form of governance. The best form, I might add. The heads of each lair hold council three times per lunar year at *Dún Dreach-Fhola*. The Archons of the Dragonists are composed of three principle archons: the Archon Eponymos, the overarching leader, who is currently Edana; the Polemarchos, the military lead, who is Kojo; and the Archon Basileus, the ceremonial and spiritual lead, who is Ruxandra. The other six, Thesmothetae, hold voting power upon the Dragonist Council. Every twenty-seven years elections are held for these seats. Only Balaurians from the lairs may cast their vote."

"And a Balaurian is...?"

"There are two classes or degrees within our order. A Balaurian, is the higher, one who is truly vampiric, not human. The Wyverians, the lesser, are human in nature, but sanguinarians."

"Humans who drink blood?"

"Precisely. They are handpicked and initiated into the Dragonist Order from covens, pylons, groves...I think you get the gist of it."

"Earlier you mentioned the name, Antonio...about tracking us?" I continued.

"I thought you were done with the questions."

"I lied."

"Women," said Ben, returning with a pile of wood he dropped near the fire.

"Hey, and men don't lie?" I countered.

"Never," he grinned, tossing a log in the fire.

"Not too much, Fireman," said Bölscem.

"Yes, Master Scribe," Ben mockingly replied.

"Antonio is an archon from our Brazilian lair. He is descended from the Mura people, whose ancestors, many ages ago, spoke of a great vulture bat that roamed the Amazon.

"He is our technical guru, versed in many computer languages. He is the one who designed our smartwatches and that implant we removed."

"Ok, last question, I promise."

"Shoot."

"*Dún Dreach-Fhola*, where's that?"

"Well, and it may sound strange, it is in the Otherworld."

"Otherworld?"

"Yes, the Otherworld, a dimension running alongside this one."

"Is that where Castle Dracula is?"

"Yes, it is."

"So, the other day when you said I couldn't find it, you were alluding to this 'world beyond.'"

He nodded. "Now let me answer your question."

"Sure."

"*Dún Dreach-Fhola* roughly translates to the 'Castle of Blood Visage.' It is an imposing, dark crystal fortress in *Ériu,* what you call 'Ireland.' It lies near a desolate pass in *Na Cruacha Dubha*, the Mounts of Black Stacks. Invisible, save only in misty times of the Betwixt and Between. The Lady Edana Sióg Fola, who rarely ventures into this world, has, for countless moons, been its keeper. She is the reigning archon.

"And on that note, I must take my leave and contemplate Edana's next move. For she surely will be enraged at my disloyalty and, at the very least, want this ring back," he said then got up. "I bid you adieu, or, as we say in Hungarian, *szia!*"

"*Szia!*" I replied. And with that, he disappeared into the woods. I clicked "stop" on my lecture recorder and pulled out the prepaid phone.

I did a search on *Dún Dreach-Fhola*. Turns out to be an obscure castle said to be shrouded in mist atop Ireland's highest mountain range. It was supposedly accessible only on Beltane and Samhain, and kept by blood sucking fairies—wonderful. Some theorized Bram Stoker was inspired by this myth and by the *Dearg-Due*, a fair maiden turned blood thirsty. As for the search on *Ruxandra cel Rău*...married royalty, date of birth: 1484. Date of death...in shock, I dropped my phone.

Au revoir :o

Imbas Forosnai

Bölcsem Kertész Naplója, 2025. Október 20

Sleep was heavily upon me when my spirit got caught up in the Otherworld. There before me I beheld the Dragonist's Archon, Edana the Dark Muse, that great *filí* and *Dearg-Due*, coming forth from her chamber, flanked by Balaurian Guards. Her cheeks were drawn, her frame feeble, but her countenance sharpened. Edana Sióg Fola had induced *Imbas Forosnai*, the Druidic seer ritual of old: shut away she had deprived herself of flesh and blood for three days and three nights. Her palms upon her cheeks, lying in respite uttering deep and dark sayings, her groanings had unnerved the very guards outside her chamber door. Now, her senses heightened, those hazel eyes penetrated to my soul. My spirit encompassed by ruddy blond locks, swirling in the misty billows. She sang:

Oh, my Master Scribe
Faithful visage no more
Oh, my Master Scribe
How are you have fallen, fallen
A bright moon amongst the stars
Adorning ties did bind
Oh, you are fallen, fallen
Once hidden amongst the clouds
Cel Rău enraged comes forth
Seeking signet ring and soul
Oh, how you are fallen, fallen
Oh, you are fallen, fallen

I jolted out of slumber, my spirit troubled. *What have I done!?* It was too late to return. Ruxandra cel Rău, like her fathers before her, was not known for mercy. To disobey her was tantamount to one's demise. My only hope, exile on *Hy Breasal*, the Isle of Maidens, where no Dragonist dared venture. Twain glimmering mounds far beyond *An Tiaracht* in the *Tír na nÓg*.

Shrouded in mist, the Isle of Youth elusive to all, save the most cunning seafarer, unreachable 'til the day in a seventh year. There, I could feast on the blood of black rabbits, living long with fair Cleena.

Whose sails were unfurled upon the seventh's time,
Shy Merope steering his way?
Yea, Brave Nisbet of Donegal
Pierced the shroud
His deed in lore had its sway.
Metals precious deep and dark
Showered we upon him,
Hence his lark.
Crave I her distant shores,
Lost in Cleena's locks.
Drunk in her repose
Amidst silver grove so fair.
Laden aureate apples
Doth it bear.

Henge Key

Magnolia's Diary, October 20th of 2025

Dear Diary,

It is the evening of day three of our isolation from the world. For now, I am enjoying this slower pace of life: no TVs, radio, social media...though I kept checking the news on the prepaid.

Darkness fell, a new moon tomorrow...I wonder if that means anything to Bölscem? Does he have a plan for us to escape our pursuers? Again, during the day—I wish I could tolerate the light as well as he—the scribe took leave of us, meandering along the James, said he needed his hesychasm to ruminate over a *geis*. *"Geis"* and "hesychasm," what's he talking about? He's so peculiar. Definitely eccentric—no, I take that back, he's *extremely* eccentric.

I inquired what *"geis"* meant. "Tingling in my ear" was the reply, something about an omen upon *Mag Mell* and how he wished he could withdraw to the caves of Tihany. *What!?* I thought, *What is he saying?* Then he spun about and vanished into the sylvan scape. Ugh!...totally bizarre...then again, am I not peculiar? Scribbling in this journal, pretending my diary is someone I can talk to. Anyway, I digress. Off he went, meandering and musing...we would meet up later down at a sandy riverbank.

Sheltered from the sun, in the Pump House's defunct hydroelectric room, Ben and I played our own version of pick-up-sticks. We fashioned wooden debris into sticks, whittling the ends. Pressing upon the points propped the other end for removal from the pile. Smaller sticks were worth more points. Of course I won most rounds, my delicate fingers and nimbleness no match for the thick and calloused hands of a fireman.

The hydro room was secured from prying eyes. To access, one must cross through the boiler room, barred by a shaft of metal padlocked across a pair of

double planked doors. Above the entry, a colorful mural of the James River Arch Bridge, nestled in a Tudor arch. The boiler's firebox and smokestack were lone gone. Past it, the hydroelectric room. The steam-powered turbine gone too, but scraps of corrugated metal sat in a pile, perhaps part of the generator, and on its north wall, the remains of a large marble-paneled control board.

Beyond it, the largest space and oldest part—the pump room—has a cathedral height ceiling flanked by Tudor windows looking out on the canal. Its northern wall featured three immense penstocks. The rushing water spun turbines, driving the pumps, now looking more like toilet seats. Drinking water navigated to tunnels under the stone walkway. Above all this, a catwalk leading to a pavilion for dancing.

Spent by our games, we ventured into the pump room's cavernous hall, now a place of placid puddles. Then to its catwalk, where Ben reenacted *Notre-Dame de Paris*. Ben pretended to be the hunchback, Quasimodo, and I the beautiful gypsy, Esmeralda. The suspended walkway was enjoyed by visitors and dancers alike. In its heyday, many wanted to see the grand aquatic operation. People would dance on the planked floor above, the pump house pavilion, with its open-aired, arched porch overlooking the creek on one side, and the shipping canal on the other.

There, Ben and I danced while I hummed an Irish ballad, *Cití Na gCumann.* The lover of the song desired to whisk her away to an enchanted glen, a wood of delicate flowers. Ben's steady hands glided me under serenaded starlight as I imagined we were at a postbellum ball. There, in the serene night, immersed in the sound of rushing water over a canal lock, we brushed lips then more of our shapes.... Oh, it was memorable; it was magical.

Later, we met Bölscem down at one of several sandy banks called Texas Beach, so named since it is accessed by Texas Avenue. Around a crackling fire we shared a rabbit he'd caught, both its flesh and blood, carefully drained into a cup before roasting. Though it was delicious, I felt bad for the cutesy little critter :(

As Ben's fire died down to embers and the river's rapids became a more distant hum than a melody in our ears, the conversation petered from light topics, such as railroad tales and Richmond history, to a continuation of Bölscem's tall tales. I secretly hit the record button as I had the night before, when I sensed the mystic monk was about to ramble on. Here, my dear Diary, I put down these tales to your parchment regarding the Society of the Dragonists. . .

"In the 1920s," began Bölscem, "a looming insecurity amongst both the Dragonists and Fomorians grew to a state of alarm, for modern man, we sensed, would soon discover us and ultimately wipe us out. Both races were appalled and terrified of the madness of Mankind in World War I, the first truly mechanized and chemically weaponized conflict. We were particularly shocked by the destruction of nature, for which vampires rely on its wildlife for blood and Fomorians for its shelter and rejuvenation. Never before on such a scale had man scorched Mother Earth. He poisoned the land and air of continental Europe using mustard gas and chlorine-phosgene to name a few. Also, the recent discoveries in science began to knock upon our Otherworld doors: Marie Curie's findings on radiation, Stark's electric fields, Einstein's photoelectric effect, and Bohr's work on atomic structure...all of it, concerned us greatly. Ruxandra, at the time being head archon, and who was more involved in men's affairs than most in our order, formed a fragile alliance with the Fomorians. We agreed to pool our resources together to find lost antediluvian artifacts of our ancestors. We did so in hopes such discoveries would solidify our hold in the Otherworld and maintain our anonymity on this planet."

"Whoa there, friar. That's a lot of rambling. Those fellas named Bohr and Stark? I have heard of Marie Curie, I do know some things, but 'antediluvian?' What's—" said Ben.

"Friar! Bölscem, if I were you, I'd call him 'Fireman Sam.'"

Bölscem looked at me sideways and said, "Who's Sam?"

"It's a cartoon character out of the UK," I laughed.

"Very well. Now, Fireman Sam, 'antediluvian' means 'events *before* the Great Flood.' When I say, 'flood,' I mean the one in the days of Noah."

"Oh, gotcha. So you found ancient relics?" said Mosby.

"Yes, I will get to that...may I continue?"

"You're alright, friar. Go ahead," chuckled Ben, tossing a broken branch onto the fire.

Bölscem continued. "Most of our exploits produced little fruit until our joint expedition into the dense jungles of the Yucatán Peninsula changed everything. Based on written accounts of the Bishop of Chiapas, among other esoteric texts, we began excavations of pre-Colombian structures and temples, some in the land of *Anáhuac*, especially along the *Río Usumacinta*."

"Where's that?" Ben piped.

"The river runs through present day Mexico and Guatemala," said the scribe.

"Fascinating! Do go on," said I, locking my arm around Ben's.

"Guided by our new found friendship with Chorti, an indigenous vampire commanding jungle and earth, the Dragonists, in league with Brannbjørn and his followers, descended into the depths of an ancient labyrinth. Later, Chorti would ascend to the Archon Council, replacing an Estrie whose long, unbound hair was the cause of her eventual demise in a Votanian boobytrap, but I digress."

"Ho, I remember him. He's that hairy fella with backwards feet. Wasn't he the

egg who brought me up without a shovel?" asked Ben.

"Yes, he is the one," Bölscem replied.

"Yeah, I read that too—yesterday, from the *Dispatch*, how they found your coffin but no shovel marks. It has set the whole town in a frenzy," I said.

"That's me! I set a town ablaze," quipped Ben, grinning.

"Hah, haha..." I remarked. "So, Bölscem, you mentioned...umm, was it 'Votanian,' you said?"

"His name was Votan. Brannbjørn believed he descended from the Fomorians. He was probably a Nephilim by nature, considered godlike. He ruled the Na Chan kingdom, the people of the Serpent. They pre-dated the Mayans.

"In short, we unearthed Votan's knowledge held deep within the earth of the Yucatán. It was good fortune, in retrospect, if we had tarried the great archaeologist, Sylvanus G. Morley, might have first discovered a Hall of Records."

"Hall of Records?" I queried. "Do you mean *the* Hall of Records? The records Edgar Cayce foretold?"

"The very same. The Sleeping Prophet also spoke of another, one buried beneath the Sphinx and one in Atlantis. If the elite amongst mankind have not found the other Records yet, it will only be a matter of time until they do so."

"Either what you're saying is meat & potatoes, or it's pure applesauce," piped in Mosby. "There's no coleslaw with you, Bölscem."

"Ah...'coleslaw?' I gather not your meaning, but, as you said, 'applesauce?' Nay, my dear Mosby, but it is, indeed, steak and frites."

"Go on," I said, giving Mosby a disapproving look.

"Well, the Hall of Records had been held dormant, deep in the nadir of the Labyrinth of Yaxchilán. What later was named the famed 'House of Darkness.' Supposedly it was built by the great Votan. Under Chorti's guidance, the wizardry of Ruxandra and Edana, and the mining efforts of Brannbjørn and his clan, great slabs and boulders were removed which blocked the passageways of that forbidden House. Many died in our excavations—cave ins, boobytraps, nefarious encounters; others went mad."

"What did you find?" I inquired.

"A sealed chamber of selenite crystal. Walls eighteen cubits high by twenty seven cubits long, containing a plethora of artifacts, otherworldly elements, scrolls, stone tablets—"

"Artifacts!? Such as?" interjected Ben, now more engaged.

"Such as a henge key," he said. Then he reached into his leather pouch and held up a bluish gray crystal glittering and glowing in the firelight. "It is a portaling device."

"Bee's knees!" burst out Mosby.

"I'll say," said I. "That's so cool."

Its shape was a tetrahedron but with convex faces instead of triangular. Three sides had varying patterns of triskelions, the fourth was smooth. "What's it made of?"

"To put it simply, it is a unique quartz crystal possessing piezoelectric qualities."

"Uhh, okey dokey then," said Ben.

"How's it work?" I asked.

Bölscem declared, "Pretend this fire ring's border stone is part of an ancient circle. Hold the key like this." He held the crystal henge key with the smooth side upon his palm. "Place it so," he rested one of the convex knobs onto a concave area of a boundary stone. "Notice the key's knob fits into a henge's concave notch. Exert pressure and it will trigger a swirling gateway; a portal, if you will. Then you simply walk through it to the other side. Of course, you have to be a 'channeled being' for this to work."

"Wha'...? Channeled being? Translation," I said.

Bölscem sighed and elaborated, "You, Ben, and I, we are channeled beings. Our spiritual bodies are open to receive the 'waters,' so to speak, of the

Otherworld the ancients called 'Tír na nÓg.' Our channels are open; they are not blocked. Most humans' channels are blocked. By channels, think electromagnetic forces, biophotons...but that's just the physical layer. Their manifestations can be measured to some extent by the scientific method. But there are other forces...those forces, too, need to be flowing. The henge key is a wonderful conductor of these forces flowing through us. The piezoelectric effect emanates from us when we apply pressure on the crystal, which, in turn, conducts the forces and vibration of our being."

"Wowzer!"

"Ah...'wowzer,' Magnolia?" bemused Bölscem.

"It's a 21st century expression, and please call me Maggie. What does it vibrate at?"

"Well, henge key in place, your feet on the ground, you begin to vibrate at one hundred-ten megahertz, Earth's frequency, then it progresses up an octave."

"What else did you find down there?"

"Well, Maggie, it was extensive. All descriptions of the relics were recorded by William Pool in a registry called, *The Records of Yaxchilán*. Among the artifacts were star maps, Enochian scrolls of magick, and powerful objects too—the Sun Disk of Aramu Muru—now hidden deep within the vault of *Dún Dreach-Fhola*, a great number of precious items, that is, with the exception of the key *Ben* has in his pocket."

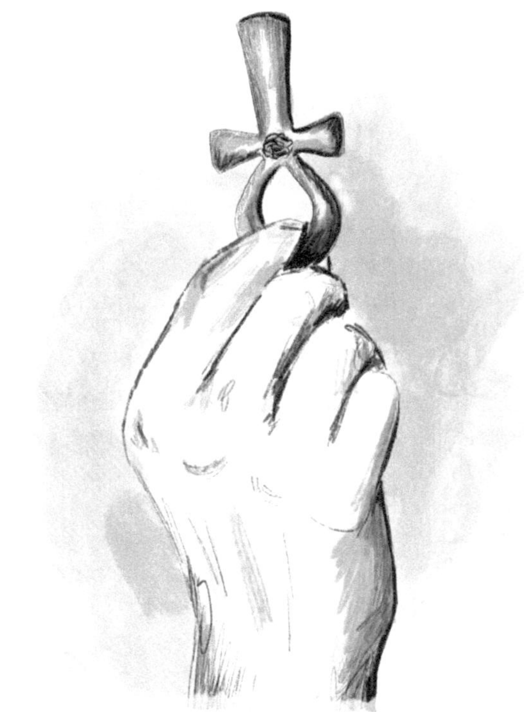

"How'd you know?" exclaimed Ben, producing a golden copper-looking ankh from his inside coat pocket. It had ruby quartz petals forming a rose at its center.

"Why else would you return to Pool's mausoleum? You figured there must be a niche in its chamber that this key fits, and you would be right."

"Hmm, you didn't tell me about this key..." I glared at Ben then looked over at Bölscem, saying, "What's it made of?"

"The ankh is orichalcum and

the petals are rose quartz."

"Orichalcum? Never heard of it..." said I.

"Suffice it to say it is an ancient alloy," stated Bölscem.

"Let's use it—high ball it outta here!" said Ben.

"High ball it?" I quizzically looked at Ben, "What's high—"

"Train talk. Back in the day, near the tracks, spheres on poles were raised and lowered telling engineers how fast to go."

"Interesting," I commented.

"Tomorrow is a new moon," said Bölscem, peering at Ben. Then he turned his gaze to the fire. "Ruxandra will return; with whom, I know not." He poked at the fire. "But before nightfall, we must leave through the portal. She will come for the Johns' fellow," stabbing a stick at other embers, "then she will come for us." With that, he snapped the stick and tossed it in the fire.

"How do you know all this?" I asked.

Bölscem smirked, gazing into the flames. "I have seen it in a vision."

"Is Charles Johns the caboose in the vengeance train?"

"Hmm. I see Ben has got you up to speed. But it's less to do with what Andromalius wants, and more to do with attaining Collette's soul. Do not let Ruxandra's ideas of justice be in any way admirable in your mind."

"Who's Andromalius?"

"An archdemon. Every city has a demon presiding over it. For Richmond, it was Choíros, until Andromalius intervened. With the death of Collette, he asserted himself. Perhaps for him, it was an opportunity to advance in that kingdom. Collette was born a hybrid: half human, half vampire. Her soul caught between two worlds, that of Hades and that of the Otherworld. We have her body, but Andromalius will not release her spirit to us, until we do his bidding."

"My family was part of that bidding?"

"Yes, unfortunately."

The flames receded; only embers cast faint shadows upon our visages. Moments later a morning ray pierced the horizon then bright beams fanned out between the tree limbs. "And now, a hundred years later, this Charles Johns is on the chopping block?"

"Exactly. He is a descendant of C. W. Johns. The one who signed off on widening the Church Hill Tunnel. He was the chief engineer for the Chesapeake & Ohio here in Richmond. If a bloodline bears a transgression, and a man has not succored the cover of grace, Hell can lay claim out to the fourth generation."

With such talk, Ben didn't want to hear any more. He stood up in disgust and went over to the river and began skipping rocks. Bölscem and I sat silently for a span, except for my occasional humming.

Soon haze blanketed the horizon bestowing on us tranquil moments before the sun's rays had their full effect. Then, in an instant, with a sunbeam piercing through the forest canopy, the calm was broken when we heard rustling in the forest.

"Do you hear people?" said I.

"I do, from over there," replied Bölscem. We turned looking up river. From the next sandy bank, an older black man approached. He was wearing a brown jumpsuit and walked with a white couple: the man had on a dark wetsuit, the woman, holding a towel.

We remained still. The older forged waist deep into the river, then the young man followed. They conversed a bit while the woman observed. Over the sound of the James, I could make out a few words: "cleansing...savior...new."

Then the older man held the younger, who was pinching his nose. It was a baptism.

Just then, my Diary, the waters about them became as blood. I let out a gasp. Bölscem and Benjamin's eyes got huge, their mouths gaped. The other party didn't notice what we beheld. Then the reverend immersed the younger, and raised him up out of troubled waters. The man rejoiced, lifting his hands, and the woman clapped and hollered. Meanwhile, the minister caught sight of us through the trees. He said nothing, just smiled as though he knew we would be there.

By and by, the reverend came to our camp. Bölscem stood up. The fire crackled one last time, the river rumbled, the sun cast a beam upon him.
He gazed upon us and uttered:

In the land of Idumea, nettles and brambles amidst thorns shall be in the fortresses thereof: and it shall be an habitation of dragons, and a court for owls. Wild beasts of desert and isle shall also meet, and the satyr shall cry to his fellow; the screech owl also shall rest there, and find for herself a place of rest. His hand hath divided it unto them by line: they shall possess it forever, from generation to generation shall they dwell therein[6]

At that, and without another word, he turned and walked away into the woods. Neither Bölscem nor Benjamin uttered a word. The scribe's eyes narrowed, his lips pursed.

"What in the world was that!?" I exclaimed.

“That, my dear Maggie, was a prophetic utterance. Idumea is for us at the End of Days. That blood you saw is blood for humans, not blood for our kind. We made our choice. Now, we must leave, for day breaks upon us! As Ben said, ‘Let's high ball it out of here!’”

With the scribe’s interpretation, my heart had other questions, but my mind could not put them into words. And with that, we embarked upon a most peculiar journey.

Au revoir :-o

Portaling

Magnolia's Diary, October 21th of 2025

Dear Diary,

As we returned from a night on Texas Beach to a new day, we were met with piercing beams upon our pale skin. So we quickened our pace through the underbrush surrounding the beach toward the railroad tracks. To cross above the tracks, we bounded up the steel and concrete stairway to a foot bridge, then halfway across the narrow truss (its sides wrapped in a diamond-shaped mesh) we bypassed a hiker. He did a double take at the sight of me. I guess he'd seen my mug in a newsfeed.

He turned around and shouted, "Hey, aren't you the chick who ditched her wheelchair?"

We came to a halt at the tail end of the bridge. "Umm—" is all that came out of my mouth.

In a flash Bölscem sprinted toward him. The hiker bolted for the stairs. I pleaded, "Leave 'em alone!"

Before the man could finish the second flight of stairs, Bölscem had pounced upon him. I heard thrashing and banging sounds, then silence. A minute or two later Bölscem sauntered across the bridge, wiping his lips with a handkerchief.

With my hands on hips, I asked, "Was that really necessary?"

"Indeed. I was famished." He grinned from ear to ear. "Besides, we couldn't take the risk of him alerting the law."

"Did you kill 'em?" snapped Ben.

"Noo. He'll come to, after a while. Now enough talk, we must make haste," he replied as a train below us cruised by. "I have a plan to get us out of Richmond, to a safe adobe, through the portal at Pool's crypt. It will buy us some time to figure out our next move."

"Fine," said Mosby, "I'm sick of sleepin' in a crate."

So, we trekked the North Bank Trail eastward. When the path meandered just below the cemetery's lookout at Waterview Avenue, we passed a jogger who, evidently, didn't recognize us, luckily for him. Once out of his sight, we ducked through the breach in the cemetery's fence Mosby had made days before. We continued to move fast, for Ben's and my skin was searing.

In the early morning light, we sprinted down Westvale Avenue toward Pool's mausoleum. Not a car to be seen; Hollywood cemetery had not yet opened. However, Bölscem spied Morrigan just ahead, who cawed an alert. Then, cut from behind obelisks, tombstones, and other mausoleums charged Mávros' pack to exact revenge for their fallen alpha.

Two beasts engaged us while the others growled. Mosby held them off, swatting them away while Bölscem unlocked the iron lattice door to Pool's mausoleum. He shut the door behind us not one moment before gnashing teeth and claws sank into our flesh.

Bölscem looked at Ben and ordered, "Give me the ankh!"

Ben handed him the ankh key and he inserted the rod part into an oval notch in the chamber wall. Then he said, "Here, take my hand, and Maggie, take Ben's hand. Hold on, do not let go!" With the other hand he held onto the key's teardrop loop. I thought to myself, *This is nuts! It's just a wall!*

But to my amazement, Bölscem's body began to vibrate, creating a chain reaction through Ben and then through me. A few seconds later a low humming sound started, then it went up like an octave making me forget about the growling dogs. I stared at the wall. Still nothing. Yet the humming and vibration continued to rise. Then, at first I couldn't believe what I was seeing: a tiny swirling, electric blue shaft emerged in the chamber wall. *This is off the chain!* Incredibly, the spiral got bigger and bigger, until it formed a tunnel large enough for us to go through. *This is so freakin' cool,* I thought. Next, Bölscem stepped into it; I saw his foot disappear into the vortex, followed by his torso. *Was this really happening?* He pulled Ben through and I followed suit. We vanished from Richmond...to who knows where.

I looked back. All I could see was a faint black speck from whence we had entered, but only briefly. I felt like an untethered kite pushed by the wind through a blue whirling wormhole. Dizziness, vertigo overcame me. *I'm gonna puke.* Up ahead, I perceived a misty gray opening. I strained to keep my grip upon Mosby

as Bölscem exited the blue vortex. He pulled Ben through, but in doing so Ben stumbled and lost his grip upon me. I drifted backwards as though the wind had changed. Then a firm hand grabbed hold of me.

"I told you not to let go," admonished the scribe, still holding my wrist. He steadied me as I couldn't maintain my footing and midway into catching my breath I puked. Ah, gross! Ben gave me his hanky to wipe off the excess. Then, my eyes adjusted. I squinted before the afternoon sun and a strong wind. I looked down relieved to feel the ground under my feet, albeit muddy grass. *At least I've got my boots on.*

"It was my fault," admitted Ben, still gaining his balance.

"All considered, not bad you two for your first portaling," quipped Bölscem then chuckled a tad.

Ben and I didn't say a word, just glaring at him. Needless to say, I was slightly pissed at the friar.

However, my agitation was quickly replaced by wonderment at the site around me. We were encircled by great monolithic stones. I gingerly placed my hands upon the great standing rock we had come out of, just to make sure I wasn't dreaming.

It was split, except at its base. Surveying the rugged treeless landscape, lochs and great stones were the prominent features. In the distance, you could make out expansive hills gradually merging with the flatlands. The air was brisk, cleaner than back home. Ben and I knew we were no longer in America, but some far off magical land. The ground was replete with puddles; here and there tufts of grass and moss.

On the opposite side of the circle, I noticed a few people; some had cameras around their necks, others with smartphones, a few with sunglasses on, all wearing coats or windbreakers. Tourists, no doubt. They looked dumbfounded on account of our supernatural arrival. An elderly woman gasped at us shouting, "How did you do that?"

Bölscem ignored her gesturing to us. "Welcome to the Ring of Brodgar." He patted the exit stone, "This is the Split Stone. Now we must go to the next gateway. Follow me." Bölscem strutted toward the center, oblivious to the gawking tourists. Ben and I followed, taking in the scene.

Ben said, "Where are we?"

"Orkney, Scotland," blurted Bölscem.

"Bees knees! Never been overseas."

"Oh, now you're a poet," I quipped; he smiled at me.

"These stone things sure beat train travel," he continued.

"Come, we must hurry," exclaimed Bölscem. "Spies as familiars patrol here!"

We crossed the circular field over to another great stone with a triangular tip.

We stopped in front of it. Bölscem ensured three rose quartz petals upon the ankh were depressed then placed the key in a notch.

"Grab hands!"

As before, we began to vibrate, then the stone. I could feel and hear a hum. The earth trembled beneath our feet. The thrum went up an octave and, just as before, the bluish electric vortex opened up within this edifice.

A young man stood nearby, undaunted by our exploits. Other onlookers steadied themselves against the stones, fearing the tremor would open up the ground underneath them. They remained afar, transfixed, as they witnessed a bright light emanate from a monolith and three beings disappear into it.

Just as I entered, I looked back over my shoulder to see a young guy running forward. He cried, "Wait, I'm coming!"

He entered, but immediately doubled over, clutching his head, his speech slurred. He quickly became a speck. I never saw him again.

For a few seconds we were smoothly drawn through the swirling tunnel, all around us layers of spiraling ripples of dynamic electromagnetic light. Sonic whooshing and crackling permeated the space. Words fail to describe the phenomenon. A few clips later the silky ride abated and it felt more like being sucked up by a UFO tractor beam. Nausea hit me hard. Struggling to hold Ben's hand, I fixed my gaze forward to maintain what little equilibrium I had left. I caught sight of an elongated speck in the distance. Staying focused on the speck saved me. Soon it became a narrow grayish slit, about six feet in height. My motivation to hold on renewed.

Bölscem squeezed sideways through the vortex's narrow exit. Ben and I did likewise. *We'd made it! What a relief!*

Immediately, we were met with a rush of warm air; a stark contrast to the wispy brisk weather of Orkney. Above, a starlit sky smiled down upon us. In front of us, no surprise, another stone circle, though much smaller in diameter than the Ring of Brodgar.

The stones were shorter and narrower, some fallen, most careening forward into the center, others gone or reduced in height. Looking back, we had materialized from the tallest one. I wondered why the latter leg of our ride here ("ride," for lack of a better description), was more turbulent than our first portal journey. I think it had something to do with this destination not having all its stones.

No one spoke as we were all gathering ourselves. Ben and I propped up against a stone till the vertigo passed. *At least I had nothing more to up-chuck. LOL!*

Bölscem grinned and said, “A seldom used passage.” Of course, neither Ben nor I were amused by this comment. I must admit slapping him came to mind.

Once stable, I thoroughly surveyed the grounds—thanks in no small part to vampiric night vision. This time, no tufts of grass and puddles; the ground was

dry, essentially a meadow surrounded by a spindly iron fence. Fortunately, there was no one around and little sign of foot traffic. Visitors must be a rare occurrence, since no tourist parking lot existed. Beyond the megalith circle were crops, and past that, a mosque. Overall, not what one would expect to find at such an ancient site.

“Where are we?” I asked.

Bölscem turned to us and said, “Welcome to northern Pakistan. The portal here is called the Asota Henge. No Dragonist travels here.”

“Yeah, I can see why,” I quipped.

“Come, we will find food and shelter with an old friend of mine.”

We began following him down a dirt road. I had taken only a few steps when the monk abruptly spun about and said, “Allow me.” Without another word, he took my scarf and fashioned it around my head. “There, you are covered well,” he beamed and then began jaunting away. “We tread upon Islamic land.”

“Who’s Islamic?” Ben asked.

“It’s a religion, Ben, not a person,” I corrected.

“Oh, sorry.”

Soon we were walking through farmland. No street lights just trees lined on one side, crops the other. The stench of livestock reached my nose. *I don't think we're gonna find a Chick-fil-A around here.* Up in the distance I could see a block style building. It was shabby. As we got closer, I could make out a gray walled structure with a flat roof. The wooden door was light blue in color, and in the window candles illuminated the stoic interior.

Bölscem tapped on the wooden door three times, a beat held between each knock, then the door opened. An elderly man with a long beard and blue turban stood silhouetted by the lumens.

"*Sat Sri Akal,*" said Bölscem, forming his hands in prayer.

"*Sat Sri Akal,*" said the grey-bearded man. "*Khush aamdeed.*" He gestured with his hands out toward the living area.

"My companions do not speak Urdu."

"*Koi baat nahi.*" He smiled, looking at Ben and I. "I am Budhjot. Welcome! Your name, good sir?"

"Ben. Benjamin Mosby."

He then turned to me, smiling. *His aura's balanced and peaceful*, I perceived to myself.

"Hello, I am Magnolia. I like your metal bracelet."

"Ah, thank you. Your skin, magnolia's petals, your eyes its leaves."

"Why...thank you. Sir."

"Sit, sit," he motioned to us. We sat on flat cushions upon an ornate rug. "Tea?"

"Yes, please," I replied.

He poured us tea. It was refreshing and fragrant with spices—definitely one of which was cardamom. We made small talk. He asked us where we were from, why we were here...then he said, "You must be hungry. Come, Bölscem! Let us prepare a meal."

At that, they got up and went outside to a clay oven surrounded by brick work surfaces. As they chatted quietly, Bölscem shaped dough into balls.

Ben said, "What's with the turban and that curved dagger? And, ah...the pajamas?"

"He's a Sikh. They believe in one god, in defending themselves, and in living a simplistic life."

"Oh, I thought maybe he was a genie."

I chuckled, "Why yes! Do you have a wish?"

"Yeah, take me back to Richmond."

"Hmm, a few problems with that, namely ravenous familiars, oh, and the FBI, jail, not to mention they'll dissect us and record the results in some x-file."

"*X-files*, I did see that show."

"How?"

"Whataya think I was doing while at Collette's shack? I watched a buncha shows on her picture radio."

"Huh-ha! 'Picture radio,' I love it! It's called a TV, a television. But, yeah, cool show."

"Weird, but I kept watching."

"Oh, and another problem: that Ruxandra chick, she wants to impale us!"

"I gotta stop her. Ain't no way a copper or some snooper's pea-shooter is gonna do it. Who's the doughboy she's after anyway?"

"It's um, well, it's Charles..."

"Yep, Johns...Charles Johns."

"Ben, are you sure?"

"'Course I'm sure. That guy's done nothing wrong. Well, maybe he has, but he can't be held to something that happened a hundred years ago."

"True..."

Ben drank some tea and looked about at the decor. "What's this country?"

"It's Pakistan."

"Oh. That near India? Wasn't around in my day."

"This *used* to be India...then the Muslims wanted their own land, so here it is."

"I see. Now it makes sense...the smell in this house reminded me of an exotic spice store on Broad Street. In the 20s, Broad was swell. You could get things from all over, including India. Anyways, Maggie, this place is too foreign for me. I don't even know what time it is," he murmured, glancing at his Elgin pocket watch. "Besides, I wanna find the reverend who was baptizing over in the river... maybe that blood'll change our blood?"

"Maybe, Ben. I'm sorry I haven't said this before, but I'm grateful for what you did."

"'Twas nothin'. Stop, will ya?"

"No, let me finish," I said, sipping some tea to wet my throat. "I'm still alive, and, and I don't need a wheelchair anymore. But at the same time, I'm not too crazy about drinking blood for the rest of my life."

"You and me both."

I took another sip and said, "We can't go back without Bölscem. Look, he knows how to deal with Ruxandra and crew, and this stone hopping business—guess I'll call it 'portaling.' Besides, it freaks me out. Without Bölscem we'd probably get stuck in a wormhole, or get lost somewhere in the netherworld."

"Otherworld," Ben corrected.

"So, you were listening."

"I'm on it," he grinned. "Hey, you're recording our jabbering on that tiny box of yours, aren't you?"

"Noo!"

"Liar."

I reached into my clutch purse and hit the *stop* button; I felt myself blush.

The old man and Bölscem returned, placing dishes on a burlap mat over the area rug.

Before us were entrées in metal bowls: Chana dal, split pea curry garnished with cumin; Channa Chaat, chickpeas with vegetables and Aloo Keema, minced meat and potato curry. Budhjot showed us how to use the round flatbread, called roti, to pick up the main dishes.

I began eating with my left hand, then Bölscem grasped my hand saying, "Don't!"

"But I'm left-handed."

"Not here you're not. In this country, the left hand is for... other things."

"Oh!"

Afterwards, Budhjot told us enchanting stories about the Asota stones, stupa-shaped craft, and people from the sky. Ben was bemused. He decided to bring the conversation back to earth and asked what Budhjot did for work. The Sikh replied he was a tenant farmer and a keeper of the stones.

Bölscem told us that at one time, every henge had an overseer. They presided over the stones, cleared out debris, chased off marauders, wild animals and such. But now, few caretakers exist, so portaling can be precarious, especially since many sites are now tourist attractions. Hence little traveling is conducted during daylight hours.

As the evening drew on, we sat outside, cross-legged around a fire pit sheltered by a canopy of stars. We shared stories. While Bölscem nicked fringes of paper, he explained fact versus fiction regarding his former master, Count Dracula. He spoke of Dr. Van Helsing, whose real name was Dr. Albert Willem van Renterghem, a pioneering Dutch psychiatrist known for his hypnotic therapies. In passing he stated, this, and the location of Dracul Castle, were made public by the Dutch researcher Hans Corneel de Roos. Fortunately, when the Dutchman and Dacre Stoker, a descendant of Bram Stoker, visited *Montură Izvorul*, they were unaware, much to the relief of Dragonists, of the natural feature which unlocks the passage to its imposing gate. When I inquired about the feature's description, Bölscem abruptly changed the subject to a broader discussion of

trespassers. Interlopers were, and continue to be an ongoing challenge for the Dragonist Order. Of note, Edana has dealt with troublesome explorers before such as W. B. Yeats and folklorist, Seán Ó Súilleabháin. Like Edana and her lair, so too has Ruxandra grappled with what measures she might take if someone traverses the Romanian lair.

Ben asked after John and Mina Harker; he fared worse than I, in that the scribe had lost the desire for such talk and declined to address that subject. *Crap! I had a thing for Mr. Harker.* Instead, a spell of music made for a perfect evening. So, Bölscem and the gray breaded Sikh played hypnotic melodies together. Budhjot plucked a lute-like musical instrument called a Rubab.

It reminded me of a banjo, but more exotic in tone. As usual, Bölscem played his recorder. However, Ben stole the show doing his best to tap away on a dholak, a two-headed hand drum.

Around midnight the Sikh went off to bed.

At that, Bölscem laid out his plans to leave Pakistan and aid us in starting a new life elsewhere. At first, to my surprise, Ben said nothing, but heard him out. Bölscem continued saying a particular Asota stone would convey us to a new place, a place called—and I might butcher the spelling—Galkanumandiya. Galkanumandiya Ruins in Sri Lanka. There, he felt, like Pakistan, it was off the grid from the authorities and the Dragonists, but its culture would be easier for us to blend in with than staying in Pakistan.

Finally, Ben had heard enough. He told Bölscem in no uncertain terms he was heading back to Richmond, to do what he'd been awakened to do. The River City was his home, and he owed justice to Richard and the other laborers, and to prevent a cave in by persuading Charles Johns to do something about it. Bölscem looked to me for my opinion. I told him it was a crazy plan but I agreed with Ben. Something had to be done, even if it meant we might not make it out alive. Then he rambled on for a bit trying to talk us out of it. No such luck, we stood our ground. Finally, the monk gave up and was resigned to our decision. Shockingly, he even promised he would help us.

Why he agreed, he never said. Perhaps he felt *bad* for what had happened to Ben, and to me, and his involvement in our life altering occurrences. Perhaps bad isn't the word, dare I say it—guilty might be a better choice—and if so, was this his way of paying amends to us? I could only assume. One thing was certain, he was vocal in his agreement with Ben and me: Mr. Johns didn't deserve to die nor did my family members. For all of Bölscem's ramblings and verbose pontifications, when he felt convicted about something, he was a man of action giving little-to-no explanation.

I confessed I had puny faith we'd stop the murder of Charles Johns. Besides, it was probably too late, given the new moon was underway and by now Ruxandra and her minions were already in Richmond. "Who knows?" I said. "By now Charles may be dead, or worse, impaled upon a pole in her castle courtyard."

But Bölscem corrected me; we were in the future. He made clear we were several hours ahead here, and that it was still yesterday in Richmond. Time was on our side; the Dragonists would not dare arrive through Pool's portal during daylight. But we would have to go back soon if there was any hope of saving Mr. Johns' skin.

To save time, Ben asked if one of the Asota stones could take us directly home. Bölscem replied it was not possible. He explained we had to return the way we came. *Ugh! I was not looking forward to such a trip. The vertigo...the bumpy ride...the tourists at the Ring of Brodgar, entering in and out of monolithic stones.* There, at Orkney, he advised, we might encounter familiars, too, for Brodgar was watched, as it served as a hub for portals all over the planet.

"Why a hub?" I asked.

Bölscem explained Brodgar's infrastructure was dependable. Most of the monoliths were mainly intact, and it still had a surrounding ditch, which aided in the conductivity of manifested vortexes. These factors, plus the fact that the Ring was situated on a major geodesic line, made it a reliable and safe henge hub, especially for usage at night, when no visitors were about.

He discerned my bemused look when he mentioned the term "geodesic line." He expounded that portals were along ley lines, part of a geomagnetic network encircling the Earth. This network, the Dragonists called "the Serpent Web." This web had existed for millennia, however, the Order had expanded it. Dragonists adept at the craft had formed new serpentine channels to monoliths, such as when Ruxandra bound the Split Stone to Pool's mausoleum. Part of the Serpent Web was beyond terrestrial, gateways existing in space, such as one recorded on a Yaxchilán tablet said to be between Earth and the Sun. A kind of interstellar Jacob's Ladder, traversed by demons and angels since time immemorial. Enoch, in his prophetic book, spoke of such portals. He himself traversed such gateways on more than one occasion. Recently, humans had discovered it, most notably, the distinguished physicist, Jack Scudder. At this, Bölscem opened to a sketch in his journal depicting a portal the Dragonists had found on a tablet in the House of Darkness.

"Interesting sketch, but don't we need to go?" I implored the scribe. He just nodded.

Soon after, under the cover of night, we bid adieu to Budhjot and began our journey back towards Richmond. As we walked the dusty road toward the Asota Henge, I could not help but think about what would happen next; Covach would arrest us then take us somewhere to be dissected. Or perhaps worse, we'd end up in some kind of Area 51 lab living out our days in a gigantic test tube of plasma, being poked and prodded at.

All that got me thinking about Bölscem's alternate plan: the wonderful beaches and balmy weather in Sri Lanka. Maybe it wasn't such a bad idea...a life o exile. But I knew, well, right now anyway, I just couldn't live there and, surprisingly, I was finding myself feeling that I couldn't live without Ben.

Oh, dear Diary, I kept those thoughts to myself.

We entered the tallest Asota monolith then, after a turbulent journey, we arrived the day before we'd left, in Orkney's Ring of Brodgar. There it was already dark, a few hours before midnight, so no astonished tourists to deal with. However, as we jaunted towards the Split Stone, Bölscem spotted a famiiar, explaining it was a black shag, standing watch on a visage-shaped monolith called the Head Stone. With no moonlight, its glowing red eyes were amplified all the more. It let out terrifying screeches and grunts, carried far by the wind.

From behind monoliths opposite us, appeared dark figures, their hooded black robes snapping in the wind. Amidst their cloaks my eye caught glimmers of armor. There were three led by a fourth who stood taller. He shouted. "Ho! Better than Fomorians, Bölscem and his merry band."

"Let us pass, Sophar," demanded Bölscem, motioning Ben and I to stay behind him. He spread his fingers, his hands began swirling at his sides.

"Time to die, scribe," declared Sophar. He drew an Egyptian style sword from his scabbard, as those behind him drew curved swords. Bölscem uttered indiscernible words, hands still twisting. The air became stale, warmer and drier; an eerie stillness pervaded. The shag held its peace.

Stare downs and flaring of fangs from both sides filled a few moments of tense silence. Sophar raised his sword, then the three. In an instant the ground trembled under their charge. Bölscem held his ground. Ben and I backpedaled. Sophar was at the Ring's center when Bölscem, still uttering, moved his left foot forward and, just as he hurled his hands before him, a great wind slammed

Ben and I face first into the ground. Peering upward, I saw that the scribe was wrapped in his long coat rooted to the earth. Armor clattering, the shag screeching, I witnessed Sophar and his vampiric escort doing tumbleweed rolls. The bird was nowhere to be seen.

As this was happening, a swirling shaft of blue light was emanating from the Head Stone. Out stepped a copper-skinned man, jet black hair, donned in black leather, his hand grasping a taller man, similarly dressed, though more vintage, with a wide brimmed hat.

Ben stood up and said, "These boys are mine!"

Before Bölscem could say a word, Ben darted at them. So swift was he, the copper-skinned man had no time to avoid the barreling fireman. Ben dashed him against the great stone. The taller one, shoulder length, ruddy hair and a blood splotched face, sidestepped the freight train, and in one motion chiseled his talon-like nails into the back of Ben's neck. Blood spattered upon stone and grass. Ben cried out, stumbled forward, and landed face first in the mud.
The towering figure reached down to grasp Ben's neck, but just as he was about to tear his head off, Bölscem swept the tempest upon him, pressing him up against the Head Stone, his hat sailing into the ditch.

"Traitor!" he hollered.

"Grzegorz! Return to your frigid hell!"

Grzegorz righted himself. Seemingly out of nowhere, a ball of sludge whacked him in the eyes. Blinded, Grzegorz stepped awkwardly into a puddle, turning his ankle. Ben pitched a perfect strike. He seized Grzegorz's head in both hands and dashed it against the monolith. Grzegorz went limp, sliding down the Head Stone, and slumped over in a tuft of grass.

Bölscem sped toward the Split Stone. "Make haste you two!"

Ben and I caught up with the scribe. With one hand, Bölscem inserted the ankh key into the notch, while his other hand opened for me to grasp. I took hold.

Just as Ben grabbed my other hand I heard a *thud* then Ben wailing. A crossbow dart had penetrated his back.

"Don't let go of him!" ordered Bölscem. The vortex blossomed about the notch. Vibrations...wailings...gusts...shag taking flight; banshee screeches mixed with the howling wind. We vanished.

Au revoir :o

Return to Richmond

Bölcsem Kertész Naplója, 2025. október 21

Ben's lower back was black and blue. He grimaced while I removed the Balaurian dart. I was amazed these two had survived the skirmish at Brodgar. Though Ben was worse for wear, it was far better than dead.

We were confined to Pool's musty mausoleum chamber until the sun abated and the voices of visitors diminished. Thankfully no one peered through the lattice gate. An occasional car drove down Westvale Avenue, but none stopped. Perhaps they were taking the road up the hill to see Mosby's empty grave.

"He's hot," said Maggie, her hand upon Ben's forehead. "Why isn't he healing?"

"The soldier's dart was dipped in *verbena officinalis*," I explained.

"Translation, please?" said Maggie.

I looked at Ben and whispered, "Keep quiet now." Ben slumped into a corner and ceased groaning. "Vervain," I replied, "is a medicinal herb to humans, but a toxin to vampires." I rummaged through my pouch.

Maggie picked up the bolt and sniffed its tip. "Hmm, citrus...will he die?"

"No, here's the antidote." I showed her a tiny brass flask embossed with a coiled dragon. "*Draconis Palm*. Mosby, stick out your tongue." Ben complied, swallowing three bite-sized crimson colored globules. "Drink." I gave him a chaser of red wine from a leather clad flask. "Now, rest." He lay back against the wall and closed his eyes.

"That looked like resin," observed Maggie.

"Correct. It is resin from *dracaena draco*, known as the Dragon Tree. It grows on the isle of Tenerife."

"Cool...how long will it take to work its magic?"

"Well, if it was me...a day or two. But since he's a strigoi, two or three hours perhaps. But we can't stay here. Darkness will soon be upon us, and with it the new moon. Then Ruxandra, and whoever else, will be coming through this wall, looking for us."

"Why's a new moon so important?"

"A new moon is a time of inception...endeavors break forth, lunar powers maligned to a dark and sinister kind. Ruxandra will draw upon such power to enhance her own. Her beginning aims to be our ending."

"Oh lovely."

"Do you think perhaps your friend Cornelius might come and fetch us?"

"I suppose so; where will we go?"

"I don't know, you know this town better than I. What do you suggest?"

Moaning came from the corner, Ben said, "I suggest the old convent on the hill."

"The old convent? What are you talking about?" said Maggie.

Just then a buzzing noise from overhead enveloped our ears.

"Stay low," whispered Bölscem. We ducked and a drone zipped by our horizon line, no doubt a police one, but it never came in for a closer look. It was soon out of sight.

"I believe Ben is speaking of what used to be a nunnery on Richmond Hill, now called Church Hill. There is a walled garden there."

"That's right, I remember that place. Just a second," said Maggie. She pulled out the prepaid and searched for it. "Yes, there's a walled garden there...it was a monastery, called Monte Maria. Now an ecumenical group owns it. They renamed it 'Richmond Hill.' I'm looking at some pics...there's a structure on its grounds...used to be former slave quarters. Hmm, a team of volunteers are restoring it...just like what we encountered at the Pump House. Looks like our next hideout."

"Good. Now call Cornelius and urge him to get over here, pronto."

"Won't they trace the call from his end?"

"No, he's too smart for that. Likely you'll end up calling another prepaid...do you recognize the contact number?"

"Nope."

"My point exactly. Now call!"

Leaving the cemetery in Cornelius' tinted SUV, the techno asked, "So, have you guys been sleeping in that mausoleum all this time?"

"No," said I, "we only do first class...we move from tomb to tomb...Sauer's, Reynold's...all the best places." Maggie glared at me.

"Cool," said Cornelius, driving toward downtown. "You didn't stay in Monroe's?"

"I should say not!" said I. "We do have some class, dear boy."

"So, why am I driving you to Richmond Hill? Why don't you guys just leave town?"

"We got some business to attend to," said Ben. "Let's just leave it at that."

"Ok, no sweat. Hey, there's another," exclaimed Cornelius, peering out his driver's window.

"Another?" said Maggie.

"Yeah. You know, another drone," said he. Now we were downtown. "That's the second police drone I've seen since we left Hollywood."

A handheld device came to life on the dash. "Squad 501. Possible hit and run, 1312 East Cary."

"501 copy. On my way."

"What da blazes is that?" said Ben.

"That's a police scanner, big guy...you know, a radio."

"Gotcha, they had radio in my day."

"Hey, since you guys left my crib, I've been scanning police telecom, and...well, let's just say, umm, through some techie backdoors...turns out police, FBI, and something called BARDA are teaming up to find you."

"That's just perfect," said I.

"Is 'BARDA' some dapper?" asked Mosby.

"Nah, I wish," said Cornelius, "it's–"

"Not now!" said I.

"Oh, okay, Mr. Monk," said Cornelius. "It's cool." He looked up through the front windshield. "So, how come I...whoa!"

"What's up?" asked Maggie. We were approaching Shockoe Bottom.

"There goes another one! But that one's a doozy...they're definitely looking for you guys. That last one's no standard spec. It's a fixed wing VTOL."

"A what?" said I.

Cornelius looked surprised that I didn't know. "It lands, takes off vertically, does surveillance, it's a fixed wing...it, umm, stays in the air longer, flies faster.... That craft's got facial, thermal, mapping, eavesdropping–it's loaded. Good thing you are all sitting in the backseats."

"Is it following us?" asked Ben.

"Nah, it's veering the other way," said Cornelius. We were now in Shockoe Bottom.

A few minutes later he drove up a steep cobblestone road. On one side stood a high brick wall with the placard, *Richmond Hill* on it. "This is it," said Cornelius. He parked on East Grace Street's cul-de-sac near the Church Hill Overlook, the best view of downtown.

"Thanks so much," said Maggie, leaning forward and pecking Cornelius on the cheek.

He smiled, "No biggie Mags."

"You're alright, radio guy," said Ben, "thanks for getting the tattoo off me."

"You got it," said Cornelius. The gas lanterned streetlight illuminated his spiked

hair. “You guys hiding out in the garden?”

“We hope to,” said I.

“Ok, well, you ought to be fine for a night or two. Look Mags, no more contact, I’m out. Sorry, but I’ve got lots going on. I’d rather no one asks about us, if you get me. If they catch you, trash the phone, alright?”

“Will do,” said Maggie. She kissed him on the cheek.

“Ok, well, good luck guys,” he said, glancing in his rearview then his side mirrors. “Looks clear; good luck.”

We got out of the truck. By this time, Ben had gathered enough strength to get about on his own. Of course, the garden gate was locked, but nothing a bit of magick couldn’t solve.

Just then, a gust of wind from the west rose up. An owl hooted three times. The new moon had not yet set, but she was here. The beginning of the end had begun.

River City Runs Red

Bölcsem Kertész Naplója, 2025. október 22

Thanks to the Portal Stones at the Druid's Altar of Drombeg, I sit here in a rocky cove admiring the diamond studded waters of Glandore Bay. Yet, I am watchful, for I wait upon a signal–the ninth wave, hearkening the arrival of the *TonnSweeper*, a twin-masted baghlah crewed by daughters of *Tuath Dé*. In the meantime, during this respite, I pen all of what transpired in the city of Richmond from the day before. . .

We had only just settled into our new hideaway when the Edenic atmosphere of Richmond Hill's garden was shattered. The sun, despite its casting of elongated shadows, was forced to witness a tumult of flame, ash and smoke. Horns of fire trucks blaring, ambulance sirens wailing, and the wobbly blasts of police cars augmented the cacophony of the raging fire. From the intersection of Grace and 23rd Street I beheld a churning column of smoke. The breeze ushered into my nostrils the scent of sage, and dragon's blood, mixed with rosemary and sulphur. Without a doubt it was the vampire safe house, Collette's flat, in particular, the alchemy and herb rooms, engulfed in flames. Alas, the athanor ruined! Would my ceramic crucibles still be of use? True to her word, Ruxandra had set it ablaze.

What secrets it held, I knew in part. Now one such secret had morphed into the wider world right before my senses. The explosion, a bouquet of vibration and debris, shook the very ground beneath my feet, even though I was more than six blocks away. Evidently, substances in my lab had married with heat and flame, making for a momentary pyrotechnics show against a backdrop of darkening sky. The sizable plume cloud would surely make the evening news.

Brilliant Ruxandra; she had created a perfect distraction for her and her minions to seize Charles Johns, who was out and about. According to his blog, his after-work jog was every weekday. There was no time to vacillate.

I hastened to our hideout in the garden; down a moss covered pathway past a stone carved bird bath embellished with ivy then descended a short flight of stairs entering the former slave quarter under restoration. A one-room shelter tucked away from the main grounds, it had a flat roof adjacent to the garden's eastern wall and small porch. The blast had awakened Ben and Maggie.

"Ben, we must go!" he sat up slowly, still rubbing his eyes.

"What was that explosion?" asked Maggie, putting on her boots.

"My alchemy lab."

"What!?"

"His furnace," said Ben.

"Hmm, indeed. That and some rather combustible material. It was in the basement of Collette's place," I elaborated.

"You said we had more time," remarked Maggie.

"I was wrong. Ruxandra and her minions must have come right after we left the cemetery."

"A surprise move," commented Maggie.

"Exactly."

"But why the house?"

"She burned it down to throw off the authorities. She knows as well as I, Mr. Johns goes jogging after work."

"I'm sorry you lost your lab."

"Maggie, stay here and watch our belongings."

"But I–"

"No buts, Magnolia. We will be back well before sunrise."

Ben put on his coat and sniffed the air. "Comin'! Hey, what's that smell?"

"Collette's herb room," I replied. I sniffed a tuft of hair from my coat pocket.

"What are ya' doing?" asked Ben.

"Smelling Charles Johns' hair...benefits of avian familiars."

"Wait a minute, what if something goes wrong?" asked Maggie.

"I will signal you in the sky; should I do so, come with speed."

"But where are you going?" she pressed.

"Down to the Canal Walk, where Charles runs."

Ben and I made haste through the garden past a great circular brick deck, jumped the wall, and proceeded down several sets of stairs in Taylor's Hill Park. From there, we hurried down Shockoe Bottom's 21st street toward the canal.

At the dead end, we crossed Dock Street, and when the coast was clear, we saddle-climbed a steel beam of the James River Viaduct, landing on a signaling platform. From there, we trekked westward along the trestle's upper deck, heading toward the Canal Walk. Once down at the Triple Crossing, an intersection of three railroad tracks, I caught wind of Johns' scent due west.

I informed Ben and we sprinted; the scent became stronger. I slowed our pace as the sound of the river rapids entered my ears. We looked down just past the river's floodwall at the beginning of the James River Pipeline Trail, and there Ruxandra was. Amazingly, she had not yet picked up our scent; the wind moved in our favor. A fog bank was settling in, undoubtedly wrought by Ruxandra. I motioned to Mosby to remain silent. Below us, in front of the floodwall, two voices conversed on the Trestle Trail: one male, the other female–Ruxandra, her Romanian accent a dead giveaway.

I peered over the trestle, spotting Charles Johns in a track suit. He was jogging in place near the wooden stairway leading downward to the James River Pipeline Walkway, known to locals as simply: The Pipeline. It was a metal mesh catwalk atop a large sewer pipe running slightly out from, but mostly parallel with, the river's northern bank. Directly above it, the railroad viaduct, from which we could pounce on Ruxandra, who was just a few feet up the trail from Charles.

"Excuse me ma'am, are you following me?" Charles asked with a disdainful tone. His aura, dark blacks and grays, signified a selfish, malignant, and unbalanced character.

"Good evening, Charles. I am a fan of your blog."

"Oh, glad you're a fan. So, who are you?"

"Just a fan...needing something."

"As you can see lady...I'm in the middle of running. What do you want?"

"Your blood!" She revealed her fangs and stepped towards him.

Startled, he took a few steps back, then turned and ran. He was heading toward the floodwall's open gate through which the Triple Crossing's lowest rail line emerges. But he stopped in his tracks at the oncoming spectacle of Lothar Neuntöter, the tall, lean, bleach-skinned Germanic vampire. His albino physique dotted with decaying open sores was quite a contrast to his nihilistic black, steel-studded attire and spiked, lava gray hair. With his gleaming fangs, he took a bite out of his own forearm. His blood stained the abalone trail. He chewed on it, then swallowed.

This put Charles in a panic. He back pedaled, darting toward the only escape, the Pipeline's wooden staircase. The stairs led to a descending steel ladder unto the Pipeline's catwalk. The horn of a train blared. I gazed down the track to see its headlight flickering. The last vestiges of sunlight were glistening on the rapids and wisps of mist.

Now out of my view, Charles must have reached the Pipeline's steel ladder while Lothar gave pursuit, followed by the sauntering Ruxandra. Once it was all clear, I motioned to Ben and we jumped off the rumbling viaduct to the floodwall door directly below, then to the door's side ladder. Between the din of the raging river, the train horn blasts, and the clattering of its hopper cars, the sound of our movements went undetected. By the time we reached the Pipeline's ladder, we could barely make out the back of Ruxandra's dark leather duster and Lothar's spiky-haired head on the walkway. We kept a good distance. Our steps on the mesh catwalk were cloaked by the train's rumbles directly above us, our forms obscured by the pockets of mist,

and our scent concealed thanks to a favorable breeze. Charles was out of sight. A light from a smartphone pierced the fog; it was coming toward Lothar. It oscillated from illuminating the metal mesh in front of it to the oncoming Neuntöter. By now we had shortened the distance, so we stopped and crouched low.

"Excuse me," said a tattoo-faced man as he approached the German, for the walkway was narrow. Lothar did not step to one side. The man looked up, peering at Lothar's visage. "Hey, are you wearing some kinda mask?"

"Nein."

"'Cause, umm, you look like the Richmond Vampire...come to think of it, you look

like that wall art over there." He pointed to one of the viaduct's pillars right behind Lothar, graffitied with a vampiric-looking character in a high collared coat.

Lothar turned and glimpsed at the urban art then faced the young man and let out a hideous laugh. He asked, *"Hat dich ein Mann überholt?"*

"Huh?"

Ruxandra caught up with Lothar and translated, "Did a man pass you?"

"Ah...yeah."

"Danke," replied Lothar then hoisted the man by his neck visible through a gap in the mist. Terror blanketed the victim's visage; gripped in a vise of elongated

bony fingers and iron-like claws meant no escape. As the Neuntöter held him, the train above us blasted out a pipe organ call, and with it came to mind Byrd Theatre's mighty Wurlitzer rising from the orchestra pit blaring the introduction of the *Toccata et Fugue in D minor.* The man's phone hit the handrail, its screen cracked on landing, and its light directly illuminated the vampire's monstrous fangs. He vainly tried to scream, wriggling his feet. Lothar lowered him, took a bite out of the base of his neck, chewed on his flesh, then sucked blood from the gash. Satiated, he hurled the ragdoll body into the James. *"Ah, sehr gut."* He wiped his mouth and continued the hunt for Charles Johns.

Ben, in anger, started to move past me, but I held him. The train's horn sounded again, adding to the screeching wheels and clanging couplings.

They were moving their heads side to side, trying to detect Charles' whereabouts. Smelling their prey would be a challenge, as the odor of ganja wafted from squatters on Pipeline's tapered beaches. Amid breaks in the mist, lights from the downtown skyscrapers peered between the viaduct's concrete pillars, revealing rapids, rocks, and sandy shoals below on either side of the walkway. The concrete columns supported a cathedral ceiling of steel rail, timber ties, and lattice girders, all of which obstinately stood their ground against the flow of the mighty James. Each pillar erected as a homage to the religion of industrialism.

The hunters proceeded along the catwalk until the handrails gave way to just the sewer pipe caked in concrete icing. They sniffed and peered this way and that. Had Charles gone this far, or had he leaped through the handrails onto the sandy banks below?

Moments later, directly ahead in shadow, a sneaker's sole scuffed the pipe, ensuing a cry of agony. Ruxandra and Lothar abandoned the safety of handrails and meshed metal panels for the bare sewer line suspended above the rapids. Though coated in concrete and flanked by the occasional shrubs and small trees, the pipe offered little footing. The night seemed to cradle this hostile and obscure place and yearned to devour unwelcome guests.

Lothar and Ruxandra forged on, embracing the denser darkness. We stalked the stalkers, maintaining our remoteness. Despite our caution, I was surprised she had not turned to check behind her. Was she so obsessed with finding Charles, she had thrown prudence to the wind? Or was her arrogance such that she feared no threat? Of course, there was always the possibility that she'd laid a trap for Ben and I, and we were walking right into it. Nonetheless, we tiptoed forward.

Soon Ruxandra's voice pierced the din of the rapids. "Get up and die like a man!"

Charles hobbled to his feet. "*What have I done!?* Is this about money? Are you working for someone?"

We crept closer until we were a stone's throw away, concealed in shadow by one of the viaduct's columns.

Ruxandra smiled cruelly. "No my dear Charles, we work for no man," she replied, "and your money's of no use to us...but your blood is."

"My...oh my god! Why!?"

"Your great-grandfather, did he not approve reopening the Church Hill Tunnel?"

"He did, but...what's that got to do with me?"

"Someone's got to pay, Charles, someone in the bloodline–not through meaningless money–but in blood. Blood was spilled and must be paid. Your grandfather knew the endeavor was fraught with doom...yet he authorized it anyway. Much like you, endorsing developer plans–stuffing your pockets but emptying others–some of whom now roam the streets of Richmond–homeless!"

"What!? What skin do you have in this game?"

"Ah, Mr. Johns, excellent question. One of my kind was in the tunnel a century ago," Ruxandra explained.

"The...the Richmond Vampire? You, you've come to seek some sort of revenge?"

"Precisely, Charles! Blood for blood–that's our currency," stated Ruxandra.

At that, a wobbling, high-pitched resonance filled the air. The rapids beneath spiked in tiny peaks. Out of the mist emerged a voluminous burgundy orb casting jagged crimson reflections upon the waters. All stood entranced by the macabre sphere. A sudden smell of sulphur fumigated the air, and a cold chill pervaded.

I whispered to Ben, "Andromalius."

"Ahh, wha–what's that!?" asked a trembling Charles.

"That, my dear, is your transport," remarked Ruxandra.

"Transport?"

"To Hades–your new home," she grinned then motioned to Lothar. He seized Charles by the neck.

Ben jostled past me, nearly knocking me into the river. Were it not for my staying hand upon a concrete pillar, I would have been soaked.

Ben burst into a sprint, charging headlong down the pipe. Ruxandra spun to see an oncoming bull in the form of Benjamin Mosby. Just as he was closing in, from above dive bombed a murder of crows consisting of Morrigan, Blackburn, and Coronis. They had emerged from the trestle works. Indeed, it was a trap!

They were led by Evermore. They tore at Ben; tufts of hair and skin went flying. He put up a forearm to cover his eyes, while with his other arm he vainly swatted at the avian marauders. Stumbling, he fell forward upon the sewer line. The grayish pipe drizzled with streams of blood. Ruxandra laughed.

Enraged, I conjured up a fierce billow. The gust sent her winged assassins toppling end over end, some crashing into the viaduct, others into the floodwall. The force either knocked them out or crippled their wings. The orb retreated into the blanket of the night. This gave Ruxandra pause.

My counterattack gave Mosby needed time to recover, and, despite a bloody face, he stumbled to his feet. His constitution hastened to heal.

"Lothar!" she called. Lothar dropped Charles upon the pipe and sidestepped in front of her. Mosby resumed his bullish charge. He gained momentum then leapt headlong into Lothar, sending the two of them barreling over onto the rocky banks. There, a sustained melee ensued.

Ruxandra's heterochromia eyes locked with mine. She unpinned her lavender hair. It cascaded down to the small of her back and blew to one side by the wisps of the wind.

Renegade! she thundered telepathically. Then cel Rău pivoted and walked away, belting out a series of high pitched shrieks. I stormed forward, gnashing my teeth. Her hands came up from her sides in synch with her voice, summoning the air. Just as I was closing the gap, a billow of fog precipitated from the blackness, embracing her with a chorus of screeching and squealing. The devilish haze headed my way.

From out of the billowy vapors, upon the pipe's apex, a stampede–a mischief of rats! Her last etheric conveyance: *If the rats don't get you, they will!*

...They? Who's...? but my musings faded at the assault of two more mischiefs. The vermin were climbing viaduct supports anchored in the sandy banks. The clefts in the concrete columns served as their footholds. As I turned in retreat toward the walkway, I felt a rodent scaling my leg then biting into my flesh...another and another. I made it to the catwalk, but I was wailing in agony, bashing back and forth against the handrails. Before me another mischief oncoming. *Was this it? Would I be eaten alive?*

In that instant, deep in Shockoe Bottom, the Poe Museum sprang to mind. Edgar's Wheel of Misfortune spun out my fate. I perceived "DEVOURED BY ANIMALS" rotating toward the ominous arrow.

With all fortitude, I righted myself. *"Noo!!!"* I roared. "This is not how it will end!"

I closed my eyes, focusing not on their gnawing nor the blood trailing down my

limbs, but upon the roiled rapids. My utterances reverberated with the elements; reaching forth, I summoned the waters towards me. Submitted depths stacked upon depths–rising river–ascending up tree trunks, touching the pipe–rising...filling my boots...shrills of vermin–roaring river–over my waist...above the handrails. The devouring ceased. I grabbed the rails; my conjuring abated.

Holding firm against the receding tide, I opened my eyes to the spectacle of countless rats swirling and shrieking in a maelstrom. Then, floating by, came a bloodied Charles Johns crying out for help and treading water. As quickly as the river had relented to my will, it had returned to the will of Mother Earth; backlashing walls of water crashed toward the opposite shore. A wave carried Charles to the shore of Vauxhall Island, not far from the Pipeline's sandy beaches. Vauxhall, part of an archipelago in the midst of the James, was a nesting site for herons; it was only reachable by boat or the Norfolk Southern truss bridge, which traverses the isle to the James River's southern shoreline.

Charles stumbled to his feet upon its sandy coast. Blood oozed from minor cuts sustained from his brush with death. His track suit soiled with blood and dirt, he glanced at me then looked upriver. Lothar was coming his way, treading water along the current. Panic came over his countenance. He bolted toward the bridgework.

A blaring horn from a Norfolk Southern train assaulted my ears. It was heading straight for the truss. Meanwhile, Lothar maneuvered to the isle's peninsula. He spooked a heron, which took flight. Then Ben floated by me and anchored himself on a boulder surrounded by rapids.

He yelled, "Where'd Charles go?"

"There!" I shouted, pointing to the railroad bridge. "But Ben, let him go..." Ben let go–not of his mission–but of the boulder, and swam toward the island. "Ben!" I hollered, "Ben!"

But it was of no use—he ignored me. He managed to make it to shore and fell forward, coughing up water. "Ben! Are you ok?" I cried, but I got no reply. Instead, he cleared his lungs, gained his footing, and resumed the pursuit.

I decided saving Charles Johns was more important than challenging Ruxandra. Besides, Ben would have his hands full against the Neuntöter vampire—a ruthless killer—and whoever else might be out there. So I hurried back to the Pipeline's exit ladder. However, my pace was not as before, not as a vampire, but as of a mere man. Summoning the waters had drained me. Nevertheless, I pressed onward. As I did so, the train's engine was now on the bridge, letting out another blast. I went up the ladder and rounded the corner to hitch a ride, but I was too late. Should I have taken the shorter way? Dove off the walkway into a tumultuous river, then treaded over to Vauxhall? Looking back now, I see that I should have, despite my lack of aquatic prowess. For, by the time I had taken the long way, the train and its short parade of boxcars were well beyond where I stood and I faced the graffiti covered "No Trespassing" signs posted before the bridge.

I caught sight of Lothar, who took hold of the last car's ladder and began climbing up to its roof. Charles Johns was barely visible; his brightly stained running gear gave away his location. He was farther up the line, on a boxcar close to the diesel locomotive.

In the meantime, while I gave chase, a good fifty meters in front of me, Ben

scurried up the steep grade onto the tracks. He did not even look back my way but instead sprinted forward to accost Lothar. I continued running as best I could to catch up.

When I had passed the last truss on the bridge, what I saw next astonished me. Charles was scaling the Manchester Floodwall Observation Area, a foot bridge above a flood gate. Evidently, his adrenaline had kicked in at the sight of the vampiric monster bearing down upon him, leaping from one car to another. He must have launched off the roof of a boxcar. Then, while at the apex of the trajectory, he grabbed hold of the bottom of the chainlink cage–a fence-like barrier preventing pedestrians from falling off the overpass. Next, he clambered over to the stair rail, descending to the westward portion of the Floodwall Walk. He was soon out of my sight.

Ben had gained the roof of the last boxcar and was heading for the Neuntöter. As Charles had done, so did Lothar. He leapt unto the overpass's metallic mesh, laden with love locks. Then he clawed his way over to the stairway. As he was about to bring a foot over the hand railing, Lothar was seized by his pursuer. Ben had propelled himself diagonally from a boxcar roof and grabbed hold of Lothar's dangling foot. The Neuntöter shook him off, casting Ben backward onto a slope of drainage boulders. Lothar resumed the hunt.

Ben lay motionless. Finally, I reached him and shook him. "Ben! Ben, wake up!" I slapped him on the cheeks. Bruises on his face from the fall were already beginning to clear up.

"Ahh, Friar," he groaned. I helped him to his feet. He looked along the wall's pathway. "Charles!" He scrambled over the boulder field to the flood door's ladder. He climbed it, tightrope walked upon the top of the gate, then jumped upward to regain the Manchester Floodwall Walk.

Though I had not the strength to keep up, my vampiric hearing was good and true, for I heard from across the river a chorus of buzzing. A drone, but not the typical police craft, it had a deeper, more guttural tone. The craft was heading our way.

"Ben, stop! It's another trap!" I hollered. He looked back about sixty meters away upon the gravel path. "Do you not hear that?"

"Bölscem, it's been good knowing you. *Szia!"* he bellowed back then resumed his rescue. Those were the last words I heard from the fireman, consumed with a burning desire to extinguish a fire he had not ignited.

Moments later, from the direction of Mayo Bridge, who should come sprinting up the walkway, but Maggie. The fringe of her scarf trailed behind her, she cried, "Ben, wait up!"

He turned, "No time! Charles is in danger. Help Bölscem!" He ran off.

"Bölscem?" she looked toward the apartment buildings.

"Maggie!"

She jerked her head toward my call and bemused, "Bölscem, what are doing down there? You look a wreck."

"Too much magick for one day. Maggie, as the daylight bids us farewell, so do I bid you adieu."

"But why?"

"There's nothing more I can do. Now go, help Ben, I fear he is falling into a trap."

"Yeah, I sensed that, that's why I came–take care. *Szia*, my friend!"

"*Szia!* Enchanting Magnolia!" And with that, she too was gone from my sight.

Vampiric Beast

Magnolia's Diary, October 22nd of 2025

Dear Diary,

I couldn't remain any longer at the Richmond Hill garden, a fog bank encroached upon the garden's southern wall. It must have been a sign. I had an overwhelming sense—an impression—my love was in trouble. Suddenly, I perceived Ben in a scuffle with some dark and imposing vampire. This vampire looked a lot like the one in the *Nosferatu* flick. Just as tall, but he was younger and definitely more ugly. All over his face and arms were bloody sores that matched his bloodshot eyes.

It had to be Ben communicating...but how? Vampiric sixth sense is all that came to mind. After all, we shared the same blood. Words, you know dear Diary, fall short in explaining how such perceptions differ from regular thoughts. I had to trust my instinct—not my doubts. He needed me.

I vacated Richmond Hill by the main entrance and descended the long cobblestone drive to Shockoe Bottom. From there I took the closest street down to the Virginia Capital Trail, its canopy the James River Viaduct, unto the Canal Walk, which snaked its way to a flight of stairs leading to the Mayo Bridge. Once on the bridge's sidewalk, I saw a Norfolk Southern train nearly finish its crossing. A strong intuition came over me; Ben was on that train. I sprinted across to the Southside, entering the footpath off of Hull Street, leading to the Manchester Floodwall Walk. It was all so strange; I knew which way to go, and all on a gut feeling like I was some migratory bird whose internal compass led the way. Once at an elevated position on the Floodwall Observation Area, the last rays of light were enough for my vampiric vision to see far. I searched for Ben on the train now meandering toward the Manchester Bridge. Not there. Then, scanning the Floodwall's towpath, I spotted him. He was heading down the hand-railed path toward the pump station, an engineering platform just off the trail, jutting out into the river. He was chasing after this black-cloaked figure closing in on a tracksuit-clad jogger, likely Charles Johns. Was the wraith the same spine-chilling vampire I'd envisioned? I cried out to Ben. He turned and hollered back to stay put and help Bölscem.

The scribe called from the slope of boulders below. He appeared diminished; all vigor gone. He explained he'd drained himself fighting against Ruxandra, who'd vanished in a shroud of mist. As to his other rivals, Edana, Kojo...he said they didn't come. His theory was the revenge train had gone too far for their liking, that it threatened the very existence of the Dragonist Order. Perhaps he was right, for what came next pointed to that theory.

As for Ben's orders, I didn't listen. I bid Bölscem farewell and darted up the gravel footpath to help in the rescue of Charles Johns. As I was catching up with darkness settling in, I heard a drone hovering over the river. It had a subtler sound than a police UAV. Glancing toward the whirling, I was surprised I couldn't see it; perhaps it had a cloaking device. Its thermal imagery must have detected an altercation up ahead, for it was flying that way.

When I caught up to Ben he was locked in a tussle with this monstrous, albino vampire covered with bloody sores. He had long claw-like nails and jagged teeth, decked out in garb like someone at a Goth party. Sure enough, just like in my vision, he looked similar to the vampire straight out of *Nosferatu*. It was Lothar, the one Bölscem warned us about. Behind the brute, in the water pump's deck area, lying fetal style under a bench, was Charles Johns. I guess he thought laying low would keep him outta sight. Of course, he'd be dead wrong; even with human eyesight under the low light of the city one could've spotted him. The neon orange apparel was a dead giveaway, not to mention an eyesore, along with his reflective jogging shoes.

Meanwhile, the Nosferatu ogre tried to grab and bite Ben, then switched tactics, catching him in the cheek. His razor nails sprayed Mosby's blood over

the pump's panel boxes. Ben, dazed, fell back against a handrail. Then, just as Lothar was about to finish him off, I yelled, "Yo! Big fella!"

Lothar turned and scowled at me. His bloodshot eyes glowed red in the misty night. *"Du bist Nächste,"* Lothar uttered, gnashing his jagged teeth. *That didn't sound good,* I said to myself. A pang of fear coursed up my spine.

Luckily, Ben recovered and put a solid right hook on Lothar's snout. *Crack!* went his nose. Lothar staggered backwards, bumping into a pump rod. He snapped his nose back into place and said, *"Nicht schlecht, aber es ist Zeit zu sterben!"*

Uh-oh, think he said, "Time to die," I thought. He lumbered forward, backing Ben into a corner. He fainted with his right then seized Ben's throat with his left. *Oh, it's always the left, isn't it?* I knew right then I had to do something super crazy.

I pounced on Lothar's back and dug my nails deep into his eyeballs shouting, "Time to be blind, Frankenstein!" I felt his acidic blood burning my fingers—mega gross! The worst part...I *broke* a nail!

"Ahhh," he cried out, dropping Ben on the deck. *"Du Zicke!"* He staggered backwards upon the metal grates, clutching his bloody eyes.

Suddenly, a shaft of light blinded Lothar. It was that drone I'd heard. It definitely wasn't police; it was larger, gun metal black, and appeared like a Klingon battlecruiser uncloaking itself. The bright beam caused smoky vapors to rise from the Neuntöter's skin. He cried out all the more, shuffling to and fro, vainly trying to avoid the luminescence. He banged into handrails then the floodwater mechanisms.

In response, emanating from the mist in the direction of Manchester Bridge, I heard the rumblings of boots and gear. Before us, the walkway bowed out toward the river, then beyond it, the first of a dozen or so body-armored goons broke through the fog bank. Their helmets bobbed up and down, peering at us with night vision goggles.

Ben went over to Charles and ordered, "Come with us, now!" He stood up, dumbfounded, and without a protest, Ben put him in a fireman's carry. We bolted in retreat toward Mayo Bridge.

The drone kept its searchlight on Lothar, who was still clutching his eyes, smoldering, and roaring with agony. From a distance, over the noise of the rapids, I made out a low frequency whirling; it was becoming louder, though I spotted nothing. Was it a helicopter, or a hovercraft? Kinda both...definitely ominous.

Soon Ben, with Charles in tow, was at the covered observation area. But I had slowed my pace, drawn by the sight and sounds of Lothar and the two crafts, so I was halfway between the pump station and the chain linked overpass. Beyond the spectacle and through the fog breaks I spotted Special Agent Covach (or is it "Kovach"?), she was wearing an FBI jacket. She bore a gun, along with Detective Breland wearing a khaki trench coat amongst a body-armored squad. It was a trap! The chopper whirling grew louder, moving up the James.

Ben hailed me to hurry up. I ignored him. I still saw no rotating blades, no craft...then, in an instant, a beam shot forth from it. The outline of a sleek clamshell hull appeared amidst the fog. It was so surreal. You can't make this stuff up!

The chopper's light was joined with the UAV's at a forty-five-degree angle, a futuristic stealth helicopter with curved blades. Lothar's skin now boiled under the luminescent onslaught, his cries amplified. He staggered onto the pathway in front of Covach and crew, banging up against another handrail, then floundered the other way and began coming my way, though his pace had considerably slowed. Whether he could still see me or whether he was listening for my footsteps, I had no time to figure out. I hastened my retreat.

The two beams continued to track him. Behind me I heard an ops guy shouting, "Stop! FBI...or we'll shoot." I glanced over my shoulder to see Lothar paying them no mind despite red laser beams dancing upon his body. Some strayed past, illuminating the pebbled path at my rear. *Bang, bang, bang!* Bullets whizzed near me. A few hit Lothar. He came to a halt, as did his pursuers. They marveled as the Neuntöter groaned and flexed his body, pushing the slugs out with a *thud, thud* onto the gravel. He did an about-face and roared at them. They retreated slightly, then the monster swiveled back toward me and upped his pace.

"Come on Maggie!" yelled Ben from the top of the observation bridge.

Covach moved to the forefront of the Kevlar mass and aimed her pistol at Lothar. "Stop, vampire," she shouted, "or I'll gun you down!"

Lothar kept on coming. He was closing in on me. Like a fool, I backpedaled to see what would happen next. Guess curiosity got the better of me.

Through the fog a faint spark; she'd discharged a round, hitting him center

mass. Amazingly, he slowed, and teetered to one side, barely moving.

"Halt!" she continued. He wouldn't. She fired two more; his chest arched forward under the impact. Lothar bellowed, wriggled, and collapsed upon his back which set in motion the abatement of the mist.

He lay there clawing at the gravel towpath, gasping for breath, contorting in a seizure. She'd used sacred bullets...she'd used *vervain* injected shells. *Whoa!*

Under the glaring beams, Covach motioned to several ops. Two cuffed Lothar while another held a syringe. The charcoal coated copter moved into position over the scene, its curved blades kicking up dust. Below it, a hoist line was lowering a biomedical isolation unit with the acronym, "BARDA" stenciled on the side.

Breland, flanked by tactical guys, moved past the capture. "Maggie! Don't move!" hollered Breland.

At that, I bolted toward the overpass thinking, *This was planned...Covach—BARDA! What is that!?*

"Maggie! We'll shoot!" cried Breland as I ascended, zigzagging up the overpass stairs. Shots dinged off the bridge's chainlink mesh. None hit me. I descended to the other side, then bounded down the flights of stairs to the trail at ground level.

I was at the bend in the path when from the apex of the bridge, Breland pleaded, "Maggie, *Maaggieee!* Please stop!"

I didn't even look back, just kept running. My mind flashed back to Bölscem's warning: you're one of us now...mankind desires to dissect us and discover the Otherworld.

Just when I thought I was in the clear, I made out the same whirling and buzzing of the drone which had detected Lothar. It zoomed past Breland and company heading straight for me. Like a burst from a stage light, its beam locked onto me. I sprinted and crossed a canal footbridge toward Hull Street. I'd hoped to elude the mechanized marauder amid the nearby buildings. Just as I reached Hull Street, I sensed a series of dialed clicks then someone deeply exhaled above me. *Bang!* A boom filled the air. I stopped and peered upward to witness rotor blades gyrating to earth along with metal and plastic parts. *Someone had shot it down!*

"Wah-hoo!" I heard someone shout. Atop an apartment building a scrappy-haired character brandished an IR sniper rifle with bipod. Next to him, a gal with orange dreads danced a victory jig, waving a night vision spotter.

"Always wanted to do that! Yeah! Got that sucker, didn't I?" he said.

"Yeah, you did," I hollered back. "Thank you...err. Hey, who are you?

"Rudy, from the boxcar! Remember me? Friend of the scribe man. Now, get outta here pronto, sweetie!"

Before I could say anything more, they were gone.

"Maggie!" Ben hollered from across the street. He was standing next to Charles at the tracks.

"Ben!" I jaywalked amongst the cars stopped dead on account of the explosion. "Hey, that was the boxcar guy! He shot down the drone!"

"Bee's knees! That ragamuffin's full-a surprises," Ben chuckled.

"I'll say! What next?" I asked.

"Hey, aren't you Roger's niece? You were in a wheelchair." stated Charles.

"That's right."

"So, ah, the govies are after you cause you're—"

"—vampires! Yeah got it," I declared.

"Weird. Say, who was the goth chick and the Frankenstein chasing—"

"—Your ass," interjected Ben. "You're welcome, but it comes with a price," hoisting Charles back into a fireman's carry.

"Whoa, hey there," Charles squirmed. "Whatta you—"

"Shut it! Or I'll bite you," I replied, shooting a wink at Ben.

"You move too slow. I'm taking you to see an old friend," explained Ben.

We bounded down the tracks past the Richmond Railroad Museum till we reached the line heading due north over the Mayo Island Bridge. It was a deck plate girder bridge sandwiched between two automobile bridges: Mayo Bridge and the James River I-95 Bridge.

As we crossed, I looked for the copter, but it was long gone, and no sign of Breland and his goons. In the meantime, the disbelief on Charles' face was comical. He was blown away that Ben could carry him so quickly and that a girl was keeping up!

We made it to the Triple Crossing. Charles piggybacked Ben, and we descended down to the ground level track line. There, Ben put Mr. Johns down.

"Where are we going?" I asked Ben.

"Church Hill Tunnel. Charles here's got some promises to keep, to an old friend of mine."

"Say what now? You ain't...are you *Benjamin Mosby?"*

"Yes sir," Ben said with raised eyebrow.

"I...ah...you're the Richmond Vampire?"

"No sir, just back on the hundredth, to put things right," Ben smiled. "Now, let's go see—"

"See who?" asked Charles.

"A mutual acquaintance."

At that, we went over the Canal Walk's footbridge, crossed Dock Street in front of Bottoms Up Pizza.

"Man, I could go for a slice," I said.

Just then a police SUV came up from behind us; at the last second it turned onto 17th before he got to us. *Whew! That was close!*

From there Ben led the way up 18th, a cobblestone street with vintage gas lamps. Charles strained to keep up in the middle and I trailed behind. No sign of cops under the canopy of lights and neon signs, one of which was The Pizza Place. *Boy, pizza was starting to sound real good...until lookin' at the back of Johns' neck made me crave something else...*

As we walked by the bar, Fallout, some loiterers dressed in Goth garb made passing remarks. One blurted a wisecrack at Ben. Another was well endowed and showing it off. She eyed him up and down and said, "Hey there, big guy, wanna bite of me?"

"Maybe next time, miss," he replied.

"I'll cut you first," I shot back hissing and flaunting my exquisite nails and for-real dental work. Oh, dear diary, you shoulda' seen the expression on that chick's face. *Ha!*

As we approached Broad Street, a fog bank settled upon the next intersection up. *Were we heading that way? If so, had Ruxandra laid another trap beyond?*

Just as I was about to express my fears, Ben came to a halt. He was spellbound by a mural of his old train. The one he'd shoveled coal into a hundred years ago. It was engine 231, coming out of the Tunnel with Tom Mason posing

as if the old newspaper, *Richmond Planet*, was taking his picture. He just stood there, taking in a flood of memories. Charles and I gave him space.

"I remember everything in those first few seconds before and after the collapse," began Ben, tears welling up. "The cries of men running, shouting...the praying. Me, yellin' at Tom to get outta the engine." Trickles of salty tears glided down his cheeks. He wiped them away with his hanky then looked at Charles and said, "It's time for you to make things right."

"With the Tunnel? I would, but how? Everyone's dead—except you, apparently," said Charles.

"Nope, the men are waiting for you. They're still diggin' the Tunnel to this very day. Keepin' it from fallin' in again."

"You mean—the ghost stories? How people late at night say they hear the sound of pickaxes, and shovels coming from the Tunnel?"

"Yes, sir, and you're about to meet 'em."

"Noo, no, nuh-uh! They'll haunt me," Charles said, shuddering.

Ben grabbed Charles by the zipper part of his track suit and exclaimed, "Now looky here, get a-hold of yourself! Be a man, Mr. Johns! Face up to what your ancestors didn't. If you don't, I reckon that's when they'll haunt your soul 'til you're in the grave." He released Charles but held his gaze.

Charles exhaled, peered up the street toward the Tunnel's western entrance, and said, "Fine, all right, I'll face my guilt." He resumed walking that way and we followed. *Guilt? What was he talking about?* I mused to myself.

When we entered a shoal of fog at the intersection of 18th and Marshall, I couldn't help but bring up the prior conversation with Mosby by asking Charles, "You said, 'guilt.' Guilt over what?"

He sighed and motioned to the state's historical marker explaining the tragedy. Once we were closer, he pointed beyond a privacy gate to the Church Hill Tunnel's western portal. The stone arched entrance was nestled between an old poultry warehouse turned apartment complex and its residents' parking lot.

He cleared his throat and explained, "I worked with city officials and developers on this site. We made it so the Tunnel entrance couldn't be approached by the public."

"So, in effect, you buried it a second time," I stated.

He nodded. "You could say that. Plus, people in the know realize the tunnel is unstable."

We stepped in front of the privacy gate. Between the gateway's bars and the creeping mist, I could make out the tunnel's western portal; a third of it cast in shadow, the rest, when not draped in fog, was illuminated by a street light showing petrified cascades of moisture, moss and mold, and some bird droppings. The gate's key code barred our entrance.

Just then a resident came from the lot. As he came toward us, he said, "Can I help you?"

"Yes," said Charles. "This fella here," he pointed at Ben, "has come a mighty long way to see this tunnel. Do you mind letting us in to get a closer look?"

"Sure, no problem," he said and put in the code. He held the gate open for me.

"Thanks," I said. He proceeded walking to his apartment, no longer engaging us as he tapped at his smartwatch.

We approached, reverently, upon a stone-tiled walkway as if we were on cemetery grounds. The tunnel's portal appeared under assault; its stone block, winged walls and archway its only defenses from the urban sprawl all around it. Above its arch, a parade of parked cars on Cedar Street, and flanked on both sides of it, the complex: residents' windows peering down on it on one hand, and their vehicles, on the other.

I felt exposed under the contemporary street lights craning their necks, spewing forth unnatural LED light. The poles were made of cold stainless steel as were the handrails bordering the building's raised walkway, and still more steel rails riding atop the portal's winged walls. The whole scene was an eyesore: a mass grave from a bygone era juxtaposed with soulless architecture.

The only remnant left memorializing this sacred site was an engraved inscription upon the entrance. It stated the year the tunnel was sealed forever: 1926. At the very least they should have inscribed, "October 2, 1925," as a fitting headstone for those entombed within. In my mind, the C&O had shown their true colors: a lasting, disrespectful sign of how the railroad company viewed the commoner's life. This didn't surprise me, though, as I thought of my own family line, whose fortunes were intertwined with that of the railroad, and its exploitation of human life in pursuit of profit. In particular, my father and his father before him came to mind; they had conveyed their disdain for the common man to me, and even more so for the sons and daughters of former slaves whom they saw as a disposable workforce. They tolerated their presence and masked their true view of these wonderful human beings with good old "Southern hospitality."

What a bizarre thing, just a few feet away, inside this sealed portal, was a vintage steam locomotive and flat cars riddled with the dead bodies of who knows how many laborers. But the bizarreness became creepy when we heard the tapping of pickaxes and the shoveling of dirt emanating from the tunnel. The mist seemed to shutter every time a tool struck the earth.

"What the hell is that!?" exclaimed a wide-eyed Charles Johns.

"That's your invitation to make things right," said Mosby. Ben edged closer to the Tunnel. Before its entrance, he stopped at an abatement wall holding in a plot of boulders. Charles stood still before a collection of outdoor tables and chairs between him and Ben. "Come on," Ben said, motioning to Charles, "they ain't gonna bite you."

"I...I always thought the ghost stories were rubbish," said Johns.

"Well, they aren't," I stated, standing next to him. "Are you a wimp?"

"No," he snapped. "I can...I can handle it." He walked up to the retaining wall, and I followed suit.

"Now, listen here," said Mosby, "once we step up onto these boulders, we're on sort of sacred ground. The digging will stop, and a dignified gent by the name of Richard Lewis will come out. He's their spokesman. Now, look here, Charles, these men are looking for rest. What I mean to say is, they're seeking a proper memorial. And you're gonna give it to 'em—right?" Ben pressed his index finger into Charles' chest.

Charles gasped, then exhaled and said, "Yes. I need to fix this."

"Good," Ben replied. "Now just wait here." He stepped over the wall and the excavation ceased. He maneuvered over the rocks until he stood under the "1926" marker. Then the mist receded from the tunnel wall, and in its wake a ghostly figure dressed in workman's clothes walked out of the portal into the wider world.

"Well, well, if ain't a' Mr. Mosby," said the ghost.

"Hey there, Mr. Lewis," replied Ben, "good to see you again."

"You're lookin' hopeful, Ben. Who's these folk with ya?"

Ben bid us come and join him. "This here's our lovely Magnolia," Ben said as Charles and I tentatively trekked over to greet Mr. Richard Lewis.

"Oh you're a sight for sore eyes Miss Magnolia," said Lewis, taking off his cap and doing a slight bow. "Glad to make your acquaintance."

"Oh, likewise," said I, hardly believing I was talking to a spirit.

"And this," Ben continued, "is Mr. Charles Johns."

"How—ah, how do you do, sir?" said Mr. Lewis.

"I'm fine, thank you," answered Charles.

"Mr. Johns here is the great grandson of C. W. Johns," explained Mosby.

"*The* Johns? The one who signed off on our fate?" said Lewis.

"The same," said Ben.

"Well, this is a surprise. As you can see, Mr. Johns, we're still at it. We, including Mr. H. Smith, get no rest. We've been workin' on this tunnel, keepin' it from cavin' in for just o'er a hundred years now. Our ghostly labor reminds folks: don't never let such a thing happen again. We sure'd like a more fittin' memorial too, than what we've got here. Are you the man who can make that happen?"

"I, I am, Mr. Lewis," replied Johns, clearing his throat.

"And how'd ya reckon that'll be?" pressed Lewis.

"Well, I rub shoulders with corporate folk who can bolster the tunnel where it's weakening. As for a monument—to you and the others—for your sacrifice. I know

people at city hall who can make that happen. Maybe even a museum, something befitting this historic place. Will that suit you?"

"Yes sir, that'll suit us just fine," Richard smiled, and a tear slid down his cheek. "Then we can finally rest, and the sweet chariot...it'll swing low and carry us home."

"Well, good, then," said Charles, who got all choked up, as did Ben and I.

"Now, gentlemen and good lady," said Mr. Lewis, "I bid you adieu," and tipped his hat. And with that, he vanished back into the portal, back into the Otherworld, before we could even say goodbye.

Au revoir!

Pool of Blood

Magnolia's Diary, October 23rd of 2025

Dear Diary,

I am weak—wounded...will I recover? Let me explain...

After our encounter with Richard Lewis, Charles Johns was grateful for what we had done. In thanks, he secured for Ben and I a driverless taxi, on his dime. Coupled with an absent moon, the cab's tinted rear windows shielded our identity. Thus we made our way to Hollywood Cemetery without a hitch, until we spotted watchful eyes at its gate.

A police patrol was near its entrance, most likely keeping a look out for us. Ben and I exited the vehicle on nearby Cherry Street then jumped the cemetery fence. We hastened to William Wortham Pool's mausoleum which, strangely enough, was not guarded. Perhaps they were staked out around Ben's grave site, the scene of media frenzy.

Under the cover of darkness, we moved from tree to tree until we arrived at Westvale Avenue before the sepulcher's courtyard fence. Before we opened its gate, we scanned the grounds, including up the slopes on either side of the tomb's retaining walls. The area was clear, so we proceeded. However, just as Ben pried open the iron lattice door, I heard several footfalls upon the hill just above the sepulcher then spied flickers of flashlights. Ben ripped apart the chain lock and opened the entry for me. An officer in mid-stride came around a bush shouting: "Halt! Police!"

I entered the chamber. "Stop or I'll shoot!" he warned again.

Bang! A shot missed Mosby and ricocheted off one of the crypt's Egyptian columns.

Ben spun around and stepped inside with me, then, just as he was closing the gate, a police dog leapt at him. He seized its snout in midair then smacked its

head against the pillar, knocking out the canine.

Ben shut the rusty door and held it fast. Flashlight beams illuminated the chamber revealing the gritty keyhole, a pointed oval slit above a crack in the south wall. I inserted the ankh's stem into the slot. Immediately, a serpentine jolt of ethereal current coursed through my arm.

More shots rang out. *"Aargh!!!"* Ben cried, falling back onto the stone floor. Blood oozed out of his chest while I took one in the leg. I stumbled but held onto the key in the slot.

"Hold your fire!" boomed an order from behind the gunmen.

I looked out between the lattice, past the barrage of flashlights and firearm smoke; the officers were making way for Detective Breland. He entered Pool's courtyard with a walkie-talkie squabbling in hand. Breland held the talk button, jabbered on it; the only word I made out amongst the police jargon was "Covach."

"Go on!" Ben told me as he staggered to his feet, "I'll hold them off!"

"Who are you?" demanded Detective Breland.

"I'm Benjamin Mosby."

"Whoa," said Breland. "How'd you do that?" witnessing Mosby's chest pop out the slugs into the pool of blood staining the stone steps.

"Are you the Richmond Vampire?" bemused Breland.

"No, just a fireman come to right the wrongs of the Church Hill Tunnel."

"What wrongs?"

Ben hesitated. Gazed at me, "Hmm," he pondered with tightened expression, then looked back at Breland and gave an unexpected response...

How many men were buried that day?
Well, C & O says just three . . .
Mason, Richard Lewis and a man named Smith,
But the survivors say it's many more, you see.
Tormented spirits to this very day
In the haunted tunnel, a train and crew,
No peace, no rest, they're in there still
As the fires of hell burn in the hill.[7]

Meanwhile, an unmarked car pulled up and Special Agent Covach got out with other agents. "Where's Charles Johns?" demanded Covach now standing beside Breland.

During all this, I had time to tune into the ankh key and chamber wall. From my body a swirling energy arose from my core, to my chest, and out my hand into the key. The key quivered then the wall itself. The power I felt was indescribable. A flicker of astral brilliance germinated from the stone slot.

Ben replied, "Charles is at—"

"Caw, kraw...eek," cried the conspiracy of Blackburn, Evermore, and Morrigan swooping down from seemingly nowhere. The avians pecked upon Ben's fingers laced between the gate's iron bars. *"Aaargh...grrr!!!"* Ben bellowed, but held his ground.

"Ben! Let go of the door!" I demanded.

"Not till I see a blue tunnel," he answered. Bits of his flesh fell to the stone steps. A vortex began forming.

"Shoot those birds," ordered Covach.

Pop! Pop! shots rang out from officers.

"Eek...caw...eek..." Blackburn and Morrigan fell in a heap against the entryway. Evermore fled.

I held firm; the vortex blossomed, its swirling celestial blue spirals encompassed the whole wall. My hand, the ankh and its rose crystals radiated.
I felt light as a feather.

"Ben, Maggie! Stop, or I'll kill you both," hollered Agent Covach, pointing her handgun at Ben.

Just then the key's notch, the nucleus of this maelstrom, burst forth, glimmering streaks engulfing the chamber and blinding Covach and company. The grounds trembled with a dazzling luminescent display. Officers stumbled, dropped their weapons and covered their eyes and ears at the onslaught.

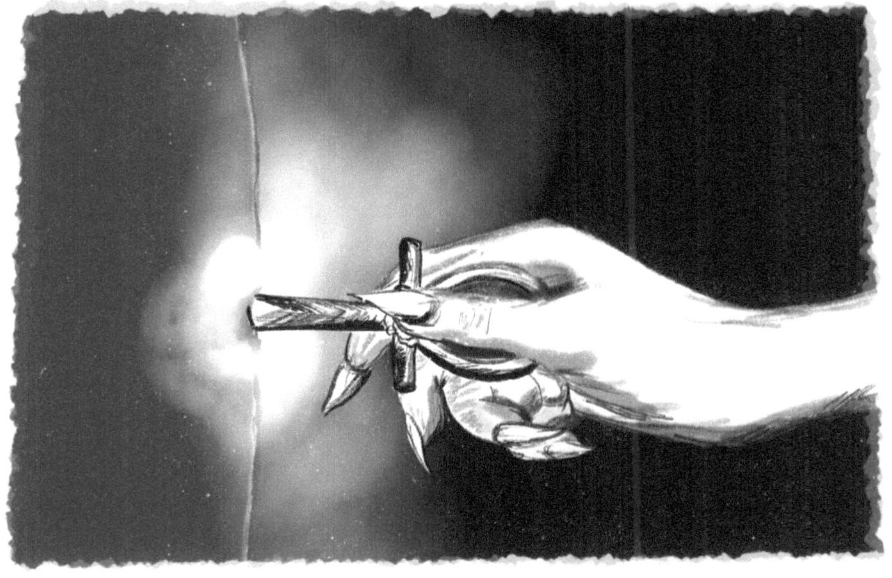

Covach and Breland staggered backwards and turned away. The portal had sensed it was under threat. It retaliated.

Despite the frigid night, the ankh was warm in my hand, there was play in the notch like the key was an alchemic rod in a molten mixture. The vortex was pulling me and the ankh inward.

I stretched out my other hand and hollered, “Ben, take my hand!”

For once, Ben listened. He let go of the gate, his bloodied hand in mine.

Covach spun around wearing sunglasses and aimed her pistol. *Bang! Bang!*

“Ahh!” I cried. A vervain bullet pierced my flesh, lodging itself below my rib cage. *Whoosh!* We were wrested by the swirling vortex.

Au revoir :-o

An Unexpected Guest

Bölcsem Kertész Naplója, 2025. November 1

At the onset of Samhain, the Beginning of the Darker Half, high above the sea in lofty *Túr Liath Faire*, a soaring grey tower, golden crowned with conical roof, I reposed in my scriptorium's Savonarola chair, stroking my black rabbit, Melchior. Finally, seated at my escritoire, I put quill to parchment; my first entry since my exile here in *Hy Breasal*, the mysterious isle far west of *Dún Aonghasa's* watchful eye in *Inis Mór*, though they of Umbanda persuasion call this place, Aruanda.

Recovered amply from my arduous journey and my lamentations over all that transpired in the New World's Richmond, I would have jotted down speculations as to the whereabouts of Magnolia and Mosby, had it not been for a wren alighting from the wind upon my sill, churring me to look forth. I did so. Now twilight on Samhain, in the Time of Betwixt and Between–when your world may visit mine–I spotted from majestic *Túr Liath Faire*, rising from the sea–just a stone's throw from shore–and taller than the Tower of Bregon, a dhow, approaching from the east. She had twain majestic blue sails, each emblazoned with a bright yellow upturned crescent moon with poised khanda sword, known as Aad Chand, amongst the Akali. Her pennants, the Nishan Sahib: a silk triangular flag bearing the Khanda with a tassel at its end. Soon I heard the footsteps of my fair apprentice, a *Tuath Dé* maiden, who was illustrating my commentary on *Theatrum Chemicum*. She announced the arrival of Budhjot, my old friend, an Akali and Keeper of Asota Henge. He requested an audience, having news of the Dragonist Order. I bid her have him ascend the tower's ivory spiral stairs.

"Sat Sri Akal," said Budhjot, forming his hands in prayer.

"Sat Sri Akal," said I, likewise in gesture. "What brings you to *Hy Breasal*, my good friend?"

"Bölscem, I bear news of the Dragonist Order; upon *Oíche Shamhna*, the eve

of Samhain, a siege upon *Dún Dreach-Fhola* has begun."

"By whom?" asked I.

"By *Doamnă Ruxandra cel Rău* and her Dacian Guards...they are aided by a faction of the late Lothar Neuntöter's lair and the lairs of Chorti and Grzegorz," stated Budhjot.

"Astounding!...how do you know of this?"

"A mole came out of his burrow in *Montură Izvorul*," he grinned.

I smiled and said, "Ah, you have a way with words, my friend. I miss my master's library."

"She means to unseat Edana as principal Archon and secure the body of Collette cel Rău," continued Budhjot. "Then, my dear friend, she will come for you."

"She knows not where I am."

"Possibly," he shrugged.

"Hmm, which leads me to my next inquiry. How did you find me?"

"A salmon swam from *Hy Breasal* and brought me knowledge of *Clíodhna's* pathway upon the sea."

"Ha! Very well, I will not press for a more forthright reply," I chuckled, peering from a narrow arched window at the westward offing.

"Most thankful, Supreme Scribe," he said, slightly nodding with his electric blue turban.

I pivoted from the window and said, "As to the matter of Ruxandra...no doubt she has made a deal with Andromalius–what is that?" I inquired, noticing in Budhjot's hand a small leather-bound journal.

"This is Magnolia's journal."

"What!? How did you come by this?" I pressed.

"She came by way of Asota Henge for healing from vervain. She requested it be placed *only* in your hands, along with this letter," he replied, handing me a tiny linen envelope, its wax seal depicting a magnolia flower.

I hastily opened the letter and read:

Dear Bolscem:

I trust all's well and you are safe in exile. Ben and I made it out of River City by the skin of our teeth... we had an altercation at Pool's portal, with, guess who — Agent Kovach + Detective Breland. I was wounded, as you would say, "by a sacred bullet," from Kovach's fireman, but we escaped to Brodgar. Surprisingly, no Dragonists were nearby. From there to Asota we secured Budhjot for healing.

With Budhjot's guidance, we portalled to Sri Lanka by way of the Ruins — don't ask me to spell it. What we will do next, who knows?

I entrust my diary with you. Why, you may ask. The answer: I'd hope you'd be moved to write a compilation of our adventures, and perhaps go back in time, publish the work, and somehow prevent all the calamity from taking place.

Ben and I wish you well...

Au revoir! Maggie

"What will you do?" asked Budhjot, handing me her journal. "Can you not go back in time, and do as she wishes?"

"Hmm..." I fiddled with my goatee, "...perhaps. I will meditate upon it."

"Surely," he insisted, "there's some simpleton in Richmond whom you can persuade to publish such a work."

"Possibly," I smiled touching the analemma on a floor globe.

Budjhot ambled over and caressed the sphere. "What if," he postulated rotating it, "by some strange means, Ruxandra discovers this isle." His finger landing on *Hy Breasal*. "What shall you do?"

"Let her come!" I grinned dangling a balaur portal key to Dracul Castle.

Rakestraw's Epilogue

Dear Readers:

As you can see, I have published a paraphrased version of Bölscem Kertész's archaic tome: a collection of various journals and reports by familiars, well before the hundredth anniversary of the Church Hill Tunnel collapse, and, more importantly, before all the gruesome events which may transpire afterwards.

I hope you have enjoyed this jaunt into the Otherworld, and in some small way or another, as your heart and Wisdom lead you, play your part in stopping these horrific occurrences from manifesting.

In many places I engaged poetic license–not as you think to distort the story-line, but rather to enhance it, as Bölscem desired me to do so. For instance, perhaps Benjamin Mosby did not recite the excerpt from Bob Harrison's song, "The Legend of the Church Hill Tunnel," as I record he does, but, in this way I feel I have captured the true heart of what Mr. Mosby was feeling.

On a final note, the bulk of Bölscem's account has been put to print, however, some of his tales I have left out. In small measure, I did this because they are not essential to the story, but in a larger measure because this work has taken a great toll on my constitution. Perhaps a revised version of the *Return of the Richmond Vampire* will be published, containing the rest of the story. Only time and fate will tell.

Many blessings to you, and steer clear of the misty Otherworld!

Yours in Wisdom,
Jon Rakestraw

P.S. - What has become of Benjamin and Magnolia? Only time will tell. As for the fate of *Dún Dreach-Fhola*, the haze of battle has yet to clear. Yet, one thing is certain, Thin Places become thinner with each passing year.

Acknowledgements

- Robert Harrison, Church Hill Tunnel Historian
- Chris and Beth Houlihan, Owners and Guides, Haunts of Richmond
- Thomas W. Dixon, Jr., Founder, Chairman & President Emeritus, Chief Historian of Chesapeake and Ohio Historical Society
- Rachel Pater, Founder, Richmond Story House
- David L. Gilliam, General Manager, Hollywood Cemetery Co.

  (Cover photo release courtesy of Hollywood Cemetery Co.)
- Chris Semtner, Curator, The Poe Museum
- Janet Holly, Teacher and Historian of Richmond's African American history
- Ned Krack, Guide, Richmond Railroad Museum, Old Dominion Chapter- NRHS (ticket stub image courtesy of Museum)
- Nick Smith, Crystals Advisor, Aquarian Carytown
- Kelly Justice, Owner, Fountain Bookstore
- Daniel Strait, Inspirer
- Steve Choisser, Bonnie & Elisse Duvall, Beta Readers
- Sally Babylon, Artist & Author, Art Legacy Publications
- Matthew Guillen, Reference Coordinator, Virginia Museum of History & Culture, Virginia Historical Society
- Lisa Wehrmann, Reference Services Librarian, The Library of Virginia

Finally, thanks be to all the family, friends and teachers
who have inspired me to write

Endnotes

1. Num. 14:18b (ESV).
2. Gerald Griffin, Hy-Brasail - *The Isle of the Blest*, in Fairy & Folk Tales of Ireland, ed. W. B. Yeats (London: Sirius Publishing, 2019), 256-257.
3. Robert Harrison. *The Legend of the Churchhill Tunnel* Recorded June 1996. Coyote Studio, 1996, unreleased.
4. Llewellyn Lewis. Excerpt from *The Train That Will Never Be Found.*
5. Russell Lawson. Excerpt from *Church Hill Tunnel.* Released November 30 2011 on Wait! There's More! album.
6. Isa. 34:13-14, 17 paraphrased (KJV).
7. Robert Harrison. *The Legend of the Churchhill Tunnel* Recorded June 1996. Coyote Studio, 1996, unreleased.

Translations

English (Invented)

endoword - to synthetically insert a word/thought into the conscious mind (usually conducted via wireless technologies)
portaling - to traverse between uber-natural portals via a wormhole
Scarletvin - adreno-infused human blood

French

au revoir - goodbye
bateau - boat; flat-bottomed river boat
canelé - cylindrical shaped custard filled rum and vanilla pastry with a caramelized crust
c'est la vie - that's life
joie de vivre - joy of living
voilà - behold

German

bitte - you're welcome
danke - thanks
Du bist Nächste - You are next
Ja, ich habe eine Frage - Yes, I have a question
nein - no
Nicht schlecht, aber es ist Zeit zu sterben - Not bad, but it's time to die
sehr gut - very good
Was meinst du - What do you mean
Wie werden wir Mosby kontrollieren - How are we going to control Mosby?
zicke - bitch

Hungarian

koporsó - coffin
kulcs a poolhoz - key to the pool
naplója - diary
szia - hello / bye
Úr. - Mr.

Irish

Dún Dreach-Fhola - Castle of Blood Visage
Dearg-Due - Red Blood Sucker
Ériu - Ireland (Old Irish form of)
filí - seer poet
Geata Ulchabhán - Gate of the Owl
geis - taboo; prohibitive; denoted a curse if committed
Imbas forosnai - prophetic illumination involving a Druidic ritual of fasting, isolation and posture.
Na Cruacha Dubha - The Black Stacks
Tír na nÓg - Land of Youth
tonn - wave
Tuama Crann Creathach - Tomb of the Aspen

Norwegian

ja - yes
ha det - good bye
tusen takk - thank you

Portugese

fica tranquilo - stay calm
obrigado - thanks

Romanian

da - yes
excelent - excellent
gogoși - filled doughnut sprinkled with powdered sugar
grevă echilibrul - strike the balance
grozav - that's great
la revedere - goodbye
mă scuzați - excuse me
minunat - wonderful
multumesc - thanks
nu - no
pa - bye
sânge nou - new blood
servus - hello (Transylvania)
sunt bine - I'm fine
vă multumesc dragă - thank you dear

Russian

dasvidaniya - goodbye
govno - shit
Urod - expression for a "freak"
zasranec - asshole

Sanskrit

Sat Sri Akal - Truth is God; greeting in Sikhism

Spanish

sí señorita - yes, Miss

Urdu

Khush aamdeed - Welcome
koi baat nahi - no problem

This is a work of fiction. Current names and characters are the products of the author's imagination with the notable exceptions of Chris and Beth Houlihan, the late Black Dog, Mark Holmberg, Hans Corneel de Roos, Dacre Stoker as well as Alexis Crawley, Tully Lozoya and Paula Chimel. Characterizations and portrayals of historical figures and their descendants namely Richard Lewis, H. Smith, C. W. Johns, William Wortham Pool, Samuel Owens, and Benjamin F. Mosby are purely fictional and in no way are to be construed as fact. Events are the fabrication of the author's imagination with the exception of the collapse of the Church Hill Tunnel.

Printed in the United States of America
Revised Edition
Library of Congress Control Number: 2021910794
ISBNs: 978-1-7371547-4-7 (Revised), 978-1-7371547-0-9 (hardcover), 978-1-7371547-1-6 (paperback), 978-1-7371547-2-3 (ebook), 978-1-7371547-3-0 (Kindle)

ILLUSTRATOR: Meam Hartshorn, meamhartshorn.com
BOOK DESIGN: Leslie Saunderlin, lesliesaunderlin.com
EDITOR: Shelia Shedd, swiftcreative.net
PROOFREADER: Roxana Coumans, proofreadebooks.com
DIGITAL ART: Jeff Glotzl, glotzl.com
PHOTOGRAPHER: John Henley, johnhenleyphoto.com, cover photo © 2021 by John Henley

Instagram / @jonrakestrawwriter
Web / jonrakestraw.com
Grey Tower Books, LLC

www.ingramcontent.com/pod-product-compliance
Lightning Source LLC
Chambersburg PA
CBHW030546310726
48979CB00010B/2058/J

* 9 7 8 1 7 3 7 1 5 4 7 4 7 *